Praise for Martyn Waites' previous Joe Donovan thriller,
Bone Machine:

'A whiplash plot combined with contemporary issues results in that rarest of feats: a blockbuster with soul' *Guardian*

'A highly entertaining, shamefully addictive read' *The Crack*

'A grisly crime thriller in which Waites's no-nonsense cop investigates hookers, gangsters and corpses with sewn-up mouths. Granny wouldn't be impressed. We are' *Maxim*

'If you like your tales dark, brutal, realistic, with a pinch of Northern humour – don't wait any longer – Waites is your man' *Shots*

'Hard-boiled noir all the way through . . . Ends with a real punch of a cliffhanger' *Euro Crime*

'The book houses an audacious energy and if you're in any way a fan of Ian Rankin or Stephen Booth, this mesmerising thriller will be right up your street' *Accent*

'The leading light of a new generation of hard-hitting contemporary crime novelists has produced a cracking thriller' *Daily Mirror*

351 738 531

By the same author

Joe Donovan series
The Mercy Seat
Bone Machine

The White Room
Born Under Punches
Candleland
Little Triggers
Mary's Prayer

About the author

Born and brought up in Newcastle upon Tyne, Martyn Waites was an actor before becoming a writer. As well as short stories and non-fiction, he has written seven novels, several of which have been nominated for awards. He has held two writing residencies, at Huntercombe Young Offenders Institution and HMP Chelmsford, and run arts-based workshops for socially excluded teenagers. He is currently Literary Fellow at the University of Essex.

Visit www.martynwaites.com

WHITE RIOT

Martyn Waites

POCKET
BOOKS

LONDON • SYDNEY • NEW YORK • TORONTO

First published in Great Britain by Pocket Books, 2008
An imprint of Simon & Schuster UK
A CBS COMPANY

1 3 5 7 9 10 8 6 4 2

Simon & Schuster UK Ltd
Africa House
64–78 Kingsway
London WC2B 6AH

www.simonsays.co.uk

Simon & Schuster Australia
Sydney

A CIP catalogue record for this book
is available from the British Library

ISBN 978-1-84739-058-5

Typeset in Bembo by M Rules
Printed and bound in Great Britain by
Cox & Wyman Ltd, Reading, Berks

For Linda again

PROLOGUE

A BETTER WORLD

Night.

He sat on the edge of the bed, unmoving. An anonymous chain hotel room. With the bed, a desk, a wardrobe. In-built and functional. Characterless. Could have been anywhere in the world.

The lights were off, the TV black. City sound drifted in through the open window. Only other noise in the room his breathing. The air pressed down, hot and heavy. Unrelenting.

He stared at the wall, face closed, mind unreadable. Hands in his lap, fingers moving against each other. The minibar had been raided.

Next to him, his mobile trilled.

He jumped, stretched out a hand, held it to his ear.

Waited.

'It's starting,' a voice said.

He listened, said nothing.

'It's not too late, you know. You can still change your mind. Join us.'

He sighed, shook his head. Opened his mouth to speak. Closed it again. The caller laughed.

'Nearly. Was that going to be a yes?'

He kept his mouth tight shut.

'It's going ahead. Whether you want it to or not. Whether you're part of it or not. So speak now or for ever, you know.'

He found the courage, opened his mouth. 'No. I'll . . . I'll stop you. You can't . . . can't . . .'

'Really?' A laugh. 'You won't. The hope only of empty men. Because this is the way the world ends. Or begins.'

Another laugh and the line went dead. The phone felt hot, heavier than lead. He tossed it on the bed beside him.

Kept staring at the wall.

Earlier.

They drove round all day looking for the right victim. Someone who fitted the profile. Someone who would be missed.

The car was a Rover 75, a few years old, with extended axle space giving as much room in the back as in the front. Stolen to order from out of town. Licence plates switched. Confident it wouldn't be traced. They drove slowly, carefully, no loud music, no revving engine. Nothing eye-catching. Nothing memorable.

Six of them. Four men, two girls. The girls curled up on the floor of the back seat, unseen from the street. No one joked, asked them for oral sex while they were down there. No one said much beyond what was necessary, talk so small as to be infinitesimal.

The men wore sunglasses, hoodies zipped up, hoods down. Windows up, air con on. It was a hot day.

Driving, concentrating.

Looking.

And then they found him.

Sooliman had never known terror. Real life-about-to-end terror. Until now.

His body hit panic attack after panic attack, blood pounding faster than a John Bonham drum solo. I'm too young to have a heart attack, he thought, not knowing if it was a feeble joke or a true statement.

His eyes were open but he couldn't see anything. His

wrists and ankles bound with plastic ties; his body jack-knifed and crammed into the cramped space. Exhaust fumes stung his nose and eyes. Lack of air made him light-headed. Tears and snot covered his face. The gag in his mouth made it hard to breathe.

His body bounced, was banged around. He repeatedly hit sharp metal, felt wet warmth on the skin of his bare arms and face. He tried to focus, breath deep; will himself away from his present, find a happy memory, anything that would give him strength to cope. Impossible. His mind held only confusion and fear.

Thoughts of sudden death.

Through the gag, he cried.

They had taken him in the park. Out playing with his friends, enjoying a game of cricket on the Town Moor after getting home from college, taking advantage of the early-summer heatwave that was as unexpected as it was welcome. Laughing, play fighting as they approached the moor. Five of them, friends since school, all from the same area. Coke and Fanta from the newsagent, cricket equipment commu-nally supplied. They had set up and started playing, two teams of two with Sooliman out fielding, knowing his chance to bat would come eventually.

Because that was the way Sooliman was. He concen-trated on college, on his clubs. Chess. Science fiction reading group. Things he felt comfortable with but not geeky. He still went out with his mates, pubbing, clubbing, sticking to the soft drinks. Not because he was a Muslim. He just didn't like the taste. And no girlfriend. Too shy to ask anyone out. Much safer to go to his clubs or stay in his room, listen to his classic rock. Be the person he wanted to be behind a closed door. A bedroom Bowie. A curtained-off Cobain. A pretend Plant. Act out his lonely dreams while in his heart he secretly, deeply yearned for love.

So when two girls came along and stopped to talk on the moor, he didn't know what was happening. They were flirty, all bare arms and midriffs. And incredibly good looking. The kind of girls he didn't even dare dream about. One blonde, one brunette, both about eighteen or nineteen, with lightly tanned skin smelling clean and wonderful. So much so he took his eye off the ball and missed a glorious catch that his friends immediately started ragging him about. He didn't listen. He didn't care.

At first he had thought they were asking directions, but it was soon clear that wasn't what they were after. They talked to him. Smiled. Giggled. He tried talking back but became tongue-tied. They laughed along with him, encouraged him. Listened to what he had to say in response. No girl had ever done that before. Sooliman's heart felt as big and as full as St James's Park on a Saturday afternoon. He was a rock god. A sci-fi hero. He tried not to stare too obviously at the flesh on display, not to respond too readily to the arm strokes and supposedly accidental body brushes, the teasing and flirting. Tried, red-faced, to hide his growing erection.

His friends looked over, lost interest in the game, switched their attention. Started walking over slowly, hip gunslinger gaits. The girls noticed, made it clear they were interested only in Sooliman. He didn't want his friends over either; they would take the girls away. Sweep them off with exaggerated stories and promises of rides in their fathers' BMWs. It always happened. So when the blonde wandered off to a wooded area, the brunette in tow, and beckoned him over, he didn't need to be asked twice. Heaven was unfolding on earth. He didn't even look back.

And that was when they grabbed him. Four of them in long-sleeved hoodies with gloved hands and bandanas tied around their faces, sunglasses hiding their eyes. Standing before a car hidden on an access road behind a thick hedge. Heaven disappeared before him. He tried to run, but his legs wouldn't move. Then they were on him. Gagged and trussed, he was thrown into the car boot. Not even time to scream.

He heard angrily spat insults through muffled metal – 'Paki cunt', 'suicide bomber scum' – then vicious laughter, the giggles of the girls running quickly away. The suspension creaked as bodies got swiftly into seats and the car was engaged, revved and driven off, the sound like the roar of the devil in Sooliman's ears.

Time passed. How long, Sooliman didn't know.

Then a violent jarring: the car had turned off a main road, was now on an unmade one. Eventually it slowed, stopped.

He waited, breath coming in snotty, ragged gasps. Heard doors slam, footsteps. Voices, words inaudible through the metal, above the thump of his heart. But no mistaking the sense of anticipation.

The boot was opened. Sooliman held his breath.

He screwed his eyes up tight, desperately willed whatever awaited him away, willed his life back to how it had been when he had woken up that morning. He tried to visualize his mother standing there, his friends, his ordinary life that he had taken for granted but nevertheless loved. He made frantic deals with an Allah he had believed in only to please his parents. He would never criticize his father's strictness again, would turn his music down when asked, never claim his business studies degree was boring. Never be mean to his little brother. Never look at a Western girl again. He closed his eyes hard, told himself it was all a dream. A horrible dream.

Opened them again. It was no dream.

Light, harsh and unexpected, made him squint. He closed
his eyes, opened them again by degrees. Took in his sur-
roundings. A garage of some kind with bright, artificial
striplights overhead. Double doors firmly closed, but
through a small high window he caught a glimpse of outside.
Night had fallen. The moon stared in, full and high and surrounded by blackness like an unreachable light at the end of
a tunnel fraught with monsters.

He could make out the silhouettes of the four men who
had kidnapped him, the harsh indoor light haloed around
them. Their hoodies resembled cowls, their faces shadowed
and empty like horror film monks. Anger and violence came
off them in waves. The terror he had felt in the car
increased. Arms grabbed him, pulled him out of the boot.
He was thrown to the ground. The fall jarred his bones,
stretched his joints, knocked the air from his lungs. The
floor was gravel and packed dirt; it bit through his jeans, his
T-shirt. Into his face.

He opened his eyes, tried to look up.

'Don't move.'

A boot kicked him in the jaw. He went down.

Self-pity, fear and anger churned inside him. Tears welled
again at the corners of his eyes. He sniffed them back in,
scared to show weakness. Scared to show them anything.

He waited.

One of the four detached himself from the group, crossed
the floor. Sooliman's head was forcibly pulled up by the
hair. The restraints on his wrists pinned his arms into the
small of his back. Another one crossed, knelt down before
him. Spoke.

'Don't worry,' the voice said. 'You'll get your reward
soon. In paradise.'

Panic welled again inside Sooliman. He felt vomit build,
unstoppable, in his stomach. Burst in his mouth. The

speaking man jumped back as vomit exploded from Sooliman's nose and around the gag.

'Cut him loose!' he shouted.

The one holding up Sooliman's head produced a long, heavy hunting knife, cut the bindings of the gag. Sooliman was dropped, retching, on the floor. Dry heaving until his stomach was empty. He finished, lay there in silence.

'Get this cleaned up,' the speaker said. 'Get him cleaned up. And then get on with it. We haven't got all night.'

Sooliman was dragged to the back of the garage, dumped on the floor. His bonds were severed but still he didn't dare move.

'Stand up.'

Sooliman did as he was told. Three of the men stood before him. Sooliman's legs began to buckle when he saw what they were carrying. Cricket bats, baseball bats, clubs. All augmented with darkly glittering metal, razors, spikes, nails. The first speaker stood some distance away at the far end of the garage. The voice sounded almost sympathetic.

'Sorry. But think of those virgins waiting to greet you.'

They rushed him. Sooliman closed his eyes as pain, sharp and enormous, started at the back of his skull, shot down his neck and all round his body like he had been wrapped in electrified barbed wire. The force of the blow knocked him to the floor. He twisted his body, turned. Another blow. Another. Pain like he had never experienced before. More hurt than he had ever felt in his life.

He couldn't scream, couldn't cry. He barely had the strength to just lie there.

Another blow. Another.

He thought of his mother, his family. Tried to imagine their lives without him. Their grief.

More blows. Hard, cutting deep.

Felt something unmendable sever inside.

Felt himself being wrapped up in a thick, black comforting duvet.

Made one last begging peace with a god he tried desperately to believe in.

Willed the pain to stop.

Felt nothing at all.

Marion looked up at the sky. No clouds. A white moon. No sign of rain, just the oppressive, clammy night, like the sky was holding everyone down. The city needed a storm. A good storm. Make everything clean again. Let everyone breathe.

She rounded the corner. Just one more street, then across the road, over the grass and up the lift to the eleventh floor and home. She was exhausted. The off-licence had been busier than usual tonight. Everyone wanting something cold to drink while they sat in their back yards or on their balconies. Too busy for her to have a break. Mr Patel had appreciated her work, said he would slip something extra into her wage packet. She had thanked him. He was usually good about things like that, a decent man to work for, Mr Patel. Didn't matter that he was a Paki.

She rounded the final corner, ready to cross the grass. Or what was left of it. Now just a dump for unwanted furniture and fridges. Some of it disappeared into other flats and houses, some of it was set alight, some of it was used as a makeshift playground until it became so fragmented it just disappeared.

Before she could take another step a car came speeding up to the grass, putting its brakes on with a screech. Three men jumped out, took something out of the boot, threw it on the ground. One knelt beside it, did something that she couldn't see, stood quickly back as the bundle caught on fire, went up in flames. Two of the men jumped back into the car. One stood, looking round. He saw her and, making an expansive gesture, threw out armfuls of leaflets, jumped inside the car and sped away.

Marion stood there dumbfounded, too shocked to move. Her eyes tried to take in the scene before her, process it. She stared at the bundle, hoping it wasn't what she feared it to be.

It was. A body. A man's body.

Marion screamed. And kept on screaming.

She was still screaming when the ambulance arrived twenty minutes later.

He sat on the side of the bed, unmoving. Beside him, his mobile trilled.

Reluctantly he answered it.

'It's started. Falls the shadow.'

He turned the mobile off, threw it like it was contaminated.

The air felt even heavier, the room hotter.

He tried to keep breathing.

PART ONE

ANGRY COMMUNIQUÉS

1

The knife danced before Jason's eyes. He recognized it, knew its purpose. Boning and filleting. Felt a pang of knowledgeable pride, then a frown of confusion. An intake of breath, as it came towards him.

'Kev . . .' he said, wide-eyed, unsure what was happening, not liking it.

'Shut up, you stupid twat.'

Kev had stripped his hard, scarred body down to his underwear. At first Jason had thought his friend was turning queer. But when he picked the knife up from the table, he understood. It was nothing like that. It was so there'd be no bloodstained clothing to be CSIed.

An old farm building, the walls wood, the floor dirty concrete. Curved knives and mean shears hung on nails, rusty and aged. Farming implements of wood and metal were propped up against the walls, cobwebbed, slowly falling to pieces. The ancient brown stains on the floor gave witness to what the place had been used for.

A slaughterhouse.

Kev crossed to the door, turned the key in the lock. Then back to Jason. 'We haven't got long. They'll be here in a minute.'

Jason's heart jumped into his throat, was strangling him by beats. 'What? Kev, I'm your mate, I'm the Butcher Boy, I'm special, they said so . . .'

Kev tried to keep his features impassive, his voice level. 'Yeah, you're special all right.'

Jason gave a little giggle. 'Yeah, I am . . .'

'Yeah. Really fuckin' special.'

Jason frowned. Kev was looking at him strangely, his eyes shining as much as the knife. 'But Kev . . .'

'Shut up.' Kev looked at the door, back to Jason. 'There's no time. Listen. They brought you here 'cos they want you to do somethin' for them.' He pointed to the coil of rope on the floor. 'I was supposed to get the process started.' He sighed, like it was hurting him. 'An' I can't. I can't let you . . . I can't.'

Jason couldn't take his eyes off the blade. He'd seen it split carcasses in the shop. Pare flesh back to the bone. He knew what it would do to him. There were only a few years between them, but Kev looked so much older handling the knife. 'But Kev, they said it was somethin' great, for the future. I'd be a hero . . .'

'You'd be dead. Fuckin' dead.' Kev hissed the words. Jason jumped back at the force of them. 'Yeah. That's what they want. You dead.'

Jason's eyes widened. 'But Kev . . .'

The blade was thrust back in Jason's face. 'You wanna live?' Jason nodded. Stupid question. 'Then shut it. I'm tryin' to think.'

Jason looked at Kev, tried not to make a sound, not even breathe. Wondered how this man, the nearest thing to family he had ever had, a brother – a father, almost – was holding a knife on him and threatening to kill him. And he would do it. No doubt.

Kev looked to the door, back at Jason. And his eyes had changed. They looked not friendly but not so scary. Jason clung to that look like a lifeline.

'Gonna give you a chance,' said Kev. He put his arms by his side, held the knife loosely. 'You know what to do. Make it look good.'

'But Kev . . .'

'Just do it, you stupid cunt,' hissed Kev. 'Do it.'

Jason, realizing he had no choice, rushed towards Kev. His big, muscled torso absorbed most of the impact and he remained standing. Kev made a grab for Jason, catching his shoulder. Even though Jason knew he wasn't using all his strength, it still hurt.

Jason fought back. Aimed a punch at Kev's stomach that Kev only made a token attempt to deflect. A kick at Kev's groin. Kev crumpled slightly but didn't yield ground. Jason knew he would have to step up, not worry so much about hurting his friend, concentrate, fight harder to get himself free.

Kev came at him, swinging the knife. Jason jumped out of the way. Kev swung again. Jason grabbed Kev's outstretched arm, forced the knife back towards Kev's body. Kev grimaced; Jason detected a smile in there somewhere.

Jason pushed hard. Kev put up token resistance. Jason kept pushing, hard as he could. It was like arm wrestling with an uncle when he was a young boy, the uncle making a show of it, letting him win ultimately. Kev seemed to be guiding the knife to where he wanted it, then, with Jason still applying pressure, let go.

The knife slid into Kev's side, just below his ribcage.

'Fuck . . .' Kev gasped in surprise. It seemed to have hurt him more than he thought it would. He slumped to the floor as the blood started to fountain out of the wound.

'Go, now . . .'

Jason looked down at his prone friend, shocked and stunned by what he had done. He looked at Kev's near-naked body, eyes taking in the tattoos that told the story of the man's life.

The Union flag. The flag of St George. No Surrender. A vicious, snarling thing that could have been half pitbull, half rabid bulldog.

And the home-made ones: 100% White. Ain't No Black In The Union Jack. SKINZ4EVA. Home-made or prison issue. Dark ink making the white skin whiter.

Jason was still proud to call Kev his friend.

'What you waitin' for? Run, you fuckin' puff.'

Jason remembered where he was, dropped the knife. Heard the door of the main house open. They would be there any minute.

He looked down at Kev once again, wanted to say something.

'Look, Kev . . .'

'Just fuckin' go . . . And don't stop, don't let them get you. They'll kill you . . .'

Jason turned the key, grabbed the door handle, took two deep breaths, opened it.

And ran.

Silence at first. The only sounds his feet, his ragged breathing. He risked a glance behind. Heard angry shouts, cries. They had found Kev. Realized what had happened. Were giving chase.

He put his head down and went.

The terrain was hard. He ran blindly, his trainers giving him speed, the hard and uneven ground impeding his progress. No idea where he was or which direction would offer safety. He just ran.

It was a moor of some sort. Away out in the country somewhere. Rough, sharp plants pricked and nicked his skin like little razors. Stung his arms like tiny bees when he stumbled against them. He ignored it all. Thought of nothing but escape. As a kid he was a good runner. But that was years ago. Smoking, drinking, drugs . . . they were more important. Thought all the rucks and fights and fucks would keep him fit. They hadn't.

Tripping and falling, he ran. The coarse, jagged, uneven

ground caught him off guard, sent pain arcing round his body. His chest felt like it had been tipped full of hot stones and every breath he took just fanned the flames. His arms pumped furiously; he ignored the pins and needles in his fingers, the aches across his shoulders.

He didn't look back. Didn't dare.

Fuelled by terror, by fear, he kept on going.

His eyes were adjusting to the dark. He began to make out shapes and mounds, places ahead. Tried to plan a path for himself, avoiding too many potholes.

A hill loomed up before him, a solid mass blotting out the stars. He launched himself at it, climbing hard, trying not to lose what momentum he had gained. He crested the ridge virtually on all fours and stood at the top, gasping, his legs steady as water.

He looked behind him. His pursuers were still there, but quite a way behind. A slight hope rose within him. He had the advantage. He could do it, get away. Hide out. Or get help.

He looked ahead again.

And couldn't believe his eyes.

At the bottom of the hill was a small forest and, next to that, cottages. Two, no three of them. Lights on, curtains drawn. And all that stood between him and them was a run down the hill.

He took a deep breath and, adrenalin and hope giving his body a fresh surge of energy, ran down the hill as fast as he could. Like his life depended on it.

Halfway down, a thought hit. He knew he was in Northumberland, but beyond that he had no idea. What if the people in the cottages owned the land he was on? Or they were friends or relatives? Or sympathizers? He would be running right back to the people he was escaping from.

And he knew what would happen then.

Changing direction mid-stride he ran towards the wood.

Jason heard sounds behind him, ran all the harder. Made the covering of the trees, risked a glance behind him. The hunters had reached the crest of the ridge, were looking around, assessing their options. He watched as they split up, some going towards the houses, some to the trees. He turned and dived into the woods.

Once inside he looked around, blinking. The dark outside nothing compared to the dark within. He rubbed his eyes, tried to get them to acclimatize quickly, assessed his options. They would be coming in soon. They didn't have torches, so they would be as blind as he was. He had to use that to his advantage. If he stayed where he was they would find him. If he hid on the ground they would find him. He looked upwards.

Almost giggled.

His eyes getting used to the darkness, he found a suitable tree with plenty of thick branches and covering foliage and began to climb.

Jason knew he wasn't the smartest kid around. Never had been. Although his memory went back only to the time his mother's old boyfriend had smacked him around so hard he had to be taken to the hospital with a fractured skull, so who knew? Maybe he had been smart before that.

Meeting Kev had been a smart thing. A good thing. The best that had ever happened to him at the time. Living rough, selling whatever he could for money. Bit of weed, coke, heroin, stuff he'd nicked, his body. Anything. Just drifting, going with the flow. Getting through life one day at a time.

He thought Kev was a punter at first. Sold him some weed first, then heroin. Didn't look the type but you could never tell. Then kept coming back, even when he didn't

want to buy. Started talking. Asking him about his family,
where he was from. With his muscles and tats he didn't look
like no social worker, but Jason couldn't be too careful.
Wary, he told him some true stuff and some lies, mixed it a
bit. Confused himself by the end of it.

Kev started looking out for him, looking after him. Kept
the local gangs off his back, the proper gangsta dealers, even
found him somewhere to live. A room in a house with three
others.

Three just like him. Homeless, rootless. Wanderers and
strays. They all congregated at a local pub. The Gibraltar.
Jason tagged along with them. Wasn't much to look at from
the outside, even less from inside. Bare walls and floors.
Only decoration the flags and photos round the place. And
there was Kev and his mates slap bang in the middle.
Regulars in the place, ruling it. Wary at first because they
looked so mean, like the kind of men who would use him
then not pay him or try to hurt him afterwards. But this lot
weren't like that. So Jason, little by cautious little, began to
go with the flow.

Eventually he came to almost trust the men. Dared to
allow himself to feel at home, even.

Then Kev had another surprise. A job. Working in the
butcher shop with him. Jason had never had a job before,
didn't know what to do. But said yes, thought it would be a
laugh. So there he was. The Butcher Boy, sharpening his
knives.

Jason kept some of himself back, ready to run at the first
sign of things turning bad, of the bill needing to be paid.
Because all of this didn't come free. There had to be a price
somewhere. But it never arrived. Instead came a strange
feeling. One he didn't have the emotions to respond to. A
sense of belonging.

Then came the meetings. At first he thought that was the

price, like the Christians making you say you believe in God
and Jesus before they would feed you or give you a bed for
the night. But it wasn't like that. They just told him their
truth until it became his.

And then he really did feel he had found somewhere he
belonged.

And now this.

They came hunting. Pulling branches off trees, fashioning
them into clubs, thrashing away at the ground, the low-
lying ferns and plants, hitting out blindly and fiercely,
wanting to hurt, to maim.

They didn't find him.

Up above, not daring to move or barely breathe, Jason
crouched, the branches snagging his clothes, ripping his
skin. He watched, listened. Heard their angry voices issuing
orders to each other, as if by shouting loud enough and
strongly enough they would make him appear.

He didn't.

Eventually they wearied. Reluctantly accepting defeat,
they retreated from the woods. Taking a few last smashes at
bushes and tree trunks as they went.

Jason still didn't dare to move. He had seen a film once
where this guy on the run was hiding and the bad guys
looking for him said they couldn't find him and left. So the
good guy went out when he thought the coast was clear.
And the bad guys had tricked him and were waiting for
him and caught him. And killed him. So he would stay
where he was. Because they might have seen that film too.

Jason sighed, as loudly as he dared, letting the tension, the
terror out. He needed a plan. Some way to stay alive.

At first he could think of nothing. Then began to wonder
how an ordinary Tuesday could turn out like this. Panic
built inside him. He would have to sit in the tree for ever,

getting older, wasting away with nothing to eat and drink and no way to even go to the toilet. Maybe he would be pecked at by birds, big birds. Maybe they had them round here, he didn't know. Or some kind of wild animal that could jump up trees.

Oh, God.

He wanted to scream and almost did, stopping himself by shoving his fist inside his mouth to stifle the sounds. They might still be there, waiting. Ready to kill him. He waited until the wave passed, removed his fist, tried to calm down, think.

His old Connexions worker was always telling him to make a list of things, look at the plus points. He had always thought that was bollocks, but he had to do something. So he tried.

How much money did he have? Not much.

Where was he? In Northumberland.

Who did he know there who could help him? No one.

Where could he go next? Nowhere.

Short and fuckin' sweet, that was it.

He put his head in his hands, curled up in a ball. About to give in to despair again, but something stopped him.

Northumberland.

He put his head up, thought back to a few weeks ago. Started rummaging through his jacket pockets, feeling the adrenalin rush building up again.

It had better be there, it had better be . . .

A few weeks ago. Who would have thought.

A few weeks. Felt like a lifetime ago.

'Oi, you. I know you.'

Jason had been sitting at the foot of Grey's Monument, waiting for something to happen, somewhere to go. His day off from the butcher's, he had a bit of a buzz on from a

couple of spliffs, a couple of rocks and was working his way
through a can of Stella. An average day. He was going to see
Kev later, see what was going on, maybe go to a meeting.
Looking forward to that. But until then, just killing time.
Watching the world go by, getting a bit of sun. Eyeing up
the girls, pitying the office workers. Knowing everything
they said and did and how they lived their lives was wrong,
knowing he was right. He had the answers.

Or he knew someone who did.

'Oi.'

The boy turned, looked at him. From the narrowed brow
it was clear he didn't know who Jason was, couldn't remember him. But Jason remembered the boy.

''S'me. Jason.'

'Yeah?' The boy shrugged.

'Father Jack's, remember?'

The boy turned pale. Jason didn't think that would have
been possible, the kid being black an' all, but he did. He
shouldn't even have been shouting at a nigger in the street,
at least not all friendly, like. Christ, he must be stoned. Or
bored.

The kid came over, looked at Jason.

'Father Jack's . . .'

'The home.'

The youth bridled. 'Man, that was never no fuckin'
home.'

The youth was big now, gangling. Must have been about
fourteen at Father Jack's then, looked about sixteen now,
same age as Jason, but where Jason was still small the youth
had shot up. But not just age; he carried himself well.
Seemed bigger in many ways. Jason felt a hard shaft of something unpleasant strike him between the ribs. He didn't
know what. Anger? Jealousy?

Jealousy? For a nigger? Yeah, right.

'Yeah,' said Jason. 'I remember you.' He thought hard for a moment, eyes screwed up. 'Jamal, innit? Yeah. You moved in an' everythin' went tits up. Police there an' everythin'. We all had to leg it, find somewhere else to live. Thanks to you.'

Jamal looked at him, shrugged like he didn't want to get drawn into talking to Jason but continued all the same. 'Father Jack was one evil bastard, man, a fuckin' pervert. Deserved to be turned over, you get me? Deserves his jail time. No question. Hope he's gettin' everythin' due to him in there.'

Jason's fogged brain was having trouble following Jamal's argument, tried to counter. 'Yeah, but . . . wasn't a bad place. Y'know. Just had to ignore some stuff, think of the good stuff. Was kinda settled there.'

Jamal looked at Jason, compassion in his eyes. 'Know what you mean, man. Comin' up rough . . . it's bad.'

Jason looked hard at Jamal. The black kid was confusing him. He seemed genuine, concerned. They weren't supposed to be like that.

'You found somewhere else?' The compassion still there.

Jason's eyes slowly lit up. 'Yeah, did. Was shit for a time. But it's awright now. Got some new mates. A job. Proper one, like.' He couldn't believe those words came from his lips. He smiled. 'Yeah. Things are cool.'

Jason involuntarily flexed his arms as he spoke, sending the new tattoos rippling over his scrawny little muscles.

'Yeah, things are cool.'

He saw Jamal's eyes jump immediately to them, size them up, make a judgement. Jason felt confused again. Jamal should be showing fear; it was the correct response of the immigrant to the tattoos. He'd been told. But Jamal wasn't scared of him. He took in the tats, the clothes, the haircut, his uniform, his tribal insignia and showed no fear. If anything there was pity in his eyes.

Another hard, sharp shaft went through Jason.

'So what you doin', then, eh?' Usually there would be some mutual compassion when he met someone who had come up like he had, the hard way. Instead he tried to build up a good wave of anger, ride it out. Use it to cope with his confusion. 'You on the dole? Scroungin'? Burdenin' the state? Lettin' the taxpayer keep you in ganja an' beer?'

It was what they told him to say to them at meetings. Would hit nerves, get them angry. Guaranteed, they said. Jason didn't know why. Personally he couldn't give a fuck about the taxpayer, whoever he was. And he loved ganja and beer.

Jamal looked at him, a reluctant fire lighting up behind his eyes, an argument he didn't want to have but he wouldn't back down from.

'Fuck you talkin' like that for? That some twisted shit you comin' out with. Don' you be dissin' me, man, I work for a livin'. Hard. Harder than you ever know.' He ran his eyes disdainfully over Jason with the last few words.

'Yeah?' Jason sneered at him, the anger mixing with the rocks and booze now. 'Doin' what?'

'An information brokerage.'

Jason had no idea what Jamal was talking about, tried not to let it show. 'Yeah? Right. Well. You got a—' what did they call them? '—a business card? Eh? Might need some a' that stuff you sell. Some information.'

Yeah, thought Jason triumphantly. Make the nigger dance.

Anger flushed Jamal's cheeks. He drew his wallet from his jeans back pocket, hands shaking angrily, pulled out a card, flicked it at him. Jason caught it, laughing as he did so, but unable to cover up that sharpness stabbing at him again.

He looked at it, tried to read it through slowly, gave up on the first line. He had never been good with words; they meant next to nothing to him. There were three phone numbers on there. And numbers he was good at. One local landline, one mobile and another one.

'What's this?' he asked, pointing to the third number.

'My place in Northumberland,' said Jamal, unable to keep the pride from his voice.

Jason looked at the card, nodding. Jamal turned, began walking away.

'Hey . . .'

Jason wasn't finished with him yet.

'Have a good life, man,' Jamal said from over his shoulder, not stopping, not even bothering to disguise the lie in his voice.

Jason watched him go, holding the card between his fingers.

A teenage nigger handing out business cards. What was the world coming to.

He felt the edges of the card, bent it, testing the weight, then pocketed it. At least it would make a good roach, he thought.

He felt all through his pockets, hoping he hadn't made a roach out of it.

He found it. Crumpled and soiled but still readable. He brought it out, but there wasn't enough light to read it by.

He smiled. Asking a nigger for help. Would have been ironic if he had known what ironic meant.

He put the card back in his jacket pocket over his chest, over his heart.

Tomorrow he would go and find Jamal. He would have to crawl a bit, maybe, explain they might have got off on the wrong foot last time they met, blame the drugs or the drink, but hey, no hard feelings. We're both mates. Both came up the hard way and know what that does to you. And then

Jamal would laugh and say that's OK. Let him stay for a few
days. Help him back on his feet. Lend him a few quid,
maybe.

Or even . . .

Jason frowned, thinking hard. An idea was forming, a
plan . . .

Yeah, a plan . . .

2

It had bad idea written all over it like a full body tattoo.

The house Peta Knight had grown up in was an old seventeenth-century rectory outside Gateshead near the south bank of the Tyne. Pulling the Saab on to the curving gravel drive brought back her usual memories: playing in the huge back garden, going for long walks through the woods, sitting by the river, watching the water ebb and flow, thinking it went on for ever. Comfort and indulgence, security and relaxation. Childhood's sacred remembrances, its safe nostalgia.

Not the place to meet a potential client. And certainly not one her mother was recommending. She wasn't looking forward to this.

Trevor Whitman was an old friend of her parents from way back, her mother had said, although Peta had never heard him mentioned before. Back in the north-east from living in London and needing someone with Peta's talents. Which were what? A delicate matter; her mother couldn't say over the phone. Why didn't Peta come and meet him? At the house? They could all have lunch. Peta didn't think it felt like the kind of thing she should be getting involved with. Not the right kind of job. Any job, her mother had insisted, voice sweet steel, was the right kind of job when it was the only job. Peta reluctantly demurred. Her mother cooed she would do lunch. Make a pleasant afternoon of it.

Peta liked to research potential clients, get to meetings

early, position herself well, take control, direct the conversation. There would be little chance of that here. But she had no choice but to accept the work. Her money stream was as dried up as a globally warmed creek bed.

Going through the front door, she crossed the black and white squared-tile entrance hall, her unfamiliar heels awkwardly clacking and echoing, handbag slipping off her shoulder, skirt tight as a rope round her knees. Pulling her cotton blouse from her sweating chest, blowing a stray strand of hair out of her eyes. Angry at having to dress up to go home, so far away from her usual comfort zone of jeans and trainers or gym sweats, she felt like a female impersonator. A very bad one.

She looked in on the front room. Same as usual. Her parents had settled on a Liberty print and Klimt look some time in the Seventies and, seeing no reason to change what worked, kept it the same over the subsequent decades. Peta often thought that was a metaphor for their relationship, a thought seemingly confirmed because since her father's death from cancer four years previously her mother hadn't changed a thing.

She called out; no one answered.

Into the kitchen, the Aga turned as low as possible in the heat. The back door was open, two figures sitting close on the wooden garden furniture, laughing. One of them saw her, turned. They pulled apart.

'Peta, darling, come on out.'

Peta went out. She noticed that the bottle of wine between them was nearly empty.

Her mother stood up, smiled. In her early sixties, Lillian Knight was a striking woman. With good bone structure and a figure kept trim and fit, she seemed ten if not fifteen years younger than her actual age. Her blonde hair was now perhaps a shade unnatural, but so what? When Peta looked at her she saw herself in several years' time and found no disgrace in that.

They kissed, both cheeks.

'You're looking well.'

'You too, Lillian.' Always Lillian, never Mother or Mum. That's how she had grown up. The era her parents were from.

'We were just reminiscing about the good old days.' Her mother turned, indicated the man sitting at her side. 'This is Trevor. Trevor Whitman.'

Trevor Whitman's hair was greying, swept back and collar length, his beard well manicured, one step above designer stubble. Medium height and build. Kept himself in shape. Dressed in a dove-grey suit with a black silk shirt beneath it.

He stood up, shook her hand.

'Hi,' he said.

She noticed how he surreptitiously took her all in. How his equally surreptitious nod indicated approval. How his eyes held hers for a beat too long. She forcefully blew the strand of hair away from her face again. He gestured to the garden table; there was a third chair. She sat, feeling uncomfortable, not liking the sensation. Trying to compose herself.

A radiant smile. He lifted the bottle. 'Drink?'

Peta shook her head. 'I don't drink alcohol.'

'I'll get you some water,' said Lillian, seeming suddenly awkward. 'Give you a chance to get to know each other.'

Lillian stroked her hand along Whitman's shoulder. Peta noticed the gesture. She felt she was meant to. Lillian slipped quickly away to the kitchen. Whitman kept looking at her.

'I must say,' he said, holding eye contact, 'you're not what I was expecting.'

'I get that a lot. It's the name,' she said. 'They expect a man.'

'I didn't mean that. I meant an ex-policewoman working

in the private sector, I thought you'd be more . . .' His fingers wriggled as if grasping for the word, smiling all the while.

'Dykey?'

He reddened. 'Well, I wouldn't have said . . .'

She thought of the way her mother had stroked him. 'How d'you know I'm not?'

He quickly took a mouthful of his drink, pretended to find his glass fascinating. Peta tried not to smile. Lillian, as if on cue, chose that moment to reappear. She placed a glass of iced sparkling water down for Peta, another bottle of wine beside Whitman's glass.

'Right,' she said with a bright, shiny smile. 'Now that you two have introduced yourselves, shall we have lunch? Catch up on gossip, then you can get down to work.'

Peta looked at her watch, told her mother she wouldn't have time for lunch. Said that she had a lot on for the afternoon, wished it were true when she said it. Lillian objected but Whitman said it would be OK.

'Fine,' she said, although it clearly wasn't. 'Right. Well. I'd better go and make myself scarce.' She turned, went back into the kitchen. Hurt but trying not to let it show.

'Oh dear,' said Whitman.

Peta felt a pang of guilt, tried to tamp it down, focus. She shrugged. 'I did tell her but she wouldn't listen. I won't take the blame.'

Whitman smiled. 'She's a stubborn one. Once she's got an idea . . .'

Peta nodded, took a sip of her water, felt her composure returning. 'I know.' And worse since she retired from lecturing, she thought, but didn't want to share that with Whitman.

'Sorry,' he said. 'About that remark before. Out of order.'

'No problem.'

'The wine, I suppose. And not very PC.'

'It's OK.'

Another smile. 'Cool. Whatever.'

She looked at him again, sizing him up, professionally judgemental now. The kind of guy who never got punk and thought great music stopped at the Stones, thought cinema was never so exciting after Fassbinder died, had a shelf full of yellowing, orange-spined Penguins, drove a sports car – probably a red one – and thought he was still hip and down with the kids because he knew who Eminem was. Peppered his speech with transatlanticisms. Had the arrogance and demeanour of an ageing rock 'n' roll rebel academic growing old gracefully, proud of not losing his rough edges. She could see what her mother and he had in common.

'Can I ask you something?' he said. 'You don't drink. I'm curious. Is that by choice or . . .'

She had been so determined to succeed when she joined the police, so eager. But whatever the PR people say, an intelligent, attractive young woman, unafraid to speak her mind, is still not welcome in the police. Or at least that was what her colleagues did their best to let her think. When she eventually admitted defeat and left she was racked with depression and a drink problem. She had also had an intense affair with a very unsuitable man that hadn't helped. She had sorted herself out, but it had taken her years.

Peta kept her face blank, her eyes unreadable. 'Let's just say the police lifestyle didn't agree with me.'

'Lillian's told me about your company,' Whitman said, pouring himself another large glass of wine. 'Albion, is it?'

'Was. It's finished now. I'm freelance.'

Whitman raised an eyebrow. 'Thought you were doing well. You and an ex-journalist. Joe Donovan, right?'

Peta kept her voice calm, her answers clipped. 'We're no longer working together.'

'Right.' Then he grinned. 'Guy or girl?'

'What?'

'Joe. Guy or girl?'

'Guy.'

'Thought I'd better ask.' Another smile, another over-long eye lock. 'You look just like her. Lillian. When she was your age. The image of her.'

Peta felt her face reddening, hoped it was just the heat. 'So who is it you want protecting from?'

He smiled, eyes going twinkly-crinkly in the corners, sun glinting on his teeth. 'Myself, mainly.'

Enough. He needed some serious mental realignment and quick focusing.

'Mr Whitman—'

'Trevor, please.'

'Mr Whitman, let's get some ground rules established. This is not a leisurely afternoon with friends and family. We're not on a date. You want to employ me in a professional capacity. So without meaning to be rude, let's talk business.'

Whitman sat back, humbled and fumbling for words. Blushing. Peta definitely with the upper hand now. She waited, her silence the tool he needed to dig himself out. From the kitchen her mother clattered about.

'I'm sorry,' he said. 'That's not what . . . I didn't mean to give that impression. Very unprofessional among other things. Yes, you're right. Let's get on with it.'

'Good,' said Peta, clearly in control. 'Now what's the problem?'

'You're an information broker,' Whitman said eventually, after searching for the right approach. 'That's what I need. Information.'

'About what?'

'Or who.' He sat back, took a mouthful of his drink.

Looked at her, his eyes cold ashes, whatever was in them earlier now burned out. The garden umbrella cast a long shadow over his face. 'What d'you know about me or my background?'

Peta's mind flicked over the notes she had made before the meeting. 'Political radical. Heyday was the early Seventies.'

Whitman winced. Peta enjoyed his reaction but didn't glory in it. She continued.

'North-eastern working-class boy, got a scholarship to university. Newcastle redbrick.'

'Where I met Philip and Lillian.'

'Became politicized there. Left, set up an Angry Brigade splinter group, the Hollow Men.'

'After T. S. Eliot. Satire.'

'And that group was responsible for acts of violence against the state—'

'Ah, now that's not fair—'

Peta continued as if he hadn't interrupted. '—including attacks on the police, various Tory MPs and the firebombing of a pub full of off-duty policemen. Eventually the Hollow Men disbanded, an acrimonious split. Repented of earlier actions in the Eighties, was never charged for anything. Attempted to become Member of Parliament for the SDP in '82, was unsuccessful. Went into teaching at university level, became a lecturer in psychology and sociology.' She sat back, smiling, trying to play down the smugness she felt. 'How am I doing?'

Whitman was impressed. 'Very good.' He smiled. 'Disbanded, acrimonious split, make us sound like a rock band.'

'Wasn't that the intention? Politics the new rock 'n' roll?'

Whitman smiled wistfully. 'Different time. When politics meant something. When rock 'n' roll meant something.' The smile faded. 'And I'd take exception to that description of crimes against the state. We were never terrorists. We were freedom fighters. Revolutionaries, not terrorists. That's what radical politics were like back then.'

'Different time.' She nodded, clearly unconvinced.

He drank his drink.

'So how can I help you now?'

Whitman seemed to think hard, then continued. 'Well, as you know, I've recently written my biography. I didn't expect it to knock *The Da Vinci Code* off the top of the best-seller chart, but I thought it might attract some interest in – shall we say? – academic circles.' His voice, once he became interested in his own words, was rich and sonorous. Yet, Peta noticed, still betrayed his north-east origins. 'Political journals, that sort of thing. I wasn't prepared for what happened.'

Peta leaned forward, interested. 'What happened?'

Whitman opened his mouth but seemed reticent to speak. He moved his lips as if auditioning the correct words before speaking them. 'I've been getting . . . phone calls.'

'What kind?'

'The . . . disturbing kind. The threatening kind.'

'Threatening?'

'Yeah. Well, not in so many words. More . . . insistent. Veiled threats.'

'Saying what?'

'Saying . . . enough to worry me. This person knows about me. My background. Knows I'm coming back up here. Wants to make it difficult for me.'

'In what way?

'Just . . . difficult.'

'So why are you back up here?'

'The book. I'm promoting it. A few local media interviews, TV and radio, a signing, that sort of thing.'

'And then what? Back home? To London?'

'No, I'm . . . I took a sabbatical. Staying up here. For a while.'

Peta leaned forward. 'Any reason?' She looked to the kitchen window, where her mother was pretending to do something at the sink. 'Family? Friends?'

Whitman shrugged. That irritating smile began to creep across his features again. 'Not much family left. Friends?' He followed Peta's gaze. 'Maybe. But really I'm just taking in the local colour. Seeing the old town. Logging the changes. That kind of thing. Might write another book about it.'

He glanced quickly at her, then away, as if his eyes were holding something he didn't want her to see. She didn't believe his words but didn't press him. It had nothing to do with work.

'Right.'

'And judging by the headlines and the TV, I picked possibly the worst time to come back to Newcastle. What with that Asian kid. And the Fascists on the march again. And that Muslim guy trying to make a name for himself.'

Peta nodded. 'Not the most stable of times.'

They both knew the story. A twenty-year-old Muslim college student had been found dead in the street after being set ablaze. Peta could still clearly recall his grief-stricken mother at a televised press conference weeping openly, having a breakdown in front of millions. The National Unity Party, a BNP offshoot, had been blamed but, with local elections in which they were expected to make significant gains upcoming, were strenuously denying it. As a result, Muslim communities, egged on by Abdul-Haq, a local leading radical, were arming themselves, patrolling the streets at night. The city was on a knife edge. Tension was high. And, Peta thought, fanning her neck and chest, the weather wasn't helping any.

'And the heat,' Whitman said. 'Wasn't like this back in the day.'

Peta suppressed a smile at the phrase.

'Yes,' she said. 'We're always going on about southerners, how they get the slightest bit of snow and barricade themselves into their houses for a week. We're the opposite. A bit of heat and we revert to angry cavemen.'

He smiled. 'And cavewomen. Let's be politically correct.'

'OK,' she said, back to business. 'This caller. Any ideas. Do you know who this person is?'

'Obviously not. If I did I would be able to do something about them.'

'All right, then. Do you suspect who this person might be?'

Whitman sighed. 'I don't know.' He took another mouthful of his drink. Refilled from the bottle. Peta noticed the wine was nearly all gone. 'I used to get calls a few years ago.'

'And it's the same kind of messages?'

He nodded.

'So why didn't you go to the police about them the first time round?'

Whitman snorted out a laugh, drank down a third of his drink, looked away. 'A firebomb ripped apart a pub in the centre of Newcastle. A pub frequented by off-duty policemen and women. Over thirty years ago.'

'I read about it. Fifteen people injured, one dead.'

'Then you'll know we were held responsible for it.'

'And were you?'

Whitman sighed. 'We were blamed for it.'

'Did you do it?'

Whitman took another drink.

Peta waited.

'The Hollow Men were blamed,' he said, stressing the

word, 'but the Hollow Men didn't do it. At least, not as far as I was concerned.'

'What d'you mean?'

'There was one of our group. Alan Shepherd. Always wanted to push things further. The most extreme of all of us. He talked about doing something like that. Really up for it. We argued, said it wasn't the way forward. Next thing we know, the pub's gone up. And Alan's disappeared.'

'So it was him?'

Whitman took another mouthful of drink. 'We always assumed he was behind it and that he'd been caught up in the flames. We never heard from him again.' Another sigh. 'And we were blamed. That was the turning point for me. I left soon afterwards.'

'And that was when the phone calls started?'

He nodded.

'To all of the Hollow Men or just you?'

'I don't know. I'd cut ties with them by then.' He sat back. 'So you see why I couldn't go to the police.'

Peta nodded. She sensed there was more; that Whitman wanted to open up. She waited.

'I assumed that those calls were from a member of the dead copper's family,' he said. 'His brother, I thought.' He shook his head, back in the past. 'Very distressing. Abusive. Late at night. Presumably when he'd been drinking. I know they made me drink.'

'Saying what?'

'Saying . . . I should never relax. That they would never forget or forgive me for what I had done. That one day, when I had forgotten, they would be there, waiting for me.'

'And you did nothing?'

'Yeah, I did. I moved away. Changed my phone number. Got a new life. The calls stopped then.'

He took another drink.

'Anyway,' he said, waving his hand wearily as if trying to dismiss the memory, 'it's all in the book.'

'And the calls stopped until recently?'

He nodded.

'And what did you do then?'

'I knew I had time owing at the university, asked for a sabbatical, planned a trip up here to coincide with the book launch. Phoned Lillian. And as luck would have it, she mentioned you. Not a detective as such, and perhaps that's the appeal. No cop vibe.' Another drink. The bottle had been drained. 'So that's it. What d'you think?' Whitman leaned forward, tried to hide the desperate edge in his voice. 'You want to take me on?'

Peta looked again at him. His earlier suave demeanour all but disappeared. In its place was a fidgety, anxious-looking middle-aged man. Very un-rock 'n' roll.

Peta looked at her sparkling water. The bubbles were rising, breaking on the surface, disappearing. Condensation had formed on the outside. She stroked her finger slowly down it, feeling the cold wet tingle it left. A tiny thrill went through her.

'I'll need your complete cooperation. Don't withhold anything. If I ask you a question I want a straight and honest answer. Right?'

He nodded. 'Right.'

Peta rummaged around in her handbag, produced her notebook. 'Good. So these calls you're getting now. Where do they come to? Home? Mobile?'

'Both.'

'Right. And what was the name of the policeman who died?'

'George Baty. It's all in the book. A matter of public record now.'

She wrote it down. 'As good a place as any to start. Now,

what about other people? Contacts, friends. From the old days, perhaps?'

'I don't know . . . I don't think so.'

'The Hollow Men were based up here, right? In Newcastle?'

Whitman nodded.

'Any of them still around?'

He shrugged, head back under the shade of the umbrella where Peta couldn't read his face. 'I don't keep in touch with any of them. Only one that I know of. Abdul-Haq.'

'The radical Islam guy? He was a Hollow Man?'

Whitman nodded. 'Changed a bit since I last saw him. Couldn't have been more surprised when I saw him on the news.'

She pushed her notebook and pen over to him. 'Give me a list of the rest. If there are any still up here I can talk to them, see if anything jogs a memory.'

He smiled. 'I can do better than that.' He reached down to the side of the table, produced a hardback book, handed it over. 'All in there.'

Peta looked at it. *Angry Young Man: The Rise and Fall of Radical Politics in the 1970s.* His name underneath it. A slightly blurred news picture of a much younger Trevor Whitman hurling a rock during a demonstration. Looking angry but something more. Vibrant, alive. Charismatic.

'Thank you,' she said.

'My pleasure. Let me sign it for you.' He took out a pen, scribbled something in the front, handed it back. 'So what are you going to do? Phone taps? Traces? That kind of thing?'

She thought of Amar. 'Albion had a very good surveil-lance expert. The best I've ever worked with. He's . . . not been well recently, but I'll see if he feels up to it yet.'

'Thank you.'

'No problem.' Peta told him how much she would charge and what he could expect. Whitman accepted everything. She stood up. 'Well, I think that's it for now. You staying here?'

He looked back to the kitchen window. 'No.' He gave her the name of his hotel, stood also.

'And if you get a call in the meantime, tell me. Straight away. Any time.'

'I will.' He had regained some of his earlier composure; the twinkle had returned to his eye. 'I look forward to seeing you again, Peta.'

He extended his hand; she took it. As they shook she experienced a frisson, like a static electric charge. Not unpleasant. Just discomforting. She was sure he must have felt it too. He smiled, let go with a certain amount of reluctance.

Lillian, as if on cue, emerged from the kitchen. 'Finished chatting?' she said, smile in place, earlier upset seemingly forgotten. 'Are you taking her on?'

'I am,' said Whitman, smiling. 'I'm sure Peta is the answer to all my problems.'

Lillian smiled. It seemed brittle. 'I'm sure.' Her hand again fell on to Whitman's shoulder. He made no attempt to remove it.

Peta felt it was time to leave. Her mother made protestations, but Peta got the feeling that she was secretly relieved to have her go.

Peta got in the car, put the book on the passenger seat next to her, opened it to see what he had written.

> To Peta: Cool name for a cool gal!
> Looking forward to working with you,
> Love
> Trevor Whitman

'Jesus,' she said, shaking her head. But smiling, all the same.

As she drove away, Whitman and Lillian came to the door, waved. Both smiling, but Peta sensed a tension beneath the smiles. She would have to speak to her mother on her own some time. Find out what was going on.

Driving away, Peta turned the radio on. The news. Police were saying they had no new leads in the murder of Sooliman Patel. Rick Oaten, the leader of the National Unity Party, was strenuously denying they had anything to do with it, despite his party's leaflets found at the scene. He had fully cooperated with the police, he said, and there was no evidence that linked him or his organization with the attack. Reports were coming in of an increase in racially motivated attacks throughout the city.

'National Unity Party,' she said under her breath. 'National Union of Pricks, more like.'

A soundbite from Abdul-Haq followed. He was angry. 'How much longer must our young men be slain? What more needs to happen before the police will act? How bad do things have to get before we legitimately take steps to protect ourselves? Our communities?'

She switched channels.

She looked in the rear-view mirror, back at the house. A cloud seemed to be hovering over it.

A song came on the radio, the Arctic Monkeys' hectic chug bringing her back to the present.

Despite all her misgivings, she felt the familiar tingle. It was good to be working again.

Whitman and Lillian watched Peta pull out of the driveway. Lillian turned to him.

'How did that go?'

'Fine.'

Lillian stared ahead, looking at the space Peta had disappeared into, breathing heavily. 'I should have been with you. Made sure you said the right thing.' She turned back to Whitman, fire still in her eyes. 'And what were you doing out there? Flirting with her?'

'No, Lillian, I was just . . .' He shrugged. 'She's a lovely girl. You should be proud.' He smiled.

'You were flirting. With *her*. Jesus Christ, what's wrong with you?'

'I was admiring her. She looks like you, Lillian. The image of you. At that age.'

Lillian said nothing, the anger in her eyes cooling slightly. She sighed. 'Hope we've done the right thing.'

'We have.'

'My little girl . . .'

Whitman placed his hand on Lillian's arm. 'Let's go back inside.'

Lillian looked at him. Made no attempt to remove his hand. 'Oh, God . . . Trevor . . .'

He stroked her arm. 'It'll be OK. Come on.'

Lillian said nothing.

Just allowed him to guide her back inside the house, close the door behind them.

3

'There. Look closer. Now. Do you see him now?'

Joe Donovan squinted through the binoculars, saw the house, trees. A car; some big, silver, planet-destroying 4×4. People emerging from it, slamming the doors loudly behind them. He zeroed in: a couple, well dressed, late thirties. And a boy.

Donovan focused in on the boy.

'You see him?'

'I . . . I see him.'

Donovan zoomed in as close as he could. The boy was dark-haired, tall. Ten, eleven years old. Wearing casual clothes – jeans, T-shirt, trainers. Either top-end high street or designer. The boy closed the car door more carefully than the couple had, picked up his sports bag, followed them inside.

'Well?'

Donovan put down the binoculars, expelled a deep breath.

'I . . . don't know. Just don't know.'

Amar Miah was in the car next to him, telephoto lens in his lap. Sitting awkwardly, his back rigid, like his body was giving him discomfort. He moved, grunted in pain.

'You OK?'

'Yeah,' said Amar. 'Just a bit uncomfortable if I sit in one place for too long.' He moved about, tried to find an easier position. 'Anyway, what d'you think? Is it him?'

Donovan stared at the house again, willing the boy to emerge, wanting one more look.

Be him, thought Donovan, be David.

Be my son.

It started with a phone call from Francis Sharkey. The solicitor had been working on Donovan's behalf to find David, had people out chasing down every lead, every half lead, every whisper.

'It's your son,' he had said simply and succinctly. 'It's David. We've found him.'

And Donovan's world had caved in. He hadn't been able to answer. Sharkey had continued.

'Or at least a very strong possibility that it's him. And he's alive.'

Questions had tumbled through Donovan's mind too fast for him to articulate. Emotions also. He felt his heart would explode.

'I've got to go to him . . . got to see him . . . now . . .'

'It's not that simple, Joe.'

'Why not?' Donovan had replied. 'Why . . . What's . . . Why . . . What's the matter with him?'

'I'm on my way,' said Sharkey. 'Don't go anywhere. I'll be straight there.'

Donovan put his mobile down, looked round. He was alone in the Albion office, standing among the debris of a recent break-in, bottle of whisky before him. He couldn't remember who had broken in, why, or what he had been so upset about. Couldn't remember anything. Before the phone call was now another time, another place.

It was a moment he had been in preparation for, in dread of, for four years. Since his then six-year-old son had disappeared.

That day in the shopping mall played and replayed in his

head obsessively. David standing behind him, queuing up to pay for a present for Donovan's wife, David's mother. He turned and . . .

There, then gone.

There, then gone.

Without a trace. As if he had never existed. Every avenue explored, every possibility considered. Nothing.

And Donovan had never stopped looking for him. Even though it cost him his marriage, the love of his daughter, his job and, in bringing him to his own personal abyss, just about his sanity.

During those years, in the dark, haunted times, in those loneliest hours, dancing on the edge, mind spinning from alcohol, playing Russian roulette, he had examined every imagined outcome, ghost-played every possible scenario.

David alive. David dead. David alive but worse than dead.

Every one he could think of, no matter how horrific. Steeling himself for when that day came. If that day came.

Now it was here.

Perhaps.

But he couldn't plan for how it felt when he heard those words.

Sharkey turned up within the hour. Donovan had made substantial inroads into the whisky. He paced the floor, unable to sit, his movement booze-blurred and unsteady. But his thoughts were in sharper relief, his mind roiling.

'Why won't you let me see him? I've got to, I've . . .'

Sharkey sighed. He was sitting on an office chair, legs crossed, immaculate as usual. 'There are complications.'

'Complications? What d'you mean . . . what?' Donovan was slurring. Standing before Sharkey, breathing whisky into his face.

Sharkey's nose wrinkled from the smell. But he didn't dare mention it.

'It's a delicate situation. This boy and his possible identity have only emerged as a result of long-term surveillance.'

'So?'

'It's part of an ongoing job. With wider implications. It can't be compromised.'

'Fuck off. This is my son.'

'And I can understand that. But let me just say, as far as we can tell, he's been well treated, not been harmed in any way. In fact, if anything he's been pampered.'

'By who?'

Sharkey hesitated. 'Why don't you put the bottle down, Joe?'

Donovan threw Sharkey a murderous look. 'Keep talking.'

Sharkey kept talking, every word hitting Donovan with the force of a brick.

'The good news is,' said Sharkey, his smooth lawyer tones kicking in, 'he's not been picked up by a gang of paedophiles, sold into slavery, anything like that. As far as we can tell.'

'What d'you mean, as far as you can tell?'

'Sit down, Joe. It'll be easier.'

'Fuck off. Don't tell me what to do.' Donovan kept pacing, whisky bottle in hand.

Sharkey continued. 'Finding him has been a mammoth task. We've had feelers out all over the country and abroad. Looking for any sightings of—'

'Yeah, yeah, cut to the chase.' Another swig from the bottle.

Sharkey opened his briefcase, took out a slim file, flicked through it, carried on talking.

'A couple came to our attention. Late thirties, well-to-do. He works in the London media in some capacity, she spends most of her time in the gym or on sunbeds. Own an old farmhouse with land just outside a small village in Hertford-shire. A perfect couple. Living the dream, one might say, if one were that way inclined. Perfect except for one thing.'

'No children,' said Donovan, still walking.

'Precisely. Then they go on holiday. And when they return, they have a boy with them. Their neighbours are far enough away not to notice at first, their friends and col-leagues mostly London-based.'

Donovan stopped pacing. 'And this boy's about, what? Ten years old? And matches what we think David would look like at that age.'

Sharkey nodded. 'Exactly.'

Donovan looked at the file on Sharkey's lap, like a hungry dog slavering after a bone. 'You got photos?'

Sharkey passed over a small stack of photos. Donovan, his hands shaking from more than alcohol, took them. They were blurred, grainy. A boy in school uniform getting out of a 4×4. The boy walking, trees, other children obscuring the shot. Going into what looked like a private school. Coming out again. Getting out of the same 4×4, going into a house.

'Long lens stuff,' said Sharkey. 'Employed a couple of tabloid paps to get them.' The side of his mouth twitched almost in a smile. 'Told them he was the illegitimate son of Michael Barrymore.'

Donovan handed them back. 'You used that computer program thing? Aged him?'

'We have. Although, as you can see, we didn't have much to go on so the results aren't a hundred per cent conclusive. But they seem pretty close. Close enough to call you in, Joe.'

'What about DNA?'

'Can't get close enough. They never let him out of their sight.'

Donovan sat down on another office chair, letting the information sink in. His heart was beating harder than the

wings of a canary trying to escape a too-small cage.
Suddenly he felt tired. 'So when can I see him?'

'Well, as I said, it's a matter of some delicacy . . .'

The couple's names were Matt and Celia Milsom. The boy
was attending a private school in the area under the name of
Jake Milsom. As far as Sharkey's investigative team could
gather, he was supposed to be the son of a cousin who had
emigrated to Bahrain, staying in Britain to complete his
education.

He mixed with the other children at school but didn't
seem to have many close friends. None came to visit; he
never went to see anyone. The Milsoms kept him close to
home.

'So if he's not the son of a cousin,' said Donovan, 'where
did he come from?'

'Looking for David inevitably involved overlapping with
other investigations,' said Sharkey. 'Information exchanges.
He came to light as part of a worldwide effort to stop the
trade of black-market children. As well as those sold into
sexual slavery, there's also a thriving market for supplying
rich childless couples. These children can come from all
over the world. Some are bought or stolen to order. Some
willingly sold, some snatched. And they can end up anywhere.'

'Even here.'

Sharkey nodded. 'Even here.'

Donovan looked at the photos once more. 'I want to see
him.'

Four months.

That was how long it took for Sharkey to smooth things
over with other agencies, to let Donovan take over that
strand of the investigation. But there was one further

complication: no more Albion. And Donovan had dreaded telling Peta the fact.

'What d'you mean?' said Peta.

'Just what I say,' said Donovan. 'No more Albion.'

She looked round the office. No one had cleared it up. Now it looked like no one ever would.

'There's been whispers,' said Donovan, 'We're going to be investigated. Coppers, law, the lot.'

'Why?'

'Because our last job should have been simple information-gathering. Instead it left at least four people dead and almost destroyed Tyne Dock in a fire.'

'We helped to stop a sex-trafficking ring and a serial killer,' said Peta. 'Amar almost died. I almost died.'

'I know,' said Donovan.

'And you think that's not on my mind every day? You think not having work is going to make it better?'

'No. I think it's all the more reason for you to ease off. It was close for me too. And police and Customs still have a lot of questions.'

'Get Sharkey to deal with it.'

'He is. But he costs money. Virtually all the fee we got from the last job has gone on him. On legal action to keep us out of jail.'

Peta looked like she was ready to explode.

'So that's it? We just walk away from it? From what we've built up? All that hard work, gone?'

'No,' said Donovan. 'We just lie low for a bit. Do some freelancing. Let it blow over, then bring Albion back.'

Peta paced the room then stopped, turned, her face lit by a harsh light. 'I get it,' she said.

'Get what?' Donovan knew what she was thinking, had anticipated this.

'It's this boy, isn't it? The one who might be your son.'

'*Is* my son.' The phrase was out before he could stop it.

Peta actually bit her lips to stop herself answering back. Composed, she continued. 'So we'll help you.'

'No. I'm doing this on my own.'

'Why? We're a team. We're in this together.'

'We're not a team. I said, we've got to—'

'I heard what you said.' Peta was getting angry. 'But we *are* a team. You, me, Amar, Jamal. We don't stop just because some lawyer says so. We work together, we—'

'I'm doing this on my own.'

'Why?'

His eyes held angry conviction. 'Because I've got to.'

Peta's hands were shaking. 'No problem. You don't want your friends, your team-mates, fine. Go play cowboy.'

'It's not that, it's just—'

'Oh, fuck off.' Peta wasn't holding back now. 'So you've suffered. We know. Well, you're not the only one. We all have. That's why we stick together. But not you. You're too fucking self-indulgent and self-obsessed to notice when people lo . . . when people care about you.'

'Me self-indulgent? I'm not the one who can't take my drink.'

Peta stared at him, for a few seconds too angry and hurt to speak.

'I'm sorry. I shouldn't have—'

'You're right, Joe. We're not a team any more. So fuck you.'

Four months.

How long it took him to get his head together enough to persuade the other agencies that, in the absence of Albion, he was able to take over this strand of the investigation.

He had phoned Sharkey, the other agencies involved, from David's room.

He always called it that, despite the fact that the boy had never set foot in there. It was a room that only Donovan ever entered; even Jamal knew not to go in.

The walls were covered with pictures of Donovan's missing son. Photos of his life up to the age of six. School, family, holiday photos. And suppositional photos: David aged, David superimposed on white sandy beaches cut out from magazines, on holidays he would never take. David. Everywhere.

Against the walls were filing cabinets. Filled with every lead, line of inquiry, dead end that the police and private organizations had undertaken. Donovan sometimes came into the room, would spend a night or a day going over the files, checking to see if something had been missed, some clue overlooked, some avenue not explored. There was nothing. There was always nothing.

Until now.

He had stood there, phone in hand, drawing strength from the walls around him, arguing that personal involvement wouldn't cloud his judgement, would only make him more focused to get at the truth.

The investigation was stonewalling, he reminded them. The investigators couldn't get close enough to the boy without arousing suspicion. It was agreed. Donovan would take over.

Four months.

Until Donovan, along with Amar Miah, his one-time colleague from Albion, could sit one Wednesday in June underneath an ancient oak tree on a country road in Hertfordshire behind the wheel of Amar's Volvo estate, watching the house and hoping they wouldn't be too conspicuous. Hoping to get some answers.

'So is it him?' asked Amar.

Donovan kept looking at the house, willing the door to open again. His mind was again in turmoil, his heart again racing. Sweat was prickling his body. He wanted a drink, something to numb his mind. Anything.

'I don't know . . .' said Donovan again. He had planned the moment in his head so long. Rehearsed it. 'I thought it would be . . . I don't know.' The excitement in his body would build and build until he saw him, then crash and burst out, a huge tidal wave of emotion pouring out of him, engulfing his son in love, making him safe once again, sweeping him home. 'I thought when I saw him that I would just *know*, you know?' But it hadn't happened. The uncertainty. The not knowing. 'That I would see him and suddenly there would be this . . . connection. This instant connection.' But the emotion was still there inside him, built up, but with no outlet. 'And . . . I don't know. I just don't know.'

Amar moved round again. His discomfort was obvious. 'So what d'you want to do?'

Donovan pulled his eyes away from the house, looked at Amar, saw from his face how much pain he was in and not letting on.

Donovan sighed, shook his head. He felt like his soul was screaming for release. 'Get you out of this car.'

'I'm OK.'

'No, you're not. I shouldn't have listened to you. I should have left you back in Newcastle resting up.'

Amar had turned up at Donovan's place when he was leaving, insisted on accompanying him. Donovan, knowing what state his one-time colleague was in, had relented, taken him along.

'I'm fine, Joe. Honest.' Amar swallowed hard as if not wanting to show Donovan how much pain he was in.

'No, you're not.'

A flash of something – anger, pain, Donovan didn't know what – registered on Amar's face. 'I have to do something. I can't just sit there—' The words froze in his mouth. He said nothing more.

Donovan looked at his lap, played with the strap of the binoculars. An awkward silence descended.

'Peta phoned,' said Amar. 'Got some work for me back in Newcastle. Freelance stuff. Surveillance.' He gave a short, hard laugh. 'Better be on the ground floor. Not too good at stairs yet.'

Four months. The same amount of time since Amar had lain bleeding his life out on to a pavement, a bullet lodged within him. Four months since a twelve-hour operation to save his life by removing his spleen, part of his lung and two ribs was deemed a success. Four months since he had been able to walk unaided and without pain.

It had stopped him going out, making casual pick-ups in gay bars and curtailed a cocaine habit that was spiralling out of control. Donovan thought he should be grateful for that.

Amar kept looking at Donovan. 'You should talk to her, you know,' he said. 'You haven't spoken for months. Come and see her.'

'So that's why you wanted to come.' Donovan shook his head. 'Did Peta put you up to it? Jamal? I thought he made himself scarce when you turned up.'

'You should call her. She's upset. She wants to help. We all do. Put the argument behind you. Talk to her.'

Silence fell like cold, hard snow.

Donovan's head was buzzing like a beehive on overtime. He wanted to just get out of the car, walk up to the door, hammer on it until it was opened, then rush inside and grab his son. Have the emotional reunion he longed for. Sweep David away to safety. To home.

Donovan blinked. The door hadn't opened. He hadn't

gone up to it. The emotional tidal wave was still inside him. 'We're going.'

'Back to Newcastle?'

'London. Bit of business to take care of in the morning. We'll stay over then I'll drive you back to Newcastle, right?'

Amar looked puzzled. 'OK.'

'Well, what am I going to do? Sit here for ever and stare at that door? Will the fucker to open and David to run out?'

'What are you going to do?'

'I don't know. Find another way. Because this one isn't working.'

He turned the engine on, drove away.

Donovan's soul silently screaming all the way to London.

4

Jamal wasn't bored. Not exactly.

Joe Donovan often said that only boring people got bored, and Jamal, not wanting to think of himself remotely in that way, had come to accept that as true. So he wasn't bored. No. Just wished he had some way of making his Wednesday night pass quicker.

He'd flicked on the TV, found only films he'd seen before, soaps he wasn't interested in, documentaries about things he couldn't care less about. Not even any gyrating honeys or bashment babes on MTV Base.

He'd played all the games he wanted to. His thumbs were worn out.

He'd started reading one of Donovan's books, *Requiem for a Dream* by Hubert Selby Jnr. He had learned that requiem meant a funeral song for the dead and, reading it, that made sense. It was one dark book, dark and depressing. About kids living rough, getting high, doing what they had to do to get by. Real life the requiem for their dreams.

Jamal knew all about that one.

It was gripping and involving and full of heart and love, the writer obviously reporting back from having lived it, but Jamal could read it only in small doses. He was also fearful of the ending, in case anything bad happened. He didn't want it to trigger any unpleasant memories of his own. Any bad endings.

But no bad endings here, he thought, looking round the cottage and smiling. Took a sip from the big glass of mixed fruit juice at his side. Fruit juice. Who'd have guessed? No drugs, no booze. Living clean, intending to stay that way. And loving it.

Donovan had phoned to say he would be back on Thursday, leaving Jamal on his own. He just hoped Amar had been able to say something, talk some sense into him. Hoped his scheme to get the team back together again had worked.

He hadn't realized just how lonely it would be, in the cottage by himself. He was used to living alone, on his wits, back in London. But this was different. Everything was different now. His mate Josh was away; there was nothing to do. Couldn't even get into Newcastle. Not that he wanted to at the moment. Streets weren't safe if your skin was dark, not since that Asian kid had been set on fire. Too much violence. Too many people looking for easy targets. Even a savvy kid like him was scared.

Jamal stretched out on the sofa, yawned. Thought about going to bed, maybe taking up one of Donovan's graphic novels. Old-school stuff, *Watchmen* or *V for Vendetta*. Or coolest of the cool, *100 Bullets*.

He stood up, made to cross to the bookshelf.

And stopped.

A noise, coming from beyond the back door.

Something scratching, rooting around.

Jamal froze. Usually when he heard something like that it was a fox foraging in the bin, or a cat on a nocturnal prowl from one of the nearby houses. Nothing to worry about.

He listened. Heard the crash of glass as bottles saved for recycling were knocked over.

Too big for a cat or a fox. Or even a badger.

But cats, foxes and badgers didn't trip over bottles. And then swear.

Jamal looked round, wished Donovan was there with

him. But he wasn't and there was nothing he could do about that.

He steeled himself, swallowed hard, cautiously made his way towards the back door. Stopped, scoped the kitchen, looking for some armament, something that would give him an advantage. His baseball bat was propped up against the back door, two tennis balls on the floor beside it. He and some of the boys from the village sometimes went out on the recreation field, played their own version of baseball. Thankfully he had ignored Donovan's nagging and not put it away. He picked it up and carefully opened the back door.

He looked round, eyes getting accustomed to the darkness. The air was still and warm, even this late. He listened. Heard only his own breath coming harsh and ragged, his heart beating fast as drum 'n' bass.

He stepped outside, bat raised. Planted his feet away from the broken glass. Stood as still as he could, waited.

A movement; heard more than seen, the bushes by the end of the garden rustling, the shiny, dark leaves catching a moonlight glint.

Jamal turned, ready. 'You better come out, man. Whoever you are. I'm armed an' I'm gonna start hittin' soon, you get me?'

Nothing. The bush remained still.

Jamal cleared his throat. 'I ain't jokin', man.' He took a step closer to the bush, tried to ignore the damp grass beneath his socked feet. 'I'm comin'. I mean it.'

He pulled the bat back, all of his strength behind the swing, let it go.

'Don't hit me!' A figure stepped out from behind the bush, cowering, hands before its face.

Jamal, unable to stop, quickly changed direction, bringing the bat down away from the figure, swinging it at the other side of the bush. It hit, sending leaves flying from the impact.

He tried to make out the face of the figure in the leafy shadows.

'Sorry . . .' the figure said. It was a male voice, scared.

Jamal stepped back, bat held ready once more. 'Step out o' there,' he said. 'Slowly.'

The figure stepped out on to the lawn. In the moonlight Jamal could make out a small frame, undernourished and runty-looking, clothes dirty and dishevelled. Eyes wide like a hunted animal's. He had no idea who it was.

'Hey, Jamal, how's it goin' . . .'

Jamal looked closer. There was something familiar about the youth.

'It's Jason. Remember? Met you in the street a few weeks ago?'

Jamal frowned. 'Jason? From Father Jack's?'

Jason nodded. 'Yeah.'

They stood staring at each other, questions bubbling to the surface of Jamal's brain, popping too quickly for him to ask them.

Jason gave a quick, nervous glance round, fear shining like silver in his eyes. Jamal caught the look.

'Can I come in?'

Jamal frowned, those questions still there. 'Uh, yeah, sure.'

Jamal pointed to the house. Jason hurried inside. Jamal reached the back door, gave a quick look round the garden, listened. Just in case. Sure there was no one there, he stepped in, closed the door behind him.

Locked it.

'Sit down.'

Jason sat on the sofa. He was filthy, like he had been sleeping rough in the woods. It was like letting a wild animal into the house. Jamal wondered what kind of mess he would make of Joe's furniture.

'Man, you're mingin',' said Jamal. 'Where you been? An' how you find me?'

'Gave us your card, didn't you? Remember?'

Jamal remembered and silently admonished himself. Must have handed out the wrong one. He had various ones with different phone numbers and addresses on them, depending on how much information he wanted the recipients to have. Jason was supposed to have got the basic model. Must have got mixed up. Would have to be more careful in future. Shouldn't have even been carrying them round at all.

Jamal studied the youth, remembered their previous encounter. Jason was wearing jeans, boots, ripped T-shirt, all filthy. His razored hair was growing back; his head resembled a fuzzy, dirty peach. His nervous, fearful eyes took in all corners of the room. Perched on the edge of the sofa ready to bolt, he looked small and young, a lost little boy playing at being an adult. Not really master-race material, he thought.

'So who's after you, bro?' said Jamal, sitting in an armchair.

'Can't tell you,' said Jason, his voice dry and cracked, his head shaking.

Despite their differences, Jamal felt an empathy with the lost boy. A street kid, come up the hard way. Done what he had to do to survive. Now scared and needing help. And Jamal knew he would give it. He had no choice. Because he'd been there. Because some allegiances went deeper than skin.

'Can I have a drink?'

'Got fruit juice. Just opened some.'

A sharp-toothed smile appeared on Jason's ratty little face. 'Got any Stella?'

'Nope. Fruit juice. Or tap-water. Maybe I could stretch

to a cup of tea.' Jamal felt good saying the words, strong. Like something Joe would say.

Jason looked at Jamal like he was from another planet. 'Fruit juice . . .'

Jamal went into the kitchen, poured two fruit juices from the fridge, returned to the front room. Jason was on his feet, looking over the CD collection, touching things. He had a hold of Jamal's iPod. When he saw Jamal enter, he replaced it on the shelf.

'Here.' Jamal handed him his juice. Jason took it, sat back down, shifty eyes darting everywhere.

'So you're runnin', yeah?'

Jason nodded.

'Who from?'

'Said. Can't tell you.'

'So why you come here? Why you look for me, then?'

Jason drained his glass, put it on the floor. Looked at Jamal, his eyes conflicted, like he wanted to unburden but found trust hard.

'You gonna tell me?'

Again, the look of confusion. That lost look.

'Got to open up some time, man. An' we was at Jack's place. We already shared some shit, you get me?'

Jamal knew what was stopping him. The experience of Father Jack weighed against what the skinheads had told him about black kids. He sat back, waited for one side to win.

Jason's inner conflict came to the boil. 'They . . . they're gonna kill me,' he said eventually.

Jamal nodded, said nothing. Just like Joe had shown him.

Jason looked away, at his glass, at the floor. Anywhere but at Jamal. 'Kev found out an' . . . an' . . .' Jason nodded to himself, his body rocking backwards and forwards, his face showing a growing incredulity at his words. He looked at the ceiling, past the ceiling, his eyes unfocused. 'Shit, I stabbed him . . .'

Jamal watched him, concern on his face. 'You stabbed him? Stabbed who?'

'Kev. Bright.' Jason's eyes focused again. He gave a little giggle. 'I'm the Butcher Boy.'

'Right.'

'I'm special.'

Weirder by the minute, thought Jamal. 'Who are they?'

Jason looked at Jamal, frowned. 'You fuckin' stupid? You know who they are. On the news all the time.'

'The NUP?'

Jason nodded. 'Aye,' he said, pride in his voice. 'An' I'm one o' them. A special one.' A shadow seemed to pass over his face. 'Well, I was.'

'Keep goin',' said Jamal. 'You were talkin' about Kev. You stabbed him.'

'Yeah. Well, anyway, he got me to cut him with the knife. Make it look good. I'm the Butcher Boy.'

'You said. Then what?'

'I ran.'

'Here.'

'Yeah. They chased us. I had to hide in trees an' shit, like, sleep rough.' He laughed with a child's glee. 'Like a proper fuckin' survivalist, you know? Livin' in woods. Then I had to find you, like. Took me a whole day.'

Jason sat back, looking comfortable for the first time. 'An' here I am.'

Jamal scrutinized him. 'So why they wanna kill you, man?'

''Cos I'm special.'

'You keep sayin' that. How?'

Jason shook his head. 'Can't tell you that.'

'Why not?'

''Cos I'll lose me money.'

'What money?'

'The money. I've had loads of time to think it through. It's the plan. I'm gonna make loads of money. An' you're gonna help us.'

Jamal frowned. 'Jase, man, you're makin' as much sense as tits on bulls. What you on about?'

Jason gave him the kind of look that ignorant people give intelligent ones when they believe they're thick. Jamal would have been upset by that once, fought back against it. Not any more. He didn't need to.

''Cos what I know, right, they don't want anyone else to know. Anyone. So we blackmail them.'

'Blackmail.'

Jason nodded. 'Aye. You see?'

Jamal was beginning to regret letting him into the house. He wished Donovan were back. 'So if I'm supposed to be helpin' you, shouldn't I know what you're talkin' about?'

'Not yet. 'Cos if I tell you now you'll run off with it an' make money.'

'Why would I do that?'

Another retarded, incredulous look at Jamal. ''Cos you buy and sell information, like it says on the card. If you had the information you wouldn't need me. I'm not thick.'

'Right.' Jamal definitely regretted bringing him into the house. He nodded, pretending to think it over. Suddenly the Wednesday night of earlier didn't seem so boring after all.

'Listen,' said Jamal, 'there ain't no information brokerage no more. It's gone.'

Jason frowned. 'So why d'you give us the card?'

Jamal shrugged. 'Frontin'.'

Jason said nothing.

'Tell you what,' said Jamal, 'why don't you come back when the boss is here, yeah?'

'The boss?'

'Joe Donovan. This is his house. He be back tomorrow, we can sort it then.'

Jason jumped up, suddenly agitated. 'No,' he said, 'no, we can't. Has to be you. No one else.'

'Why not?'

'He'll take the money, won't he? Take it away. Might even be in with them.'

'Don't think so, man. Not Joe.'

Jason laughed. 'Aye. Not takin' the chance, like.'

'OK,' said Jamal, standing up. From his brief acquaintance at Father Jack's he remembered that Jason wasn't the sharpest tool in the box. Obviously something had happened to him since then, made him worse. Drink, drugs, whatever. That, coupled with the earlier abuse, must have sent him over. He had seen it happen before. Jamal felt sorry for him, it was sad, but he didn't want to get involved in someone else's paranoid fantasies. 'Come back tomorrow, yeah?' he said, walking towards the front door, 'We'll talk about it then. You want money to get home, yeah?'

Jamal reached the front door, turned. Jason hadn't moved; his fearful eyes darted around the room again.

'Don't make us go out there,' he said, his breathing getting harsh. 'Please, Jamal. Let us stay. You've got to let us stay . . .'

Jason crossed quickly to Jamal, put his hands on his arms, gripped tight. Up close, Jason smelled of woods, fields, pig-pens, farmyards.

'Man, you stink,' said Jamal. 'You need a bath.'

'I'll have one. Yeah. Please let us stay an' I'll have one. Please, Jamal. They're out there, lookin' for us. Tryin' to kill us. Honest. But they'll never think of lookin' here.' He smiled as if he had thought up a master plan. 'An' not with you.'

Jamal looked into Jason's pleading eyes. He didn't find the madness he'd expected, just fear and desperation. He saw not the tough skinhead Jason wanted people to see but the scared little boy who had been bullied and victimized at Father Jack's and probably before that too.

Jamal could more than sympathize with that. 'OK,' he sighed. 'You can stay the night. An' then we talk to Joe, yeah?'

Tears appeared in the corners of Jason's eyes. 'Yeah, whatever . . . thank you. Thank you . . .'

He tried to hug Jamal. Jamal stepped back. 'Yeah. Good. Bathroom's upstairs, first on the left. Go an' run it. Should be some hot water. Gimme your clothes, I'll stick them in the machine. Get them washed an' dried.'

'Thank you.' Jason's face was beaming. 'You've saved me life.'

'Whatever. Go an' get a bath.'

Jason made his way upstairs. Jamal went up too, to get a duvet to lay on the sofa. On the landing he stopped, looked at the closed bathroom door. Heard running water.

He crossed to the window, looked out. The night was warm, heavy and still. No one there. No car headlights. Nothing out of the ordinary. He let the curtain fall back into place.

Just checking, he thought. Just checking.

Jamal woke early, sunlight streaming in to his room and with it heat. Another glorious day. He was getting sick of them. He checked his bedside clock. Five thirty. He groaned, flopped back on the pillow.

He had tossed and turned all night, unable to sleep for long periods. The windows had been open to counteract the heat, but it probably had more to do with his guest. He reckoned Jason would still be asleep if he had had as rough a time as he claimed. Donovan would know how to deal with him when he returned.

He felt wide awake, couldn't get back to sleep. He threw back the covers, got up. He needed the toilet. He would try to go quietly so as not to wake Jason.

He crept out on to the landing, tiptoed over to the top of the stairs, expecting to see the youth fast asleep below him.

But he didn't.

The sheet was thrown off, the sofa empty.

Jamal went downstairs, looked around the front room. Jason was nowhere to be seen. He went into the kitchen. The washing machine had been opened, his dried clothes taken. He went back into the front room, looked at the shelves.

His iPod was gone.

'Shit . . .'

He searched the room. Other things were missing too. CDs, ornaments. Small objects. Things that could be sold or fenced. One of the pillowcases was gone. He looked round again. Saw a note left on the mantelpiece. He picked it up, saw the semi-formed letters, the childish scrawl. Read it.

sury but ave go. i feel bit bad but i need muny. you bin good an we stil partnus if yu want. but mybe not cuz who you r an who i m. but thnks for cleynin mi clohs.
                                                              jason

Jamal threw the note on the floor. He felt worse than angry. He felt betrayed, cheated. By one of his own. He would never have been taken in a few years ago; he must be getting soft. A trusting idiot, like the kind he used to rip off when he was desperate.

He looked round the room again, tried to calm down. Just wait until he told Joe . . .

Shit.

Joe. He didn't want him to know what had happened. Didn't want him to know how he had been taken in. He picked up the duvet, ready to carry it upstairs, then stopped.

Better have a look round, see what else Jason had taken.

Hands shaking, he got his notepad and pen, started making an inventory.

5

He waited for the fire to engulf him. It never came.

Before him bodies were burning, twisting in pain, mouths open, screams drowned out by the noise of the flames. Flesh bubbling and hissing first to jumping, liquid red then unmoving, charcoal black.

No longer a pub, now just a scene from Dante's *Inferno*. And in the middle of this hell, he stood.

Untouched by it.

Life burnt out before him. Faces implored him for help.

He couldn't save them. And if he couldn't save them, he wanted to burn along with them. It was only right. He stuck his arm into the flames. They danced around him, away from him. He tried again. The same thing. He walked towards the fire, ignoring the charred crunching underfoot. It parted, gave him space to move.

'You can't!' he screamed, his words only heard inside his head. 'It isn't fair. Don't leave me behind. Don't take them and leave me . . .'

One of the burning bodies turned, faced him. Skin and muscle gone, now just a flaming skull. 'Let me be no nearer in death's dream kingdom,' it said.

'I didn't do it . . .'

'Let me also wear such deliberate disguises . . .'

'Listen to me . . . *I didn't do it* . . .'

''Til that final meeting in the twilight kingdom . . .'

The burning body loomed. He screamed again.
And it stopped.

Trevor Whitman awoke, tangled up in his bedding, sweat sticking him to the bed.

He sat up, heart racing, looked around. Saw the hotel room, flopped back on the bed, breathing heavily.

'I didn't do it,' he said. 'I didn't do it . . .'

He stared at the ceiling, unmoving.

Joe Donovan sat in the car and stared at the house.

They had stayed the night in London. He had left Amar at the hotel.

Fresh morning sunlight, warm air. The leafy, affluent, North London suburb of Crouch End seemed alive with possibilities, new chances even.

The house looked the same as he had last seen it. Big, Edwardian. Permanent and solid, lasted for years, would last for more years to come. Safe. A proper house for a proper family.

His old house.

He watched the front door, heart beating fast, breathing heavily like a prizefighter about to step into the ring, focusing himself for the task ahead.

Talk to his wife, daughter. Tell Annie she would have a son again. Abigail a brother.

They barely spoke now. Donovan's obsession with finding their missing son and his subsequent breakdown had strained the marriage past breaking point. Running, he had ended up in a semi-derelict cottage back in his native north-east, staring into the abyss, ready to jump. Only the arrival of Jamal into his life and the creation of Albion had pulled him back. Now he no longer looked into the abyss but was still near the edge. And he knew: one good shove and he would stumble and be lost. Possibly for ever.

Like the boy in the house in Hertfordshire. He could pull Donovan away from the abyss. Or shove him into it.

Annie would be pleased when he told her. Could imagine her wanting to share his hope. Join him in taking the first steps towards being a proper family again. Movement at the front door of the house pulled him back from his reverie.

Out stepped a figure. A girl with long, dark hair pulled back, tied in a loose knot at the back, wearing school uniform. His daughter, Abigail. So grown up he almost didn't recognize her.

His heart was pumping like he was losing blood. She hated him and he didn't really blame her. Why had he gone looking for David? Thought it must be something she had done wrong. What had happened was awful, a nightmare, and going on with life was difficult, but why couldn't her dad be content with her? Just her?

He was, he wanted to tell her. He still loved her and her mother with all his heart. And he wanted them all to be together. The four of them. A full family. A proper family. So he kept looking.

And Annie and Abigail had never been able to accept that. But that was OK. Because he wasn't sure he could accept it himself.

She walked down the path to the gate. Tall and confident. He gave a choked-sob smile, pride and guilt inextricably linked.

He had the car door open, heart in mouth, legs shaking and ready to get out, when another figure appeared. A man, late thirties. Casually dressed with short hair, glasses and designer stubble. Michael, he presumed. Annie's new partner. Donovan closed the car door, sat back.

Michael pointed his keys at the Fiat Multipla in front of the house. It responded, unlocking to allow Abigail in. Michael walked to the driver's side, said something to

Abigail that made her laugh, got in too. The front door closed. Annie was double locking it. She put her keys in her bag and walked towards the car, flicking her dark hair out of her eyes. Just like she used to do.

Donovan felt a knife stab his heart. He wanted to rush out, grab hold of Annie, tell her he was here, tell her who he'd found.

The knife twisted. His hand was on the door handle, ready to fling it open, run into the street, jump in front of that stupid fucking car . . .

And twisted, thrust in deeper. Tell Abigail he loved her, she didn't have to hate him any more, he'd found him, they were a family, a real family . . .

The Multipla drove past him. None of them even glanced in his direction.

Thoughts of Annie and hope disappeared like a half-remembered dream exposed to daylight. His face was wet. He didn't know he had been crying. He felt a weight on his chest, like hands shoving him.

Backwards.

He sat in the street, head on his steering wheel, openly sobbing, hands held as fists to his forehead. His tears eventually dried up. But not their cause. He waited until his hands had stopped shaking. Drove away.

Stuck a CD into the player, the first one that came to hand – Richmond Fontaine: *Post to Wire* – to drown out the noise in his head. Listened to Willy Vlautin tell him that not everyone lived their life alone, not everyone gave up.

But knew from the sadness in his voice and the funereal tune that he didn't mean it.

6

Rick Oaten walked through the hospital like a Hollywood star on a red-carpet premiere. Waving hello to this one, blowing kisses at that one, smilingly ignoring another one who spat angry words at him. Basking in the fame of being the NUP leader. Two slabs of awkwardly suited, shaven-headed muscle lumbering in his wake just added to the effect. Medium height, balding and getting jowly and paunchy, in his mind he was a six-foot-plus well-thatched Adonis. He stopped outside a closed door, greeted two young men who were waiting there, one with a notebook, one a camera.

'Now here, Mr Coulson,' he said to the one carrying the notebook, 'you will see the reality of the situation without the spin of political correctness. What we're really up against.'

Coulson the reporter nodded, stifled a yawn. Tried not to let his distaste of Oaten show. Too much.

'And you, Mr McKean, can get some excellent pictures to show to your readers. Bring the horror into the homes.'

McKean ignored him, pretended to be fiddling with his aperture.

Oaten flicked his thinning floppy fringe back from his forehead, hoping it covered his bald spot, turned and opened the door with a flourish. Kev Bright lay in the bed, propped up on pillows, drip attached to his arm, pyjamas covering his torso, eyes open, watching. A heavy-set woman in her mid-thirties was sitting in an armchair reading *Take a Break*. Hearing the door, she threw the magazine aside, jumped up

and almost ran to the bedside, where she began stroking
Kev's hand, heels clacking on the floor like horses' hooves.
Her ample body had been squeezed into the clothes of an
eighteen-year-old on a Friday night out down the Bigg
Market. She sat down, her miniskirt riding all the way up
her thighs. She left it there.

The two young journalists exchanged glances, raised eye-
brows, tried not to smile, let alone laugh. There would be
some serious payback going on when they got back to the
newsroom.

The door slammed; the two bodyguards remained stationed outside.

'What a beautiful picture,' said Oaten. 'How devoted.
You can start snapping now.'

'Can you ask her to put her tits away?' said McKean.
'We're from the *Chronicle*, not *Razzle*.'

Oaten's face flushed from anger and embarrassment.
Another flick of the hair and he crossed to the woman. He
tried keeping his voice low, but the reporters still heard his
words, the anger behind them.

'Diane, what did I tell you? No heels, no low-cut tops.
Jesus Christ, what's the matter with you?'

The woman looked scared, flinched at his words like they
were accompanied by slaps.

'Sorry, Rick. I'll ... I'll go home an' change,
like ...'

'You fuckin' stupid cow,' he hissed. 'There's no time. Just,
just make yourself decent.'

Diane began some detailed rearranging of her copious
breasts. McKean looked tempted to start snapping. Coulson
gave him a look of mock admonishment.

'Right, lads,' Oaten said, turning back to them with forced
bonhomie, 'this is Kevin Bright. Hard grafter, a proud working man. Salt of the earth. A true, yet unsung, working-class

hero. And a very good friend of mine. And his . . . girl-friend. And what happens two nights ago?' Oaten thrust his head at the two reporters, eyes wide. 'What happened? He gets knifed, that's what. Knifed.'

Coulson and McKean waited. Oaten gestured to the notepad.

'Write that down. Knifed.'

Coulson didn't move.

'Go on.'

Coulson sighed, scribbled something on the pad, looked up again. Oaten was walking round the room, building up to some dramatic announcement. While his back was turned, Coulson showed McKean what he had put on the pad: a cartoon of an erect penis spouting sperm. McKean tried not to laugh.

Oaten reached the bedside, turned back to them. 'And who knifed him?'

They waited.

'Will you tell them, Kevin, or shall I?'

'You,' said Kev, his voice sounding genuinely weak.

Oaten patted him on the arm, gave what he presumed was a smile. 'I shall. Youths. A gang of them. How many, Kevin? Five?'

Kev nodded.

'Five. Five pieces of scum against one honest, hard-working man. A totally unprovoked attack.' Oaten began pacing the floor again. 'And you know what else? They were Asian. Indian. Muslim, in fact. You see? That's—'

'How do you know?' Coulson asked.

'What?' Oaten clearly wasn't happy at being interrupted.

'They said. You see—'

'What did they say?'

Oaten hid his anger as well as glass hides sunlight. 'Jihad. Something about a jihad.'

Coulson tried to speak again but Oaten ignored him. He declaimed his rehearsed speech, not stopping for any interruptions. 'You see what we're up against? You see? An unprovoked attack. You call us racist? I say we're realist. You say we breed hate? I say we're honest about the situation. You say we're angry? You're right there. We are. Angry. And defending our territory. Making our streets safe for honest, law-abiding citizens to walk down.'

Oaten stood back, looked victorious.

'Any questions?'

Coulson turned over a page in his notebook. 'Yeah,' he said, lazily scratching his cheek with his pen. 'I'd like to ask the honest hard-working etcetera whether he fought back.'

Oaten looked uneasy. 'Why?'

Coulson shrugged. 'I just thought someone who has two convictions for football hooliganism and a life ban from St James's Park would have put up a fight. That's all.'

Oaten looked like he was ready to explode. His upper lip slipped back over his teeth in a snarl, like a wild animal ready to attack. Struggling to control his temper.

Flash.

The camera went off full in his face. And again.

The two journalists nodded to each other. Coulson flipped his notebook shut. McKean slung his camera over his shoulder.

'Think we've got everything here, thanks,' said Coulson. 'We'll be on our way.'

They turned and left, closing the door behind them.

No one spoke, no one moved. They could hear laughter trailing down the hall, running feet. Oaten was still red in the face, his body shaking.

The door opened. In stepped a man; thin, suited, in his fifties, his hair close cropped, rimless glasses.

'Bastards, fucking bastards . . .' Oaten's fists clenched and unclenched. He noticed the new arrival in the room, stopped. 'Mr Sharples . . .'

'I told you to wait for me,' said Mr Sharples, his South African accent making all his words guttural and harsh. 'Why didn't you fucking listen?'

Oaten stared at him, too angry to speak.

'I'm sure they made you look a fool. And I'm sure you did your best to help them.'

'Don't . . . lecture me . . .'

A hard, cruel light ignited behind Mr Sharples's eyes. His voice was calm, all the more menacing for it. 'Let's get this straight. I'm not here to give you good ideas or make valid points. I'm here for you to fucking listen to me. Got that?' His accent turning the words into verbal machine-gun bullets.

Oaten stood there, shaking. 'This is my party—'

'And you'll run it the way I tell you. Got that?'

'Don't fuckin'—'

'Got that?'

Looking into Mr Sharples's eyes was like staring into Rick Oaten's worst nightmare. His head dropped. He nodded.

'Good.' Mr Sharples crossed to the door. 'Right. We do this professionally. A full press call on the steps of the hospital. TV, print media, the works. No chance for argument or answering back. And if you want to be the fucking party leader you start behaving like it. Or I'll find someone who can.' He looked at his watch. 'If I leave now I might catch them. Stop them printing.' The overhead lights glinted on the frameless glass before his eyes. Made his eyes hard, inscrutable. 'Try not to fuck too much up when I'm gone.'

He closed the door silently behind him.

Oaten's fury hadn't diminished. It still needed an outlet. He turned to Kev.

'You, you fucker. I want you out of that bed. Now.'

'But Rick, I've been stabbed. Jason Mason—'

'Don't fuckin' "but Rick" me!' Oaten was screaming in Kev's face now. Diane shrank away in fear. 'You get up out of that fuckin' pit. I want you on the street. I want you to find that kid, that little cunt, before he can do any damage.'

'I've got the boys lookin' for him . . .'

'The boys?' Oaten leaned across, put his fingers inside Kev's mouth, grabbed his tongue, pulled on it, hard. Twisted. 'Don't fuckin' talk . . . don't . . . say . . . fuckin' *any-thin*' . . .' Incoherent with rage, struggling to regain control.

'The boys,' he said eventually, gasping. 'The boys. You're gonna join them. You're gonna find him an' bring him to me. That clear? You got that?'

Kev, spittle oozing from the sides of his mouth, mutely nodded.

'Good.'

Oaten dropped Kev's tongue, stood back, breathed out heavily. Kev massaged his aching mouth. Diane stared in horror.

Oaten tried to regain what passed for equilibrium. When he could trust his own limbs he walked to the door.

'Fuckers,' he said. 'Fuckers.'

The door vibrated in the frame when he slammed it behind him.

Abdul-Haq stood on the hastily erected platform and looked out before him. He saw faces: concerned, frightened, angry. Mostly brown faces, a smattering of white ones, a few very dark ones. He saw people worried about their futures, their ways of life. He saw TV cameras, print journalists.

He saw a crowd, ready to be worked.

When they saw him take the stand they stopped talking. He waited patiently, giving their conversations a chance to subside, replacing the noise with an expectant silence. Ready to swap fear for reassurance.

He glanced behind at the seated couple, well but conservatively dressed, the woman leaning into the man for support, the man with his arm around her, comforting her. She crying; him trying not to. He gave them a reassuring smile.

Behind the platform, almost out of sight from the main crowd, were Waqas and Omar. His personal bodyguards. Well muscled, wearing black T-shirts and black jeans, their earpieces barely visible. Waqas's T-shirt was long-sleeved, the shiny patches of pink skin, the burn marks covered up on Abdul-Haq's order. People were scared by them, intimidated, offended. Waqas agreed. That was why he put them on display, along with his scarred face. Omar, with only a scar running down his left cheek, had got off lightly by comparison.

Abdul-Haq stepped up to the microphone. 'Peace be upon you.' His amplified voice, rich and rounded, echoed round the crowd. They responded, ready to listen.

He looked around again, saw a drab, run-down, redbrick street in the Arthur's Seat area of Newcastle. A poor area, predominantly immigrant, whether Asian, African, Eastern European or university student. Those already there too poor to leave. The kind of disadvantaged area where poverty outstrips opportunity, where fear turns to hatred faster than work turns to wealth. A place ripe for investment and redevelopment.

He opened his arms for emphasis. 'I'm standing right on the spot where Sooliman Patel was murdered. By racists.' The word emphasized with a strong hand gesture. 'And with me—' he gestured to the seated couple behind him '—are his parents. It has cost them a lot to come here today. More than I hope any of us, with the grace of Allah, will ever have to experience. But they wanted to do so to share this moment with you. To make sure it never happens again.'

Mrs Patel's shoulders heaved as another bout of tears overtook her. Mr Patel's arm tightened around her shoulder.

'Sooliman Patel was playing with his friends just over there.' He gestured in the vague direction of the Town Moor. 'Playing cricket. When he was snatched from us by Fascist bullyboys. By racist thugs. And murdered.' He leaned forward on the final word, pitched it up, heard it ring out over the crowd. He shook his head. 'Was he a criminal? Had he done something to anger these boys? No. Then why? What was his crime?' He scanned the crowd again, waiting, knowing no one would give the answer, knowing they were waiting for him to supply it. 'Being Asian. Being a Muslim.' Again his head forward, his voice raised, the words unmistakably emphatic.

He went on. Gave a brief precis of Sooliman Patel's life. A loving son and brother. A fine student. A good boy. Mrs Patel wept all the more; Mr Patel held her all the harder.

Abdul-Haq looked round, caught the eyes of the crowd. Felt that familiar tingle inside, knew he had them. They were listening to his words, ready to obey his commands, ready to believe whatever he told them, even if it contradicted the evidence of their own eyes. He never tired of having that power.

He pointed to the ground, ramping up his oration. 'This is where he died. This very point. His body was found here.' He flung his arms out. 'Look around you. What do you see? Who lives here? We do. The West End of Newcastle was not a prosperous area before Muslims moved in. Before even Sikhs, before Hindus came. Before we set up shops for our own people, providing food, clothing, jewellery. If this area is prosperous now it is because of what we did. How we changed it.' Another hard, unblinking look out at the crowd.

'And there are those who want to stop that. Who *hate*—' again his head forward, again the word unmistakably emphasized. '—*hate* what we have done here. And want to stop us. And we are not going to let them.'

He stood back, waited for the applause. It wasn't long in coming.

Sooliman Patel hadn't lived in those run-down streets. Abdul-Haq didn't live there. There were a few quite prosperous businesses, but not in a great way. But no one pulled him up on it. Everyone wanted to believe in what he said.

Everyone wanted, he thought, to find a target to hate.

He started speaking again. Knowing what he was going to say, knowing what they wanted to hear. Luxuriating in the power that he could control a crowd with just his voice. His mind skipped to old newsreel footage of Hitler, of the Führer driving what seemed like thousands of people into frenzies of ecstasy with just his voice. Understood how seductive that was. People wanted to believe in something. Wanted to still the rational voice in their heads, be part of something that they have convinced themselves is right.

Our streets aren't safe.

Our way of life is under attack.

If we have to defend ourselves it is our right.

More applause.

Abdul-Haq became aware of some kind of disturbance at the back of the crowd. Most hadn't noticed, their attention so focused on him. He had only noticed because of a sixth sense honed through years of street oratory. He glanced briefly in the direction the noise was coming from, sized up the situation immediately. A couple of skinheads, drunk, chanting racist slogans. The applause was drowning them out but people were starting to look, draw the attention away from him. That couldn't be allowed to happen.

A surreptitious hand gesture and Waqas and Omar

detached themselves from the back of the platform and swiftly skirted round the outside of the crowd. The skin-heads were dragged away from the crowd, before even the TV cameras could follow. Abdul-Haq knew what would happen to them next. He didn't expend too much thought on their fate. They had brought it on themselves. Instead he turned to the crowd again. Smiled.

Announced a candlelight vigil at the mosque on Grainger Park Road. All would be welcome. Spoke words of healing, of conciliation. Laced them with threats of unequivocal action. Held hands with Mr and Mrs Patel, asked the crowd to pray with him.

Hoped the sound of the intruders being dealt with wouldn't ruin the ambience.

It didn't.

Eyes closed, Abdul-Haq listened to the silence, smiled.

The people were his.

7

Peta had always had a soft spot for Newcastle's Civic Centre. Standing on the corners of Barras Bridge and St Mary's Place in the Haymarket end of the city, it had been built in the Sixties during the T. Dan Smith era and, unlike most of the brutalist concrete monoliths of the period, was something quite beautiful.

It looked like a huge, secular cathedral. White and circular, it was designed round a courtyard with an imposing twelve-storey main block rising out of it. Capping the block was a copper lantern and beacon with three castles from the coat of arms. And the bit Peta loved best: sea horses. All round the top. So completely unexpected they made anyone looking up smile.

She walked into the reception area, up to the desk. Her sunglasses hooked over the front of her T-shirt. Now back in her regulation work uniform of trainers, T-shirt and, in a concession to the heat, black linen combats instead of jeans, she felt more herself. In control.

Peta had gone straight from her mother's to the gym. Swimming, thirty minutes with weights and the treadmill, her regular tae kwon do session; her usual method of sorting her head out, even more dependent on it recently. Then a phone call to Amar to find he was still away. She was getting fed up with leaving messages for him. Then work, researching and reading.

Her university psychology course was on hold, lack of money since Albion's demise. She was glad of the distraction, stopped her thinking of floodlit cellars and body parts, of dead women and knife-waving killers.

So, coffee and notepad beside her, she had sat at the kitchen table and opened Trevor Whitman's book. With some trepidation, looking for mention of her mother and father. Relieved to find none, she got down to work.

Prioritizing, she decided to leave off playing *Where Are They Now?* with the Hollow Men until later and concentrate on finding anyone who had a grudge against Whitman.

That was the plan. However, she had become sidetracked. Whitman's story, his life, had drawn her in. With strong, clear and compelling writing, he told of a working-class kid from Byker in Newcastle who was the first in his family to go to university.

He wrote of the sacrifice and the hardship. His father had worked in a factory manufacturing asbestos, a job that eventually killed him. His mother had pursued the company for compensation, like so many others in the country had successfully done, on the grounds of wilful negligence, and got nowhere. Shark-like lawyers had circled, eating up the funds, disappearing and leaving only bills in their wake when the claim failed. Whitman believed this had contributed to his mother's early death.

Angry and disillusioned, yet impassioned for social justice, he had been given a scholarship to attend Newcastle University. He chose politics and law. She imagined the young Whitman, hurt, alone and angry, surrounded by people from more affluent backgrounds, the offspring of those responsible for his parents' death even, there by dint of hard work, not favour, nursing and nurturing a huge chip on his shoulder. It took no imagination at all to see how he became caught up in radical politics.

She had put the book down, tried to concentrate on the work at hand. Picked it up again. Found what she was looking for, followed it up with an early-morning visit to the city library to scour old newspapers.

George Baty.

The policeman in the pub firebombing. He had been twenty-three when he died in 1972. Married with a baby son, six months old. A wedding photo accompanied the article, a young couple smiling out from the ancient blur of old newsprint. A radical group called the Hollow Men were blamed for the atrocity. Attention was focused on Trevor Whitman. There was a photo of him too. Long-haired, bearded, fist raised; obviously taken at a demonstration where he was angrily denouncing something. The difference in photos was effective but hardly subtle.

She read on. Despite the efforts of police, they were unable to secure a conviction. There was veiled talk of them being too heavy-handed in their attempt to bring him to justice, too keen to get a confession. Considering how brutal Seventies policing was, she thought, that must have been something.

The case dragged on, then eventually disappeared. Other things took its place. The Birmingham pub bombings. The three-day week. The first miners' strike. There was a piece about six months afterwards, an interview with Trevor Whitman in which he put his side of the story. Talked up his innocence, mentioned the threatening phone calls. Alluded to George Baty's brother, Colin. It was clear from his words how unsettling they had been. The police had been reluctant to investigate thoroughly.

George Baty's widow, Marilyn, had remarried, cutting all her ties with the Baty family. She would now be in her fifties, the son in his thirties. And so far untraceable. Peta wrote it all down.

An internet search brought up information about Colin Baty. At the time of his brother's death he had been a low-level street thug working manual jobs for the council, getting drunk, taking out whatever anger he had on whoever was at hand. But his brother's death obviously made him reassess his life. He changed, became driven. Stopped fighting, reined in the drinking, retrained. Set up in business. Telecoms. Became a local Labour councillor. Married with two children. Both girls, both at university.

Colin Baty had been on TV recently, in the papers. Asked for comment, reaction to Whitman's book. His anger over his brother's death and whom he blamed clearly hadn't diminished. Was developing quite a fledgling career in punditry. Blamed Whitman's reappearance for the fact that he was on long-term sick with stress. Peta thought him a logical person to start with.

'Hi,' said Peta to the receptionist, 'I'm here to see Colin Baty.'

'Is he expecting you?'

The receptionist smiled, but Peta imagined it was calculated. She was middle-aged, smartly dressed and she looked sharp. She obviously had to deal with lots of people trying to get in, knew all the ways to stop them. That was why Peta had phoned ahead.

'He is,' she said. 'Peta Knight.'

The receptionist rang up, talked. Peta waited.

The TV was on behind the desk, local news. Rick Oaten was standing outside the Royal Victoria Infirmary hosting a press conference. Peta caught some of the words:

'You call us racist? I say we're realist. You say we breed hate? I say we're honest about the situation. You say we're angry? You're right there. We are. Angry. And defending our territory. Making our streets safe for honest, law-abiding citizens to walk down.'

The news package rounding off with a clip of Abdul-Haq, creating a thin veneer of balance. Standing on the spot Sooliman Patel was murdered, his face full of righteous anger: 'Rick Oaten is talking nothing but lies. This is a vicious fabrication. Where is his proof? Where are his witnesses? Where is the police report? Nowhere. Because whatever happened to this man was not a racist attack. Was not a Muslim attack. If he wants answers he should be pointing the finger at his own kind.'

And back to the studio. Peta didn't doubt Abdul-Haq's legitimate anger, but it didn't play well on the screen. Next to Rick Oaten's slickly couched hatred, he looked like just another scarily angry militant. More likely to repel than be embraced. And the location of his oration too manipulative. Oaten, conversely, had looked sincere, statesman-like, his suit immaculate, his hair perfectly coiffed. A winner with the electorate. Peta instinctively hated him even more.

The receptionist rang off. Smiled again, this time with genuine warmth for the legitimate guest. Gave Peta directions, pointed to the lifts. Peta followed the directions, found herself walking down anonymous corridors, stopping to gaze out at the view of the city. She found the room she wanted. Knocked.

'Come in.' A voice: gruff, male, middle-aged.

She entered. Colin Baty was sitting behind a desk looking important. She imagined it had been done for her benefit. The room was bright, airy, with another wonderful view of the city. Colin Baty was a thickset man in his mid-fifties, dressed in chinos and a white shirt, tie askew, red-faced, with curly salt-and-pepper hair that a bad journalist would have described as tousled.

'Mr Baty?' Peta entered the room, extended her hand. 'Peta Knight.'

He smiled at her, or rather at her breasts. She noticed, decided to let it go.

'Colin Baty. What can I do for you? You were a bit vague

on the phone. But first, can I get you a drink? Tea? Coffee? A cold drink?' He almost winked. 'Something stronger?'

'No, thanks, Mr Baty.' Peta decided it was time to be straight, no messing about. 'I want to talk to you about your brother's death.'

She dug out one of her old Albion cards, hoped he wasn't aware of them, handed it to him. He snatched it from her, read it quickly, turned it over, back again.

'You said on the phone you were some kind of investigator. Says nothing about that here.'

'We're an information brokerage. That covers a multitude of activities. Right now Trevor Whitman is one of our clients.'

Colin Baty's already red face got redder. Whatever was left of his smile disappeared. Peta thought he had all the makings of an imminent heart attack. She would definitely be getting no tea.

'He's back. I know. On the TV, in the paper. Bloody everywhere.'

Peta didn't remind him of his own recent media appearances.

'Murdering bastard. I've tried to get him banned, but there's nothin' I can do about it. Never did time, comes back up here and they treat him like some kind of hero.'

'No one's treating him like a hero.'

He pulled his lips back from his teeth. And Peta saw the one-time streetfighter. Anger still there, just channelled differently. He jabbed his finger at her.

'You lot are. Taking him on as your client? Can't do that with my brother, can you?'

'Look, Mr Baty, I know this can't be easy for you . . .'

'Say what you've got to say and get out.'

'Phone calls,' said Peta, standing her ground. 'Threatening phone calls.'

A spark of worry flashed across Baty's eyes. 'That was years ago,' he said. 'And nothing was ever proved.'

'I don't mean years ago,' she said. 'I mean now.'

Baty frowned. 'Now?'

'Trevor Whitman is receiving threatening phone calls. Now.'

'What kind?'

'You tell me.'

Anger built within Baty, threatened to burst, but he stopped. Instead a smile spread across his features, followed by a laugh. It seemed so alien to his face, Peta would have preferred the anger.

'Oh, I get you. I get you. Someone with a long memory's saying nasty things to him about what a murdering scumbag he is and he's so scared he's come running to you for protection. To a woman.'

His eyes went to her breasts again as if to emphasize the point. Not bothering to hide it this time. Well I think much more of you for that, she thought, hoping the distaste didn't show on her face.

He moved his eyes back to hers. 'And you think it's me.'

Peta folded her arms, gave him the look she had perfected during her time on the force. 'Is it?'

Baty didn't speak straight away. Instead he seemed to be auditioning possible responses. Peta waited, doubted he could supply an answer she hadn't prepared for.

'Is he really scared?'

Peta didn't reply.

'I hope he is. He deserves to be.' His anger ebbed slightly. He looked tired.

It must be tiring, thought Peta, carrying that intensity of hatred around with you.

'It's not me,' he said. 'But I wish it was. And I wish him more than just threats. I wish he'd been through what I've been through. I wish he'd been through what my brother had been through.'

Peta nodded. The office no longer seemed light and airy, the brightness gained only by casting darker shadows. 'Right.'

'My brother was a good man. He did a job that helped people. Kept them safe.'

Peta said nothing, waited.

'Trevor Whitman was a waster. In his hippie commune. Shagging all his birds, kids all over the place—'

'What?'

Baty looked at her, frowning. 'What I said. Shagging his hippie birds. Left kids all over the place. Read it in the papers.' Baty smiled. 'Didn't you know?'

Peta felt like she had been winded. 'We must read different papers,' she managed to say.

With that, he moved her to the door, closed it firmly behind her. Peta stood outside for a few seconds, steadying herself, then made her way back to the lift and out of the Civic Centre.

The sea horses didn't make her smile this time.

She wished Albion was back together, all of them working together again.

She wished she had someone to talk to.

8

Kev Bright clutched his bandaged side, grimaced as the Land Rover bounced over pothole after pothole. Tried to swallow, but that just reminded him of the pain in his mouth.

What he deserved, he thought. For betraying the party. Even for Jason, the lost boy. It wasn't what a Knight of St George did. A foot soldier of the revolution.

Then maybe he wasn't one.

The thought hit him like a well-aimed brick in the face. For years the party had been everything. His life. It had saved him from his dull, tower-block existence. Given him a job, a sense of comradeship, of belonging. Kept the doubts down. But now they were back.

Growing up in the Benwell badlands of the West End of Newcastle, where fists spoke louder than words. And that suited Kev fine. He was king of the streets, anyone else the subject of his anger. He ruled. Anything to put off going home. Back to the ninth floor of the tombstone tower block. His dad's alcohol-powered swinging fists. His mother's screams.

Then his mother was gone, off to Peterlee with some Paki postman. Well, Greek, but the same thing. Then his dad lost his job in a warehouse in Tyne Dock and with it his heart. And he was too old to retrain, didn't understand computers, couldn't afford one. So just sat in his vest rolling fags, watching Trisha, shouting back at Jeremy Kyle if he was up early enough. His brother Joey was the clever one in the family, the one who would go far. Now lying all day in bed, the heroin monkey on his back. Not that fucking clever.

Kev was happy being out all hours. Ignoring kids he'd gone to school with, hurt, nicked stuff off, bossed around, seeing them getting good jobs, driving good cars, leaving the area. Ignoring the fact he had trouble reading and writing. Ignoring the fact that he couldn't get a girlfriend, didn't find them attractive the way the other lads did. Telling himself that none of it mattered; as long as he could go to the football, bully a ticket off someone smaller, have a ruck, he was happy. The press of bodies all round him, male muscles connecting with male muscles. Twisting, grappling. Pleasure and pain. Belonging. Ignoring the rage and fear, the candle burning inside him that he couldn't blow out. The voice that was telling him he was going nowhere, doing nothing. Ignoring all that. Until he met Gary.

Gary.

Standing over him one day in the shopping centre off Scotswood Road, Kev sitting there, knocking back can after can, trying not to think about the rest of his life. Gary stood over him, blocking out the sun, light haloed round him. A vision. A god.

Shaved head, eighteen holers, jeans and T-shirt so tight they showed off the curves and contours of his muscled body. Relaxed, in control. His jacket off, showing the tats all over his forearms and biceps. He looked, to Kev, perfect.

Said five words: 'I know what you need.'

He did. And Kev had taken it gladly.

Gary gave answers. Told Kev who was to blame. For his mother running off. For his brother's heroin habit. For the fact that he didn't have a job, a future. Put it all in context with the global Zionist conspiracy. Put it closer to home with pictures he could understand: the Pakis. The niggers. The asylum seekers.

Gary showed Kev the world through his eyes. Saw crumbling concrete, burned-out brick. The whites depressed, huddling about. The new kids coming up either fuck-ups or meltdowns. Smug Pakis smiling to each other, treating the place like it was their community. Or newer foreigners from fuck knew where with dark skins and big, round, scared eyes. Jabbering away in other languages, all of them. Sticking to their own.

His neighbours.

And something moved inside Kev, an emotion coming into focus.

'I feel your anger,' Gary said, 'understand your hate.'

The way he said 'hate'. Sounded just right to Kev.

Gary knew some others that felt the same. Why didn't Kev come along later? Meet them?

Kev did.

And never looked back.

The pub Gary took Kev to was just off the West Road in Benwell, the Gibraltar. On the walls behind the bar were flags, photos, framed letters from people Kev had never heard of but would soon come to revere as heroes. David Irving. Nick Griffin. An outward manifestation of what was inside the regulars, what was written on their bodies in scar and ink.

Then upstairs for the meeting. Sitting there, Kev felt the same rage and fear coming off all the others in the room. Felt, for the first time in his life, he could relax.

And out in front of them walked Rick Oaten.

Rick Oaten told it like it was. Rick Oaten told the truth.

Kev listened. And it all made sense.

'I'm a Knight of St George,' Rick Oaten said. 'We're all Knights of St George.'

That got a round of applause, some cheering, a few chanted *heils*.

He went on. 'The West End of Newcastle is like this

country in miniature. It used to be a good place where families could live in harmony and everyone knew everyone else. But now it's a run-down shithole full of undesirables and people who've given up trying to get out. No pride any more. No self-respect. Our heritage sold to Pakis who've just pissed on us.'

Another cheer when he said that one, like they'd been waiting for him to say it.

He went on. The liberal elite government. Feminism. Teaching homosexuality in schools. Human rights for terrorists. Free NHS treatment only if you're an asylum seeker. All conspiring against the white working class. Another cheer.

'Anybody live in a tower block?'

Kev's head jerked up.

'High-rise cages where they put animals. Stick them on—' he paused '—the ninth floor . . .'

Kev's heart missed a beat.

'The ninth floor, and hope they throw themselves off, save them the expense of housing them.'

A huge cheer. This time Kev joined in.

'Love your country like it used to be,' Rick Oaten said, 'but hate it like it is now.

'And I do,' Rick Oaten said, his voice, his fist raised. 'Both. With all my heart.'

Another cheer. Kev was with them now.

'We are one crisis away from power. One crisis away from moving in, taking over. That crisis will happen. Sooner rather than later. And then we'll reclaim it. Make this land a proud place to be again. A land fit for heroes once more. And you, my lovely boys, will be the ones to do it. The foot soldiers of the revolution.'

And they were on their feet, Kev among them.

There was more, much more. But that was the bit Kev remembered. Word for word.

Kev felt valued, like he belonged, like he was wanted.
Kev felt like he had come home.

He hit a pothole, winced at the pain.

Gary was long gone. After what happened he had no choice. Things like that weren't just frowned on; they had a habit of becoming nasty. Really nasty. Gary said he had seen it before. Body-in-the-concrete-foundations-of-a-new-quayside-development kind of nasty.

Kev told himself he didn't mind. Kept telling himself he didn't mind. Kept his head down, concentrated on what he'd found instead.

Himself.

And a job. Frank Bell. A butcher, a party member and man short. Couldn't take a Paki or a wog, obviously, so he asked Kev. Kev was terrified, but the job didn't involve much reading and writing and Frank Bell taught him how to use the till, recognize the numbers and let the computer do the adding.

And best of all he got to handle knives.

Cut flesh away from bone. Slice skin from fat. Pare muscle from sinew. He loved it. Especially delivery day when the new carcasses arrived.

Then came the whispers: Rick Oaten was forming his own party. The NUP.

Things were moving: Kev felt it. He offered his services. Was accepted. A recruiter. Security. A trusted foot soldier.

'OK,' Rick Oaten had said. 'You're loyal. You've got a true heart. I might need you sometimes. For special jobs.'

Kev had said he could be relied on. Rick Oaten said he knew. Smiled again, like he could see something Kev couldn't.

'But things are going to be a bit different this time. A bit different.'

And they were. The NUP were different from what Kev was used to. There were new, posh offices. Secretaries. A spin doctor, Mr Sharples, drafted in to advise on policy. When Kev first heard Rick Oaten on TV talking about the new party he thought he had been betrayed. There was no anger, no righteous indignation. Just measured discussion, reasoned and reasonable response.

But then Kev saw what Rick Oaten was doing. Playing to the mainstream. Make yourself electable and you get elected. People want to believe. Give them what they want to believe in.

With Mr Sharples standing behind Rick Oaten all the time, a living shadow. A puppeteer.

It worked. Membership was up. Newspaper reporting was increased. Kev and his mates still got in the Gib, had their traditional fun there, but without Rick Oaten. But that was OK. Everyone understood.

And then there was the plan. The big plan. Codename: Thor's Hammer.

Kev was in on that too. No longer just a foot soldier, now a trusted lieutenant.

But then two things happened: the special jobs and Jason Mason.

Poor little Jason Mason. The lost boy.

Kev didn't want his brother Joey roaming the streets on his own, looking to score drugs, wasn't safe. So Kev used to go and get them. He didn't want to, but as he saw it he had no choice.

He used to see this boy, living rough in a derelict house just off the West Road. But it wasn't until he saw him out on the town late at night with some middle-aged bloke that he realized what the boy did for a living. And in that instant Kev's angry heart had gone out to him. It might be too late for his brother and his dad. But he had to save the boy.

He started talking to him when he saw him, asked him along to the Gib. Tried to share the sense of community, of belonging that had been extended to him. Bring him along the right path. It was easy. The boy was hungry for a new life, a better one. And when he saw Jason saluting at meetings, chanting and shouting, when he saw him rucking with liberals, puffs and niggers, he felt so proud.

Like the son he thought he'd never have.

And Jason loved it, became a favourite with the others. Like a mascot. In him they saw their future. That made Kev even more proud.

And then he had found out what Rick Oaten meant by special jobs. At first he didn't think it would touch him, thought his anger, his loyalty, would carry him through. But that was before he saw the Asian boy's face spread all over the concrete floor. Saw his blood pouring from his body, his bones snapped and sticking out. Saw him burning in the street. When he closed his eyes. When he went to sleep.

Now nothing seemed so straightforward any more.

He sat in the Land Rover going over pothole after pothole in Northumberland, clutching his side, swallowing hard. Each bounce, each swallow brought another question, another conflict to his mind. Pain hit him as bad as the knife had. But he couldn't let it show. Not in front of Cheggs and Ligsy. Pain meant weakness, and weakness didn't deserve respect. He was in charge. Respect was vital.

His doubts were a new candle burning inside him, one he couldn't blow out. He tried to ignore them. He had a mission. No matter how unhappy he was with it, he had to do it. Find Jason. What he would do when he found him was a bridge to be crossed another time.

They hit another pothole. He tried not to cry out.

★

Donovan was driving out of Newcastle, into Northumberland, when it hit.

He pulled the Scimitar off the road, banked it on to a verge, sat there.

His chest ached, his heart sambaed and skipped, the bones in his legs and arms felt like lead. Stars danced before his eyes.

A panic attack. At least that's what he hoped it was.

He turned the engine off, sat there, arms by his side. Tried to steady his breathing. Focus.

He had dropped Amar off at his apartment, picked up his own car from there. A Reliant Scimitar, dark green. A Seventies classic, but it never felt old. Handled like a racing car.

But not today. He wasn't in the mood.

The CD was still playing, Jim White singing about how he'd found someone he loved more than the rain. A song he wrote for his daughter. Donovan made no attempt to turn it off.

Surprised he had held it together as long as he had. All the way up from London.

No good, he thought, no good.

His vision was still blurred, his heart still jumping. The panic attack not receding. He tried breathing deeply again, held the steering wheel. Concentrated. Hoped it was just a panic attack.

Oh, God, not a heart attack, please, not a heart attack . . .

He gripped the wheel, eyes screwed tight, breathing through his teeth.

I can't do this on my own, he thought, gasping. I need help.

Peta. Amar and Jamal. All together, Albion functioning like it used to. He wanted that back again. Needed it.

His family. His other family.

He pitched forward against the steering wheel as another spasm lurched through him. He fumbled in his pocket for his mobile, tried to bring it out, key in a number. Peta. Dropped it.

Closed his eyes.

Opened them again.

He looked around, sat up. Feeling in his arms, his legs again. Breathing normally. It was over. He had ridden the panic attack out.

The CD was still playing. He frowned. Two tracks down.

He had blacked out, sat there unconscious for over five minutes. He shook his head. Over five minutes.

He turned on the car, put it into gear. Drove away.

Couldn't do this alone any more.

He needed help.

9

Mr Sharples took his usual booth at the Café Roma on Mosley Street, espresso before him. Neat, grey-suited, mid-fifties with close-cropped steel-grey hair and rimless glasses, he was invisible to the mass of commuting customers filing in and out. How he liked it. Power, he knew, lay in the shadows.

He sipped, the hot, black bitterness scalding down his throat. He licked his lips, relished the feeling. Took out his black leather notebook. Planning ahead.

Things were going well. After Oaten's talking to. Only one minor problem. But that would be dealt with soon.

His mobile trilled. He checked the name on the display. Answered it.

'I hear the boy has escaped,' the caller said. 'Do we need to talk?'

'No.' Mr Sharples didn't like talking on mobiles. Any phones for that matter. Even if it was as secure a line as money could buy.

'Do you need that particular one? Have you a replacement?'

'No. We need him. And we'll get him. He's being programmed.'

'Not very well, from the sounds of it,' said the caller. 'We need to step it up. An event. Another diversion. Another crisis.'

Mr Sharples took another sip of espresso. 'What did you have in mind?'

'I leave that to you.'

The line went dead. Mr Sharples folded his phone, slipped it back into his jacket pocket. Took another sip.

An event. A diversion.

A crisis.

He smiled. Licked his lips.

He knew just the thing.

Jamal knelt in the front garden, fingers digging in the dirt. He and Donovan had meant to do this for ages, been putting it off. He worked furiously, ripping and pulling, soil spraying everywhere. Gardening tools, plant pots, bags of compost and bedding plants in polystyrene trays were strewn all around him.

He had checked all round the house. It was like he had first feared. Both his and Donovan's iPods were gone, some CDs and ornaments, Jamal's wallet with cash and his debit card. Jamal had ripped people off in his time, back in the day when he was on the streets. But that was OK, expected. They were johns, he was a hustler. All part of the harsh, grim game. But now it had happened to him and he hated it. He was no john, no soft target. Hated it even more that someone who'd been in the life like him, should have known better, had done it. Someone he was trying to help.

There were rules about these things. Jason needed to be taught them.

And Jamal didn't know what to tell Donovan. Was dreading his return. He just knew he should be occupying himself with something.

So he was ripping weeds out of the front garden.

He worked on and morning became afternoon. Became lost in what he was doing. So lost he didn't notice the Land Rover pull up at the end of the road, the three men get out.

But they saw him. They walked towards the cottage,

checking all round, the fields, trees, bushes, as if searching for
something.

Or someone.

Jamal became aware of their nearing presence, looked up
from where he knelt. Three pairs of steel-toecapped boots
met his gaze. His eyes travelled up the bodies. Dirty, faded
jeans, tight, long-sleeved T-shirts, white but thin; Jamal
could see swirls of blue ink and bulked muscle beneath.
Faces full of cruelty. Cropped heads.

Jamal swallowed hard. Skinheads had always made him
nervous. Especially big ones. He looked up.

The leading one, hair not quite as short, spoke. 'Is the
master of the house in?'

The other two laughed like it was the funniest thing
they'd ever heard but tried to stifle it. Sounded like they
were farting through their noses, thought Jamal.

'No,' he said.

Jamal's answer made them braver. 'You the gardener? The
hired help?'

'No,' said Jamal. 'I live here.'

The lead one looked at the door. 'Your mam in? Your dad?'

Jamal said nothing but his face gave away the answer.
The three shared glances, no mistaking their intention this
time: we're going to have some fun.

'Just you, is it, little black boy?'

Jamal was scared. He'd met kids like this before. But these
were adults. And could hit harder. But he was proud of his
house and he wasn't going to let anyone intimidate him on
his own property. So, thinking attack was the best form of
defence, he stood up.

The three squared up to him. Bristling, ready. He faced
up to them.

'Yeah,' said Jamal. 'Just me.' As he rose he grabbed a gardening fork, clutched it hard in his hand.

The leader took a step forward. He winced as he did so, putting his hand to his side. Jamal saw padding, guessed there was a bandage or dressing under his T-shirt.

'Gone out an' left you alone, eh? Risky. Anythin' might happen.' He sniffed the air. 'Surprised they let niggers live in the country. But they get everywhere now, I suppose.'

'Yeah,' said one of the other two, 'why don't you fuck off back to where you came from?'

Jamal answered with a strength he wished he possessed. 'You mean Streatham?'

The two looked at each other, confused, Streatham seemingly as far away and exotic as Africa. The leader gave a pained look. Jamal surmised it was either his injury or the fact that he was with a couple of idiots.

Sensing, however small, an upper hand, Jamal kept talking. 'This is my property,' he said. 'Get off or I'm callin' the law.'

'A fuckin' nigger brat tellin' me what to do?' said the leader, stepping closer. 'In my own country? Your property? You need a fuckin' lesson from your massa, boy.'

The other two shifted on their feet, eager and ready for trouble.

Jamal, terrified, his heart pumping like it wanted to escape his chest, gripped the fork as hard as he could. Sweat pooled in his armpits, flooded his back. He looked around to see if anyone was on the road. A cyclist. Ramblers. A Parcel Force van. Anyone. No one.

He was going to get hurt, he knew it. Perhaps worse.

The three skinheads were grinning, savouring what was coming. No one moved. The sun beat down on all of them.

High Noon in Northumberland.

The three didn't take any notice of a car behind them.

'Look behind you,' Jamal said.

'Fuck off,' said one of the three.

'I mean it. One step nearer and you're fucked, man.' He smiled as he said it.

His conviction convinced them. They looked round.

'Good afternoon, gents,' Donovan said, smile in place, leaning over the car door. 'Help you with something?'

The three turned, unsure who he was and whether he required politeness, but sure there was only one of him and three of them.

'Lost? Need directions?' Donovan kept the smile in place. Jamal wasn't fooled by it. 'I'm guessing you're a long way from home. Don't get out and about in this fine country of ours much, am I right?'

The leader of the three turned to face him, walked between the other two. Jamal noticed how painful it was for him to move, sure Donovan had seen too. The leader approached Donovan.

'You're blocking our Land Rover.' Then, as an after-thought: 'Sir.'

Donovan smiled even wider. 'Don't call me that. Makes me sound like my dad.' The smile curdled, like cream gone sour. 'Yeah, I'm blocking your car. Care to tell me what you're doing on my property?'

The leader frowned, tried to find an acceptable answer. While he was doing that, Donovan looked at Jamal, mouthed, 'OK?' Jamal felt a warm glow spread inside him, nodded and smiled. Donovan was here. He wasn't scared any more.

Donovan looked at the leader. 'Well?'

'We're . . . we've lost something. We're looking for it.'

'On my property?'

He shrugged. 'Round here.'

'Round here.'

The leader nodded.

'Then I suggest you look somewhere else.' Donovan stepped up, face to face. 'Right?'

A jerky dance of conflicted emotions passed over the leader's face. The civilized response was to nod, turn and walk away. But the base, feral part wanted to stay. It was clear to Jamal that he wanted no part of the first option.

'OK,' he said aloud. Then, under his breath: 'Nigger lover.'

And that was when Donovan, who until that point had kept his left arm hidden, brought up the heavy metal American police torch he kept under the seat of the car, smashed it hard as he could across the leader's shoulder.

The skinhead sighed like he was a novelty inflatable the air had been let out of, crumpled, an expression of pain and surprise on his face. The two followers didn't move, just stood there dumbstruck. Awaiting orders that wouldn't come.

'What did you call me?' said Donovan, eyes lit by an angry light. 'Wanna say it again? Eh?'

The skinhead curled up into a ball. As he went down his body jerked, causing pain to buckle round his middle. He didn't know which injury to hold the most. Red spots began to appear through his top.

'Wanna say it again?' said Donovan, louder this time.

The skinhead shook his head.

'Anything you do want to say?'

The skinhead said nothing.

Donovan raised the torch again. 'Eh?'

'S . . . sorry . . .'

'Thank you.' Donovan's smile was back in place. He pointed to Jamal. 'That's better. Now say it to him.'

The skinhead spat on the ground, face sour with pain and rage.

Donovan sighed. 'Oh, dear. I had hoped we wouldn't have to go down this route.'

He raised the torch again. The skinhead shrank away, the other two watched dumbstruck.

'Wait,' shouted Jamal.

They all turned and looked at the boy. He had almost been forgotten with everything else that was going on.

'Let him go, Joe.'

Donovan frowned. 'Why? He was going to hurt you, Jamal. They all were.'

'Yeah, I know. But look at 'im, man. He's a piece o' shit. He ain't worth it.'

Donovan looked down, saw what Jamal saw. A huddled specimen of humanity in pain. Bleeding. Bruised.

'Get up,' said Donovan. 'Get out of here.'

The skinhead tried to raise himself, couldn't do it. He beckoned to the other two for assistance. They hauled him roughly to his feet.

'Now get out of here.'

Jamal walked down the path to join Donovan. 'An' jus' remember,' he shouted to the departing threesome, 'was a black boy saved your ass from a whippin'.'

The lead skinhead turned. Anger, rage, humiliation and pain were etched vividly on every feature. He clearly wanted to scream, hurl abuse, attack and hurt. But he could do nothing. Instead he said: 'You need to move your car.'

Donovan got in the Scimitar, moved it. The Land Rover roared off, accelerating angrily. Donovan parked the car properly, walked down to where Jamal was standing.

'Everything OK while I was away?' he asked.

Jamal smiled, shrugged. 'Bit borin'. Know what I mean?'

Donovan looked at the front garden. 'Been busy. Don't let me stop you.' He turned, looked at the cottage. 'Gasping for a coffee. Want anything?'

Jamal shook his head.

'Know what they were after?'

Jamal opened his mouth to speak. Weighed up whether

to tell Donovan or not. Donovan spotted his hesitation, picked up that something was wrong.

'What? What's up?'

Jamal sighed. 'Oh, Joe, man, I think I done a bad thing.'

Donovan smiled. Jamal noticed he looked really rough. Black rings round his eyes, his hands shaking from more than the recent excitement. 'Come on inside,' he said. 'Let's talk about it.'

Donovan walked into the cottage. Jamal turned to follow, realized he was still clutching the gardening fork tightly in his hand. He opened his fingers, let it drop to the path, followed Donovan inside.

10

Lillian felt him on top of her, his body pressed against hers. It had been so long. It felt so good.

Their mouths found each other's. Kissed, deep, long. Broke apart. His mouth trailed down her neck, kissing as he went, pulling gently with his teeth. She moaned slightly, pushed her body closer to his, encouraging him to go on. He kissed her shoulders, moved his tongue down to her breasts, found each nipple, sucked, squeezed, nibbled in turn.

Behind her closed eyes, the years fell away. They were no longer pushing sixty. She saw them as they had been: young, vital, sexually hungry beings. She held on to the image, held on to him, dug her nails in further.

His head lifted from her breast, moved down her body. She soon felt him nuzzling at the tops of her thighs. She pushed her pelvis towards his mouth, put her hands on his head, guiding him to where she wanted him. He kissed her. She sighed. She felt his tongue arousing her, sighed again. Lay back, ready to enjoy what was to come.

When the doorbell rang.

Trevor Whitman jumped up. Their eyes met. Lillian got off the bed, crossed to the window, looked down. She turned back into the room.

'It's Peta,' she said.

Peta stood before the front door. She didn't know why she had rung the bell. Usually she just walked straight in but seeing the way Lillian had been with Trevor Whitman the

last time she was there it somehow felt inappropriate. It just
felt like their relationship had shifted and she didn't know
what was going to happen next.

She had things to ask her mother, questions she wanted
answers to, conversations she hoped they could have.

The door was opened by Lillian in her towelling dressing
gown.

'Oh.' Peta looked at her. 'You OK? Not . . . disturbing
anything?'

'No,' said Lillian, holding the robe tightly closed with
her fist. 'Come in. I was just about to have a shower.'

Peta stepped inside, followed her mother to the kitchen.

'Tea? Coffee?'

Peta asked for tea. Her mother set about making it. Two
Earl Grey teabags, two Penguin mugs. Virginia Woolf: *A
Room of One's Own* for Lillian, Graham Greene: *Brighton
Rock* for Peta.

'Used to be Dad's mug,' said Peta.

Lillian said nothing. Waited for the kettle to boil.

'So,' said Lillian, sitting at the kitchen table once the tea
had been made, 'social call? Or were you looking for
Trevor?'

Peta sat next to her. 'I wanted to talk to you, actually.'

Lillian blew on her tea. 'What about?'

'What d'you think? Trevor Whitman.'

Lillian said nothing, waited.

'Are you seeing him, Lillian?'

Lillian took a moment to answer. 'Yes, Peta, I am.'

'Right.'

'It's four years since Philip died.' A note of defensiveness
had crept into her voice. 'It's a long time to be on my own.
I'm not that old, you know.'

'I know. It's just . . . it was a bit of a surprise, that's all. You
didn't tell me.'

'Do you tell me everything that's going on in your life?'

They both knew the answer to that one. Lillian had been there for Peta during her darkest alcoholic days, but the help had come with conditions that Peta hadn't wanted. Since she got sober she had tended to keep her mother at arm's length. Lillian certainly didn't know everything that had happened on Albion's last case. She wouldn't have let Peta walk the streets on her own if she knew that.

'No,' said Lillian. 'Thought not. Trevor's an old friend. And . . . he's been good to me since he came back into my life. He makes me happy.'

'Good.' Peta said the word but she wasn't sure whether she meant it. Something was still bugging her. Still not quite right.

'How's the investigation?' Lillian's words were hidden by her mug.

'Yeah, it's started.' She told Lillian about Baty, how she thought that might be a dead end. 'But he did say something. About Trevor.'

'What.' Lillian put her mug down, sat as if expecting a blow.

'Probably nothing much, probably doesn't mean anything at all. Just that Trevor Whitman had a lot of women. A hippie commune full of them. I mean, it's ridiculous, I know, and none of my business really, but were you . . . you know . . .'

'I wouldn't believe what he says about Trevor. He hates him.'

Lillian and Peta both looked up. Trevor Whitman was standing in the doorway wearing jeans and a T-shirt, hair and stubble distressed. He looked like a walking Gap ad.

Peta looked between him and her mother, clocked again her mother's bathrobe. Got the picture.

'Hello, Trevor,' she said without much enthusiasm. She

suddenly felt unwanted. Knew she had been right to ring the doorbell and not walk straight in. Like things had changed and she wasn't sure where she stood.

'How's the investigation going?' Whitman said.

Although there wasn't much to report, Peta told him. He listened, smiling. 'Thanks for that. Keep up the good work. You read my book yet?'

'Some of it. Very good so far.'

Whitman smiled.

The room had suddenly got very hot, the atmosphere oppressive. Peta stood up. 'I'd better be off.'

Lillian looked as if there were things she wanted to say to Peta. She rose also. 'I'll see you out.'

'No need. I'll see myself out.'

Even the hot air outside felt better than the prickly awkwardness of her mother's kitchen. She stood by her car, gulping in a few mouthfuls of air, then got in, drove off.

Still with so many questions unanswered.

The Forth was busy; the usual mix of students and professional city bohos sitting and standing round the old, mismatching tables, the long, dark bar. The same clash of music as always: the ultra hip, the ultra arch. Peta sat on her own, ignoring the noise. Eyes only for the drink in front of her.

She knew it was the wrong thing to do, but felt so stressed, with no one else to talk to, nowhere else to turn. No friends around, except her old one.

So she sat staring at her gin and tonic. She ran her finger down the side of the glass, felt the cold, wet thrill of condensation. Saw the bubbles rise to the surface, pop and disappear. She imagined lifting it to her lips, feel the sweet, sharp, iced liquid roll down her throat, bringing its cold comfort to her body. Her mind.

Her fingers gripped the glass.

She thought again of floodlit cellars and body parts, of dead women and knife-waving killers.

Of her mother wanting to tell her things.

How she had wanted to do this for so, so long.

Her phone rang.

She moved her fingers away, ready to grab it in her bag. Then stopped. Might be her mother.

Her hand fell back. She would ignore it.

It kept ringing.

She looked between the drink and the phone. Saw the number. The phone won out. Taking a deep breath, she put it to her ear, answered.

'Hi,' said a voice she knew on the other end. 'It's the biggest twat in the universe here. And it's costing me a lot to do this so please be nice. I'd like to talk to my friend Peta, please.'

Peta smiled, a tsunami of relief washing over her.

'Hello, twat,' she said. 'What can I do for you?'

And Donovan told her.

She finished the call, pushed the drink away, stood up.

Left the pub, feeling happier than she had in a long time.

11

Safraz Rajput opened his eyes. Looked around. He must have still been asleep, still been dreaming, because he didn't know where he was.

He was in a car, that much he knew. But not his car. He drove a nearly new Peugeot 307. Silver. This one was bigger, older. Dirtier.

He shook his head. Slowly: it felt like he had been drinking heavily and he had a hangover. He rubbed his face, sat back. Had he been drinking? He couldn't remember. No, he hadn't.

Then how . . .

He blinked, willing his fogged mind to clear, tried mentally to retrace his steps.

He had been playing five-a-side at the leisure centre in Gateshead. With his mates from work in a local league, their usual Thursday-night game. They won, beating a team of technicians from the college six–two. A couple of celebratory pints in the bar, then home.

Home.

He frowned. He couldn't remember going home. He remembered going to his car, reaching for the door handle then . . .

Nothing.

Safraz had to get out.

He tried the door handles. There weren't any.

Tried pulling the button up to release the catch. Nothing there. No buttons to open the windows. Nothing.

He looked outside. It was dark, somewhere he didn't . . .
Was he in the West End of Newcastle? It wasn't somewhere
he was familiar with. No one about. Began hammering on
the glass, shouting.

Nothing.

Put his shoulder to the door, his whole body weight
behind it. Wouldn't budge. He punched the windscreen,
got nothing but sore knuckles.

He heard a small whimpering sound, like a wounded
animal crawling off to die, realized it was him.

A phone rang.

He checked his pocket. His own mobile had gone. The
noise continued. He looked round. On the back seat was a
black nylon rucksack. The ringing was coming from there.
He leaned over, picked it up, unzipped it.

'Wha—'

The explosion tore the thought from his mind as it tore
the skin, blood and muscle away from Safraz Rajput's bone.

The Albion offices looked like a ghost building.

Most of the old Edwardian buildings on Somerset Terrace
off Westgate Road had all been gentrified to some degree and
were now home to various architects, lawyers, accountants and
mortgage advisers. But the Albion offices, boarded up, with
the remnants of age-dirtied blue and white police tape still
fluttering from the front gate, just looked haunted, derelict.

Amar Miah walked down the lane from Westgate Road,
his walk uneven as his cane navigated the cobbles. He
stopped outside the front door, the cane supporting his
weight, getting his breath back. Physically he was feeling
better all the time. His strength returning, his body repairing
itself. But his mind, his spirit, was another matter.

Coming so close to death had made him reassess everything in his life. He thought he had died at one point, lying

on the pavement, life flowing out of him, only to be brought back by the paramedics and doctors. As a result he had given up his heavy drug habit. Even stopped cruising the gay clubs and bars. It had been difficult, but after experiencing first hand how easy it was to die he had clung that bit harder on to life. And now, stronger, more focused, he just wished he had something to do with his life.

Peta's call was unexpected. He had thought she was phoning about the job she wanted him to do and she had mentioned it but there had been more.

'Come to Albion,' she had said, giving him a time.

He had tried to argue, at least ask why, but no more details had been forthcoming.

'Just come along. We'll talk then.'

And here he was.

He tried the front door, expecting resistance. There was none; it was unlocked. He pushed it open, went in. Down the hall, still strewn with rubbish and debris, layered with dust. He looked into the front room, what used to be the client room. The big, chocolate leather sofas now slashed and spewing stuffing, mildewed through neglect. Boards at the window throwing selective shafts of early-evening sunlight round the room. No one there. He walked on towards the office. Opened the door.

And stopped.

There sat Joe Donovan on a packing crate, Peta sitting on a partially destroyed office chair next to him. Jamal stood, back to the filing cabinet, hands in pockets. They all looked up as Amar entered. Donovan stood, smiled.

'Glad you could make it,' he said.

'What's going on?' said Amar.

Peta stood also. Jamal gave him his full attention.

'We've been talking,' said Donovan.

Amar waited.

Donovan and Peta shared a look. He spoke first.

'Fuck Sharkey,' he said, 'and fuck waiting for the dust to settle.'

'And fuck taking on your own crusades when you've got a team to help you,' said Peta.

Donovan couldn't meet her gaze, looked instead at Amar. 'Peta's in, Jamal's in. I'm in. All we need is a techie. And, of course, we want the best in the business.'

Amar smiled. 'Where do I sign?'

Trevor Whitman was in the back bedroom at Lillian's house. He had given up his hotel room; now that Peta knew where he was with her mother there was no need to keep it on.

Philip had used the room as an office, and Lillian hadn't touched it in the four years he had been dead. Dust covered everything. A computer that had once been state of the art but now looked like something from prehistoric times took up most of the desk. Whitman had cleared most of the peripherals away, made space for his laptop. He was looking over his schedule for the next few days, a three-quarters-empty bottle of red wine beside him, Coldplay playing through iTunes on the laptop. One of the few modern bands he actually liked. He hummed along with the lyrics, something about seeing the world in black and white.

He could get used to this. Lillian downstairs, the promise of good food, conversation, more wine and physical comfort. Almost get used to it. Just one thing to get out of the way first, then he could relax.

His mobile rang. Putting his laptop aside, he picked it up. Peta, perhaps, with an update.

'Hello.'

Silence.

Whitman's heart skipped a beat. He knew who it was. He

looked round. Not in Lillian's house, he thought, anger and fear building within. Like he was being invaded, violated.

He said nothing more, waited for them to speak.

A small laugh came down the line. 'This is the way the world ends,' the voice said. 'This is the way the world ends.'

Whitman returned the next line, couldn't stop himself. 'Not with a bang but a whimper.'

That laugh again. 'Oh, it'll be a bang. A fucking big one. And the hope of empty men won't stop it.'

The phone went dead.

Whitman stared at it, the only sounds in the room his breathing and Chris Martin's voice singing about the black and white world again and how it wasn't painted right.

He threw the phone as hard as he could at the wall. It shattered and fell.

He started on the wine again.

The night closed in. The heat still oppressive.

He felt it was about to get hotter.

PART TWO

DAYS OF RAGE

12

Newcastle was still heating up. And didn't Detective Inspector Diane Nattrass know it.

The sun over the city was like a magnifying glass held over an anthill, the rising temperatures setting the inhabitants aflame. As people lost sleep, focus and patience with each other, as small irritations grew to large grievances, conflict flashpoints were everywhere. Road rage, abuse, assaults, fights all on the up. And that magnifying glass still overhead, unrelenting. The city was working its way to the brink.

And with the city's emergency services overstretched, particularly her city centre-based department, the last thing she needed was this.

She looked round, took in the sight. The blast had completely wrecked the car, atomized the body inside, blackened and cracked the road and pavement around it, put all the windows out down the street. Those that remained. The area was beyond being run down; it was derelict. It was a run-down street in Fenham, bordering Arthur's Seat in the West End of Newcastle. The houses were old and terraced, mostly boarded up, roof tiles missing, tagged by street gangs. Thank God, thought Nattrass, that it hadn't happened on a more populated street.

Blue and white police tape cordoned off what was left of the car itself. Uniforms were out doing door to door in the surrounding streets. SOCO were all over the scene, sifting, bagging, brushing. Looking for occult clues to stop it being a scene, to turn it into a story.

She hadn't been able to stop the press running with the
story: SUICIDE BOMBER KILLS SELF IN BUNGLED BOMB
ATTACK. She had been able to keep the TV cameras and
print media out of the area. Another area cordon had
secured that.

'Boss.'

She looked round. Stevie Fenton, her new detective sergeant, was coming towards her. He was young, eager,
ambitious. Conscientious and good at his job. She had no
complaints about him. But his very professionalism just
made her miss her old DS.

'Yes, Stevie,' she said, turning.

'Forensics have come up with a name.' He looked down
at his notebook. 'Safraz Rajput.' He looked up. 'Sounds like
he fits the bill.'

'Don't jump to conclusions,' she said, pressing down a
mild irritation with him. 'Go on.'

'Born here, third-generation Indian. Described himself as
British, more than anything. Married to a librarian.'

'Kids?'

Back to his notes. 'One son. How can he do that, eh?'

'Anything else?'

'Lived in Gateshead. Uniforms over the water have had a
word with the wife. Worked in IT, played five-a-side on a
Thursday, supported Newcastle United. Went out occasion-
ally with his mates on a Friday night, took his wife out to
dinner on alternate Saturdays when they could afford it and
get a babysitter.'

'Religion?'

'Muslim, but vague. Only really went to mosque on special occasions. Family stuff and the like.' He looked at the
rest of the notes, frowned. 'Says here he had a sizeable DVD
collection. Liked American cop shows. *The Wire. The Shield.*
Sopranos. Stuff like that. He was a gadget freak, loved his sat

nav. CDs in his car: Kaiser Chiefs, Franz Ferdinand, James Blunt.'

'His car?'

'Yeah. Funny thing. Still parked outside Gateshead Leisure Centre. Went for a game of five-a-side with his mates, never seen again until this.'

'So this wasn't his car.' Nattrass looked at the burned-out, blackened shell.

Fenton was looking around, clocking the faces nervously watching them from the ends of the street. The brown faces. 'Maybe he came up here, got his orders from someone round here.'

'How?'

'Someone picked him up. Brought him here.' Another look round. 'Gave him his orders, sent him on his way. If it's goin' to happen anywhere, it's goin' to happen round here. Lucky for us they're amateurs.'

She looked at Fenton, could almost see what he was thinking. Al-Qaeda cell. Go in guns blazing, breaking down doors, drag some bodies down to the station, get them to talk. Have a major terrorist threat foiled by Stevie Fenton.

'Let's not get carried away with hysteria. Let's examine all the angles first, DS Fenton.' Not for the first time she wished her old DS was still there. For all his faults, and there were many, Paul Turnbull was a man she could trust.

The city was on a knife edge. The murder of the student, Sooliman Patel, at the hands of racist extremists was bad enough. Now this. The youth's brutal death had shocked the whole city. He was young, photogenic; he played well on TV. He became a story, a symbol. Different things to different people. Parents saw a dead child. Students saw one of their own. Racists saw one less Paki.

There had been street rallies, demonstrations. A candlelit vigil was planned in the cathedral in his memory.

That would be another potentially explosive meeting. They needed to keep the lid on this as much as possible. It was the kind of thing that would have the city tearing itself apart.

Young, angry Asians were already patrolling the streets around Fenham and Arthur's Seat, tooled up, telling the media, themselves and anyone who would listen they were there for the protection of the community, making the streets safe for innocent people to walk in at night. Demarcating their territory. Warning the police not to interfere. The fact that Sooliman Patel wasn't even from that area, that he had lived on a mixed, affluent housing estate in Gosforth, miles away from the west of Newcastle, both culturally and geographically, didn't matter. Just as long as the club felt strong in a young man's hand, she knew, the blade felt sharp in his pocket and his heart burned with righteous anger, there would always be an excuse.

Nattrass wiped the sweat from her brow. It was going to be another long day. She felt sure overtime would be sanctioned for this. She didn't see what the alternative was.

Fenton's mobile rang. He answered it, talked, hung up. Looked at Nattrass.

'Just heard. Abdul-Haq's organized another street rally.'

Nattrass sighed. 'Oh, brilliant. That's all we need.'

'He's trying to get it down this street, marching on us.'

'Let him fucking try.'

'Boss?' Fenton stared at Nattrass. She was usually in control, hardly ever swore unless it was necessary.

'Sorry. The heat. Right, get Community Liaison to talk to him, try to head it off. We haven't finished here yet, he knows that. He's just causing trouble. Let's hope he hasn't got the cameras with him.'

Fenton gave a small laugh. 'What's the chances of that, eh?'

Nattrass nodded. Her mobile rang. Without checking the screen she answered it.

'Hi, Di,' said a voice she couldn't immediately place. Gave another sigh. Joe Donovan. Not the last person she wanted to talk to, but very close.

'Hello, Joe,' she said, her voice not even disguising her irritation. 'I'm very busy. I can't talk right now.'

'I know you are, making the streets safer for us innocent members of the public—'

'I only wish you were.'

'You love working with me and you know it. Unofficially, of course.'

'What d'you want? Make it quick.'

'I know.' Donovan's voice changed, became more serious. 'I need Paul Turnbull's address. Can't find it anywhere else.'

'Why? What makes you think he wants to talk to you?'

'Because I've got work for him, Diane. A job.'

Nattrass didn't take long to make up her mind. She gave him the address, broke the connection. Smiled. He was a good man, Joe Donovan. Irritating bastard, but a good man. She became aware that Fenton was looking at her.

'Boss?'

She sighed. 'Right. Get Liaison to talk to Abdul-Haq. Get Forensics to hurry up with their report. I want to interview Safraz Rajput's wife myself. I want toxicology . . .'

She went on.

The sun still burning in the sky.

Unrelenting.

13

Ex-Detective Sergeant Paul Turnbull sat staring at the TV screen, impotent anger raging inside him.

Car finance. Accidents at work that weren't your fault. Debts consolidated into easily affordable monthly payments. The working classes airing their personal lives on chat shows like dirty laundry on some high-rise balcony. Trisha Trash. Kyle Cunts. Mouth breathers, the lot of them. The middle classes finding cash in the attic, a home in the sun, going on bargain hunts. A black and white film nostalgic for a world that never was. Philip and Fern just filling in time until the viewers died.

Daytime TV. He hated it.

This wasn't who he was.

This wasn't where he was supposed to be.

He flicked it off, got up, found he had nowhere to go. The flat was small, shabby, rented. Not a home. Never a home.

He listened. Heard traffic going past on Chillingham Road. The sound of people who had to be somewhere. No noise from below, the pizza place not open until evening when the walls would judder as the current was diverted and the ovens turned on, the ancient, overloaded wiring struggling to cope. Then the smell of cooking dough would waft upwards.

He avoided the place at first, thinking it not just literally but figuratively beneath him, worried even that he would meet some lowlife he had nicked, but that smell began to entice him down. Now, it was his staple diet. And talking to Iqbal the proprietor was sometimes the only human interaction he would experience for days.

He paced the room, a caged animal. It wasn't right. He should be out there, in the wild, on the streets. Back on the strength. Looking for the killer of that murdered Asian kid. Looking into that suicide bomber. He bet his ex-DI, Di Nattrass was deep into the investigations and he should have been there with her.

He sighed. Di Nattrass had really gone to bat for him. Put her own job on the line. It had really surprised him. But ultimately even her intervention hadn't saved him. They had still thrown him out.

Turnbull's last case as a member of Northumbria Police had brought down a sex-trafficking ring and the successful arrest of a serial killer. But instead of the expected commendations, he had ended up out of the service. Too many dead bodies. Tyne Dock ablaze. Too cavalier, too maverick. Not by the book. Transparency was all now, and his methods couldn't be held up to public scrutiny. A walking time bomb. Too much potential embarrassment.

For his superiors, not for him.

And now all he had was a soul full of bitterness, a heart full of broken dreams. And daytime TV.

He thought of making a cup of tea. Or coffee. Gave a shuddering self-pitying sigh. What his life had come to.

He caught his reflection in the mirror over the mantelpiece. Once so sure of himself and his opinions, now he didn't recognize the face staring back at him. He used to be Mr Monochrome in every sense: his clothing, his views, even his football team black and white. Now just a slurry of sludgy, blurry greys. His once neat hair greasy and untidy, more grey than black. His weight increasing from lack of exercise. His shoulders sagged. His T-shirt stained, dirty. His beard beyond designer stubble. And jogging bottoms. Jogging bottoms. But the eyes were the worst. They showed a man who had given up. On himself. On everything.

He hated the Trisha Trash and the Kyle Cunts. And feared that was what he was becoming.

Then: a knock on the door.

Turnbull turned, unsure whether he had heard correctly. He stood, unmoving.

It came again. Unmistakable.

He crossed the room, made his way downstairs. Tamping down the small surge of hope in his chest. It would only be Jehovah's Witnesses. Or canvassers ahead of the election. Still, he could send them off with a mouthful.

He opened the door, insults charged and ready to hurl. They died in his mouth. It was the last person he expected to see. Joe Donovan.

'Hello, Paul,' Donovan said. 'Bastard of a job tracking you down. Almost like you didn't want to be found. Can I come in?'

Turnbull stood mutely aside, let Donovan enter, followed him up the stairs. Donovan looked round. Turnbull saw the flat from Donovan's perspective: a collection of rooms decorated with carpet remnants and trade-only paint and wall coverings, containing geriatric charity-shop furniture and an air of despair and hopelessness. Turnbull felt a bile-ball form inside him.

'What d'you want?'

'Cup of tea would be nice,' said Donovan, sitting down on a sofa that had last had a brush with fashion when Thatcher was coming to power, trying to ignore the cloud of dust that rose as he did so.

Turnbull didn't move. Donovan was taking it all in.

'This where you end up when they chuck you off the job?'

'They didn't chuck me off. I resigned.'

Donovan nodded. 'Right. Made their job a lot easier, then.'

'Fuck off.' He looked away from Donovan, embarrassed by his sudden outburst. Donovan said nothing.

'Traffic division,' Turnbull said bitterly, as if vocalizing an ongoing internal conversation. 'Fuckin' traffic division. That's what they offered me. That or a desk job somewhere down in the fuckin' bowels. May as well have just said they were movin' me to the fuck-up squad. What choice did I have?'

Turnbull sat down in an armchair, armrests holding so many cigarette burns they seemed part of the pattern.

'And then Karen throwing you out,' said Donovan.

Turnbull stared at the floor, nodded. 'Changed the locks one day when I was out, threw all my stuff into the street. Can't see my kids, nothin'.'

'Bad,' said Donovan, genuine empathy in his voice.

Turnbull looked up. 'What the fuck would you know about it?'

Donovan didn't have to answer. Turnbull stared at the pattern on the carpet, wondered what sort of mind had ever considered the sickening swirls and clashing colours a good idea.

'How d'you find me?' Turnbull asked eventually.

'Phoned Di. She didn't want to give your address out but—' He shrugged, smiled '—I insisted.'

Turnbull nodded absently. 'Diamond. Only one who kept in touch. Rest have backed off like I'm fuckin' Typhoid Mary. Like my bad luck's goin' to rub off on them.'

'Suppose you can't blame them under the circumstances.'

Turnbull's anger broke again. 'What the fuck d'you want? Did you just come here to make—' he moved his hands around as grasping words from the air '—judgements you're not qualified to make?'

Donovan shook his head. 'No.'

'Mister Smartarse. Mister Cunt. Mister I-don't-need-to-operate-within-the-law-because-I'm-better-than-all-of-you.'

Donovan bit back words, stood up. 'Call me when your head's in a better state.'

Turnbull looked at Donovan. They weren't friends. Didn't even like each other. But there was mutual respect there, trust even. And Turnbull couldn't say that about many people. Certainly not his former colleagues.

'Wait.'

If Donovan walked, Turnbull wouldn't find out what he wanted.

And he would be alone again.

Turnbull eyed again the hideously patterned carpet. 'Sorry.'

Donovan sat back down, tried to shrug it off. 'OK.'

Another silence stretched between them.

'Why did you come here?' said Turnbull. 'I doubt you're concerned about my welfare.'

'You're a friend, course I am.'

The words hit. Turnbull couldn't look up. Couldn't trust himself to say anything.

'But there was something. Got a job for you.'

Something fluttered inside Turnbull's chest, like a sparrow trapped in a cage breaking for freedom. He looked up. 'A job?'

'Yeah. If you want it, that is.'

'What kind?'

'One that requires discretion, tenacity and patience.'

Turnbull attempted a laugh. 'But your go-to guy for that wasn't available, so you came to me.'

Donovan smiled. 'Jesus, that's a first. Self-deprecating humour from Paul Turnbull.'

'Fuck off.'

Donovan laughed. 'That's more like the twat I know.'

Turnbull smiled. Stretching muscles he hadn't stretched in weeks. Months, even. The sparrow fluttered harder. Then stopped.

'Last time I worked with you I got kicked off the force.'

'You can't blame me for that, Paul. So. D'you want to know about it?'

'Tell me.'

Donovan told him of the couple in Hertfordshire who had turned up one day with a son. 'There's talk it might be some kind of international child-smuggling operation. But I'm not interested in that. I just want to find out who the boy is and where he came from. So what d'you think?'

It sounded so easy. All Turnbull had to do was say yes and he could start living again. He opened his mouth; no words came out. The fluttering started again. Bigger this time, harder. He was scared. He had left more than his job when he left the police.

But he couldn't let Joe Donovan see that. 'So that's it, is it?' His voice was loud, words wrapped in a hard carapace of anger. 'You come along and . . . and plug my life-support system back in, and everything's fine again? Yeah?'

He had more but Donovan cut him off. 'Look around you, Paul. This isn't a place to live. This is a place you go to die. Listen, mate, I know what a struggle it is day after day just to get up. I know what it's like to have a whole load of nothing stretching out in front of you and think this is it, this is my life.'

'Good for fuckin' you.'

'Yeah, good for fuckin' me. An' I'll tell you. It's a deep, dark pit and you haven't begun to reach the bottom yet. Not even halfway.'

'So why's this job so important you want me to do it?'

'Because I want someone I can trust. Because the boy that this couple have got? I think it's my son.'

'What?'

'You heard. So what d'you want to do? Stay here or climb out?'

Turnbull swallowed hard, not trusting himself to speak. His hands were shaking. He struggled to bring himself under control. 'Climb,' he said, his voice sounding like someone else's.

Donovan smiled, relieved. 'Good.' He held out his hand. 'Consider yourself on the payroll. Welcome to Albion.'

They shook.

Turnbull smiled, caught his eyes in the mirror. No longer saw a man who had given up. Saw someone whose eyes held, no matter how small an amount, hope. 'I'd better get a shave, then.'

14

'You should have called us sooner, Trevor.'

'Why? You didn't even have the trace in place.' Whitman was sitting on the sofa in the old rectory, Lillian perched on the arm, her hand draped protectively over his shoulder.

The curtains were drawn to keep out the heat. It just succeeded in making the room feel more claustrophobic.

Peta looked at Amar, shrugged. It was true. They had been in the process of doing that when Whitman had received the call.

Whitman put his glass to his lips with shaking hands. Drained it, swallowed hard, grimaced, the whisky going down burning. Lillian held him all the harder. His shirt looked like he had slept in it, his hair was all over the place. He looked like Wayne Coyne after a particularly intense Flaming Lips gig. Eyes sunken black and red, like ragged wounds in his face. Enough newspapers lying around to mop up an incontinent pet. Despite the reservations she had about him, Peta felt pity for the man.

'So what do we do now, then?' Whitman said.

'Ask questions.' She sat down next to him, switched on the Dictaphone in her pocket. 'Did you recognize the voice?'

Whitman drained his glass, sat forward, head in hands. Sighed.

Peta looked to Amar who was sitting on the chair by the fire. He gave her a nod, handing the play to her. She would be good cop, he bad. Or at least she sympathetic, he flippant. They were roles that had worked for them in the past.

'Was it Baty again? Is that who it sounded like?'

Whitman shook his head, gave a small whimper.

'Who, then? Did you recognize it?'

Whitman covered his face with his fingers, grimaced behind the mask. 'T. S. Eliot . . .'

Peta and Amar shared a look, frowning.

'What?' said Peta.

'T. S. Eliot . . .'

'I don't think so,' said Amar. 'He died years ago.'

Whitman looked up. His eyes were red for any number of reasons: tears, fatigue, intolerance at Amar's wilful stupidity. 'The person on the phone. Quoted T. S. Eliot at me.'

Silence fell in the room while that fact was digested.

'Not that one about the cats, was it?' said Amar. 'Went to see that show with the school. Piece of shit.'

Whitman turned his attention to Amar. 'No. Not the one about the cats. The one that used to be a code for my old group.'

'The Hollow Men,' said Peta.

'Right.'

Peta leaned closer. 'So what did they say?'

Whitman reached for the whisky bottle. Peta gently moved it out of his grasp. 'You can have that in a minute, Trevor. I just need to know what they said.'

His eyes couldn't meet hers. 'They said . . . they said . . . They're planning something. And I was too late to stop them.'

Questions tumbled through Peta's head, all sparked off by Whitman's words. She didn't know which to come out with first. 'Too late in what way? Planning what?'

Whitman shook his head. 'I don't know . . .'

'Did you recognize the voice?'

Whitman sighed. 'I don't . . . I might have done.'

'Male or female?'

'I don't know. It sounded familiar. But different.'

'Like it was distorted?' said Amar.

'Yeah,' said Whitman quickly, latching on to the phrase like a drowning man to a life raft. 'Distorted. That's it. Like they wanted me to hear it but not recognize it.'

Peta looked at Amar, shared a frown.

'Give us some help here, Trevor. Did you recognize the voice?'

Whitman looked up, about to speak. Then put his head down again, shook it, sighed heavily. 'No. But I think it was one of the Hollow Men,' he said weakly. 'Try them.'

'Which one?' said Amar.

'I don't know.' His hands were flexing and unflexing. Practising reaching for the whisky. 'Just get the trace set up. Please. Soon.'

Peta sat back, looked at Amar, shrugged. That seemed to be all they were getting. Whitman, sensing their talk had come to an end, reached for the bottle. Peta didn't stop him.

She stood up, looked at Lillian. Her mother seemed haggard, weighed down with worry, like she had aged several years in the space of a few days.

'Thanks, Trevor,' said Peta, turning off the Dictaphone, 'Amar'll get the trace set up straight away. He's brought his stuff. Next call that comes in, we'll be on to it.'

Whitman nodded, whisky glass to his lips.

Peta turned to her mother. 'Lillian, can I have a word . . .'

They walked into the kitchen together. Once inside, Peta shut the door, faced her mother. 'How are you bearing up?'

Lillian picked up the tea towel from the table, began to pleat the edges in her fingers. 'Fine,' she said. 'Well, as fine as can be expected, you know. It's a stressful time at the moment.'

Peta nodded. 'Look, I want you to tell me the truth. Does Trevor know more than he's saying?'

Lillian began pleating harder. 'What d'you mean?'

'Does he know who's making the phone calls? Is there something stopping him from telling us?'

Lillian looked like she wanted her daughter to leave. Peta didn't move.

'Lillian?'

'I . . . I don't know. He . . . If he does, he hasn't told me.'

Peta opened her mouth to say something more but got nowhere. Lillian slumped down in a chair, head down, caught up in a burst of sudden, intense tears. The sobs racked her body, shoulders heaving, head bobbing.

Peta didn't know what to do, how to comfort her. She sat down beside her, put her arm round her. Lillian fell into the embrace, sobbed further.

'This . . . this was supposed to be a happy time for me,' Lillian managed between waves of tears. 'I huh-hadn't seen Trevor in years. I wuh-was so looking forward to get-getting . . . to seeing him again. And now this, now this . . .'

Peta kept her arm round her.

Any further questions, and Peta had lots of them, put on hold.

'I think he knows,' said Peta, 'but he's not telling us. Neither of them are.'

Donovan swallowed his mouthful of food and looked at her and Amar. 'Any ideas why? Either of you?'

Amar shrugged. Peta said nothing.

Pani's in Newcastle. Situated down a cobbled street between the sweeping Georgian splendour of Grey Street and the ripe-for-gentrification Pilgrim Street. Laid back enough to be comatose, and with its stripped wooden floors and adobe décor, chatty baristas and model-grade serving staff the Italian café was doing its usual brisk lunchtime trade.

It was a regular haunt for Donovan. For meeting clients, the rest of the team, or sometimes just by himself with a book. Pubs and bars had always been his haunt of choice, but booze, isolation and thoughts of his son didn't mix well. So coffee, food and work filled that gap. Stopped him obsessing. For the moment.

Peta had played the tape. They had all listened.

'So,' said Donovan, 'thoughts on Whitman. I've not met him yet, so what to make of him.'

Amar looked thoughtful. 'Can't decide what kind of twat he is. Special one or common or garden.'

Peta smiled. 'They're all special. In their own way.'

'So largely negative, then,' said Donovan, taking a mouthful of iced cappuccino. 'But why would he lie if he knows who this person is? And why would your mother?'

A shadow passed over Peta's features. 'I don't know.' She sighed. 'I tried to ask her, didn't get the chance.'

'OK, not to worry.' Donovan turned to Amar. 'By the way, shouldn't you be off monitoring calls, or something, instead of sitting here feeding your face?'

Amar held up his mobile, patted his laptop bag at his feet. 'Got it all routed here. The marvels of GPS. Mobile tracking station. Anything happens, I'll know about it.'

Donovan smiled. It felt good to be working, the old team back together again.

'So what were you doing this morning that was so important?' said Peta.

'Sorting out someone to go to Hertfordshire.' He told her who.

She made a face. 'Paul Turnbull? You sure?'

Donovan shrugged. 'I trust him, believe it or not.'

Her head went down, she stared fixedly at her lunch. 'Great. Just make sure you keep him well away from me.'

'He's single again since his wife chucked him out.'

'Good.'

Donovan looked at Peta, said nothing. Turnbull's not my ex-lover, he thought. He didn't leave me with a drink problem and force me to resign from the police force.

Donovan scrutinized her. Her jeans and white T-shirt showing off her toned body, sunglasses perched on her head holding her blonde hair off her face, she looked good, he thought. Better than himself in his baggy Levi's, once-white Cons and vintage X Men T-shirt. Then he studied her more closely. Her eyes were slightly dark-rimmed, as if she had been losing sleep over something. He knew that feeling well.

They finished their meal.

'So what now?' said Donovan.

'I'm off home,' said Amar. 'Scan the airwaves.'

'OK. I think you and me—' Donovan gestured to Peta '—had better start hunting down the Hollow Men. And reading his book.'

'Great.'

Donovan and Amar exchanged glances. Peta looked worried.

'D'you not want to?'

'My parents might be in it.'

Donovan smiled. 'Right.'

'I've scanned the index and flicked through: no mention, but you never know.'

'And you don't want to come across them. I see.' Donovan and Amar exchanged smiles. 'Could traumatize you for life, that.'

'Yeah,' said Amar, picking up the riff. 'Those bad haircuts, Afghan coats, Gong albums under one arm . . .'

'Worse than seeing them naked when you're a kid.'

Peta reddened but managed a smile. 'Piss off. You know what I mean.' She smiled, but Donovan noted its fragility.

'By the way,' said Amar a moment later. 'Where's Jamal?'

'Around somewhere,' said Donovan. 'He came into town with me. He's a bit down at the moment. Let someone stay the night, ended up ripping him off.'

'What?'

Donovan told them about the visit from Jason Mason.

'He's taking it very hard,' said Donovan. 'Feels he's been abused, violated.'

'Poor kid.'

'Think he's gone looking for him.'

'To get his stuff back?'

'Yeah. To get his pride back, mainly. Let this kid know you can't go around doing that.'

It was time to go. Amar picked up his laptop and left. Donovan took the bill in his hand, produced a card. He and Peta both stood up. As he went to pay, he accidentally brushed against Peta's bare arm. It was the closest they had physically come to each other since their enforced separation. She looked at him as if the touch had produced a spark, an electric charge. His eyes met hers. Their gaze held.

'I'd better pay,' said Donovan.

'Right,' Peta nodded. They both looked away, the moment broken.

That thrill again. Neither had acknowledged it, not even to anyone else, but it was always present when they were together. A frisson neither dared to take further. Because it could either be the start of something beautiful, or the end of it.

Donovan paid. They met at the door.

'Right. Home,' she said. 'Got a book to read. What about you?'

'Find Jamal. Head off. Get ready to hunt down the Hollow Men with you tomorrow.'

'Don't take the Metro. In fact, don't take any public transport.'

Donovan sighed. 'Jesus Christ, not you as well. You haven't fallen for that, have you? We're besieged by suicide bombers? They want you to think that way. They want to keep you scared. A scared populace is a pliant populace. Don't give in to that way of thinking. Any of it.'

'Yes,' she said, 'I agree. Of course. But I'm ex-police, remember. I know what goes on that the public never get to see. And wouldn't want to see, either. If they did, they'd never sleep safe in their beds again.'

'Yeah, all right.' Donovan didn't want an argument.

'Look,' she said, uncomfortable with the words. 'Why don't you and Jamal come back to mine tonight? You can stay over if you want and we'll be ready to go in the morning. I'll cook.'

'Or we could get a takeaway.'

Peta smiled. 'Thought you liked pasta carbonara.'

'I do. But I like other things than pasta carbonara too.'

'It's my signature dish.'

'It's your only dish.'

Peta pretended to be angry. 'If you feel like that . . .'

There was something behind her words, Donovan knew that. She didn't want to be alone. That was fine. Neither did he.

'I'd love to,' he said. 'And I'm sure his nibs would too when I find him.'

'Great,' she said, a smile of relief spreading over her face. 'It's a date.'

Jamal stood in the amusement arcade feeling like a hundred years had gone by, feeling like no time had passed at all.

It was where he had first come to when he had arrived in Newcastle. The only place he knew to come to. Where he could work, trade. Where all the rent boys went; to pick up johns, to score, to get money to get stuff to make them forget.

A step back in time, but also like a glimpse into the life of another person, someone he used to be, someone who didn't exist any more. A lost boy. A dead boy.

He looked round. The familiar pings and howls, squeals and jingles, ringtones and death knells. Once, this place, or somewhere just like it, would have been his home, his theatre, his office. Where he worked and played, where he lived. Where he died.

His street sense was right back, had never left. He spotted them straight away: the hustlers, the punters, waltzing round the machines, round each other, circling closer, power-playing.

The arcade glittered like a subterranean diamond mine. The sounds like literal sirens drawing the wary and the unwary, those who couldn't help themselves, those who didn't want to be saved. Jamal felt a thrill course through his body. He could see the attraction, understand the allure. Because it had been in him. Was still in him.

Would always be with him.

He had to accept that, push it to one side. His life was different now. Safe. And he was thankful for that, every day. But he had work to do.

He wanted to find Jason Mason. And this place seemed like as good a starting point as any. He wanted to find him for various reasons. To get his stuff back. To teach him a lesson. To find out what this big secret he claimed to know really was. And because what Jason had done was just wrong.

But Jamal was out of the loop. There was no one he

could ask. And he was too dark to move in some of the circles he supposed Jason Mason moved in. But he could come here, watch, pick up clues. This was the likeliest place for the boy to come to. All that time working with Albion had taught him something. He scoped out the place, trying to find something, a groove, a rhythm to latch on to, get into.

It made him angry. Not just the punters but the boys as well. Selling themselves. Allowing their bodies to be violated. He knew there were arguments, well constructed ones. Conversations with Joe and Peta and Amar had straightened him out. But that anger was still there. And this place was making it flare up inside him.

He became aware of the man at his side before he actually saw him. That punter shuffle, that sour smell of old sweat and twisted needs. The thrill of transgression, of putting desire into action.

Jamal made to walk away but stopped himself. An idea, a plan, sprang into his mind. He stayed where he was, let the man approach. Make the first move.

'You . . . working?' Eyes running over his body like hot, clammy hands.

Jamal turned to face him. Saw not the man, just the need. So typical as to be almost a stereotype. Nondescript. Bland. Middle-aged. Suited and tied. To the office. To the family. To his secret desires.

'Depends,' he said.

The man realized he was going to have to work at it, was excited by the fact.

'You're a beautiful boy . . .'

Jamal's stomach turned. He kept his face stone-blank.

'Yeah,' he said, cutting off any more words. 'You got money?'

The man's excitement level rose. 'Yes.'

Jamal looked round, saw a darker area of the arcade near the back. Unpopulated. 'Over here,' he said. 'Show me.'

Jamal walked, the man followed. Once in the shadows the man made a clumsy lunge forward. Jamal stopped him.

'Money first,' he said. 'Wallet out.'

The man, slightly aggrieved at having to stop, pulled out his wallet, opened it. Before he could extract any notes, Jamal grabbed it from him.

'Hey—'

'Shut it, you fuckin' perv,' said Jamal, snarling round the words. 'You don't speak until I fuckin' tell you to. Got that?'

The man looked around, unbelieving, as if seeking some official he could approach for redress. Jamal grabbed him, pushed him up against the back of a machine. Away from the crowds, daylight, the CCTV cameras. The man let him. A black youth, tall but wiry, was evidently something he was scared of.

'No one gonna help you now. You got no friends here. Do as I say an' you get out alive. Got that?'

The man swallowed hard. The darkness at the back of the cave suddenly real. No glittering diamonds here. Nodded even harder.

'Good.' Jamal opened the man's wallet, took out his cards. 'OK Mr . . . Sean Williams. That you?'

The man nodded.

'Good. You like the boys, do you? Like them young?'

Sean Williams said nothing, too scared to reply.

'Yeah, bet you do. Now you gonna do somethin' for me Sean Williams. I'm tryin' to find a boy, you get me? He be on the streets, maybe even sellin' his body. Maybe even to scum like you. I wanna know when you see him.'

'What . . . what's he look like?'

Jamal didn't have a photo, so he described Jason to him.

'Little kid, white. Got tattoos, skinhead shit. You know, Nazi. Can't miss him. Think you could recognize him?'

Sean Williams nodded.

'Good.' Jamal knew the man would say he was King Zog of Albania just to get out of the building. He needed an extra incentive. A bit more leverage. He pocketed the wallet.

'What—'

'I'll hang on to this,' said Jamal. 'Just to be sure we understandin' each other here. Bet it's got all sorts of personal shit in it. Home address, pictures of your kids, your wife . . .'

Sean Williams looked like he was about to expire in a puddle.

'Business cards? Phone number?'

Sean Williams nodded.

'I'll call you tomorrow. You'd better get out there an' start lookin'.'

'What . . . what if I can't find him?'

'You better find him. Otherwise wifey gets a call. You get me?'

Sean Williams nodded again.

'Now get outta my fuckin' sight, you piecea' shit.'

Sean Williams almost ran from the building.

Jamal watched him go, feeling a thrill of power run through him. It didn't last for long, though, as it was soon replaced by another feeling. One of being soiled, unclean.

He shook his head, left the arcade.

Joe would have been proud of what he had done.

He hoped.

Donovan was waiting for Jamal by Grey's Monument. 'Did you find him?'

'Naw, man, not yet.'

'You going to keep looking?'

Jamal shrugged.

Donovan told him they were off to Peta's.

'Not that pasta shit again.'

'Hopefully not.'

Jamal nodded. 'Safe.'

Jamal stared off down the street, couldn't meet Donovan's eyes.

'You sure you're OK?'

Jamal's head snapped back. 'Yeah, man, I'm cool. Let's go.'

He began to walk off. Donovan frowned, watched him go, then followed.

15

The pub was long gone. Burned out and boarded for years, then bought cheaply and refurbished, sold as generic business premises. It had been many things in three decades and was now the offices for the NUP.

The front windows were again boarded, cheaper to replace wood than glass. A dark, conservative blue. A discreetly displayed sign. No flags, no confrontational slogans. No outward display of aggression.

Restraint and subtlety continued inside. Two heavy old desks, computers on both, two cheerful-looking, modestly dressed temps behind them. A portrait of the Queen. The Union flag, unfurled, at the side. The place contriving to reek of age and tradition.

Then the recruiting room. Two large, dark chesterfield sofas dominated, the atmosphere relaxed but not casual. Where anyone, in response to carefully worded and targeted leaflets, could pop in for a friendly chat, voice their concerns and fears over the way the world was going with professionally trained greeters and recruiters. Just as Mr Sharples had planned.

Mr Sharples. Worth every penny to get him from South Africa. Gave the NUP confidence, a credibility they would otherwise have lacked. Made them a winning proposition.

A proposition in danger of crumbling.

No understanding words in the recruiting room today. Rick Oaten paced the floor, head shaking from side to side, lips mouthing internal monologue. Mr Sharples sat on the studded leather chesterfield, sipping his single malt.

Mr Sharples watched Oaten, eyes unblinking behind his glasses.

'That fucking kid . . . that one little fucking kid . . . he could ruin everything. Everything.'

Mr Sharples ignored him, rolled the whisky around his mouth, felt that sweet sting, swallowed. Oaten continued.

'Everything we've built . . .' His hands grasped the air, angry fists hitting out at nothing. 'Supposed to be the best we've got, and they couldn't fucking find him! But they did manage to find the only nigger in Northumberland and get roundly humiliated by him. Humiliated. By a fucking . . . a fucking . . . *nigger*.' The word spat out like it was something diseased in his mouth

'Rick.' Sharples spoke without moving.

'He could be anywhere now, little cunt . . . anywhere . . .'

'Rick.' Mr Sharples's eyes flashed hard and cold. The words held razors.

Oaten stopped walking. Looked over, panting but not daring to speak.

'We all have a part to play. Concentrate on yours. We'll take care of everything else.'

Oaten wanted to speak, but the words were too scared to emerge from his mouth before Mr Sharples. So he stood, tense and rigid, swaying, the ship he captained ready to capsize. He looked about to burst into tears. Something extra was called for. Mr Sharples stood, crossed, put his arm round his shoulder.

'Don't give up now, Rick. Look what you've achieved. Look at it.' His voice, smooth and sinuous, wrapped itself round Oaten like the grip of a boa constrictor. 'The BNP, the NF, the RVF, Combat 18, all the rest . . . none of them have come close to what you've done with the NUP. Up here, in your little corner of the country. Just you. Bigger and stronger than all of them put together. A force this country will sit up and take notice of.' The grip tightened. A smile. 'Whether they want to or not. Quite an achievement. Be proud of that achievement.'

Oaten sighed. 'I am, but . . . all this is nothing. We need that kid . . .'

'And he will be found.'

Oaten nodded. Mr Sharples's tone left him in no doubt as to how.

'Now. The meeting tonight. We need you on top form. The preacher to his congregation. Convince them that not only can they win but that they *will* win. We need Rick Oaten the great political orator again. Can you do that?'

Oaten stood immobile.

Mr Sharples suppressed his first response, kept his voice honeyed. 'Can you do that?'

Oaten nodded.

'Good.' Mr Sharples looked at his watch. 'Then go and prepare to dazzle the *Daily Mail* readers. Leave the boy to me.'

Oaten nodded again. Mr Sharples ushered him out. His smile disappeared. The hard, steely gaze back in place.

'Fucking idiot,' he said.

This boy was a problem. And Oaten's thugs clearly weren't capable of dealing with him. Something would have to be done.

He took out his mobile, speed-dialled a number, waited. It was answered.

'The boy,' he said without introducing himself. 'He's still a problem.'

'I thought you had the matter in hand?'

Mr Sharples sighed, an angry exhalation of breath. 'The mouth-breathers couldn't find him. Couldn't find their arses with both hands. We don't need arguments and recriminations; we need to be together on this one. So I want you and your boys to get out and look for him too.'

The voice on the other end gave its assent.

'By the way,' said Mr Sharples before hanging up, 'what did you think of my diversion?'

The voice laughed. 'How very apposite.'

'I thought you would think that.'

'Anything else planned I should know about?'

Mr Sharples laughed. Like razor-sharp ice breaking. 'What do you think?'

He broke the connection, sipped his whisky.

Kev had locked himself in the toilet cubicle. He didn't want to come out, couldn't come out. Not yet. Not when he knew what they wanted him to do next.

He closed his eyes and saw the boy again, the Asian boy. Saw fists smashing into his face, pain and blood seeping from his body. Screams. Smelled his flesh burning.

He opened his eyes again, rubbed them hard. No good. The rage, the guilt. Back again. Coiling and twisting in his guts. He couldn't do it.

He was in the toilet block by the converted stables on the farm in Northumberland where he, and the rest of the boys, had stayed the night. He heard voices outside. Ligsy and Cheggs and the rest, on the way to the van, piling inside. Fighting and shouting, getting each other, themselves, psyched up for what they were going to do. Getting their blood up, their testosterone levels high, their cocks hard. Heard Major Tom's posh voice hurrying them along, getting them in line.

The toilet door was knocked on, hard.

'Come on, haven't got all fuckin' day.'

'Yuh-yeah, just comin' . . .'

Kev looked round. Wanted to hit something, smash it into pieces.

Wanted to burst into tears.

He breathed in deep, felt the movement hurt his stomach. Tried to think of something to get his anger going. That fucking black kid. And his nigger-loving boyfriend. Showing him and his boys up like that. He should go back there, tear their place apart, rip their fucking hearts out, teach them both a lesson . . .

But he wouldn't. He couldn't summon up the hatred.

He slumped against the cubicle wall, tried to think. He couldn't do it, couldn't join the rest of them. Had to have a way out. Another deep breath, another pain in his stomach.

An idea.

He looked down, saw the bandages underneath his T-shirt. He rolled his T-shirt up, slowly pulled the dressing away from his skin. The bandages were taped on, gauze and padding over the wound. He took it all away, laid it on the top of the cistern.

Took a deep breath. Another.

And stuck his fingers in the wound.

The pain lanced through him like he was being stabbed all over again. Blood began to seep out over his fingers, down the back of his hand. He pushed harder, moved his fingers around, grabbed at the tender, healing flesh on the inside of the wound.

His face grimaced in pain, screwed his eyes tight shut, saw black stars bursting behind his eyelids, feared he would pass out from the pain.

He held on. Felt blood pour from the wound now, down his hand to his wrist. A voice inside told him it was enough, it would do. Another voice told him it was never enough, he could never atone for what he had done.

He removed his fingers, felt the pain slide out with them. Hastily stuck the dressing and bandages back in place, opened the cubicle door. Started to limp out holding his side. He didn't have to act, the pain was real.

He went outside. Major Tom was standing at the back of the van. Tall, imposing, he looked and sounded like the kind of British army officer always interviewed on the BBC. Even dressed in jeans, boots and bomber jacket he looked military. Mr Sharples had brought him in. He was one of the most disciplined, ordered and sadistic bastards Kev had ever met.

'About fucking time.' Major Tom turned to Kev, eyes widening as he saw him clutching his side, the blood spreading through his white T-shirt. 'What the fucking hell happened to you?'

'Knife wound . . . it's . . . it's opened again . . .'

Major Tom sighed. 'Well, you're no fucking use to me in that state.' He slammed the back of the doors on the Transit van. 'Stay here. Get that cleaned up.'

Major Tom walked round to the front of the van, got in the passenger side. The van drove out of the farm and away.

Kev slumped down to the ground, watched it go. He looked up at the sky, saw cloudless blue. Felt the sun on his face. Breathed deeply. Once. Twice. Felt pain flash all round his torso.

He smiled. Pain had never felt so good.

He had never been happier to be alive.

While Rick Oaten was wowing the faithful at a fund-raising dinner and talk at the Assembly Rooms, the candlelit procession to honour the life of Sooliman Patel was just starting out.

They moved slowly, their steps contemplative, their candles held in front of them, through the city. They had gathered at the mosque on the corner of Elswick Road and Grainger Park Road where the imam had read to them from the Koran. Then, waiting until darkness had finally fallen, had lit their candles and made their way into the city.

Through Scotswood, down Westgate Road, into the centre of the city. Passing the Assembly Rooms, unaware that Rick Oaten was inside, along Mosley Street, coming to a halt before the cathedral. Singing softly as they went.

Sooliman's parents led the way, neither of them holding a candle, instead holding each other. Mrs Patel breaking down as they passed the end of the street where he died. The news cameras making sure the moment didn't go unrecorded.

Local religious and political leaders were, for once, content to let the spotlight be on someone else. Abdul-Haq kept his distance from the Patels, only walking alongside them after they asked him to.

They reached the cathedral. The Bishop was waiting outside, ready to begin the remembrance service. It had been decided to hold it outside, to make it as open as possible, to encourage people to join in not just to honour a dead boy but to demonstrate that the majority of people in the city wanted nothing to do with extremism, were in no way racist.

The make-up of the marchers reflected that: white, brown and black faces all walking together. Young and old. Atheists and agnostics alongside the devout. Together for a bigger purpose. The overriding feelings loss and remembrance, but out of those there was a chance for peace. For love. All the marchers felt it.

The Bishop gave a heartfelt, solicitous greeting to the Patels. 'This is a real chance for peace,' he said to them. 'If any good can come of your terrible loss, then let us hope this is it.'

They waited in front of the cathedral, candles burning low, waiting. Across the closed-off street, the police had erected barriers, were standing in front of them, ready for any trouble.

It wasn't long in coming. A white Transit van reversed fast up the Side, back doors opening, bodies spilling out. The police saw what was happening, ran over to contain the situation.

And were met with tear gas.

Coughing and choking, they fell back and the occupants of the van were on them. Bats, fists, chains. Taking out anyone who was in front of them. They wore jeans and bomber jackets like a uniform, bandanas and balaclavas covering their heads and faces.

More tear gas thrown, this time into the procession.

People screamed, scattered. Ran into each other, over each other, tried to get away. The masked raiders wading through the crowd, hitting indiscriminately, causing pandemonium.

The police radioing for backup, reinforcements.

At a signal from their leader, the raiders ran back to the van, piled inside. The van revved up and roared down the Side on to the Quayside and away.

Carnage and chaos. Injury and anger. All that was left of the peaceful procession. The love long gone.

Ambulances were called, wounded and shocked attended to. Abdul-Haq had pulled the Patels inside the cathedral when the violence erupted. Mrs Patel was beyond crying now, looking like she was on the verge of nervous collapse.

The news cameras had captured it all.

No doubt as to who was responsible: the shouts of *Sieg Heil* as the raiders boarded their Transit giving the game away.

The peace shattered.

Perhaps irrevocably.

16

Newcastle, past three thirty a.m. The sirens, the flashing lights were gone. Areas were cordoned off as police searched through the night for any signs of the march's attackers. Shock waves had rippled out from the event: the city was sleeping, but uncomfortably, all sodium light and shadowed darkness.

Pubs and clubs long since closed. Fast-food shops and vans shut, their grease mopped up, their meagre takings counted, their waste and wrappings left where they were dropped. Skeleton crews of taxis dotted about on city-wide ranks, drivers reading, standing together, radios throwing their voices into the transistorized void. Occasional night workers moved purposefully along the pavements, drunks and stragglers wandered home or away from home. Stone, steel and glass ticking, cooling, gathering a collective breath before the next day's heat hit.

Paul Turnbull cruised the city streets, driving slowly, moving forward purposefully. One thing to do before he went to Hertfordshire. And no amount of civil disruption would get in the way of who he was going to visit.

Out of the city centre, up to the West End of Newcastle, patrolling, looking. No sign. One last place to check. Back to Newcastle, parking up round Gallowgate, walking down Stowell Street. The Chinese restaurants that lined both sides of the city's mini Chinatown were closed, their neon and gold signs now flat and unenticing, the dragon banners hanging still, lifeless. The smell of fried food and oriental spices fading away on the air.

It didn't take long for Turnbull to find her. She was down a back alley on her knees, working away at a punter. Turnbull didn't look at the man, didn't want to. He turned away, tried not to listen. He waited until she was finished and her client had left before approaching her.

'Hi, Claire,' he said, 'it's me.'

She was taking a long drink from a Bacardi Breezer in her handbag, swilling it round her mouth before swallowing. She looked up. The streetlight made her face look even gaunter than when he had last seen her, the hollows underneath her cheekbones and eyes almost skeletal. Her eyes, even in this light, he noticed, were pinwheeling.

It took her a while but she recognized him. 'Paul.'

'Yeah.'

'What d'you want? What have you got that I want?' Her fingers played against his chest in an approximation of flirtatiousness that she had been doing so long it was now automatic. She giggled in attempted coquettishness.

He shut his eyes, shook his head. He hated to see her like this, fought hard to be non-judgemental about her, to just talk to her.

'Listen, Claire, I just wanted to let you know, I'm going to be away for a while. Work. Don't know how long for.'

'But what about me?' She grabbed the front of his shirt.

Turnbull took a second before answering her. Addicts were so selfish, so unappreciative of everything anyone ever did for them. Yet still he did it. He had no choice. He had promised. She was his responsibility.

'Just listen a minute,' he said. 'There's someone you can contact if you need anything,' he said. He handed her a card. 'Joe Donovan. You've met him before. You probably can't remember. Call him if you need anything. Right?'

She nodded, trying to focus her eyes on his face.

Turnbull stood back, took her in. So thin, her clothes as

worn out as she was. He had seen that downward spiral so depressingly often.

'I thought you were going to that clinic. Getting yourself cleaned up.'

She sighed. 'I am. I was. It's just . . . Don't keep going on at me. I'll do it. In me own time.'

'OK. I've got to go.' He didn't hug her. He didn't know how. 'Bye.'

She replied.

He turned and left. Behind him, another man was already approaching her.

Jason Mason couldn't sleep. Not because of the rats gnawing nearby, or the smell of the bins although they were bad enough. But because of what was going on in his head.

The sleeping bag was on the floor in the back of a second-hand shop. Insect- and animal-chewed mismatched carpet squares, offcuts and bare boards competed to see which could hold the most dirt. Around him were battered metal shelves holding cardboard boxes filled with old, used cameras, mobile phones, video game consoles. Plus bigger pieces: electric guitars, keyboards, amplifiers. Even a dismantled drum kit.

The shop was a front. Norrie was a fence. A go-to guy for Newcastle muggers, burglars and boosters, he kept smackheads and crackheads solvent. Anything saleable went in the window, was soon snapped up. But he was a victim of his own success: too well known to the police to handle anything big and valuable, so he had been forced to improvise. He now made most of his money through stolen credit card details, selling identities, working online. But he still kept the shop supplied. For appearances, if nothing else.

After leaving Jamal's place, Jason had gone straight to him with the iPods.

'Good resale, no problem sellin' this.' Norrie looked it over, down at the other one on the counter next to it. He was short, round, with thinning, steel-wool hair unsuccessfully flattened down to his scalp, big glasses, greasy thumbprints glinting off them in the weak light. Behind the glass his eyes blinked continuously. A nervous habit, Jason reckoned. 'Anything on it worth keepin' that I can download? Sell separately?'

'Dunno. Listen, Norrie' he had said, looking round anxiously all the time as if expecting someone to run in and grab him, 'I need to ask you a favour.'

'Don't do fuckin' favours.' He was scrabbling about in the till for notes. 'You'll wanna be my fuckin' friend next.'

Jason had expected Norrie to say that. He had to try harder. 'No, listen, this is . . . this is good. I've got somethin' else. Somethin' big, y'knaw? But I need somethin' in return for it.'

Norrie didn't look up. 'Not jewellery. Can't shift that stuff at the moment. Prices aren't worth shit.'

'Naw, better than that.'

Norrie sighed. 'How much and what is it?'

'Information.'

Norrie looked up. 'What information?'

'The party.' Jason could hardly keep the excitement out of his voice. 'They're plannin' somethin' big. Thor's Hammer, it's called.'

'So?'

'I mean big. Really big. A lot of people would pay loads to know what they were plannin'.'

'Oh, yeah? An' how d'you know all this?'

'Because—' *I'm the special one.* He nearly said it. Stopped himself just in time.

He had got to know Norrie through the boys in the Gibraltar. Their fence of choice. For the cause, they had always said. His shop was on Westgate Road, sandwiched between two motorbike shops. Just a hefty stone's throw from the Gib. Not that Norrie was a fully paid-up member of the party – they wouldn't allow it; they thought he was Jewish, although he was actually Scottish – but he did say he was sympathetic to their aims. Kev had once said he would be sympathetic to anybody's aims if there was money in it.

Jason couldn't tell him. Because if Norrie knew that, then he would just phone someone up, tell them he knew where Jason was, wait for the reward. And he knew what would happen to him then.

'Because what? What d'you know? What information?' Norrie was starting to get angry. Eyes blinking faster. Jason had just stood there with his mouth open.

'Can't tell you now,' he said.

'Well, you're fuckin' useless, then, aren't you?' He looked at the iPods. 'Give you fifty for the pair.'

Jason nodded. Norrie moved over to the till.

Jason had looked round the shop, an idea forming in his head. He had to think quickly if it was going to work. 'Listen, Norrie.' Another look round to check there was no one after him. 'I need . . . somewhere to stay. For a bit.'

Norrie blinked behind his filthy glasses, counted out bills. 'Salvation Army's that way.'

Jason screwed up his eyes, thought harder. This had to work. Had to. The alternative didn't bear thinking about. 'I've got a . . . a prop'sition. For you.'

Norrie looked at him. Waited.

'Yeah. Yeah. I stay here, right? You let me stay here. I know you do that.' Norrie had given a few wanted faces a place to stay until things had cooled off for them.

'Not any more. Too fuckin' risky.'

Jason thought hard. 'I'll work for you, right?' He looked at Norrie, a hopeful little smile on his face. 'Stay here an' work for you. Yeah?'

'Fuck off. Can't afford to pay anyone else.'

Wasn't working. Jason shook his head quickly, tried to get his brain functioning. 'Naw, naw, not like that . . .'

'What like, then?'

Yeah, he thought, what like, then? 'On the street, like. Nickin' stuff. Cards an' that. Bringin' them back, an' you sellin' them.' Jason stood still. He grinned this time, pleased with his quick thinking, his brilliant idea.

Norrie looked at him. Jason could almost see the numbers rolling around his eyeballs like they did in old cartoons. He waited. Eventually Norrie nodded.

'Stay in the back there. I'll pay you what I think stuff is worth, take your rent out of that. Food you find yourself. You don't like that, you can fuck off.'

Jason nodded his head vigorously. 'Yeah, yeah, I like it. 'S great.'

Norrie folded the pound notes up, put them back in the till. 'Your first bit of rent.'

Jason watched the money disappear back into the drawer. He said nothing, not wanting to jeopardize his position already. Norrie looked at him.

'What you still standin' there for? Fuck off out of it an' get some work done.'

Jason had done as he was told.

That was a couple of days ago. Now Jason lay there, as far away from sleep as he was a concept of home. He couldn't keep living like this, running like this. He just wanted peace.

He thought of Jamal's house. It had seemed so cosy, so comfortable. How come he had somewhere like that? How come it was always other people?

Never him.

So he lay there in his sleeping bag, listened to the rats, tried not to smell the bins behind him. Bullying back the tears. Tried to will himself to sleep.

And dream of a better future.

17

The TV news was white hot the next morning, and the run-up to what was just another boring local election was taking on almost national significance.

Images of police clashing with balaclavaed rioters were on every channel, along with footage of screaming, terrified marchers running into the cathedral. Rick Oaten's face followed, an interview held immediately after his dinner at the Assembly Rooms: 'We are a legitimate political party with respectable policies. Like any other party. We are not responsible for acts of random violence such as this, which I join you in condemning.'

He seemed calm and reasonable, debonair in his bow tie and dinner jacket. Unruffled. His words matched his appearance. Abdul-Haq, however, appeared as the opposite. Interviewed in the cathedral directly after the attack, he was visibly shaken, his mood alternating between fear and anger: 'This was a peaceful march in memory of a young boy's life. A boy murdered by racist thugs, the kind of thugs who did this to us! This is not who we are! We are men of peace! Peace!' His face, in wide-eyed close-up, failed to match his words.

And back to the studio.

Donovan turned from the TV, shouted into the kitchen. 'Don't think we'll be getting an interview with Abdul-Haq today. Might be a bit busy.'

Peta walked in, two mugs of coffee in her hands. 'You never know,' she said, 'might want to talk to as many journalists as possible.'

She sat down next to him, watched the remainder of the bulletin. A long piece about the proposed razing and rebuilding of the West End of Newcastle, replacing terraced houses and crumbling tower blocks with what they described as 'an urban brownfield regeneration scheme'. The screen showed computer-generated images of sculpted parkland with cutting-edge blocks of housing, shopping complexes and offices dotted about on it. It was a multi-billion-pound project. If it ever went through. Talking heads' pieces from local councillors showed it was having trouble being passed.

'Hey, there's Colin Baty,' said Peta.

The screen was filled by his round, red face. 'Obviously there are things we need to look at, but in principle the proposal's sound. It'll mean much-needed jobs for a deprived area and, at the end of the day, better housing and better amenities.'

'Yeah,' said Donovan, 'if you can afford to live in them.' He turned to Peta. 'That's who terrified Trevor Whitman?'

'You want to see him on full power.'

The weather came up next. More heat.

'Right,' said Peta, snapping the TV off, 'to work.'

The previous evening they had ordered an Indian takeaway instead of eating Peta's pasta. Jamal's relief had been apparent, earning him a scornful look from Peta. He had eaten and gone to bed. Not like him, Donovan knew.

'Did you have much luck finding him?' Donovan had said, knowing what was on the boy's mind.

'Nah, man.'

'You going to try again tomorrow?'

Jamal had nodded.

'OK. When this case is finished, I'll give you a hand. We'll all get on it, yeah?'

Jamal had nodded, gone in the living room to watch TV.

Donovan and Peta had sat either side of the dining room table and got down to work, Donovan through the pile of photocopied old newspapers Peta had brought back from the library, Peta surfing the net, then through Whitman's book, more thoroughly this time. There was no mention of Peta's parents. The relief on her face had been palpable.

They had then planned what to do next. Peta showed him a photo in the book of the Hollow Men. 'And they weren't all men, either,' she said.

'How very patriarchal for such heavy progressives,' Donovan had replied.

'Indeed. Five men, one woman.' She showed him the photo.

Five people, young, idealistic and full of hope, taken at a party some time in the early Seventies judging by the clothes. Trevor Whitman stood in the middle looking suitably charismatic in leather jacket, white kaftan and faded Levi's. An urban Jesus Christ Superstar. Next to him was a young Asian man with the obligatory long hair, wearing a velvet jacket and holding a cigarette in one hand and a glass of red wine in the other.

'Our friend Abdul-Haq,' said Peta. 'Or Gideon Ahmed, as he was known then.'

'In less strict times, obviously.'

'Looks like Cat Stevens,' said Peta, smiling. 'You know, I still have a problem with all this.'

'All what?'

'Well, religious extremism. Political extremists you can cope with. They're not usually ready to die for their beliefs. But religious extremists, you can't reason with them. Because God tells them to do it. And anything you say or do against them is just a test from God.'

'Not just Muslims, though. Look at the American

Christians. Censoring free speech, burning books, blowing up abortion clinics and, worst of all, voting for George Bush.'

'You've got a point.'

'When the political extremists start blowing themselves up, that's when we've got trouble.'

They went back to the photo. A woman stood on Whitman's other side, gazing up at him like she was basking in the light from his halo. With long dark hair and flowing Indian-cotton-print dress, she looked the archetypal hippie chick.

'Mary Evans, I presume,' said Donovan.

Peta looked at her notes. 'Now a community activist. Well respected. Gets things done. And a poet. Award-winning, apparently. And a lesbian. Big advocate of gay liberation, women's rights, that sort of thing.'

'The way she's staring at our Trevor here, she doesn't look too lesbian,' said Donovan.

Peta ran her finger down the notes again. 'Late convert from what I can gather given some of her quotes. Says men abused her, systematically, for years. Would never trust them again. Only trust women. Lot of anger. Channelled it into her poetry.'

'Strange how you can shift your whole sexuality like that.'

'Not really,' said Peta. 'I don't think we're as hard-wired as you think. There's been times in the past when . . . never mind.'

Donovan smiled. 'Really?'

Peta reddened. 'Get your mind out of the gutter and back to work.'

'I was joking.'

'Yeah. The sexist male's first line of defence. Anyway, Mary Evans is still in the north-east. The West End of Newcastle, to be precise.'

'Crops up a lot at the moment.'

'It's a deprived area,' said Peta. 'She wouldn't be a community activist in Jesmond, would she?'

They looked at the photo again. There were two others, a man at either side. One, duffel-coated, had a well-fed face and a wide smile. Like it was all just a really good laugh. His hair, although long, looked well groomed.

'Maurice Courtney. Little rich boy playing at being a revolutionary. Left uni, got bored, went back to the family business. Big noise in the City, London. Doubt he'd be able to tell us much.'

'You never know,' said Donovan. 'Maybe I should pop down and see him.' And see how Turnbull's doing, see when my son can come home. The thought was never far from the front of his mind. Peta's face showed she was thinking the same thing but she said nothing. Donovan looked at the photo again.

'Who's the other one?' he said.

'Richie Vane.' Peta pointed to the last one. He too was staring up at Whitman. Face slack, expression unfocused. Waiting for orders. Or just loaded. 'Bit of a casualty. Drugs. No current address, just last known hostel.'

'We can check hospitals, charities, that kind of thing. Maybe receiving treatment. You said six. Where's the other one?'

'Alan Shepherd. Disappeared at the time of the pub bombing.'

'The supposed bomber. Caught in the blast. Or did a runner. Presumably he took the photo.'

Donovan put the photo down, looked up, smiled.

She looked at him, lips slightly parted, waiting. 'What?'

'Just like old times. This. Albion back together. Good, isn't it?'

Peta nodded. She leaned forward again. Donovan tried to

keep his eyes on her face. She kept hers on him, smiling. They both sat there, neither seemingly wanting to be the first to break it, wondering just what each one was finding in the other's eyes.

The door opened.

''M goin' to bed. Spare room's mine, yeah?'

They both sat back as if they had been caught doing something they were ashamed of. If Jamal noticed, he didn't show it.

'Yeah,' said Peta, 'you take the spare room.' She looked at Donovan, composure returning to her features. 'Joe can take the sofa in the living room. Can't you?'

Donovan shrugged, his face as blank as possible. 'Sure.'

And that had been that for the night.

They had their plan for the day. Peta was going to talk to Mary Evans, Donovan was going to try to contact Abdul-Haq.

'Fine by me,' said Donovan. 'At least I won't have to listen to your God-awful music in the car.'

'There's nothing wrong with James Blunt.'

'Oh. That well-known cockney rhyming slang.' Donovan hated Peta's taste in music. Couldn't understand how such an interesting person could listen to something so bland. Actually go into a shop and buy it.

Peta picked up her keys, made for the door. 'And what would you suggest, O great arbiter of taste?'

Donovan moved with her. 'What about the Drive By Truckers? You still got that one?'

She stopped walking, gave him a look equalling the one Jamal had received the night before about her pasta. 'It's still on the shelf next to Richmond Fontaine and Jim White and Sparklehearse—'

'Sparkle*horse*.'

'I've heard them. And all the other rubbish you burned for me. Johnny Dowd. For Christ's sake, the man couldn't carry a tune if it was in a bucket. I'm going.'

Arguing with her, Donovan knew from experience, would be like arguing with the Tyne Bridge.

She went out, slamming the door behind her.

Donovan watched her drive off, smiled. Another brilliant-blue morning sky, he thought. And another day nearer to being reunited with his son.

He went to sleep thinking about him, woke up the same way. Everything else, the job with Albion, helped to take his mind off it for most of the day, but it was the beginnings and endings, or the times when he was on his own, that were the hardest. When he couldn't get him out of his mind.

He went into the kitchen, brewed up some more coffee, focused on the day ahead. Jamal was still asleep, would be down soon. In the meantime he went into the living room, picked up the phone.

Tried to get through to Abdul-Haq.

The walls had thudded, the floors shook, the crowd slammed off each other in aggressive ecstasy. The pounding, tuneless, atonal rhythm of White Jihad, a skinhead band from Poland, had transformed the upstairs of the Gibraltar into an angry mosh pit. The crowd had shouted, chanted, screamed along as the band thudded and ranted from the stage, the racist, white supremacist lyrics to their signature song 'Boot Party' known off by heart:

'With their turbans and their bombs –
Send them back where they belong –
Boot party!
Boot party!
Show the niggers white means right –

Shoot the black bastards on sight –
Boot party!
Boot party!
Boot party!
Boot party!'

Rage transcendent, the audience bound by communal hatred, prejudices mutually confirmed, the cruel comfort of belonging.

And Kev hadn't been touched by any of it.

Not so long ago he would have been in the thick of it, arms windmilling, booted feet stomping, giddy from the crush of hot, heaving bodies pressing against him, muscled male flesh against muscled male flesh, emerging eventually, skin wet with sweat and blood, both his own and others, carrying injuries and bruises like rare treasure.

The event was true believers only, a treat for Major Tom and the foot soldiers. Kev, although unable to join them on their raiding party, had been driven from the farm to the pub, was still expected to work the door and he had: frisking, checking for concealed cameras, recorders, weeding out undercover coppers or reporters. But even the true believers looked different now. Better dressed, designer labels. Happy with their lives. No cheap clothes, no conflict or doubt.

Groupie Diane had offered him sex, rubbed up against him, her hands on his cock. It hadn't hardened. All he could do not to throw up. She looked like something from his butcher's shop, big tits sagging down like udders, arse and belly and thighs ready to be sliced off the bone like pork. Smelling of rancid meat. She revolted him.

Kev wondered where Jason was, what he was doing. Felt a void within him, an aching loss he couldn't explain. He wanted to talk to him, see he was OK.

But that was all the night before. Kev had left early, gone

back to the flat. That made it even worse. His stinking dad, his stinking brother. He had to get out.

Now, in the front room with Jeremy Kyle having a go at some cuckolded chav, Kev's head was pounding. He had to get out. Go somewhere, anywhere. Do something, anything.

He needed to talk to someone.

And he knew who. It was a risk, but a risk worth taking.

He left the flat, slammed the door behind him.

Hoped he never had to go there again.

18

Jason Mason decided not to open his eyes. If he did he would have to get up. And face Norrie. And go back on the street again.

Too late. Norrie had looked into the back, seen him.

'Oi, get up. Yeah, you, you lazy cunt. Come on, you've got work to do.'

Jason quickly weighed up the options. Decided he had no choice. He opened his eyes, sat up. Felt like he hadn't slept. He looked down at his sleeping bag. At least it didn't appear to have any more teeth marks in it. That was something.

'What you still hangin' around for? Fuck off out of it an' get some work done.'

Jason got up. Rolled the sleeping bag as small as he could make it, stuffed it behind one of the shelves.

'Out.'

Jason went. Dragging his feet as he did so.

Leaving Jamal's place had been a risk. But then so had staying there. He didn't know who this Donovan bloke Jamal wanted him to meet was. Or whose side he was on. So he had weighed it up. Wait, take a chance and maybe make some big money, maybe not, or cut and run with cash in hand. No contest. Result.

But once he had got back into the city he couldn't face going back to the street, so Norrie's had been a good idea. Bit of pickpocketing, bit of boosting, stuff he was good at. Working bars, roaming streets after closing time when people were too pissed to know what was going on, even giving the come-on to perverts and running off with their wallets. Easy targets. And Norrie had been pleased with the haul.

But Jason was starting to see the risks. If the law pulled him in, word might get back to Rick Oaten. In fact, word definitely would get back. Jason knew what some of the party members did for a living.

So he had become even extra cautious. Pickpocketing was out. He was down to rolling drunks and setting up perverts. They were the least likely to complain.

He walked down Westgate Road, sun beating down on his back, the heat making him aware that he hadn't had a bath since Jamal's. Glancing round all the time, ready to run at a second's notice.

But it was still in his head. The information. He had to think how to use it. And quickly. His old Connexions worker's words came back to him. Make a mental list. Tick off the plus points and the minus points. Plan.

He did that all the way into town. Stopped off at McDonald's for a burger, some fries and a strawberry shake. He always ate at McDonald's. Knew that whatever else he was guaranteed some good food.

He reached the amusement arcade. Went inside. The hall was dark and cool, welcoming after the glare and the heat outside. He stood at one of the slot machines, feeding it with coins, not really looking at what was coming up, just playing automatically.

He became aware of someone behind him. He turned. A middle-aged businessman, suited and anonymous. Easy prey. Jason said nothing, waited.

'Are you . . . are you working?'

Jason turned. 'Might be.'

'Good.' The perv was sweating. Must take the heat really badly. 'What . . . what's your name?'

Jason almost gave his real one. 'Kev,' he said.

The perv looked disappointed.

'Why?' said Jason. 'What's yours?'

The perv licked his lips. All that sweat on his face, and his lips were still dry. 'Sean,' he said.

'You got a place?' said Jason.

Sean shook his head.

'Come with me, then.'

They walked out of the arcade, down Clayton Street towards the Central Station, where it would be easy to run, get lost in the crowds.

Piece of piss, thought Jason. Money in the bank.

Peta pulled the car to the kerb, stopped the engine. She got out, looked round. A block of new flats in front of her constructed of sickly yellow brick. Small patches of arid grass ringed the ground floor. Cars, small and new, took up most of the communal parking spaces. A huge canvas billboard was erected on the Stanhope Street side of the development showing a young, photogenic couple lounging on boxy, beige furniture, grinning perfect smiles at each other over a moderate glass of wine. IF YOU LIVED HERE, the banner said, YOU'D BE HOME BY NOW.

If I lived here, she almost said aloud, I'd be dead by now.

She was in Arthur's Hill in the West End of Newcastle. The area seemed quiet, like it was braced for the next thing to hit it. Opposite the new flats was an old council estate: Seventies, flat-roofed boxes. She locked the car, checked the piece of paper from her pocket, began walking towards the community centre.

Mary Evans was founder member, and head of, the local branch of COU, the Citizens Organizing Union. A grassroots community organization based in the north-east, it formed and encouraged local alliances between religious groups, schools, students and trade unions. With notable success: the streets were safer and cleaner, housing more affordable, drugs down, crime down, schooling up, local businesses committing to a minimum living wage and regeneration.

Or so the press release said. As she walked down the road to the community centre, Peta was struck by just how well maintained the estate looked. No furniture or household appliances littered the street, no broken windows. Front doors painted, gardens well tended. An obvious, but understated, pride. It looked if not a great place to live then the best it could be.

Peta had read up on Mary Evans. After she'd left the Hollow Men the police had pulled her in, tried to get her to roll over on her old colleagues. They bent laws to keep her in custody, questioned her illegally without a solicitor, subjected her to all manner of indignities, threatened herself and her family. She never gave in. Reluctantly, they released her. But her silence cost; she suffered a breakdown and, following a suicide attempt, had been hospitalized.

She had stated that it wasn't solely due to the police: it was the culmination of years of abuse. Family, university lecturer, even fellow Hollow Men, she had claimed. Men. Always men.

Her poetry writing started during therapy and she had discovered a real talent for it. Several volumes had been published, at least one of which had won a literary prize.

Following classic patterns, Peta thought. Feminism, man hating, lesbianism. The poetry channelling her anger outwards. Peta could relate to that. She had been serious in what she had said to Donovan.

She reached the community centre: a one-storey brick building, the paintwork on its doors and sign looking fresh, the grass around it well tended. The interior was all blond wood, old but well cared for. Clean and brightly lit. It smelled of polish. Offices led off to the side, the main hall ahead of them. From beyond the double doors came the sounds of children playing. Peta put her head round the door. Pre-school-age children were running around playing, parents and helpers alongside them. Everyone seemed happy.

'Can I help you?'

Peta turned at the voice. A woman, old, small and thin, was standing in a doorway. It took a few seconds but Peta recognized her from the photo.

'Mary Evans?' she said, smiling.

'Yes.' She looked apprehensive, tried to mask it with a smile. 'What can I do for you?'

'Can we go in?' said Peta, looking round. 'Easier to talk inside.'

She opened the door wide, they went in. The office was brightly painted, papered by primary-coloured wall planners and posters advertising various politically worthy causes. The furniture was old, mismatching, goodwill donations. She sat behind the desk, pulled her chair up slightly higher than the chairs at the front of the desk that Peta took. She had stayed loyal to her old dress sense, was still swathed in printed cotton, scarves and bangles. There had been strength in her voice, but her eyes darted and fluttered like trapped sparrows before alighting on Peta. But she sat purposefully, like she had forced herself to be strong.

She looked at the card. 'Peta Knight. Albion. Are you trying to sell me something?'

Peta tried for a reassuring smile. Evidently missed from the look on Mary Evans's face. 'I'm here on behalf of Trevor Whitman. He's one of our clients.'

Her face crumpled in on itself. Now she looked even older. 'Yes,' she said. 'I saw he was back here.' She nodded, seemingly unaware that her head was doing it. 'Trevor Whitman. God. What does he want with me?'

'He's been getting some threatening calls,' said Peta. 'We're looking into it for him.'

'And you think I did it? I need a cigarette.' She fumbled one out of the carton, lit it with shaking hands and inhaled deeply, eyes closed as if sucking down strength along with the smoke.

'Of course not,' said Peta. 'We're just talking to people up here who know him or used to know him.'

Breathing out, she looked at her again. 'Why the hell would I want to talk to him?' Her voice dropped, a dark bitterness. 'Threatening phone calls? If I'd wanted to hurt him I would have done it sooner. And better. What are you looking at me like that for?'

Peta looked taken aback. 'I'm sorry,' she said. 'You just seem to have a very deep well of anger for him.' And you accessed it so quickly, she thought.

Mary Evans seemed to realize how she must have looked. She attempted a laugh. 'Well. He's a bastard and a bully, Trevor Whitman. And a misogynist. And if he wants to fuck you up, he'll really fuck you up.'

Peta frowned. This wasn't the way she had expected the conversation to go, but she went with it. 'How d'you mean?'

Mary Evans dragged frantically on her cigarette, putting a cloud of smoke between her and her guest, trying to disappear behind it. 'I joined the Hollow Men because I believed in its ideals. And I left because I realized that it was just an excuse for middle-class boys to get into fights and behave like football hooligans. And take drugs. And use women. They called it free love . . .' Her face twisted into an ugly sneer. 'But let's call it what it really was. Rape.'

'Right,' said Peta, not wanting to get caught up in that argument. 'What about blowing things up?'

Mary Evans smiled. 'Their answer to everything. A very male answer to everything. Things needed to change. Make no mistake. But you can't create a new world using brute force. There are more subtle ways than that.'

'Such as?'

'Did you see the new housing development opposite?'

They both nodded.

'One of our initiatives. Wasteland we bought from the council then sold to a private developer. For a much higher price.'

'Sounds more capitalist than socialist,' said Peta.

Mary Evans smiled. 'I prefer the term pragmatic. The Malcolm X approach. By any means necessary. Now we're working with local housing associations to ensure those flats have a high proportion of affordable accommodation. For local working people.' She sat back, looking pleased with herself. 'Sometimes whispers are louder than screams.'

'Very good,' said Peta. 'I think I saw something on the news about it this morning.'

An emotion Peta couldn't trace flitted across Mary Evans's face. Fear?

'That's . . . that's something else.'

'OK. Back to Trevor Whitman. Do you know anyone with a grudge against him from back then? Anyone he upset?'

Mary Evans gave a short, hard laugh, rattling the tar in her lungs. 'How long have you got? He pissed off everyone.' She stubbed her cigarette out in an already crowded ashtray, taking pleasure in watching it fall apart.

'How?' said Peta.

'Because he's a manipulator. Of people. He pretends to be friends with them, then twists them all out of shape until they're mangled and useless. That's the kind of person he was. And probably still is. So there's your answer.'

Peta thought of him with Lillian. The smiles she gave him. Wondered how long it would be until she was twisted out of shape.

'D'you ever see anyone else from those days?'

Her eyes misted slightly. 'Richie. Richie Vane.' She gave a sad smile. 'He was the only decent one among them. Poor Richie.'

'Drugs and drink, wasn't it?' said Peta.

Mary Evans shook her head. 'The party never ended for Richie and the clearing up never began. I still see him now and again. Try to help him when I can. But . . .' She shrugged.

'We're trying to track down all the old Hollow Men. D'you know where we could find him?' said Peta. 'Just to talk.'

Mary Evans thought hard, reached a decision. 'When d'you want to see him?'

'Soon as.'

Nodding to herself, she picked the phone up, made a call. Peta tried not to listen but picked up phrases, especially ones about her: 'I think so . . . she seems on the level . . . trustworthy . . . genuine . . . well, we'll see . . .' She put the phone down. 'You're in luck. He's still attending his courses at the centre.' Mary Evans wrote an address on a piece of paper, handed it over. 'Two o'clock this afternoon.'

Peta took it, smiling. 'Thank you. I really appreciate it.'

A smile played across Mary Evans's features. 'No problem. Perhaps you might be in a position to do me a favour one day. Have you spoken to Gideon yet?'

'Abdul-Haq, you mean? Not yet. We thought he might be a bit busy at the minute.'

'I refuse to call him by that pathetic name. But I'm sure he's never too busy to talk about himself.' Another unreadable smile. 'Especially to a pretty young thing like you.'

Peta felt herself blush. 'Right. What happened to Alan Shepherd? Trevor's book doesn't go into much detail.'

Mary Evans's face darkened. 'Alan Shepherd. Christ. He

was . . .' She sighed. 'I'm sorry. I don't think I want to say anything more. I hope I've proved I'm not your anonymous caller.'

Peta, realizing this was all she was going to get, stood up. 'You have. Well, thanks for your help. If you think of anything in the meantime—'

'You look familiar.' Peta stopped. 'What did you say your name was?'

'Peta Knight.'

Mary Evans frowned. 'Knight.'

'My dad was Philip Knight. Married Lillian Wallis.'

'Wait.' Mary Evans got hurriedly up, walked round the desk until she was in front of Peta. She reached up, touched Peta's face. 'Lillian,' she said. Peta hardly breathed.

Mary Evans's hand stroked her cheek, slowly, compassionately, her eyes alive and dancing with secrets and tenderness, the years dropping off her. 'Yes. Lillian. You look just like her.'

'Lots of people say that.' Peta's voice was suddenly hoarse and croaky.

'You do,' said Mary Evans as if she was looking into the past, seeing something long lost. 'I see it now. Oh, you do.'

A light came on in Mary Evans's eyes. 'Did Lillian introduce you to Trevor?'

Peta nodded, unsure of her voice.

Mary Evans nodded. She almost smiled. 'Of course. And that's why you were chosen.' It was less of a question than a statement of confirmation.

'He . . . spoke to my mother, yes. And she . . . she contacted me.'

'Of course she did.' She sighed. 'Oh, Lillian. He got you too.'

Mary Evans stood back, took her hand away from Peta's face with seeming reluctance. She looked to Peta like she was just coming out of a trance. Suddenly embarrassed, she went back behind the desk, busying herself with her cigarettes.

Peta stared, confusion etched on her features.

Mary Evans lit up, breathed out a cloud of smoke like a huge sigh of relief. 'I have work to do.' She studied some paperwork in front of her. 'I'm sorry.'

Recognizing her cue, Peta turned to go.

'But be careful. The past—' Mary Evans stopped herself. Peta waited. 'Just be careful,' she said and went back to her work, her wall of smoke.

Peta couldn't get out of there quick enough.

19

Turnbull sat outside the house in Hertfordshire, hoping they hadn't seen him. The road was quiet and leafy, just as Donovan had said it would be. The sun beat down, the branches barely moved. He found a good spot with plenty of shade and sat unobserved, making notes. U2 playing quietly on the stereo, absently nodding his head to the beat.

Before driving down, he had run a thorough check on the couple, discovered nothing more than Sharkey's earlier investigation. But he hadn't let that deter him. Because he had the beginnings of a plan.

He looked down at his notepad, read back what he had written.

School. DNA. Be careful.

Get close to the boy, some hair or something, kiss off a Coke bottle, get it pulled, matched up and Bob's your uncle. He looked down at his notes again. The plan was there, he just needed a way to make it happen.

He turned the stereo up. *Elevation*. Helped him think.

Kev stared at the house, not believing he had the right one. On a new housing estate just off the A1 in Grimley, between Gateshead and Chester-le-Street. Boxy and modestly sized, with no shops, pubs or schools nearby, the houses looked like they had just sprung out of the surrounding fields. Just an ordinary housing estate.

Where Gary lived. His old recruiter. His old lover.

He had walked round, building himself up, rehearsing

imaginary conversations in his head, mentally exploring every possible outcome. Now commuters were returning home, mainly suited and carrying briefcases, getting out of shining silver cars, turning off rock music. He had always prided himself on not living that sort of life, thinking it was living hell, or not living at all. Unimaginative zombies incapable of thinking freely. That's what the party had always told him. But they didn't look like that. Good cars, good jobs. Good money. Living in good houses, miles away from anywhere, where you could lock the door behind you, keep the world at bay. They weren't zombies. They looked happy.

A van pulled up. Kev hid. It had Gary's name on the side, with the word BUILDER underneath and some kind of logo, crossed roof rafters. Gary picked up some papers and a clipboard from the passenger seat, went inside.

Kev hadn't seen Gary in over two years. He had been tautly muscled before, with a wiry energy; now his body looked heavier, more relaxed. Comfortable in his own skin. Kev waited a few minutes, then followed him. Walking up to the front door, butterflies flipping, trying to escape from his stomach, he rang the bell. It was answered.

'It's me.'

Surprise didn't adequately convey the look on Gary's face. So many conflicting emotions, Kev couldn't recognize all of them. But he knew fear when he saw it.

'What the . . . What . . . what d'you want?'

'I need to talk to you. Can I come in?'

Gary looked up and down the turning, checking no one was watching. It was clear he didn't want him there, certainly not inside the house. Nevertheless he ushered him in, closed the door behind him.

'How did you find me?'

'Went through the files in the office. Wasn't easy.'

'You shouldn't have bothered.'

The words hurt. Kev tried to ignore them. 'You a builder now? Did you do all this yourself?' Gary nodded. The hall-way was well decorated. 'Nice.'

'Thank you. So what d'you want?'

Now that he was here, with Gary, he couldn't find the words. 'I need to talk to you.'

Gary looked round, ushered him upstairs into a small bedroom that was kitted out with fake beechwood office furniture. 'In there.' He put Kev inside, closed the door. From elsewhere in the house came the sounds of the TV. He heard Gary say something, heard a muffled response by a female voice. Then Gary came back up the stairs, came in. Closed the door behind him.

'I've told Rebecca you want some work doing.' He sat down in the desk chair, rubbed his eyes with the palms of his hands. When he took them away the fear was still there. 'You're the last person I expected to see. The last person.'

Kev nodded, hurt again by the words. His wound was starting to ache again. 'I wouldn't have come if there was another way. I'm sorry.' Kev tried to smile. 'Nice place.'

'I've worked for it. Things are good.' He leaned forward in his chair. 'What d'you want?'

'Your . . . your help.'

'About what?'

'The party. I've got doubts.' He saw the Asian boy's body in flames, the blood pooling underneath his dead body. 'Doubts about what I'm doin'. I'm worried.'

Gary breathed what seemed to Kev a sigh of relief. 'Which party? The NUP?'

Kev nodded.

'I'm nothing to do with them any more. That part of my life's over.' He gave Kev a pointed look as he said those words.

'They told me you'd moved on. You were workin' for them somewhere else.'

Gary shook his head. 'They lie to you all the time, don't you know that?'

Kev looked at him, still confused. 'So what happened?'

'I left.'

'Why?'

'Because I found something better.'

'What?'

Gary's voice dropped, became more confessional. 'God.'

Kev's confusion increased. 'What?'

Gary sat back. 'God. I couldn't go on doing . . . what we had been doing. So I went away for a bit. Met Rebecca.' Gary smiled. 'And here I am.'

Kev stared at him, speechless.

Gary told Kev about going to a Pentecostal church at Rebecca's invitation. How he didn't want to go but she had kept on at him. He knew something was lacking in his life, so he went. 'And there were all these people there and they looked so happy, and I thought, I want some of that.' The speech sounded well rehearsed. His testimony. 'They were so welcoming and so . . . full of the spirit. And I knew. They were somewhere I wanted to be. Because I was in a bad place, Kev, a very bad place.'

Kev expected him to stand up, lift his voice and start preaching. Kev noticed that Gary couldn't look him in the eye as he spoke the words 'bad place'.

'Very bad. So I sat down and listened. And when the time came I prayed. Can you believe that? Prayed. Me.'

Yeah, thought Kev, the way you're talkin' now I can well believe that.

'So when I prayed—' he pointed his finger at the professionally textured ceiling. '—He heard. God heard my prayer. Then everything fell into place. And I realized I'd been wrong. So He showed me the right thing to do. Gave me the courage to do it. I left, married Rebecca. And I've never been happier. She's pregnant now.' He gave a beaming, beatific smile, arms spread before him. 'And all because I dedicated my life to Christ.'

Kev looked at Gary's arms. There were patches of smooth, shiny, hairless skin. White and translucent on top, with red embers below the surface, a fire not yet gone out.

'You've had your tats removed.'

Another smile. 'More than that. I've had my soul cleansed.'

Kev felt uncomfortable, bewildered. He wanted to talk about things he knew, hear Gary talk about them too. Reassure himself who was in front of him.

'D'you not miss it?'

Gary's brow creased in thought. He seemed to be giving the question real thought. His features took on a wistful quality. 'Maybe the football. The rucks.' He nodded, smiling at the memory. 'Yeah.' His nostalgic smile was replaced by his new beatific one. 'Not for the violence. Just the . . . the workout. That's all. And I get plenty of exercise in my day job now.'

Kev didn't know what to say next. He sat in silence.

'I don't miss the politics,' said Gary. 'Because it's all wrong. So much *hate*.' The word said like it was a foreign thing in his mouth. 'Man's way, not God's. It's easy to hate, to destroy. Harder to create, to love. That's why I became a builder. And lots of Christians want a builder they can trust. Got lots of work – too much, in fact. Yeah. You see, the only person who holds us back, the only person we should hate,' he said, 'is ourselves. Not the Asians, or the asylum seekers or the blacks. You. Me. No one was going to offer me a living; I had to do it all myself. And once I had, and money was coming in, all the other stuff just . . . didn't matter any more. I've even got an Asian girl working in the office. Couple of Polish lads on site.' He gave a short, hard laugh. 'What would the old party say about that, eh?'

Kev didn't know. He didn't know what he would say about that.

Gary stopped, looked at Kev. 'So you want my advice? Get out. Now. They're liars. No, worse than liars. Don't trust them, have nothing to do with them.' Gary's expression changed. 'In fact, I can help you.'

'Yeah?' Hope sprang up inside Kev like a small light glimpsed at the end of a tunnel.

'Yes.' Gary leaned forward once again, his expression, his body language solicitous in a personal yet impersonal way. 'Pray with me. God'll help you. Give your life to Him and the fear just disappears.'

Kev just looked at him. That small light at the end of the tunnel now an oncoming train. 'No . . . That's not what I meant,' he said. 'I just wanted things . . . I just . . . Remember how we used to be? You and me . . .' Kev reached out his hand, touched Gary's knee.

Gary recoiled from the touch as if a python had just slithered around his thigh.

'Don't do that, Kev. It's wrong. Wrong then and wrong now. Wrong thoughts and wrong feelings. An abomination before God.'

'No, it's not, Gary. It wasn't wrong, it was right. We were right. The only fuckin' thing in me life that's ever been right . . .'

Gary's voice, face were flat. His voice like spit hissing on a hot griddle. 'No. It's *wrong*. Those bars, those clubs. What we did when we were alone. With our bodies. All wrong.'

Kev felt tears welling behind his eyes. 'You really enjoyed it. You did. And so did I. It was the only time I've felt happy . . . You said the same . . .'

'I told Rebecca. About . . . us.' His eyes, body were hard, rigid. Like cold stone encasing hot lava. 'Because we agreed, no secrets before God. And she understood. We spoke to the church leader. And he arranged for counselling. A reprogramming course. And that's what I did.'

He looked up, smiling hard at Kev, baring his teeth.

'And I've never felt happier.'

Kev just stared at him.

'Take the course, Kev. I'll get you on it. And you'll have joy like you've never experienced before.'

Kev couldn't get out of the house quickly enough. He ran down the road, oblivious to the tears on his cheeks.

More lost than ever.

Jamal dialled the number, waited.

'Sean Williams,' the voice said, slightly breathless.

''Sme. What you got for me?'

There was a shuffling noise, like he was walking away somewhere. A muffled voice. 'I've found him. He's here.'

Jamal's stomach flipped over. He nearly dropped the phone. 'Where's here.'

'Outside the Central Station. We're . . . I'm going to find a room somewhere.'

Jamal looked round. He was sitting on the steps at Grey's Monument, eating a Mark Toney's sugar cone, listening to the *Big Issue* seller's cry of 'Shoosa' to everyone who walked past.

'I'll be there in ten minutes,' he said and stood up.

He handed his ice cream cone to the *Big Issue* seller and took off down Grey Street as fast as he could go.

20

Norrie sat behind the counter in his second-hand shop. No customers had come through the door all day. Customers never came through the door. He looked out of the window, thinking. His mind was clicking over all the time, cogs and gears whirring and grinding, just a piece of machinery calculating how to make more money.

Jason. The boy had a good idea. Go out, work the streets for him. Could even get a whole team of kids doing it, be a regular Fagin. Just the wrong time. He had let Jason stay, thinking about what he would do with him, calculating the angles. He had information about the party. Good. Norrie could sell that. But that might make the party angry with him. And he did a lot of business with them. And they might not take kindly to him harbouring Jason from them. So really there was only one thing to do.

He reached across, picked up the phone, dialled a number he knew, like all of his numbers, by heart. It was answered.

'It's Norrie. I think I've got some of your merchandise.'

The person on the other end started to speak rapidly.

'Wo, wo, wo. Hold your horses. This bit of merchandise is valuable to you, right? You'll pay to get it back, right?'

Norrie listened. A smile spread across his face. It was like an old leather ball splitting open.

'Good. Then let's talk business . . .'

★

Donovan struck lucky. Abdul-Haq was in. And receiving. Installed in the meeting room of his company like a visiting Hollywood star on a press junket.

His offices were located on Dean Street, heading down to the Quayside. It was an old, Victorian building with heavy wooden double doors at the front, wood-panelled walls and an open atrium inside. An antique cage lift took Donovan up to the third floor. The hallway, light and airy, was carpeted. Another double door, this one with an entrance buzzer at the side, awaited him. He pressed the buzzer.

'Joe Donovan to see Abdul-Haq.'

He was buzzed in. Inside was an IKEA-modern reception that could have been anywhere. Abdul-Haq's day job, Donovan had been surprised to learn, was in property development. He didn't know why he was surprised; he just imagined someone so community orientated would be working on a more grass-roots level. Framed pictures of housing developments adorned the walls.

He took a seat, waited. Went over what he knew of Abdul-Haq.

Born Gideon Ahmed in South Shields, to a Yemeni father and white English mother. Brought up Catholic. Found Islam after he left the Hollow Men, swore off booze, drugs, women, turned to the Koran instead. Took the name Abdul-Haq, meaning Servant of the Truth. Joined a pretty extreme bunch. Links to al-Muhajiroun, the hate-preaching deported cleric Omar Bakri Mohammed's outfit.

Describing himself as a community spokesman, he was often in the papers calling for Britain to be under Sharia law, bigging up the 7/7 terrorists, claiming Western civilians are legitimate targets. More recently he had played down his radical connections, at least to a mainstream audience. Inviting rumours that he believed in Islam as much as Tony

Blair believed in the Labour Party. That he was just a cynical, ruthless, manipulative operator furthering his own interests and that he would have claimed he was a tuna fish sandwich if it would have got him noticed.

Donovan had laughed at that description, agreed with it. Abdul-Haq had managed to be both a credible and outspoken mouthpiece for the Muslim community while simultaneously managing to run a prosperous business and dealing with non-Muslims on a daily basis. Whatever else he was, he was a shrewd operator.

Donovan thought about what he wanted to achieve with the meeting. He doubted Abdul-Haq was the one behind the phone calls, but from what Trevor Whitman had said it was someone using Hollow Men codes which made him think something was being planned. And since they were most famous for a bombing and Abdul-Haq had spoken in favour of bombings, he thought it was as good an approach to take as any. Get in there. Rattle him.

A door down the corridor opened and Abdul-Haq, resplendent in his best robes, ushered a journalist out. He looked serious, statesman-like, as he shook hands, let the journalist know the audience was at an end. He looked down the corridor, saw Donovan sitting there. He moved towards him like Norma Desmond coming down for her final, demented close-up, sweeping down the hall in his robes, smiling like a benevolent god.

'Mr—' he referred to a piece of paper in his hand '—Donovan?'

Donovan stood up, smiled. 'I'm your twelve thirty.'

They shook hands. Abdul-Haq gave him a searching look, scrutinizing him.

'Come in.'

They went into the meeting room. A large table surrounded by chairs. Anonymous office furniture. Overhead striplighting. Abdul-Haq sat at one end, composed. Donovan sat halfway down the side.

'Well, Mr Donovan,' said Abdul-Haq. 'From the *Herald*.' He smiled. 'I'm pleased that the national press are taking an interest in the affairs of a part of the country they usually ignore.'

Donovan smiled. 'Ah, I may have misled you slightly, I'm afraid.'

Abdul-Haq's smile disappeared.

'I used to work for the *Herald*. I'm now . . . freelance.'

Abdul-Haq's voice had lost any trace of warmth. 'So this interview won't be appearing nationally.'

'No.'

Abdul-Haq waited, said nothing.

'I actually work for a company called Albion,' said Donovan, knowing he had about thirty seconds before he was removed from the building. 'We're an information brokerage. We take on clients, perform services for them. Involving information. At the moment one of our clients is Trevor Whitman.'

Abdul-Haq's expression changed. There was still no warmth in it but a definite curiosity. He moved forward, listening. 'Go on.'

'He's been receiving phone calls. Threatening ones. I don't suppose for a minute you're behind them—'

'I am not. Why did you not tell me this was the real reason for your visit?'

'Because if I did you might not have seen me.'

'I wouldn't have done.'

'So are you going to throw me out?'

Abdul-Haq regarded him like an ancient emperor would regard a slave whose life he was deciding to spare. 'Not at the moment.'

'Good.'

'But if you do not believe I am responsible for the phone calls, why come to see me?'

Donovan shrugged. 'Curiosity, I suppose. Heard a lot about you. Knew you were in the Hollow Men. Wondered how you got from there to here.'

Abdul-Haq sat back. Smiled. Was there relief in that smile, mingled with the conceit? Donovan wasn't sure.

'Hard work and perseverance. Great British values.'

'Is that what the Hollow Men taught you?' Donovan smiled when he said it, but there was seriousness behind the words.

'The Hollow Men taught me lots of things. Mainly that the political way alone is not the right way. To be truly effective it must be allied with something else. Like faith. Islam is a peaceful religion. I am a man of peace.'

'But weren't you brought up Catholic?'

Abdul-Haq looked genuinely impressed. 'I see you have done your homework, Mr Donovan. Yes, I was. At my mother's insistence.'

'Bit of a radical conversion, then.'

Conceit returned to Abdul-Haq's features. 'Islam is the one true faith. I had been running from that. All my life. It was time to stop running. Time to embrace it.'

Donovan nodded. 'Right.'

'Not that it matters since you are not a journalist, but I sense you do not believe me, Mr Donovan.'

'Since I'm not a journalist, does it matter what I think?'

'Let us imagine, for a moment, that it does.'

'OK. Well, let's just say you used to be involved with a group that was blamed for bombings. And you've recently spoken out in favour of suicide bombers. You see what I'm doing here? Bit of a link.'

Anger flashed in Abdul-Haq's eyes. He tamped it down, worked with it. 'The Hollow Men never bombed anywhere.

There may – and I stress the word may – have been a rogue element involved in one bombing but no more. Suicide bombers are a different thing. If you have an army you are a general. If you have a bomb, you are a terrorist.' He shrugged. 'It is all a question of perception and interpretation. As a journalist, or even an ex-journalist, you should appreciate that.'

He seemed unflappable. Donovan would have to try a different approach. He looked round the office.

'Long way from South Shields to here.'

'Perhaps not. Do you know your history?'

'You tell me.'

'South Shields was the first place to have race riots. Not just in the region but the whole country. Sailors from the Yemen who lived here, who had fought in the First World War for this country, were treated like dogs, like scum, on their return. My grandfather among them. We wanted equal rights. We got police truncheons.' He took in a deep breath, stuck out his chest proudly. 'That is why my work is still important today.'

'But there aren't any Yemeni sailors left now,' said Donovan.

Abdul-Haq regarded him with a level stare. It said: you don't want me as an enemy.

'I am still needed because of attitudes like yours. Because of wilful ignorance like yours. My community need spokesmen. Strong, forthright spokesmen who will not let their voices be drowned out. Trampled on.'

Donovan said nothing.

Abdul-Haq's voice took on a dangerous edge. 'We want our views to be heard. We want you to listen. Above all, we want respect.'

'Respect has to be earned.'

He stared at Donovan, who returned his unblinking gaze.

'Trevor Whitman is the past. The Hollow Men are the past. Long may they remain so.' He stood up. 'My courtesy is ended. Please leave.'

Donovan knew there would be no handshake. He turned to the door.

'Mr Donovan.'

Donovan turned.

'If you harass myself or any of my employees again, whether by impersonating a journalist or just being yourself, you will be arrested. Or worse. Do you understand?'

'Loud and clear,' said Donovan.

'Then leave.'

Donovan left.

As he walked along the corridor, he passed two men. Muscled, both wearing black T-shirts, both looking like they could handle themselves. One had a scar running down the left side of his face, the other, disfigured by fire, seemed to be wearing his muscles externally. Neither looked at him as he went.

Reaching the door, he turned for one last look. Abdul-Haq was out of the meeting room, standing in the hall talking to the two men. From the direction of their eyes it was clear who they were talking about.

Donovan gave a little wave and, not wanting to admit he was slightly unnerved, pushed the door open and left.

21

Newcastle's Central Station, busy as usual. Behind the stone-fronted façade and the huge wooden, metal-studded doors was a modern concourse with a central ticket office and the usual food, drink and retail outlets dotted about.

Jamal stood behind a pillar by the entrance, risked a glance round, checking for signs of Sean Williams or Jason Mason, not wanting to be seen. This was where they had agreed to take Jason on the pretext that there were hotels nearby. A public place, less likelihood of Jason doing anything to attract attention.

He saw them, sitting outside Burger King, Sean Williams sweating, looking at his watch, Jason wolfing down a burger, juice dripping all over his hands. Sean Williams caught sight of Jamal out of the corner of his eye. He froze. Jason, into his burger, slurping on his milkshake, didn't notice.

Jamal felt that familiar thrill of excitement at Williams's unease. About seeing Jason again he was less sure of his emotions. He thought he would have felt triumphant, but it was nothing like that. He couldn't describe what he felt watching the boy drink his shake with such joy, like it was the only good thing happening in his day. And the state he was in, even worse than before he had taken a bath at Joe's house.

Jamal didn't move. Because he had been so hung up on Williams getting him there, he didn't know how to approach him. He had no plan. He thought quickly. Run up to him, jump out, give the boy the fright of his life. Then demand his stuff back. He took a deep breath. Yeah. That would have to do. That would be a plan.

He walked over to them, grabbed a spare chair from a nearby table, pulled it over, sat down.

'Mind if I join you?'

Jason looked up. Jamal saw the terror in his eyes as he realized who it was. Terror followed by the urge to run. Jamal put his hand firmly over the boy's wrist. 'Don't. I just wanna talk.'

Jason didn't look convinced but didn't move. He looked round frantically; Jamal knew what he was looking for. Backup. Others. Plotting a route out of there, checking for any obstacles, looking for the path of least resistance. Jamal knew, because he had done it himself so many times.

'How . . . how d'you find us?'

Jamal's eyes flickered over to Sean Williams, who was now sweating so much he was in danger of melting. 'Threatened to tell his wife what he liked to get up to when he was supposed to be at the office.'

'Yes,' said Williams, 'speaking of which, I'd better be getting on. You've, you've got what you wanted. Now . . .'

'Shut up,' said Jamal, enjoying the moment perhaps too much. 'You ain't goin' nowhere. Stay where you are, pervert.' He turned his attention back to Jason, tightening his grip but dropping his voice. 'I just wanna talk. That's all. You left pretty quickly the other night. Didn't say goodbye nor nothin'.'

'I . . . I was in a hurry, like.'

'Not too much of a hurry. You had time to pick up a few things on the way.'

Jason's head dropped down. 'Sorry.' The word was mumbled, lost in a clanging train announcement overhead.

'Yeah.'

Jason looked up. 'I didn't mean to. You'd been, like, good to us an' that. But, y'know. Y'know what it's like.'

'So where you stayin' now?' Concern had entered Jamal's voice.

Jason shrugged. 'Gorra place.' He sighed. 'Reckon I can't go back there now.'

'Why not?'

Jason looked at him like he was thick. ''Cos you've found us, why d'you think? 'S'not safe there any more.'

'I won't tell anyone.'

'So what d'you want?'

'My stuff back for starters. An' . . .' Jamal thought. He didn't actually know. 'An' to make you see you can't keep rippin' off them that's tryin' to help you, y'get me?'

Jason nodded.

'Good. We'll start with the iPods.'

'They've long gone.'

'How much you get for them? You can give me the money.'

Jason shrugged, his eyes sliding down to his unfinished food. 'Twenty quid. Each.'

Jamal laughed. 'Don' lie, man. Look, I'm tryin' to help you here.'

Jason's eyes were out on stalks. He wanted to believe Jamal but he was just waiting for the catch. Lies came easy to him. Trust came hard. Jamal knew that. He had lived in that world long enough.

'No bullshit, man. I'm tryin' to help you.'

Jason's eyes narrowed. 'Why?'

''Cos way I see it, someone gave me a break an' I wanna pass it on. Straight up. You're in trouble an' need help. Don' turn it down when it's bein' offered.'

Jason looked between the two, down to his food again.

'Got to be better than goin' with him.' Jamal jerked his thumb at Williams.

Jason smiled. 'Wasn't goin' to. Not really. Just ganna nick his wallet then run.'

'You got a fence?'

Jason nodded.

Jamal smiled. 'Got news for you, bruv. He ain't got a wallet. I've got his wallet here.'

Still holding on to Jason's arm, he dug into his back pocket, pulled out Williams's wallet, threw it on the table. Williams made a grab for it but Jason was quicker. He picked it up, slid it away into a pocket before Williams could look up.

'That . . . that's my . . .'

Jason looked at him. 'What?'

Williams turned to Jamal. 'You're not going to let him get away with that, are you? We had a deal.' His voice had taken on a wheedling, whining tone.

Jamal shrugged, felt power in the gesture. He understood. It wasn't about turning people into victims, going from abused to abuser; it was about the transfer of power. He had stood up to an abuser. Helped Jason to do the same. He had broken the circle. He smiled.

'I don't do deals with paedophiles. Think yourself lucky all you're losin' is your identity. You could have lost a lot more than that.'

Sean Williams looked pained, like he could hear his carefully constructed life crashing down around him. Jamal felt another thrill of power run through him.

'Gimme your mobile.'

Sean Williams, as if in a dream, meekly handed it over. Jamal opened it up, removed the SIM card, passed it over to Jason. 'Have that too. Give you a head start before he starts cancellin' his cards.'

Jason laughed, took the phone.

'That enough to convince you?'

'Yeah.' Jason nodded.

'Can I take my hand away?'

Jason nodded. Jamal removed his hand. 'What happens now?' said Jason.

'Finish your transaction with your fence, then we'll go an' see about gettin' you sorted out. You gone wrong. You need to get right again. But you got to give me my money back first, yeah? Debts have to be paid, y'get me?'

Jason got him. The two of them stood up to go. Williams, snapping out of his trance, got angrily to his feet.

'And what about me? That's it? You go off hand in hand and leave me?' He stepped forward menacingly towards Jamal, his voice rising. 'You little black shit. You think you can get away with this? Do you?'

He made a grab for Jamal's T-shirt. Jamal ducked out of the way, grabbed the shake off the table and threw it in his face. Williams was too shocked to move. Jason grabbed the remains of the burger, shoved it in Williams's mouth.

Laughing, they both ran out of the station.

Norrie was waiting. He knew they would come. Sitting in the back of the shop, looking around, mentally taking stock. He was always taking stock. Food was fuel, sleep was a necessity in order to help him go on working.

He was waiting. For Jason to return, for his money to arrive.

The phone call had been successfully concluded. There would be someone along to give him his blood money in return for Jason. Perhaps somewhere deep down in what remained of his soul he felt a small pang of guilt, but if so he chose to ignore it. Thinking like that wouldn't get you any-where. There was no money in it.

He had put the phone down smiling. Money in the bank

and still in with a lucrative source of cash. A win/win situation.

Norrie's mind was still travelling along these lines when he heard the front door of the shop opening. This was them. With his money. He stopped dead.

Two Pakis were standing there. Well built, looking like they could handle themselves. Both dressed unobtrusively, one with a scar down his cheek, the other with pink blotches on his face like he had been in a fire. Neither smiling, they just stood there.

'Sorry,' he said, 'I'm closed.'

They didn't move, just stared at him. Norrie began to feel uneasy.

'Just haven't got round to putting the sign up. Bolting the door.'

Nothing. Like talking to two statues.

'Been busy, you see.'

Like two slabs of meat.

Norrie swallowed hard. Hoped the lads from the party would turn up soon. He moved towards the door. 'So I'll just do it now, if you'd like to step . . .'

They didn't move. He couldn't get past.

He began to sweat.

'You are locking up?' One of them spoke. Scarface.

Norrie nodded. 'Yeah. Yeah. So if you'll just—'

'Allow me.'

The Paki turned and slid the bolt across the door. Turned back to Norrie. Norrie was getting very frightened. Where were those NUP lads?

'Look, I'm . . . I'm waiting for someone. You don't . . . don't want to . . . to be around when they get here. No. No, you don't—'

'I don't think anyone else is coming,' said Scarface. 'No one will be arriving to disturb us.'

He moved forward. Norrie put his hands to his face, opened his mouth to scream.

He didn't get the chance.

'So what's this big secret, then?' asked Jamal as he and Jason walked up Westgate Road.

'Ah,' said Jason. 'I'm special, that's what it is. Thor's Hammer.'

'Right.' The boy was making even less sense than he had originally. 'Want to give me a few more details?'

'Later. Let's get this sorted out first. I'll see if I can get your iPods back an' all.'

They reached the shop, stopped.

'This where you been stayin'?' said Jamal, running eyes over the filthy front.

Jason nodded. 'I'd better go in on me own, like. Norrie doesn't like . . . he's a bit . . . it's better if you don't let him see you.'

'Right,' said Jamal. He pointed across the street to a motorbike shop. 'I'll go an' look in that window, yeah?'

Jason nodded and entered the shop.

Jamal waited. Smiling to himself. This wasn't working out so bad after all.

Jason tried the door. It was unlocked. He went in. The shop smelled as it always did, old, damp, like it was on the verge of rotting. He looked round. No Norrie. 'Norrie,' he called out, 'it's me. I've got some stuff for you, Norrie.'

No reply.

'An' . . . an' then we've got to have a talk. You an' me, we've got to have a talk.'

Nothing.

Must be in the toilet, thought Jason. But if he was, why had he left the shop door unlocked? Frowning, he moved towards the back room. The door was closed. He turned the handle. It felt heavier than usual, like there was something propped up against it. He pushed. It swung inwards.

He stepped inside. There was something on the floor, some liquid. He slipped in it, almost fell over. Looked down. Deep red and black. Was that blood?

Jason was starting to panic now. Norrie must have had an accident, run off to the hospital or something. Must be bad for him to leave the shop door unlocked like that.

The door swung heavily closed. Jason turned. Hanging on the back of the door was Norrie. Pinned there by a coat hook that had come right through the back of his head and was sticking out of his mouth.

Jason couldn't move. He was rooted to the floor by fear and revulsion.

He saw a black shadow out of the corner of his eye, turned. Too late. It fell on him, hard, fast, and then he didn't feel anything.

Jamal waited. Ten minutes. Fifteen. Something was wrong.

Jason had told him not to come into the shop. There would be a problem with the owner. Jamal knew what that meant. He weighed things up. He could stand where he was and do nothing, or he could go over there, bite the bullet. What was the worst thing that could happen? Take some shit from some old wanker. Like that hadn't happened before. Mind made up, he crossed the road.

The shop was deserted. He looked round, listened. Nothing.

'Jason?'

No reply.

'Come on, man, what you playin' at? I been outside now nearly half an hour. Where you at?'

No reply. Jamal looked round again. The door to the back of the shop was closed. He pushed it open, slowly.

Saw what was there.

And ran out of the shop and down Westgate Road as fast as he could.

22

Turnbull sat in his car on the opposite side of the road and watched the school kids walk out. Anyone asks, he thought, I'm just a dad on the school run.

His own kids came into his mind. And his wife, Karen. How he'd fucked it all up. Blinked hard, pushed them out of his mind. He was on a job, he was working.

The school was private, boys only, in Bishop's Stortford. You could see the money in the cars the parents drove, the Mercs, Audis, Beamers and 4×4s. Almost smell it coming off them as they waited, windows down. Bastards. He hated them. All of them. Thinking they were protected. Thinking that because they had money nothing would ever go wrong in their lives. Nothing would happen to their kids or their jobs or their marriages. They wouldn't get cancer or get made redundant or come home early one day to find their wives shagging the postman. Or the paperboy. Or the IKEA delivery man. Because money protected them, put up an invisible force field to keep all the bad stuff out.

And the thing was, most of the time it worked.

That was why he hated them.

He saw the Milsoms' 4×4 waiting. The boy walked through the gates, got in. Didn't walk out with anyone, wave to anyone, smile even. Just got in the car.

Turnbull saw Mrs Milsom turn in her seat, smile at him. He returned it, but it was a small smile, edged with sadness, not reaching his eyes. A response only. Mrs Milsom's smile widened as if to compensate. She leaned over, kissed him on the cheek. He took it, smiled again. This time it might have seemed real.

They drove off.

Turnbull had hoped the boy might have walked down into the town after coming out of school as some of the other boys did. Gone round the shops, through the park. Because that was how he was going to get near him. Find a can he had drunk from and bag it, perhaps some discarded chips that might have had a trace of saliva on them, a sweet wrapper maybe. Perhaps even get close enough to pick up a stray hair. Or catch him at some after-school club. A football team. Make off with his sweat-stained T-shirt. But there was nothing. The boy just got in the car and went home.

Like he was a prisoner.

Turnbull felt pity for him. All that money and the force field stopped him from getting out.

Turnbull waited a few seconds then pulled out after the 4×4.

There was no hurry. He knew where it would be going.

The sign said St Hilda's Trust in black plastic hard-wearing, functional lettering. Peta switched the engine off, looked out. Eyes directed at the building, gaze fixed on something else.

Thoughts were tumbling over in her mind, snatches of conversation coming back to her.

Colin Baty: *'Trevor Whitman was a waster. In his hippie commune. Shagging all his birds, kids all over the place . . .'*

Mary Evans: *'And that's why you were chosen. Oh, Lillian. He got you too . . .'*

Over and over, the words not leaving her alone. And their meaning . . .

She had phoned Donovan but he had been unavailable. Left a message on her mobile saying he was off to interview

Abdul-Haq. She was amazed he had managed it at short notice, but remembered Mary Evans's words about how much Abdul-Haq loved to talk about himself. Maybe she shouldn't be surprised.

She looked at the building. Old, stone and bay-fronted, it looked like it had once housed a firm of Dickensian lawyers. And in its way the street, with its overflowing rubbish bins and garbage-strewn pavement, was twenty-first-century Dickensian. The buildings alongside it were now mostly cheaply rented flats, all peeling paint and rotting old wood. An archetypal run-down inner-city neighbourhood. The checklist: a convenience store, all brittle, broken lino, selling out-of-date fruit behind smeared windows in mildewed aluminium frames. An off-licence broadcasting low prices for undrinkable, death-hastening chemical stews. A betting shop. Cash Converters. Opposite was an abandoned park, empty but for a drinking school gathered around two benches.

St Hilda's Trust had a large, heavy-looking front door, a buzzer at the side, a keypad underneath.

She locked the car, switched her mobile off, walked to the door, pressed the intercom. Waited. Some of the drinking school had detached themselves from the group in the park and were slowly making their way to the entrance, sucking down the dregs of their cans, landlocked Popeyes imbibing strength from tins of spinach.

Peta was buzzed in. The door slammed closed behind her. Inside was a foyer: reception, chairs, water cooler, toilets, keypad-operated doors behind reception. Anonymous. Could have been a police station, the DSS, anywhere. She approached the desk. An elderly woman with sparkling eyes looked up at her expectantly.

'Hi, I'm Peta Knight. From a company called Albion. I'm here to see Richie Vane.'

Her eyes became immediately guarded. Peta knew what she was thinking: police.

'Can I ask what it's concerning?'

'Mary Evans of COU made an appointment for me.'

The woman's attitude softened. Peta had said the magic words. 'Wait there,' she said and left the desk.

As she waited, the reception area filled up. The drinking school from the park came in, were joined by others. Some, their faces scarred and scabbed over, looked like they had slept in their clothes; others had attempted to look smart. They were in good humour, happy to be there, chatting with passing staff, the security guard. The atmosphere seemed friendly and relaxed, but they didn't attempt to engage Peta in conversation.

Eventually the receptionist returned along with a dark-haired woman, dressed casually, with sharp, intelligent eyes behind tortoiseshell glasses.

'I'm Kaye,' she said, shaking hands. 'Come with me.'

Peta was ushered through a door, up a flight of stairs. The walls, in contrast to the reception area, were covered with primary-coloured murals depicting an idealized, child's view of a multi-racial, multi-ethnic world. Characters were smiling, sharing possessions, enjoying a happy, if unrealistic, life.

'Some of our students' work,' Kaye said as they walked up. 'The art class is one of the most popular we run here.'

'What kind of students have you got?'

'You saw some of them in the foyer,' she said. 'Anyone who's fallen through the net, basically.'

'What kind of problems?'

'The usual. Homelessness, abuse, alcohol, drugs. Mental health. Sometimes all together, sometimes in different combinations. We run all sorts of courses, help them back on their feet and into society.'

'Good success rate?'

Kaye shrugged. 'We try to perform miracles every day.'

They reached the first floor. Kaye took Peta into a large room with chairs and tables stacked against one wall. Kaye closed the door behind them, pulled two chairs from the stack, sat down. Peta did likewise.

'Mary Evans told me about you. Now, as Richie's case-worker I should say that he's responding very well to the work he's doing here. Very well. He's stopped drinking, is attending AA and taking art and computing classes. So if you're going to say something that'll upset him, trigger off a relapse, then we won't be going any further.'

'We're not police' said Peta. 'He hasn't done anything wrong. We just want to know if he's got any ideas about who's making these calls.'

Kaye looked at her watch. 'Ten minutes. That's all I can allow. If you want to speak to him further it'll have to be another time. And I'll be in the room too.'

'Fine. You work with vulnerable people. I don't want to compromise that work.'

Kaye smiled. 'Exactly.'

Kaye left the room. Peta glanced around the room, reading posters on the walls, absently scratching her arm. It was like the kind of treatment centre she had attended to control her growing alcohol addiction and to receive counselling. It all came back. She knew they had been trying to help but it had still felt like going to the doctor, waiting to be told she had cancer. She shivered at the memory.

She knew that the guys in reception, the drinking school, weren't a different species. They could be anyone. Just one wrong turn and it's there but for the grace of God.

The door opened. Kaye led in one of the men from reception. Not one of the drinking school. He sat down next to her. Tall, rake-thin, skin red and blotchy, his face

unshaven. Wearing supermarket jeans and T-shirt, hair
sandy-coloured and thinning, short. Looking at least in his
sixties, his face lined, his breathing laboured. But his eyes
drew Peta. Pale, watery blue, holding intelligence and a
hard-won compassion; they had seen things no one rightly
should, but they were determined not to harden over. He
smiled, stretched out a hand.

'I'm Richie.'

Peta shook, introduced herself.

Richie Vane's hand was warm, clammy. Peta could feel
it vibrating as she shook it. Richie Vane's whole body
was shaking slightly, like he was just in focus. Peta didn't
know if it was the cumulative effect of years of self-abuse
or just nerves at meeting new people. Probably a bit of
both.

'Mary said you'd be comin' to see me,' he said.

'Did she tell you why?' said Peta.

Richie Vane nodded. 'Trevor Whitman.' He smiled. Peta
saw damage in that smile, wondered how much of it was
irreparable. 'Trevor Whitman. Blast from the past.' His
accent had traces of the north but was mostly flat, neutral.
Could have come from anywhere, belonged nowhere.

Peta's notes on Richie Vane: a true believer in the Hollow
Men, but along the way that belief had been perverted. The
loyalest of the loyal, he had begun to separate from the
group, head off on his own, claiming to be undertaking
some shadowy, secret work. Dangerous and daring missions,
potentially lethal. The others had laughed it off, but suspicions had grown. Maybe he was Special Branch, MI5.
Feeding stories to the media, even. They froze him out, not
trusted. Uninvolved.

Then the real reasons became apparent. Drugs. Harder
than hard. Heroin and cocaine speedballs for the highs,
prodigious amounts of acid for the trips, cannabis, beer and

whisky for the comedowns. A self-medicating pharmaco-
logical experiment. That was Richie Vane's dangerous,
daring and potentially lethal mission.

They cut him loose. Drugs they didn't mind; instability
and unreliability they did. Richie's spiral had been a swift
downward one. He had remained lost for years, presumed
dead, until a chance encounter with Mary Evans had led
him on a slow climb up rehab mountain.

'Have you spoken to Mary?' said Peta.

A small smile crept around the corners of Richie Vane's
face. He nodded. 'Trevor's been havin' some nuisance calls.'

'That's right.'

'Why? Why's he think that?'

Peta frowned, wondering how much to tell him.
'Because . . . because the person said something, apparently.
Something from the Hollow Men.'

'Like what?'

Richie Vane seemed sharper than Peta had been led to
believe. 'Some old password, I think. I don't know for sure.
He didn't tell me.'

Richie Vane nodded, the smile creeping around his
mouth like ivy on a crumbling old building. He rocked
slightly, back and forth. 'Right. Aye. She's a good 'un, Mary,
a good 'un.'

'Right,' said Peta. 'So any ideas?'

Richie sat back. 'About what?'

'Who's making the calls.'

Richie let out a guttural, phlegmy sound from his ruined
lungs which may have been a laugh. 'You're jokin', aren't
you?' Another smile, the grin of a dry alcoholic. 'Ancient
history. All that happened to another man, not me.'

'You don't keep in touch with any of the old crew?" said
Peta.

'Just Mary. My fairy godmother. Checks on me now an'

again. Makes sure I'm on the straight an' narrow.' He sounded like it was both an inconvenient arrangement and paradoxically one he drew strength from.

'None of the others?' said Peta. 'Abdul-Haq?'

Richie made a face. 'Wanker.' Kaye leaned forward, looked at him. 'Not expressin' a racist slur. My opinion is not based on his ethnicity or religion.' He sounded like it was a well-worn phrase. 'Was a wanker when I knew him, he's an even bigger one now that he thinks he's doin' God's work. Can't turn on the telly without seein' him shoutin' about somethin'.'

It seemed like Richie Vane was going to go on a tirade that would take some time when he abruptly stopped. 'What they said on the phone. Was it T. S. Eliot?'

Peta's mouth fell open, momentarily taken aback by the abrupt change. 'Well . . .'

Richie Vane smiled. There was some kind of twinkle in his eye. 'Was, wasn't it? T. S. Eliot. Bet it was from "The Hollow Men". Bet it was.'

'Why?'

'Bomb code.'

Peta leaned forward. 'What?'

'Bomb code. When somethin' was gonna happen, some-thin' was planned, there would be a phone call. Quotin' a few lines. Bomb code, we called it.'

'Always for a bomb?'

'Not necessarily. Anythin', really. But it meant there was somethin' about to happen.'

Peta was about to ask another question, but Richie's mind had taken off at another tangent. 'Heard Trevor was back. Always liked him. Good bloke. Very fair.' He looked at the floor. 'Y'know. To me, like. Not gonna badmouth anyone for, you know. Not now. Not after all those years.' He was shaking even more than he had been when he had first entered the room.

Peta leaned forward to question him further, but Kaye looked at her watch. 'Sorry. I think that's all the time we can allow you. Don't want to overdo it.'

'OK. Thanks, Richie.'

He nodded, body shaking slightly less, coming to a stand-still now that the ordeal was over.

They shook hands. Kaye stood up to usher Richie out but he didn't leave.

'So, eh . . .' Richie Vane looked at his hands, the shakes not completely gone. 'What are you, like? Private detectives? Somethin' like that?'

'Something like that.'

'D'you wanna new recruit, like? Eh? Someone to work the streets? I could do it, you know. Got contacts I bet you could never get.'

'I bet you have,' said Peta.

He made a phone sign with his shaking fingers, nodded. 'Bear it in mind,' he said. 'In the meantime, if I hear anythin' where can I get in touch with you?'

Peta handed over her card. Kaye looked concerned as she did so. Peta imagined it wouldn't be in Richie Vane's possession for very long.

Richie Vane touched his nose, gave a wink. 'If I hear any-thin' . . .'

'Right you are.'

He looked hard at Peta. Smiled. 'Mary said.'

'Said what?' Peta's voice flat, uninflected.

'Lillian's daughter. God, yeah, family resemblance is strong.' He nodded. 'She nearly joined the Hollow Men.'

'Lots of people say I look like my mother.' said Peta.

'Spittin' image.' He scrutinized her again. 'And your father.' Another nod.

'Philip Knight.'

Richie Vane frowned. 'Who?'

Peta's chest fluttered. 'Philip Knight. He was my father.'

Richie shrugged, no recognition of the name in his eyes. 'Don't know him. No, Trevor was—' Seeing the look on her face, he said nothing more.

'What?' Peta said, her voice rising.

He nodded at Kaye, agitated. 'I want to go now.'

'What d'you mean about Trevor? Trevor was what?'

'Please don't excite Richie,' said Kaye.

'Him?' Peta was almost shouting. 'What about me?'

Richie was on his feet, Kaye guiding him to the door. 'Sorry.' He shrugged as he was escorted from the room.

Left alone, the colour drained completely from Peta's face. She looked like a ghost. Kaye returned, saying something about not antagonizing her client, but Peta didn't listen. Kaye walked her down the stairs and out of the building. Peta didn't hear a word she said. She got straight in the car, slammed the door, locked it behind her. Put her face in her hands.

'What did he mean?' she said out loud. 'What do they mean, all of them? What are they trying to tell me?' Tears were welling, panic rising. She tried to keep it all in.

Put her head back and screamed.

23

Peta didn't know how long she sat there in the car, waiting for the tears to stop, the wave of fear to ride out of her body, but it was beginning to get dark when she opened her eyes again. She took a deep breath. Another. Looked at her hands. They were shaking as much as Richie Vane's had been.

She rummaged in her bag, reached for her mobile, powered it up. She needed someone to talk to. She had a message.

'Hi,' said Donovan's voice, 'it's me. Hope you're OK. Listen, I've been trying to reach you. I had that meeting with Abdul-Haq. It went, well, I'll tell you when I see you. Thing is, this is what I've been trying to reach you for. I've tracked down Maurice Courtney. The last of the Hollow Men. He's in London and he can see me tomorrow. I know that we should get together and compare notes from today, but I thought it best to follow this up. So I'm off to London tonight. I know I won't see him till tomorrow but I thought it . . . there's some things I need to take care of down there. First.'

She knew what that would be.

'So I'll see him tomorrow, then come straight back. Give me a ring when you get this. Actually, do it later. I'll be driving. I won't hear you.' He gave something that sounded like a sigh and a laugh. 'Oh, well. Hope you're OK, like I said. Speak to you later.'

She put the phone down. Sighed. Picked it up again, called Amar. Got voicemail.

'Amar, give me a ring when you get this. I'm . . . Just give me a ring.'

She was about to try Jamal but just didn't have the energy to press the buttons.

'Oh, what's the fucking point?' she said out loud.

She switched the phone off, threw it on the passenger seat. She wanted to talk to her mother. But she didn't dare. In case she said something Peta didn't want to hear. But she needed something. She needed help. She looked at her shaking hands again. Listened to what her body told her.

She knew what she wanted. Knew where she had to go.

Started the car.

Drove into the city centre.

Jamal didn't know what else to do. He had tried everyone's number, got voicemail for all of them. What was the point of having a mobile if it was never on? He hadn't left messages. He didn't know what to say.

Instead he had walked down to Amar's flat, rang the bell. No reply. Beyond a joke now.

He let himself in with his key. No Amar. His laptop was set up, lights blinking away on it. He must still be monitoring Whitman's phone, thought Jamal, routing the signal to his work mobile. The one Jamal had been calling was sitting on the table.

He sighed, sat down. Didn't know what to do with himself. Who to talk to. He couldn't call the police; they would trace it, haul him in. No one to talk to, to help. There was nothing he could do. He knelt on the floor, started going through Amar's DVD collection. Hoped he could find something there to lose himself in. Get those images out of his head.

Knew it wouldn't work.

It was going to be a long night.

*

Amar stood at the bar in Camp David, the rhythm of the music pulsing through his body. He felt connected. Happy. Alive.

He had sat in his flat all afternoon, monitoring the airwaves, letting his mind wander, reaching conclusions. Getting shot and nearly dying had changed his perspective on things. He had been happily throwing his life away before the shooting, out of his head with drugs and casual, unprotected sex, playing Russian roulette with his body. Nearly dying had caused him to reassess that. He hadn't had a drink, taken a pill, done a line or had sex for months.

And it was starting to affect him.

Because the shooting had taught him something else. Life was too short. It was for living, for taking hold of life and getting everything you possibly could out of it. So there he had sat, watching lights blink, listen in to ghost conversations, wait for Whitman's phone to spring to life. And it hadn't happened.

Yeah, he had thought, his hand unconsciously stroking the pitted skin of his stomach through his T-shirt. Life's too short. So he had put the phone on relay, stood up, walked to the bathroom without his cane, got ready and gone out.

He stood watching. Groups gathered round small tables on square stools that he didn't think he would be able to get up from if he sat down. So he stood at the bar, the lights bouncing off bare brick wall, sipped from his bottle of Becks. The alcohol, long absent from his body, hit like a liquid endorphin rush. He had been eyed up on entering, just as he had done. He took another swig, tried to ignore the clichéd house remix of a Scissor Sisters track pumping out of the sound system, looked around. A few possibles, some definites, some definitely nots.

He smiled to himself, back in the swing. Like it was only days, not months.

Men smiled, threw him glad eyes. Mostly definitely nots, so he ignored them. Kept looking. Clocked a guy at the end of the bar, half in shadow. Big, muscled, with short, razor-cropped hair. Jeans, T-shirt and denim jacket. Promising.

Amar took his drink, moved slowly along. Stopped in the man's line of vision, waited. Eventually he looked up. A rough face, nose broken a couple of times, not reset too well, a flecking of small scars. But his eyes. Soft. Lost. Something broken in there.

Amar found an instant connection.

He caught Amar's glance, turned away. Amar waited, kept looking. The man slowly turned his head. Hurt eyes on Amar. Amar smiled, moved nearer.

'Hi,' he said. 'Buy you a drink?' Just like he'd never been away.

He said nothing, just looked scared. Amar knew what scared him. Himself. Wanting to connect, seeing only what holds him back. We've all been there. One time or another.

'Just a drink,' said Amar. 'I'm having one.' He motioned to the barman.

'Same . . . same as you,' the man said. He pushed his empty beer bottle along the bar towards Amar. Hand shaking.

Amar smiled, ordered the drinks.

'First time here?'

The man nodded, eyes on the bar. 'For a while.'

'Don't worry. I won't bite. Not unless you want me to.'

He looked like he wanted to smile but couldn't. Took a mouthful of beer instead. Amar reckoned those beers weren't the first of the night.

'So what's your name, then?'

His mouth opened. Amar waited. This would be the turning point. The rest of the night decided on whether he gave a truthful answer. And Amar would know.

'Kev,' the man said. 'My name's Kev.'

'Amar. Nice to meet you.'

And Amar knew he was telling the truth.

Peta opened the door of the Forth, paused for a few seconds on the threshold, entered.

She walked up to the bar, music pounding in her ears, people all around her. Fear of suicide bombers and riots hadn't stopped drinkers coming out, enjoying themselves. But then, as she knew, there wasn't much that stopped drinkers coming out.

She waited patiently to be served, the queue at the bar three deep in places. She had ample time to back out, to listen to that voice in her head, getting smaller the nearer she got to the bar. Someone was served, turned, took their drinks away. A space. She grabbed it.

She could have still turned round, walked out. She didn't have to get the ten-pound note out of her purse, put it between her first two fingers, wait with her elbow on the counter for service.

She didn't have to tell the tall, young barman with the dyed hair and the pierced face that she wanted a gin and tonic, double. But she did. She didn't have to pay him, take the change and go to find a corner of the bar where she wouldn't be bothered. Where she could look at the drink, gaze at its beauty. See how bright and clear and inviting it looked. Bubbling and sparkling and fizzing.

Her heart was beating like an express train was going to come steaming through her ribcage.

She placed it on her lips, felt the bubbles pop on the front of her face, the promise of enjoyment. She tried to smile.

The drink got closer. She tipped it forward, closed her eyes, her head back, ready to receive. She could almost taste it, almost feel it run down her throat into her stomach. Rounding the edges off her anxiety, muting the sound of the questions in her head. Knew it would go down quickly, be followed by another. And another.

Her lips were wet with the liquid. All she had to do was swallow.

One gulp. Down.

She opened her eyes. Looked at it.

Couldn't do it.

The glass fell from her fingers, smashing on the floor. People looked round, frowned. Peta didn't see them. She ran for the door, out into the night.

Running like her life depended on it.

24

Every time Jamal had closed his eyes he had been back in the shop.

The hanging body covered in horror-film gore. The mess, blood everywhere. And Jason nowhere to be seen. At first he had thought the boy was dead too, but he had replayed the events over and over in his mind and he was sure Jason wasn't there.

His next thought: had Jason done it? No. He was only small and it would have taken some strength to hang that guy on the back of the door. So whoever had done it had taken Jason. That meant his secret was real.

Jamal had drifted in and out of sleep, waking with a start each time he saw that hanging body again. He was never so pleased to see morning, had lain there watching the sun come up.

He couldn't wait to tell Amar. But Amar's bedroom door was firmly closed. So Jamal had taken a shower and was just getting dried when he heard voices outside. Amar's and another. OK, cool. He had been round the bars and brought someone back. No problem. Just as long as they leave soon. What he had to say couldn't wait.

But the voice was familiar. And not in a good way.

Unplaceable but with unpleasant associations; someone bad.

Dripping wet and naked, Jamal padded to the door, unlocked it, pulled it open slightly, looked out. He could see a sliver of hallway, voices coming from the kitchen at the end. A glimpse of movement as Amar and his guest went about getting breakfast ready. He tried to tune in, listen.

'Some serious tattoos.' Amar's voice.

'If you'd seen them, would you have talked to me?'

Amar again after a pause. 'You didn't have them on show. You didn't want them seen.'

A sigh from the guest, then: 'Somethin' I did. When I was younger. They're just . . . there.'

'That's OK,' said Amar. 'You don't have to explain yourself. I'm just some bloke you met in a bar. A one-night stand.' There was a pause. 'Aren't I?'

The other man didn't answer.

Jamal closed the door, stood with his back against it. He thought, hard:

Tattoos. Tattoos. The kind Amar didn't like. Tattoos.

Played back the voice in his head again. Combined with tattoos.

He shivered, suddenly cold in a way that the warm bathroom could never reach. He had recognized the voice.

The skinheads who had abused him the other day, outside the house. Until Joe had seen them off.

It was him. The leader. Shit.

Jamal locked the door, grabbed his towel, wrapped himself in it. He looked round frantically, knowing there wasn't another way out. He needed to think. No way he could tell Amar anything now. Had to get some clothes on, get to his room without the skinhead seeing him. But it meant passing the kitchen.

He carefully undid the bolt, cracked the door open. Listened.

The sound of physical movement, as if they were pulling apart from each other. Then Amar's voice: 'D'you want a shower or anything?'

'I'd . . . I'd better be off. Get goin'.'

That was something, thought Jamal.

'Sure I can't tempt you?'

The skinhead said he couldn't be tempted. That he had to go.

Movement. Jamal quickly shut the door, locked it again.

He waited, listening intently for the footsteps he knew would go past. Soon. Any second. Waited. Now, surely.

Nothing.

He opened the door again, listened. From the kitchen came unmistakable sounds. The skinhead wouldn't be going anywhere any time soon. More movement, the two of them going to Amar's bedroom. Jamal waited until the bedroom door shut, then, after counting to a hundred very slowly, made his way cautiously out of the bathroom.

He tiptoed down the hall, ignoring the damp trail his feet were leaving, crept round the corner to where the bedrooms were. The door was open slightly. He risked a glimpse inside. Saw Amar taking his robe off. He looked away, saw the other man.

It was him. No doubt about it.

He joined Amar on the bed. Jamal hurried on to his own room, closed the door firmly behind him.

He got ready in record time, pulling on jeans, trainers and T-shirt so fast he barely knew if they were the ones he had planned on wearing.

Pushed the door open, crept slowly out.

Closing the front door of the flat behind him, he ran down the hall and outside. Looked around.

Didn't have a clue where he was going to go.

Just hoped he could reach Joe or Peta on their phones. Didn't know what he would do if he couldn't.

Mr Sharples sat in the corner of his favoured coffee shop. Customers streamed in and out, ignoring him. Not seeing him. He sipped his espresso, picked up his knife, sliced his almond croissant down the centre. Halved that. Precisely: making sure each piece was an exact quarter. He lined the pieces up on his plate symmetrically, regarded them. Almost a shame to eat it.

His fingers were poised over the top left-hand square, working in his usual order, when his phone rang. Irritated, he answered it.

'Sharples.'

'There have been some interesting developments.'

He waited.

'A pair of investigators from a firm called Albion have been making nuisances of themselves, asking about old associates of Trevor Whitman. And threatening phone calls.'

A small shock ran through Mr Sharples. He compressed it until there was nothing to show but a tiny tic in his left cheek. It pulsed once, then no more. 'Do they have tapes of the voices?'

'No, only Whitman's word.'

Another pulse appeared on Mr Sharples's face, this time at the sides of his mouth. A smile. 'Whitman thinks he is a clever bastard.'

'How shall we persuade him otherwise?'

Mr Sharples looked at his quartered croissant. Touched it, toyed with it. Moved the squares of pastry into separate areas of the plate, leaving a geometric cross in the centre. 'We must act soon. Swiftly and decisively.'

'One of those asking questions was the daughter of Lillian Knight.'

Another pulse in Mr Sharples's cheeks. His eyes glittered darkly. 'Clever fucking bastard. He thinks that's an advantage.'

'Let's hope it isn't.' The threat in the caller's voice was obvious.

'Give me an hour. I'll call you back.'

Mr Sharples broke the connection, pocketed the phone.

He looked down at his plate, at the neatly divided sections. He was no longer hungry. He piled them one on top of another, carefully balancing them, then picked them up with his right hand. And squeezed. As hard as he could. His face expressionless. Eventually he could squeeze no more. He opened his fingers, let the pulpy pastry drop to the plate. It lay in an inedible lump.

He drained his coffee cup, licked his fingers clean.

They weren't ignoring him now.

He stood up, left the coffee shop.

Work to do.

Peta opened her eyes. Sunlight hit with an almost physical force. She closed them again, groaned. Opened them slowly.

She was in a bed and it wasn't her own. She felt under the covers. Naked. She lay back, groaned. She was alone. She looked round the room, saw her clothes discarded in a trail from the door, male clothing lying around also. She tried to think. Nothing. She was in the Forth almost downing a large gin and tonic, then . . . nothing. A dark blur.

The bedroom door opened. In walked a man, early twenties she guessed, wearing a towelling dressing gown and carrying a tray with two mugs of coffee and two plates of toast on it.

'Morning,' he said.

'What time is it?' she asked.

He set the tray down on the bed, took his dressing gown off. He was naked underneath. Peta tried not to look. Failed. He wasn't bad looking, that was something, with a fit body. He got into bed next to her. She moved as far away from him as possible. He smiled at her.

'Feeling all right?'

Peta felt numb, braindead. 'Yeah,' she said. 'Fine.'

'What a great night,' he said, biting into his toast.

Peta said nothing. Closed her eyes. Things were falling into place. Frames, images slotting themselves into the blackness of her memory. Glimpses: being in a bar somewhere, a club, her head pounding, music playing. Someone talking to her. Looking at him as if from down a long, dark tunnel. Dancing, flinging herself around on the floor. An arm round her, supporting her. Then the weight of a body on top of her, her on top of the body. Alongside.

She sighed. She had done it. Got drunk. Picked up a guy and had sex. And she couldn't remember any of it. She couldn't believe it.

'Not hungry?' he said, pointing to her toast.

'Yeah . . .' She tried to sit up. Her head spun, her stomach lurched. Oh, God, oh, God . . .

'You were putting it away last night,' he said. 'Like you were trying to rid the world of alcohol by drinking it.' He laughed, looked concerned when she didn't join in. 'You OK?'

Peta looked at him, not knowing what to say.

Realization dawned on his face. 'Oh, my God . . . You don't . . . you don't remember . . .'

Peta shook her head. 'No . . . nothing . . .'

'Oh, my God . . . oh, my God . . .'

'What?'

'We . . . we had sex.'

'I kind of figured that,' she said.

'No, I mean . . . you wanted it too. In fact, it was your idea. You said—'

'Don't tell me.' It came back to her, another jigsaw piece slotting back in. *I want to fuck your brains out.* She groaned.

He fell silent.

She stared at the ceiling. 'What happened? Exactly. When we got back here. What happened?'

He looked at her, embarrassed now. 'You . . . you said—'

'Yes. I know. After that.'

'We had sex. Lots of . . . of sex. Then you curled up. Looked sad. I put my arm around you. You cried as you . . . as you went to sleep.'

Peta sighed. 'What's your name?'

'John. I'm a student at . . . at Newcastle Uni.'

'Peta.'

'I know. Look . . . I'm not . . . I don't usually do this kind of thing. And to be honest I couldn't . . . couldn't believe my luck. I mean, you were, you . . .' He sighed, eyes dropping to the half-eaten toast. 'I don't often get, you know . . . someone as classy as you.'

'Classy? A drunk bitch throwing herself at you?' She didn't even try to keep the self-loathing from her voice.

'No,' he said quickly, 'I meant someone as good looking. You know. Bit of style.' He blushed when he said it.

Peta smiled. 'Thank you. Well, I'd better get going.'

'Oh. Right.' He got out of bed again, left the room. Peta, as swiftly as her hangover would allow, picked up her clothes and put them back on. She felt dirty. Consumed by self-hatred. Then thought of her mother and Whitman. And felt like breaking down. The drinking hadn't helped, hadn't given any comfort. She knew it wouldn't.

She looked back at the bed. Oh, God. What had she done? The first sex for ages and she couldn't remember it. And with a stranger. Had they used protection? She needed an STD checkup. A pregnancy test. Oh, God. She sighed again.

Tears were welling up inside her. She didn't want to let them out. Not here, not now.

She opened the bedroom door. John was loitering, not knowing what to do with himself. She saw his face. He looked genuinely concerned for her.

'Are you OK?' he asked.

'No, John, I'm not.'

'Oh.' He really looked worried. 'Look, it was OK. We used protection. I . . . I insisted. I meant it. I don't do this kind of thing usually.'

'Neither do I.'

She asked him where she was. He told her. Fenham. She could have guessed. Student central. She asked him about her car.

'Dunno. We got a cab back. Must have left it at the club.'

'Which was?'

'Tiger Tiger.'

Jesus, she thought. I could have chosen somewhere a bit better to have a meltdown in.

She thanked him and left. The warm air fell over her body like a blanket. The walk would do her good, clear her head.

She needed help. She needed to confront things head-on.

She went to pick up her car.

Kev felt better than he had in ages. A new man. When he slept he hadn't seen that burning student. His wound hadn't given him any pain. And someone had held him all night. He wished his life could always be so good.

Perhaps it could.

He walked through the city, feeling the sun shining down on him. Feeling glad to be alive.

His side was starting to hurt again, guilt trying to stab him, but he ignored it. He had thought guilt would have consumed him like an obese kid eating a Big Mac for shagging a Paki poof. If he had been a socialist it would have been everything the party hated in one go. But he didn't feel guilty. He felt good. Right.

The best he had felt since Gary. Even better.

He heard again Amar's voice in his ear, his mouth on his mouth. Flesh against flesh. Pleasure in reliving pleasure.

He wanted to do it again.

He would do it again.

Amar's voice in his ear, his mouth on his mouth. Flesh against flesh.

Hard again just thinking about it.

Maybe he should go for a drink. Sit somewhere and think. Make some decisions. Sort his life out.

He turned round, headed back down to the kind of pubs he knew he shouldn't go in but knew he would.

His phone rang. He ignored it. And again. He ignored it. And again. He had to answer it. Just to shut it up. He opened it, saw who it was on the display.

Rick Oaten.

He stopped walking, looked at it. Turned it off, pocketed it and kept walking.

Down to the bars that he shouldn't go to.

Unable to believe he had actually done that. Feeling like his life had just entered a new phase.

'Wake up.'

Jason opened his eyes. He was in some kind of cell, lying curled up on the floor. He was cold, shivering. Two men were in front of him, dressed from head to foot in black, black balaclavas covering their heads. The light too dim to make out any features.

Jason did as he was told, sat up.

'You don't run away again,' said one of the balaclavas. 'Got that?'

'Huh-who are you?' he said.

'I asked you a fucking question,' screamed the balaclava. 'You don't run away again. Got that?'

'Yuh-yeah.'

'Good. Let's make sure.'

Before he could say or do anything further, the room seemed to be filled with bodies, rushing at him. They grabbed him, pulled the clothes off him, kicked and punched him as they did so. Left him lying in a heap on the cold stone floor.

'Try runnin' now,' said the balaclava.

They started to file out of the door. Jason stayed where he was, curled on the floor, shivering, hurting.

'This isn't over,' said the balaclava. 'This is just the start.'

He slammed the door behind him.

Jason didn't move. Didn't even cry.

25

Donovan sat outside the house again. The street still looked the same in the afternoon sunlight. The front door remained closed. The Multipla missing, the house empty.

He wished he could just walk inside, put his briefcase by the door, make a coffee, sink into an armchair, read the paper. Ask the kids how their day at school had been, kiss his wife, all sit round the table and eat dinner.

But he couldn't.

The further he had driven from Newcastle, the more the Whitman case had diminished. He had to meet Maurice Courtney later, but right now that was the furthest thing from his mind. David was back firmly in his head. It was like the boy, or the hope of the boy, was a last branch sticking out above a raging river that was sweeping him away to an uncertain future.

He rubbed his face, ran his fingers through his hair. Exhaled. Yearning grew inside him again. He wanted to walk up that path, get his key out, touch the front door, feel it swing open under his hand, feel the change of air on his face as the outside world ended, home began.

Bitter, pointless anger welled up inside him. Impotent rage at the unfairness of life. He gritted his teeth, forced it back down. And away.

No good. He had to do something.

They weren't home. It wouldn't hurt. Just look in the windows, see a glimpse of his old life. Hopefully soon to be his new life. Do it.

Donovan got out of the Scimitar, crossed the road. Reached the front gate, stopped. Heart beating out a samba, hands shaking, he pushed it open. It groaned slightly, still needed oiling. One foot tentatively in front of the other, he walked down the path.

The front door. Hand in midair, thinking about touching it. It had been painted but the leaded glass was still the same. The tree at the side had grown, shadowing him from the road.

He breathed hard, his chest tight. It was like confronting something that had only ever existed in his mind, a dream come prosaically true. There all along. All he had to do was reach out, touch it.

He reached out. Touched it.

Solid. Firm. Locked.

He sighed. Felt suddenly foolish. He could look in the window but knew things would be different. New furniture, new carpets. Life continued without him. He didn't want to see. And besides, it was a Neighbourhood Watch area.

Stupid, he thought. Pointless. What had he expected?

He turned round to go back to his car, his hotel, and the first drink of the evening. And walked straight into Abigail. His daughter.

She jumped back, startled. He did the same.

Her expression changed as she realized who he was. The surprise and fear of meeting a stranger loitering in front of her doorway gave way. At first Donovan was convinced she looked pleased to see him. He would have sworn a smile jumped into her eyes. But it soon went. Replaced by her default setting for him: dislike. Distrust. And that unforgiving anger over his departure rekindled.

'What d'you want?'

'Hello, Abigail.'

She looked round, as if scared someone would see her talking to him. 'What are you doing here?'

Donovan shook his head. 'I . . . don't know. I was . . . passing, in the area, thought I would . . . just . . .' He sighed. 'I don't know. I wanted to see you.'

Her eyes narrowed. 'What for?'

Because I think I've found your brother. Because we can all be a family again.

'I just . . .' He shrugged. 'Do I need a reason? I had some business down here. I couldn't not stop off.' He looked at her in her school uniform, book bag slung over one shoulder. And felt very proud that she was his daughter. Then ashamed. Her upbringing had nothing to do with him. 'You're looking well.'

She sighed, put her head down. Her hair hid her face. Her features were unreadable.

'How's . . . things?'

'Things are good,' she said.

'Good. Listen.' Donovan looked round. 'D'you fancy a coffee or something?'

She looked warily at him. 'Why?'

'Just . . . instead of standing here. Sitting down. We can talk.'

'About what?'

'Look, Abby, let's just be friends. Let's talk.'

She didn't look convinced. But she agreed. 'OK.'

They found a Crouch End village coffee shop that was trying hard not to be Starbucks and fought their way through the yummy mummies with their parked baby carriages that looked like the child equivalent of 4×4s. They found a table, sat down. Donovan had a large cappuccino with an extra shot, Abigail a skinny latte.

'You don't need to lose weight,' he said. 'You look fine as you are.'

She stared straight at him. 'What d'you care?'

He took a mouthful, set his cup back in the saucer. Bit back what he had been about to say. 'So,' he said instead, 'how's school?'

She shrugged, not wanting to open up to him. 'Fine.'

'And . . . everything else?'

'What are you trying to ask?'

'Nothing. Just . . . I'm as surprised as you to be sitting here. I'm sure you're finding this difficult. So am I.'

She nodded, took a mouthful of coffee.

'It's really good to see you, Abby. Really good. You're looking . . . lovely.' He smiled as he said it.

A smile almost flitted across her face. Then the wariness returned.

'How's Mum?'

'She's fine.'

'Good. And . . . Michael? How's he?'

She looked up, features hardening. 'He's nice. He's . . . He makes Mum happy.'

'Good. She . . . needs a bit of happiness in her life.'

'Well, she wasn't going to get that from you.'

Donovan looked at his cup. He had been expecting this. 'Look, I'm . . . I think we should talk. Look at, at the future. I'm sure your mum hates me. And she's got every right to. And you too. But things are never . . . You probably weren't told everything that happened. You just got your mother's side.'

Abigail said nothing. Blew on her coffee.

'Things haven't been easy for me either. It's not what I wanted. So maybe it's . . . maybe it's time we all sat down. Talked.'

Abigail looked around, as if suddenly uncomfortable with the shift in conversation. She drained as much of her latte as she could, grabbed for her bag. 'I've got to go. Mum'll be home soon.'

'OK. Listen.' Donovan stood also. 'I'm really glad I

bumped into you. Really glad. And that we had a chance to, you know, just talk.'

'You did the talking.'

'Well, whatever. Maybe, maybe we can do it again. Some time soon.'

She made a production of gathering up her things. 'I've got to go,' she said. 'You don't have to come with me. I know the way.'

'OK.' Donovan sat back down.

Abigail turned back to him. 'And you're wrong. Mum doesn't hate you. Even though she's got every right to.'

'Really? What about you?'

'I've got to go.' Her face tried hard to be a mask of stone. Her eyes betrayed her. She looked at him, then away. 'See you.'

She left. Donovan watched her go.

He waited, then stood up. Reluctantly made his way to his appointment with Maurice Courtney.

The pub was heaving with braying City workers divesting themselves of the trappings of the office. Loosened or missing ties, removed jackets. Spilling on to the pavement outside, laughing loudly and shouting. Talking up the day's desk-bound exploits like soldiers on leave after an arduous but victorious tour of duty, stationed on some Cyprus air base rather than a boozer beside Liverpool Street Station.

Donovan stood apart from them, waiting. Pushing everything else out of his mind, concentrating on work. He didn't think he would be waiting long. Maurice Courtney wasn't, Donovan reckoned, an unpunctual man.

In a way he was pleased the meeting with Maurice Courtney was straight away. It would stop him going over the conversation with Abigail, playing it back word for word, looking for meanings he hadn't gleaned the first, second, third time around, not being content until he had squeezed every last emotional nuance from the meeting. Knowing also that it was the last thing he should be doing.

Donovan looked at the photo in his hand, tried to reconcile the smiling, happy-looking hippie with the super-confident voice on the phone. From Hollow Man to City stockbroker. Should be an interesting journey.

Donovan checked his watch again. The City boys and girls were still braying all around him. What did they do with their lives, their jobs that encouraged so little introspection, self-analysis? Why did they do it? Or was it just him – did he think too much? Did he—

'Mr Donovan?' The voice from the phone.

Donovan turned. The person standing before him bore little resemblance to the youth in the photo. This man wore middle age like a badge of honour. What was left of his hair was greying and swept back, his forehead rapidly encroaching on it. His red face and comfortably corpulent stomach showed his indulgence at the richer end of life's spectrum. His hand-cut suit showed, in an understated way, that he had no trouble affording it.

'Mr Courtney?'

Courtney nodded. They shook hands.

'How did you recognize me?' said Donovan.

Courtney smiled. It made the recipient feel like he was his best buddy ever. 'You stood out. Not many City workers wear Silver Surfer T-shirts and old jeans. At least not during office hours. Shall we?'

He gestured to the back of the bar. Donovan picked up his drink and bag and followed. Courtney led him through a dark wooden doorway, down a panelled corridor to a private room. They entered. The place was old. Floor carpeted but uneven beneath. High-backed, well-worn leather armchairs beside a fire that was mercifully unlit. The kind of place secret deals had been done in for centuries. Power granted or taken over a snifter of brandy. The Hellfire Club's headquarters.

'Please sit down, Mr Donovan.'

Donovan sat, feeling even more out of place in his Levi's and T-shirt than he had in the front bar. He placed his pint of Stella before him.

Courtney announced they should be drinking something more suitable and summoned a hitherto hidden waiter to fetch a bottle of wine. Donovan didn't catch the name but knew it would be something red and old.

It arrived. He was right. It was poured, he drank.

'Beautiful,' he said. A world away from the Sainsbury's three ninety-nine special-offer stuff he usually got.

Courtney smiled as if he expected nothing else. 'A favourite haunt of mine,' he said. 'I'm dining here with a friend later.' Another smile. 'I certainly don't mind getting a head start on him. Cheers.'

'Cheers.' Donovan drank.

'So,' said Courtney, settling into his armchair, 'what can I do for you?'

Donovan explained again. Trevor Whitman, the phone calls, the Hollow Men code. Courtney listened, face set hard as if to stop his jowls from moving. Donovan showed him the photo.

'We've talked to everyone else. You're the last.'

Courtney took the photo from him, studied it. A smile spread slowly across his features. 'Good Lord!,' he said. 'Like looking into some long-lost tribe of David Attenborough's.' He handed the photo back, his smile now wistful. 'All but extinct.'

'Not that extinct,' said Donovan.

'Oh, the people may be alive, Mr Donovan, but the thought, the . . . ethos, that's long gone. What are they up to now?'

'You don't keep in touch?'

Courtney shrugged. 'Why ever for? The foolish indulgences of youth, that sort of thing.'

'I've only met a couple.' Donovan gave him thirty years of Trevor Whitman and Abdul-Haq in fifteen minutes, sketching in Mary Evans and Richie Vane. Maurice Courtney listened, enrapt. Eyes widening or narrowing depending on Donovan's words.

Finishing, Donovan sat back, took another sip of his wine. Wondered how many other people had done the same thing down the centuries. He felt comfortable there. He could get to like this.

'So there you have it,' said Donovan. 'Like speed-dating at Friends Reunited.'

Courtney smiled again.

'Abdul-Haq,' Courtney said. 'Good Lord!, What a name.'

'What about you?' said Donovan. 'How did you . . .'

'Get from there to here? University was where you experimented.' He shrugged. 'Tried on different personas, sexualities. Characters. Get it out of your system before getting on with life. I mean, if you can't be a socialist at nineteen, when can you be one? Still . . .' He looked again at the photo. 'Halcyon days, I suppose.'

Donovan, sensing what the answer would be, asked him again about the phone calls.

'Sorry, can't help.' He kept looking again at the photo, looked up. 'Of course, there is one other person you haven't mentioned.'

'Who?'

'The one who took this. Alan Shepherd.'

'Dead, supposedly. Killed in the bomb blast in that pub in Newcastle.'

A curious look came over Courtney's face. 'Perhaps.'

Donovan heard echoes of all the ghost stories that had

been told beside that fireplace over the centuries. Felt he was about to hear another one. 'Go on.'

'As I said, it was all just a bit of a laugh to me. But Alan always wanted to take things further than the rest. Go to extremes.'

'In what way?'

'Remember, this was the time of the Baader-Meinhofs. The Red Brigades. The Weather Underground. Bombings, kidnappings, hostage taking. Compared to what was happening in Europe and America, dissent was in its infancy in this country. Alan Shepherd admired the hell out of those groups. Loved them.' Courtney took another sip of his drink. 'He called himself a socialist. But then, so did Hitler.'

'What d'you mean?'

'What I said about extremes. About taking things further. I doubt a bomb would have finished him off.'

'So he isn't dead?'

'A few years ago, I was approached by an . . . organization for help with funding. They wanted venture capital, wanted a meeting. I told them that wasn't what my arm of the bank did, but they were very insistent. I acquiesced.'

'And?'

'A new political party was being formed. They wanted funding.'

Donovan leaned forward, interested. 'The name?'

'The National Unity Party.'

'And they came to you? Why?'

'I must confess I was surprised myself. Whatever the journey I've made in my life I've never been that way inclined. I met them. And turned them down. But one of the people in the delegation looked familiar. Much older, of course, and with hardly any hair to speak of. Bespectacled. Rail-thin. Looked just like him.'

'Alan Shepherd.'

Courtney leaned forward. 'You have to understand, Mr Donovan, Alan and I never got on. There was something . . . unpleasant about him. He made me shiver. And when I saw that man at the meeting . . . like seeing a ghost.'

'Was it him? Did you ask him?'

Courtney shook his head. 'He didn't contribute much to the meeting. And when he did speak it was with a South African accent. And he claimed no recognition of me. But he kept staring at me, like he knew secrets.' He took another drink. 'He got under my skin. Even in that short time. The way Alan used to. And I've never forgotten it.'

Neither spoke.

Courtney looked at his watch. 'Mr Donovan, I don't wish to appear impolite, but . . .'

Donovan stood up. 'Of course.' He thanked Courtney for his time.

'Sorry I couldn't have been more help.'

'On the contrary. You've been a great help.'

'That photo. Could I keep it? I don't have anything from those times.'

Donovan took his address, said he would get a copy made. They shook hands. He left.

On the way out he brushed past someone he thought he knew and smiled automatically. It was only when he had reached the end of the corridor and was about to head into the bar that he realized he knew the person only from the TV and newspapers covering their exploits at Parliament.

Maurice Courtney's dining companion was as high up the political tree as it was possible to get.

He checked his messages, intending to go back to the car, then the hotel. Then the bar. Stay another night.

But the message from Jamal had him jumping in the car and heading back to Newcastle as fast as he could.

26

Peta drove over the Scotswood Bridge out of Newcastle through Gateshead. Towards her family home.

She turned up the radio, let Kasabian's thud and blunder drown her thoughts out, add to her headache. Hard enough to concentrate on what she had to do.

She reached her childhood home, got out of the car, pulled her thin denim jacket around her, looked up at the house. Thought of turning around, walking away, leaving questions unanswered. Couldn't. She popped a mint into her mouth, hoped it disguised the alcohol that she could still imagine emanating from her. Took one deep breath. Two. Went in.

Lillian was in the sitting room watching TV. Glass of red wine on a small table at her side. Whitman on the sofa, his own glass of wine beside him.

'Didn't figure you for a *Deal Or No Deal* fan,' Peta said, walking into the centre of the room, voice shaking as she said the words.

Lillian looked up. 'Hello, darling.' She took a sip of wine. Smiled, her features tense. Like she was expecting a blow. 'Sit down, make yourself at home.' She looked at the TV, glad to have her attention away from her daughter. 'It passes the time. I can't see any skill in this. He talks about a game plan, a strategy, but really there's nothing to it. There is no game plan. There's no way to play this thing.'

'And yet it's compulsive.' Whitman also had his eyes fixed to the TV.

Peta took another deep breath. 'Turn it off, Lillian.'

Lillian looked at her, uneasy.

'I don't want to talk about strategies and game plans. I just want some answers. Turn it off.'

Lillian pressed the remote. The screen went dead. Her mother scrutinized her, frowned. 'Peta, have you been drinking?' Incredulity in her voice.

'Yeah. Yeah, I've been drinking,' said Peta. 'Course I have. How else would I cope with this?'

Lillian cast an anxious glance at Whitman. 'Peta, please don't shout.'

'Don't shout? Don't fucking shout? After what you've done?'

Neither of them spoke.

'I want answers. Or one answer in particular.' She rounded on Whitman. 'Are you my father?' Her voice cracked as she said the words.

Whitman's mouth fell open. His lips moved, lost for words. The effect was comical.

Peta didn't laugh. 'Are you?' Her voice was breaking, her hands, legs shaking. 'Are you?'

'Peta, darling,' Lillian began, 'please.' She too seemed to be having difficulty finding the right words. 'Come and sit down.'

Tears were running down her cheeks, hot and angry. 'I don't want to sit down.'

'Please. I think it would be better if you did.'

Peta looked round for a seat. Whitman moved along the sofa, leaving space for her. She deliberately pulled over a dining chair from the other end of the long room, sat on that, as far away from the two of them as she could get and remain in the same room.

She looked at them both, waited. Shaking.

'You chose me for this,' Peta said, trying to keep her voice in check. 'You sent me on a wild fucking goose chase, just so I could find out for myself. Didn't you? You wanted me to do all your dirty work for you. Save you telling me to my face.'

Lillian sighed. 'It . . . it wasn't like that . . .'

Peta turned to Whitman. 'Have there been any calls? Has anyone actually threatened you?'

Whitman again struggled to find the words. 'It's . . . complicated.'

'I'll bet it fucking is.'

'Peta . . .'

'Don't "Peta" me! I asked you a question and you still haven't answered it. Is he—' She pointed at Whitman but kept her eyes fixed on her mother '—my father?'

Lillian looked at Whitman, who with a look passed over all authority to her.

'Yes,' said Lillian, her voice quiet.

Peta felt another layer of the world peel away and she was falling down through it. She put her face in her hands.

No one spoke.

Peta's mobile rang.

Lillian and Whitman shared a look. The tension had been broken. Peta made no move to answer it.

'Shouldn't you . . .' her mother ventured.

'No.' The word spat through fingers.

The phone kept ringing. With a loud sigh Peta took it from her inside pocket, glanced at it, put it to her ear. It was a number she didn't recognize.

'Hello.' A greeting with no warmth.

'Sorry to call at this time of the day,' Mary Evans said. 'I hope I'm not interrupting anything.'

Peta didn't know what to say, the truth or a lie. 'What . . . what can I do for you . . .'

'I've . . . What we were talking about the other day. Remember?'

'Yes.'

'Well, I've got something for you.'

'OK.' Peta waited.

'No,' said Mary Evans, the words rushing out in an urgent gasp, 'not on the phone. You have to come here. See . . . for yourself.'

'Right. I'll call round in the morning.'

'No.' Again that breathy urgency. Almost fearful. 'As soon as possible. Please come as soon as you can.'

Peta looked at Whitman and her mother sitting there. 'It's a bit . . . difficult right now.'

'Please.' Almost a pleading urgency. 'Please. You, you must come tonight. It's important.'

Peta closed her eyes, rubbed her forehead. Sighed. 'OK. Where?'

'At . . . at my office.' Then her voice dropped, took on a different tone. 'Please hurry. Please.'

The line went dead.

Peta put the phone back in her pocket, looked at the other two. The atmosphere in the room was as flat and oppressive as the early-evening light creeping around the curtained windows.

'I've got to go. Work.'

'But, Peta,' said her mother, 'we need to talk. Stay. Please.'

Peta looked at her, saw a woman who now looked like a stranger to her. 'I'd rather go.'

'Who was that?' said Whitman.

'Mary Evans.'

Whitman looked at Lillian, back to Peta. 'Could I come with you? D'you mind?'

'No, you can't and, yes, I do.'

Whitman stood up. 'Please. Let me come with you. It would be, would be good to see Mary again. And we could . . . could talk. On the way.'

'I want to be on my own for a while.'

'Peta,' said Whitman. 'You said yourself you've been drinking. It would be safer if you had someone with you. I could drive you.'

Peta let out a harsh, bitter laugh. 'What are you now, my father?'

Whitman flinched like he had received a physical blow. 'Please, Peta. We can talk on the way.'

Peta looked again between him and her mother.

'Talk. Until I don't want to listen any more. And when you get there you keep out of the way, let me do my job.'

Whitman tried a smile. 'Deal or no deal?'

'Fuck you.'

She turned, made her way to the door, turned back to her mother. 'This isn't over, Lillian. Not in the slightest.'

She left, not waiting or wanting to see her mother's reaction. Whitman hurried after her.

Turnbull waited until the lights went out in the house, then got slowly out of the car.

He checked the road, made sure no traffic was around. Hardly any during the day, none at this time of night. He crossed the road, zipping his thin, black jacket all the way up, turning the collar, keeping his head down, trying not to show any skin.

He reached the front of the house, looked up the driveway. The 4×4 was parked alongside a smaller car, an Audi. All in for the night. He began to walk slowly up the drive.

He had drawn a blank at the school. They didn't take him anywhere else. If he were to get something it would have to be from the house. Or the rubbish. Find something in there that could be either a positive match. Or a negative one.

Keeping close to the hedge, he edged his way along, careful to make as little sound as possible. Any he did make could hopefully be rationalized away as some woodland creature. They were sure to have them in the country.

He reached the house. It was even bigger close up. Bigger than he could afford. Or ever would be able to afford now. The garage was detached, set away from it, and he had seen them putting out bin bags behind it. That was where he would start his search.

He found them without too much trouble, his eyes growing accustomed to the dark. He hoped he wouldn't have to use his penlight. Three wheelie bins: kitchen waste, dry recycling, non-recycling. God bless environmentally friendly local authorities, he thought. Making his job even easier.

He flipped back the lid of the non-recycling bin. Took several deep breaths. The smell wasn't as bad as he was expecting, but it was bad enough. He snapped on a pair of latex gloves and prepared to thrust his hands in.

As he did so, the garden lights went on.

He looked round: nowhere to run. The car was too far away, and it would take too much time to get it started. A high hedge and fence bordered the back of the property. He could probably have attempted to scale it but he wasn't sure where it led. There was a wood behind the house, and fields. He would still have left his car out the front, still have compromised himself.

So he hid. Round the side of the garage, as far from the house as he could get. Pressed in to the brick, willing himself to disappear.

He heard a key turn in a lock, the back door open.

Held his breath, looked round again.

Footsteps. Coming towards him.

Turnbull didn't dare move. Heart racing like it wanted to escape his chest, he closed his eyes.

Waited.

Opened them.

Matthew Milsom was standing in front of him, fully dressed. They hadn't gone to bed at all.

Their eyes met. Turnbull thought of running but realized there was no point. He had been caught.

Matthew Milsom sighed. 'Suppose it had to happen some time,' he said.

Turnbull frowned, said nothing.

'We've been expecting you. You'd better come in.'

Milsom turned towards the house. Turnbull, relief being overtaken by confusion, followed him inside.

27

Amar opened the door to find Jamal standing there. 'Not got your key?' he said.

Jamal looked nervously around him into the flat. 'Just wanted to check you were alone, man.' Then back at Amar. 'Are you?'

Amar saw the fear in Jamal's round eyes. He looked tired. 'Yeah, I'm alone. What's up? You OK?'

Jamal almost fell into the apartment.

'No, man, I am definitely not OK . . .'

Amar shut the door behind him, guided Jamal to the sofa, sat him down. The boy looked like he was ready to collapse.

'Oh, man . . . oh, man . . .'

'Take your time,' said Amar. 'Tell me what's up.'

Jamal took his time. He told him.

Everything.

Peta drove the car on to the estate, pulled up in front of the community centre, cut the engine. Whitman had tried to talk to her on the drive. She had listened up to a point, then silenced him.

'Look . . . This is a shock for you. It's uncomfortable for me too.'

'If you're going to talk, spare me the fucking clichés.'

'Sorry. Yes, Peta, I'm your father.'

Peta kept her eyes on the road. She had insisted on driving, wanted to have something to concentrate on. 'No, you're not.'

'I am. I'm not lying. It's . . . it's beyond that now.'

'You may have fathered me,' she said, swerving to avoid a pedestrian who was taking too long on a zebra crossing for her liking, 'but you're not my father. And you never will be my father.'

Whitman sighed. 'Listen . . .'

'No, you listen. My father was one of the greatest men I've ever known. *The* greatest man. Always there for me, always understanding. Put up with Lillian for God knows how many years. He was gentle and kind and loving and . . .' The tears were coming freely. A car blared its horn: she had strayed too far into the middle of the road. She righted it, blinked her tears away, tried to focus on the road.

'Yes, he was,' said Whitman. 'And he always will be to you in your memory.'

'Yeah. And now he's an even better man because he . . . brought me up when I wasn't even his daughter. And you . . . you're just a piece of shit who fucked some woman then pissed off when he found she was pregnant.'

The crying started again, unfettered this time.

'Look, it wasn't like that, honestly. When Lillian and I—'

'Oh, just shut up. Shut up. I don't want to hear any more. Shut up.' The words were screamed at him. 'You might have fathered me, but you'll never be my fucking father.'

Whitman sat silently in the passenger seat. He looked hurt and wounded, like he was on the verge of tears himself. Peta saw none of that. She wouldn't look at him.

They continued in that uncomfortable silence until she pulled up in front of the community centre.

The street was quiet, city darkness hiding what it could. Lights on in houses, flats. Faint traffic sounds from the West Road. TV and CD noise carrying on the breeze. The estate at what passed for peace.

'Inner-city estate like this,' said Whitman, trying to break the silence, 'should be all chavvy hoodies out happy-slapping and joyriding. Quiet. Kind of . . . peaceful. This where she works?'

'And lives. She's done good here,' said Peta, more defensive than she should have been at Whitman's words.

Whitman nodded. 'Always knew she would be the one to really . . . change things. Make a difference, as we used to say.' His voice brimmed with sadness, regret. Like he knew he could never match Mary Evans's level of commitment. Knew there would always be something of himself in the way.

Peta opened the door. 'Stay here.'

'But I want to see her.'

Something nagged at Peta about the phone call. Something not right. She hadn't taken too much notice at first, other things taking precedence, but now her gut instinct told her to go cautiously. 'I'll go in first. If I give you the nod, you come in then.'

Whitman's forehead creased. 'You think there might be something wrong? Well, I should definitely come in with you. You'll need protection.'

Peta almost smiled. 'Get real,' she said, and got out of the car.

She walked to the door of the community centre. It wasn't right. Nothing she could place, just years of experience telling her senses to be on alert. She walked cautiously, eyes scanning the area.

Peta reached out, grabbed the handle of the double doors. The old wooden door swung easily open, releasing the small sound of creaking hinges to float away on the air. She stepped inside. One single light illuminated the hallway. Similarly weak light seeped out from under the door of Mary Evans's office.

She thought she should call out but stopped herself. She turned, walked outside, got her mobile out, speed-dialled

Amar. Backup wasn't a bad idea, she thought, looking at Whitman sitting in the car, frowning at her. Proper backup.

He motioned to her, thinking it was time for him to enter. Peta shook her head, waited for Amar to answer his phone.

Voicemail.

'Shit,' she said aloud and, deciding not to leave a message, broke the connection.

She re-pocketed the phone, steeled herself. Went back inside.

Whitman watched her go in. He felt helpless sitting there, inadequate. And scared. Everything had fallen apart now, all bets were off. But this in particular didn't feel right at all.

His phone rang.

The laptop gave out a loud beeping noise.

Amar and Jamal, both sitting on the sofa talking, turned to look at it. Then at each other.

Amar moved as quickly as he could to the desk, pulled on a pair of headphones, sat down. Listened. He turned to Jamal.

'We're on.'

Whitman jumped at the noise. He almost hit his head on the ceiling of the car, was pleased it was a soft-top. He pulled his phone out, checked the display. A heavy wave of fear rippled through him. He put it to his ear.

'It's not too late,' a familiar voice said.

'Just . . . just fuck off . . .'

The voice laughed. 'Perhaps it is too late.' The laugh faded. The voice when it spoke next sounded like electronic steel down the line. 'You think you're so clever, Trevor, but you aren't. Your plan isn't going to . . . plan. Is it? Ours is.'

'I'm warning you . . .'

'Not me you should be warning, Trevor.'

Whitman looked at the doorway. No sign of Peta.

'Between conception and creation falls the shadow. It's too late. For someone.'

The line went dead.

Whitman stared at the phone, at the doorway to the community centre. Frozen by indecision.

He put the phone away, aware his hand was trembling so much he almost missed his pocket. Another look. Sweat had broken out all over his body. He was aware of it under his arms, at the backs of his knees, beneath his hairline. Another look.

He opened the car door and, with legs that were almost too unsteady to carry him, set off for the community centre.

Peta slowly pushed open the door to Mary Evans's office.

The desk lamp was on, the only source of illumination in the room. The room looked just as it had when she had visited it a few days ago. Like Mary Evans had been working at her desk and just popped outside. No signs of struggle, no blood.

Peta relaxed slightly at that. But only slightly: no sign of Mary Evans either.

She stepped into the room, made her way towards the desk. Wishing, not for the first time, that Amar was with her. Or Joe.

The door closed behind her.

She turned. Too late.

Shapes detached themselves from the shadows at either side of the closed door. Came towards her. And when she did notice them and start to react, it was too late.

A blur.

Then darkness.

*

Whitman heard a noise from inside the community centre. It wasn't Peta.

He had been standing in front of the door, ready to open it. Instead he ran to the side of the building, flattened himself against it. Waited, trying not to breathe too heavily.

A van pulled up, white, anonymous. The doors of the community centre were flung open. He saw two men, big and burly, carry out a lifeless bundle, throw it into the back of the van.

His breath catching, he tried to look closely at the carriers but couldn't get a good look beyond the fact that one of them had skin that caught in the streetlight. It looked cratered and uneven, like he'd been badly scarred by acne. Or badly burned.

They locked the back doors, hurried round to the cab, jumped in.

The van sped off.

Whitman let his breath out in a long sigh, gulped in replacement air.

He knew what had been in the bundle.

Or rather who.

He pushed himself off the wall, began to move towards the front of the building, desperately trying to formulate what he thought was the correct response.

Hands grabbed him from behind, forced him back against the wall. He tried to struggle, to scream, but they pushed harder. A face appeared before him. It spoke, its voice harsh and hushed.

'Hello, Trevor,' it said. 'Long time no see.'

It took a while but he recognized it.

The face smiled.

Richie Vane.

PART THREE

KING MOB

28

Paul Turnbull followed Matt Milsom through the conservatory. Lights were put on as they went, illuminating a house that was still in transition. Boxes and crates were piled around, pushed out of the way, while some rooms had been tastefully, fashionably and expensively decorated. He was led through to a small room. Full bookshelves and comfortable armchairs, stereo system in the corner, cushions all around, rugs artfully overlapped. Diffused lighting, a Moroccan-influenced décor. Turnbull could see why it had been finished first; it gave a taste of what was to be done with the rest of the house. The kind of room where sitting in on an evening, relaxing with a glass of wine and a good book, something mellow on the CD would be a pleasure. Turnbull felt an unexpressed scowl build within. He would never have this kind of house.

Never have this kind of life.

'This is the den,' said Matt Milsom, pointing to an armchair. 'Please. Make yourself comfortable.'

Turnbull sat. Under other circumstances, he would have had no trouble making himself comfortable.

'I'm Matt Milsom. You are?'

'Turnbull. Paul Turnbull.'

'Can I get you a drink, Mr Turnbull?' asked Matt Milsom.

'Sure. Whatever you're having.'

'I've got a good bottle of malt in the cupboard. That seems appropriate somehow. I'll get two glasses.'

He left the room. Turnbull watched him go. For someone who had just been caught out, Milsom didn't seem very
uncomfortable. He returned with the bottle of whisky and
two glasses, poured generous measures into each, passed one
to Turnbull.

'Cheers.'

Turnbull nodded, threw a mouthful of it back, regarded
Milsom. Mid- to late thirties, tall, dark-haired. Jeans and a T-
shirt, but clearly designer. Black-framed glasses. Just what
Turnbull would have imagined a media person to look like.

But calm. No sense of panic or despair. If anything, a
trace of amusement.

No sign of the boy or Mrs Milsom.

'It's about Jake, isn't it?' said Milsom, putting his glass
down on a hand-painted Moroccan side table.

Turnbull kept his face straight, his eyes blank. Falling
right back into police training. 'You tell me.'

A smile danced around Milsom's face. 'I find you on my
property going through my bins. You tell me.'

'Yes, it's about Jake.'

Milsom looked at the floor, then back to Turnbull. 'Are
you police?'

Turnbull shook his head.

Milsom looked at Turnbull, pointed a finger, like it was a
guessing game. 'But you were police.'

Turnbull gave a small nod, acceded that much.

'So, what? Immigration? Home Office?'

Turnbull thought before answering. How much to give
away. 'Privately employed.'

Milsom nodded and smiled, pleased he had got the
answer correct. 'Right. Well, at least that's something. Do I
get to know who sent you?'

'I'm working for a private client.'

'And what's his interest in Jake?'

'Again, that's private.'

'I think I have a right to know.'

Turnbull's features hardened. 'I'll have to check with my client.' He said nothing more, letting Milsom know that was the end of the matter.

Milsom persisted. 'What if I call the police? Tell them of your intrusion?'

Turnbull shrugged. 'Up to you.'

Milsom sat back, nodded. His bluff called. 'OK. Fine.' He sighed, took another mouthful of whisky.

Turnbull did the same. It was good whisky. He waited.

'So,' Milsom said eventually, 'you want to know about Jake. Where he came from. How he suddenly showed up. You don't believe he was the cousin of a relative who was emigrating?'

'Your story,' said Turnbull, sipping the whisky.

Milsom smiled. 'OK. Two years ago, I was in Eastern Europe. Making a documentary about the orphanages in Romania. I was there on a follow-up to one I made about ten years ago. Yeah, I know, it's been done to death, but it's something I've got a bit of a passion for. That first one changed lives. Which was incredible. I mean, how many times can you do that with a TV programme? I mean, it didn't make things perfect but—' he shrugged '—you know, a lot better for some.'

Turnbull nodded. He remembered the documentary, if that was the one Milsom was talking about. It had affected him deeply. How could it have not? Children in appalling conditions, many with mental and physical problems. Children in pain, neglect. Charities had been set up, aid sent out there. New orphanages built, lives changed for the better. If Milsom was behind it, it was a fine thing he had done.

'But, you know, you move on to other things. Nature of the job. But I kept in touch with some of the kids, even sent

stuff, made donations, you know, to orphanages they were
in. I suppose I had one eye on making a follow-up, but I was
genuinely interested. Kept going back over there, that sort of
thing.'

Another slurp of whisky for the two of them. Turnbull
noticed his glass was empty. So did Milsom.

'Refill?'

'Don't mind if I do.' It was the best whisky Turnbull had
tasted in a long time.

Milsom left the room, returned with the bottle. 'Best
just leave it here, I think.' He smiled, poured, topping his
own up too. Settled back into his chair. 'Where was I?'

'You keep going back over to Romania,' said Turnbull.
Would take more than a good whisky for him to forget
what he was there for.

'Right. Well, yeah. To cut a long story short, I saw Jake,
as I called him. Jakob was his real name. One of the bright-
est kids in there.' A smile spread across Milsom's face. 'Once
we'd sorted him out. Always happy, cheeky, you know?
Laughing and smiling. And clever. Just a joy to be with.
When I saw him this time well, he, he wasn't in a good way.
He'd been . . . let down by his environment.'

Turnbull put his drink down, leaned forward. 'How
d'you mean?'

Milsom's eyes darkened. 'Jake has . . . Jake's HIV-positive.
Not his fault, obviously. And he was, was in a lot of pain.
Not being properly looked after.' He picked up his glass,
swirled the liquid round, slowly, watching it. 'And it just . . .
pained me to see him like that. Like I almost didn't recognize the same smiling little boy. I told Celia. We talked about
it, and we, we came to a decision. And that's why he's here
now.'

Turnbull took another sip, swallowed what he had just
heard along with the whisky. Questions began to form.

'I know what you're thinking,' Milsom said. 'Why didn't I just adopt, go through the proper channels. Why didn't I keep him in his own country, make sure he received the care he needed over there.' He shook his head. 'I don't know. Maybe I should have done. But that all takes time. Something he might not have. So . . .' He shrugged, sat back. 'So here he is.'

Turnbull looked round as if expecting the boy to make a dramatic entrance. He didn't. There were just the two of them. And the whisky.

'So there you go,' said Milsom, sitting back. 'Are you going to tell all that to your mysterious employer?'

'Yes.'

'And will that be enough? Will you leave Jake alone?'

Turnbull took another pull of the whisky. It was slipping down very smoothly. He was starting to feel comfortable. Always a dangerous sign. 'That's up to him.'

Milsom's eyes hardened as he took another mouthful of whisky. It wasn't the answer he had wanted to hear. 'Well, I think it's only fair,' he said, 'since I've told you everything, you tell me why your employer is so interested in Jake.'

Turnbull wondered whether some kind of exchange was in order. The man seemed genuine and his whisky was certainly good. But years on the force had left Turnbull naturally suspicious. He didn't give in that easily. 'Sorry, can't say.'

Something flashed in Milsom's eyes. Fear? Anger? Turnbull didn't catch it.

'Have you a photo of Jake I could take with me?' Turnbull said. 'If you don't mind.'

A smile nearly made it to Milsom's lips. 'I don't think so.' He stood up, his glass empty. The warmth had dropped out of his voice. 'I'm sorry you wasted your time. But I hope that'll be an end of it.'

Turnbull rose also, draining his glass as he did so. 'Let's hope so,' he said.

'Could I ask you for a bit of . . . circumspection as regards to Jake?'

'How d'you mean?'

'He's been through a lot. We just want to make sure the rest of his life's as good as we can make it. We'd appreciate it if you didn't go mentioning this to the school or the media or . . . anything like that.'

'I shouldn't think that'll be a problem.' Turnbull looked at the whisky, checked the label. Thought of buying some for himself. Jura. Ten-year aged malt. Good stuff.

Milsom walked him to the door. They shook hands.

Turnbull walked back to his car. Milsom had seemed sincere, he thought, but there was something . . . something not quite right. A little further digging was called for.

He drove away, unaware that Milsom was still at the door, staring intently as he went. The moonlight glinting off his glasses, his eyes twin balls of cold, bright flame.

Donovan blinked, turned the Drive By Truckers up further and sang along to 'Blessing and a Curse', windows open letting in as much air as possible. Forcing himself to stay awake as he drove up the M1 back to Newcastle. He had the road virtually to himself: too late for the night drivers, too early for the morning.

It felt like a twister was in his head, spinning the last few days around, giving him a headache. And now Jamal's message to get back there as quickly as possible: something bad had happened.

He was thinking all this, pushing the Scimitar as hard as he could, paying no attention to the black 4×4 with the tinted windows overtaking him. He started to become aware of it when it didn't overtake, just sat alongside him, matching its speed to his.

He looked at it, puzzled. He was doing seventy, the Scimitar flat out. He imagined the 4×4 could easily top that. He dropped back slightly to allow it to pass. The 4×4 did the same. Donovan speeded up. The 4×4 did likewise.

He looked round. Panic began to rise. The 4×4 was staying with him for a reason.

It didn't take him long to find out what.

It edged slightly in front of him, then pulled over towards him. Trying to catch the front of his car, force him to spin off the road.

'Shit . . .'

Fully awake now, Donovan slammed on the brakes, hoping that no one was too near behind him. Luckily there wasn't. The 4×4 did likewise. Donovan speeded up again, tried to pull round the 4×4.

No good. The black car anticipated his move, went with him.

Donovan flew out into the third lane, flooring the accelerator as hard as he could. The 4×4 sped up, easily caught him. Started to pull over to the right, push him into the crash barrier.

Donovan held tightly to the wheel, checked his mirrors for other traffic. There were cars and articulated lorries in the two other lanes. He couldn't just speed up or drop back; he might hit something. He kept his foot pressed down hard.

The 4×4 edged closer to him.

Donovan kept going. The 4×4 matching him.

He looked up. A slip road signposted, half a mile ahead. A desperate, reckless plan began to form. He looked round, tried to calculate the distance between himself and the traffic behind him, the 4×4 edging closer all the time.

The signs for the turn-off appeared.

Three bars . . .

Two bars . . .

One . . .

Donovan slammed the brakes on, skidded almost to a standstill. The 4×4 was slow to react, slammed to the right, collided with the crash barrier, sent up a shower of sparks as it dragged along.

Donovan didn't dare stop, didn't dare look round. He slammed the car into gear, crossed diagonally over the road, eyes virtually closed as horns blared, brakes squealed.

He opened his eyes again. He had made the turn-off.

Barely slowing down, he hit the roundabout at the bottom, went round to the right and off down whichever road he was on. No time to check where he was. He kept driving, throwing occasional glances into the mirror.

No 4×4.

Eventually he reached a small town, pulled the car off the road, drove into a pub car park and parked up as far from the road as possible. Waited.

No 4×4.

He got out of the car, sighed.

Walked over to some bushes. Threw up.

When he was ready he continued his journey home.

By minor roads.

29

Richie Vane sat in the passenger seat of Peta's Saab convert-
ible. He looked through the windows, at the dashboard, the
CD player, even the door handle and seat belt. A dislocated
smile played on his face. 'Lovely car, this, lovely.'

'Shut up, Richie,' said Whitman, not taking his hands off
the wheel, his eyes off the road. 'I have to think.' And fast,
Whitman knew. He had to get away. Put as much distance
between them and where they had come from as fast as they
could.

Outside the community centre, Richie Vane had let his
hand drop once Whitman had realized who he was.

'What the fuck? Richie?'

Richie had put his finger to his lips, kept Whitman
pressed up against the side of the community centre until the
van was well away. Once it had gone he relaxed his grip.

'What the fuck's happening? Why are you here?'

'They've got her. Peta, her name is.' Richie's face was
grave in the shadowed streetlight. He looked at the door.
Sadness came into his eyes. 'Nice name. Unusual. Did you
choose it?'

'What? Richie we've got to . . .' What? What could
Whitman do now? 'Let's go and see Mary. Is she still
inside?'

Richie frowned. 'Mary isn't in there. I saw them come in
an' wait. So I waited. But no Mary.'

'Who are they?'

'Them two?' Richie pointed along the street the van had

disappeared down. 'Abdul-Haq's strongarm boys. Seen them with him before.'

'Gideon?'

'Abdul-Haq now.' Anger came into Richie's eyes. 'Twat would be a better word.'

'Where have they taken her, d'you know?'

Richie shook his head.

Whitman paced in a circle. 'Shit . . . shit . . .' He stopped, looked at Richie. 'Why are you here?'

Richie gave another cockeyed smile. 'I was watchin'. Like I told Peta I would. Be her eyes and ears. Her word on the street. I came here 'cos I thought somethin' was up.'

Whitman's eyes narrowed. 'What do you know, Richie?'

'About what?'

'About what's going on?'

Richie frowned. 'About . . .' He shrugged. 'Peta told me you were gettin' phone calls from the old days. I said I would ask around.'

Whitman scrutinized him, tried to see if he was telling the truth. Decided he was. Richie was many things but duplicitous wasn't one of them. Unless he had changed a lot.

'OK . . .' Whitman looked around. The van was now long gone. He was in internal turmoil; emotions churning, he didn't know which one to latch on to, go with first. 'We'd better get out of here, do something about finding Peta.'

Richie nodded, followed Whitman to Peta's car.

He drove away, thinking hard, trying to get his mind in some semblance of order. To find a hook he could hang on to. He turned to Richie.

'So, Richie, long time no see. How've you been keeping?'

*

Rani Rajput couldn't sleep. She didn't even know if it was time for sleep. Days and nights were becoming one long medicated somnambulant blur. Ever since he died.

Ever since her husband was revealed to be a suicide bomber.

The police had taken her in for questioning, held her for two whole days. All she did was break down in tears, try to tell them through the sobs that it wasn't him, they must have the wrong man. He would never do anything like that. Even told them that they hardly ever went to mosque, just on special occasions – family things, birthdays. Like Christmas and weddings for Christians, she said. They hadn't listened.

Her son had gone to stay with his grandparents, but even he was questioned by a family liaison officer. Rani would never forget the looks of the police: stone-eyed hatred disguised by a veneer of professional courtesy. Even the few Indian ones, they were looking at her like all she and her husband were doing was spoiling it for the rest of them.

They let her go eventually to find that they had seized Safraz's computer, CDs, books, everything that they could. The house had been gone through thoroughly, like a polite bomb had hit it. She had just sat down in the centre of her living room and cried.

The bank she worked for in the city centre told her not to come in for a few days. Take as much time off as you want. She knew what they meant. Don't come back at all. And all her friends, the white ones especially, didn't want to know her any more.

She had tried to get herself back together, tidied the house. Gone to Tesco. But she heard the voices. They didn't bother to whisper, just said it straight out to her face.

Told to go back to where she came from.

Now that her husband was gone she could go to Iraq and fuck Osama.

That she should have her son taken away from her by social services in case she infected him with her hatred. She was an unfit mother.

Spat on her.

Not crazed, right-wing Fascists, just ordinary people.

She had gone back home, slammed and locked the door behind her. Vowed never to go out again.

And then the rumours had started. They hadn't gone on holiday to Greece last summer. Safraz had been on an al-Qaeda training camp in Afghanistan. All that drinking and not going to mosque was just a cover. Playing football with his mates, all a cover. That's what they wanted people to think. And the wife was in on it too. How could she not be? How could all that be going on and she didn't know?

She didn't know. That was it. She didn't know.

She didn't believe he was a suicide bomber. He couldn't be. He had gone to play football and ended up in a part of Newcastle they never went to, didn't know anyone there. Safraz wasn't hiding anything from her. He was terrible at keeping secrets.

The tears came again. And again.

She had refused to talk to the media, but now, with things mounting up against her, she decided she had better put her side of the story. She gave an interview to the local paper. Turned down lots of money from the nationals because she didn't know how they would treat her. How they would twist her words.

She just wanted to give her side, have her say. Let them know what a loving husband Safraz was, a good father. And voice her suspicions too, get them out in the open.

The reporter had set her mini tape recorder down, gently asked her questions, listened attentively, nodded encouragingly. Afterwards, Rani felt good about it. Like her side of the story was finally going to be put. Maybe now people would leave her alone. Maybe now people would believe her.

And then the story came out:

SUICIDE BOMBER WIFE REVEALS: HE HAD SEX WITH ME
BEFORE EMBARKING ON CAMPAIGN OF HATRED

The media had embarked on a feeding frenzy. The local journalist sold her story, the interview went everywhere. Everyone was now beating down her door.

And Rani couldn't cope any more.

So now she lay on the bed, not sleeping but not awake either, a picture of her husband and son clutched to her chest, tears in her eyes and a bottle of sleeping pills next to her.

She didn't want to die. But she didn't want to live either. She just wanted something to take the pain away. She didn't want to be hated any more.

She looked at her husband, her son, through wet, blurred vision. Her son would understand one day. She hoped.

Another pill, dry-swallowed. Another step nearer to nothing.

Rani cried. And cried.

Until she could cry no more.

Richie kept slipping away, like real life was too much for him in anything but small doses. He contented himself with looking round, playing with the radio and CD player.

'You put a CD here,' he said, staring intently at it, 'and it just sucks it in. Takes it off you. Watch.'

He held a CD at the opening on the player. It sucked it in. Richie laughed. 'Clever, eh? Like it's hungry an' wants feedin'.'

The car was filled with the sounds of Kasabian at full volume. Whitman reached over, turned it off.

'We don't need that. Just think, Richie. Think.'

Richie sat there, humming, the song still in his head. Or a song.

'What do you know, Richie? Eh? About what's going on. What do you know?'

Richie slowly looked at him. 'I don't know. Anythin'. Somethin's happenin' but I don't know what it is.' Richie gave a small smile. 'Do I, Misterrr Jonezzzzz . . .'

Whitman shook his head. Brilliant. Stuck in a speeding car with a brain-fired, Dylan-singing acid casualty. Things had gone badly wrong, out of his control. The plan was torn up. He needed somewhere to hide, to think. He needed protection.

'Richie . . .'

Richie was still humming. Whitman had to say his name again, sharper this time. Richie turned his head.

'We need somewhere to hole up. Somewhere we won't be disturbed. Know anywhere?'

Richie frowned. 'You mean a bar? I'm not supposed to drink any more. It's bad . . . bad for me.'

'I know that, Richie. I'm not asking you to drink. Just take me there.'

Richie thought for a moment. 'OK.'

'Good.' Whitman looked at the road, the night. They were out there. Waiting. Watching. Ready to attack at any moment. 'And Richie?'

'Yeah?'

'D'you know where I could buy a gun?'

Jason was pulled up, a hand round his throat choking the air out of him. He was thrown into a hard wooden chair. He sat forward, gasping for breath. He was naked, no idea of how long he had been there. He was hungry and tired. He had been trying to sleep on the floor, his shivering keeping him awake. He rubbed his neck, tried to spit. Looked up.

There were two of them. Major Tom and another man. No balaclavas this time. They both looked angry. He tried smiling at them but they didn't return it. Jason was scared, more frightened even than when the two Pakis had taken him from the shop.

'You ran away, little cunt,' said the man he didn't know. Shaved head, dressed in green army clothes. He looked and smelled hard.

'Wuh-what's goin' on? What's happenin'?'

'Did we say you could talk? Eh? Did we?'

The hard-faced one slapped him. It felt like a punch. Jason's head snapped sideways, his cheek stinging like a hundred razor slashes.

Major Tom came round behind him, put a sack over his head, began to twist it at the neck. Jason tried to pull a shuddering breath of air into his body, couldn't. He smelled and tasted old earth, dirt and dust. His hands went to the edges, tried to pull it away. Major Tom's grip was too strong. He tightened it.

Jason felt himself being roughly pulled to his feet, spun round. He felt sick, light-headed. Round and round. Someone kicked his legs away from him. He fell to the stone floor, the remaining breath smacked out of his body. Stars danced, exploded, before his eyes. He felt himself blacking out.

The sack was ripped from his head. He gasped in lungfuls of air, kept his eyes screwed tight shut. Curled into a foetal ball. Forced the tears not to form at the corners of his eyes, didn't trust them not to come streaming down his face.

He groaned.

'I said no talking.'

A kick to his ribs. Jason gasped, girdled by pain, curled up even more.

'Open your eyes.' Major Tom this time. 'Open them.'

Jason did as he was told. Found himself looking down the barrel of a gun. A revolver. Major Tom opened the chamber, showed Jason the bullet, replaced it, spun it. Pointed it at Jason's face again, pulled the trigger.

Jason screamed, tried to move out of the way. Couldn't. The hard-faced man held him by the neck, kept his face on the barrel of the gun.

Click.

Jason squealed.

Another spin, another pull of the trigger.

Click.

Jason felt his bowels go.

'Filthy fucker . . .' The hard-faced man jumped out of the way, smacked him in the back of the head.

Jason fell forward, sprawled on the floor.

'Are you going to run away again?'

Jason shook his head.

'What?' Another kick. 'Can't hear you.'

'No . . .'

'Have you been chosen for something special?'

'Yes . . .'

'Are you going to do it?'

Jason hesitated. The kicks started again. Jason kept his eyes closed, body as still as possible.

'Are you going to do it?'

'Yes.'

Jason held his breath, didn't move. The two men left the room. Jason still held his breath, didn't move.

Didn't dare do otherwise.

30

Amar and Jamal sat at the desk. Amar pushed keys on the laptop, watched the screen intently. Jamal watched Amar watching. Donovan stood behind them, can of beer in his hand. His second one. Calming him down, keeping him going.

'Play it again,' he said.

Amar did so. Whitman's voice came out of the speakers along with that of the caller. The tense conversation was relived, clicked off, ended. Amar turned round. 'What d'you think?'

'That accent the caller's got,' said Donovan, taking another mouthful, 'I'm guessing South African.'

'But he kinda goes into it an' out of it,' said Jamal. 'Like he's puttin' it on.'

'Maybe he's taking it off,' said Donovan. 'Maybe that's how he speaks now and doesn't think Whitman will recognize him with the accent so he tries to lose it.'

'So what does that mean?' said Amar.

Donovan told him about the conversation he had had with Maurice Courtney mentioning the meeting with the mysterious South African representative of the NUP.

'So?' Jamal looked confused.

'He said the South African looked like Alan Shepherd, the Hollow Man who went missing after the bomb blast. In fact, he thought it was him. If that's the case, this nails it, don't you think?' Another swig of beer. His can was empty.

It was late, past midnight. Donovan had driven straight to

Amar's flat, his nerves recovering the nearer he came to home. Jamal's phone call had told him things were happening and to get back soon as. There was also a note of fear in Jamal's voice that gave Donovan extra impetus. He had told them about the attempt to force him off the road as soon as he arrived. But he hadn't had time to question Jamal further because Amar had played the recording.

'You managed to get a trace?' asked Donovan. 'Any idea where he was calling from?'

Amar shook his head. 'Didn't stay on the line long enough. Sorry.'

'Shame.' Donovan looked around. 'Where's Peta?'

Amar's face showed concern. 'We don't know. We phoned on her mobile, no reply. Landline, nothing. Tried Whitman, same thing.'

'D'you think we should be worried? How was she getting on with the interviews?'

'Don't know,' said Amar. 'Never heard from her. That was all you and her.'

Donovan dumped his empty can in the bin, cracked open another. He saw the look Amar gave him. 'What? I'm thirsty and I've had a near-death experience. What else am I supposed to do?'

Amar gave a half-smile. 'Nothing. Just imagining what you'd say if it was me doing that.'

Donovan bit back his answer, gave a grim smile in return. 'OK. Fair enough. Right. Let's play catch-up. What we got?'

'Jamal first,' said Amar.

Jamal looked between the two, began talking. He told Donovan about finding Jason Mason. When he told him what method he had employed, the anticipated anger from Donovan never materialized. Instead a look of pride spread over Donovan's face. He smiled.

'What?' said Jamal. 'What you look at me like that for?'

'Nothing. Just pleased to see you using all that teenage anger constructively.'

Jamal, relieved, continued. He told them about going to Norrie's shop, his grisly discovery.

'Then I ran, man, down that street an' away like I'd never been there.' He was panting, reliving the experience in his head. Amar, sitting next to him on the sofa, slipped a comforting arm round his shoulders. He relaxed slightly.

'Did you phone the police?' said Donovan.

Jamal shook his head. 'Naw, man. I was outta there. A black kid with previous turnin' up at a murder? Open an' shut, bro.'

Donovan nodded. 'And no sign of Jason.'

Jamal shook his head.

'Could he have done it?' said Amar.

Another shake of the head from Jamal. 'Doubt it. He's, like, tiny. He couldn't even reach that high, never mind holdin' a . . . a . . .'

His head went forward, Amar's grip tightened.

'OK,' said Donovan. 'Jason said he was being hunted. We saw that at first hand a few days ago. I reckon that's who those skinheads I dealt with were looking for.'

'Yeah,' said Amar. 'There's something about that too.'

He told Donovan about picking up Kev, bringing him back. Jamal joined in, said he recognized him.

'You sure?' said Donovan.

'Unmistakable, man. You don't forget someone like that.'

'Even had a bandage on his side,' said Amar. 'Gave his name as Kev. The same . . .'

'The same name Jason said,' finished Jamal.

'Right,' said Donovan. 'You have been busy. My turn now.' He told them of his meeting with Abdul-Haq and subsequent meeting with Maurice Courtney. 'And Peta,' he said, finishing up, 'went off to meet the other two. And we haven't heard since.'

'We could try her mother,' said Amar.

'Bit late, isn't it?' said Donovan, checking his watch. 'D'you want to know what I think on what we've put together so far?'

They did.

'Alan Shepherd, the Hollow Men's maniac bomber, did that pub in 1972, then disappeared afterwards, got as far away as possible. South Africa, from the looks of things. And now he's back, calling himself Sharples and allying himself with the NUP.'

'That's some journey,' said Amar. 'Anarchist to Fascist.'

'Not that far,' said Donovan. 'Apparently he was always like that. I get the impression that the rest of them were scared of him. Not quite sure what he was capable of. Anyway, he comes back, gets involved with the NUP. Now, the NUP have got something planned. What, we don't know.'

'Something to do with the elections?' said Amar.

'Very possibly. All we know is that Jason was due to play a major part in it. It seems like his friend Kev found out, had an attack of conscience and let him go.'

'But Jason stabbed him,' said Jamal.

'Maybe they had a fight. Or maybe he had to make it look real,' said Amar. 'His cronies wouldn't have believed him otherwise. Bit drastic, though, if it is.'

'I'm sure you'd do the same for me,' said Donovan.

'So why was Kev leadin' the bullyboys comin' to get Jason?' said Jamal.

Donovan shrugged. 'Don't know that bit.'

'Maybe it was his job,' said Amar. 'Couldn't let them down, couldn't lose face.'

'Did he say anything when he was with you?' said Donovan.

'Yeah,' said Amar. 'He was sick of that life. Wanted out. Wanted to apologize for what he'd done. Kept saying that, wanted to apologize. I told him he'd done nothing to apologize for. He said he had but wouldn't go into it. I left it at that.' He frowned. 'No, not apologize, atone. That was it. Atone for what he'd done.'

Donovan became thoughtful. Drank his beer. 'So where does Abdul-Haq fit in? Does he fit in? And where are Peta and Whitman?'

'Call her mother,' said Amar.

Donovan looked at his watch. Well past one now. He made a decision. 'OK.' Dialled the number, waited.

It took less time for an answer than he had expected. Lillian picked the phone up. 'Hello?' Her voice was nervous, like she was expecting bad news.

Donovan told her who it was, why they were calling. 'Is she there? Obviously I won't disturb her if she's asleep.'

'No.' Lillian's voice was balanced on the fine line of frantic, ready to tip over with the slightest provocation. 'I haven't seen her since . . . she was here earlier. Then she received a call. And she and Trevor left. I haven't seen them since.'

'Who was the call from?'

'Mary Evans.'

Donovan couldn't read the emotion in Lillian's voice as she said the name.

'Mary Evans? What did she want?'

'Just wanted Peta to go and see her. Trevor wanted to go too.' A sigh, then: 'She wasn't in the strongest frame of mind, I'm afraid. She had just received some rather life-changing news.'

Donovan's heart skipped a beat. 'What?'

'That's . . . up to her to tell you. When you see her.'

He asked her again whether she had any idea where Peta

was or if she had heard from her. Lillian replied that she hadn't.

'But Mr Donovan,' she said, swallowing down the panic in her voice, 'please find them.' She tried to laugh, didn't even convince herself. 'I'm sure I'm just being a stupid woman but I think there may be something wrong.'

'Why?'

Silence on the line.

'Mrs Knight?'

'Just find them, please.'

She put the phone down. Donovan turned to the other two.

Shit,' he said. 'We need a plan.'

One thirty, and Amar was driving Donovan's Scimitar through Newcastle. Donovan had wanted to drive it himself but, since Donovan was already three cans in, Amar had insisted.

They were heading towards Mary Evans's office. See if she was still there; perhaps her, Peta and Whitman were talking into the small hours. Reminiscing about the old days. That sort of thing. Somehow Donovan doubted it.

Donovan read the map, gave Amar directions. They had left Jamal back at Amar's flat, monitoring the phone, telling him to get some sleep. They knew he could be relied on to do one of those things.

'Down here,' said Donovan, pointing towards a turn-off into an old council housing estate. 'Should be a community centre somewhere . . . there it is.'

Amar pulled up next to it. It was in darkness, the front doors closed.

'Well,' he said, 'scratch that idea.'

'Maybe not.' Donovan got out of the car, looked around. No one about. Good. He went up to the front doors. Another look around, then he knocked.

No reply.

Again. Nothing.

He pushed. They were unlocked.

He turned, pointed to the boot of the car. Amar got out, lifted the boot, brought out the American police torch Donovan kept there that sometimes doubled as a weapon. He joined Donovan on the step.

They went inside. Donovan switched on the torch, shone the light around. They saw a doorway, weak light creeping out from underneath. They looked at each other, nodded. Moved towards it.

They stood at either side of the doorframe. Donovan stretched out his arm, knocked on the door. Nothing. He reached for the door handle, turned it. It opened inwards. A glance at Amar, then he went in.

Mary Evans's office was neat and tidy. The desk lamp illuminated a small patch, papers and files on it. They stepped inside. Looked round. They were alone.

Donovan moved towards the desk, checking for any sudden movement out of the corners of his eyes. Amar joined him. Donovan opened the files on the desk, shook out the papers, unfolded them.

Property development plans. Razing whole areas of the West End of Newcastle, building new offices, flats, shopping and leisure complexes in their place. He rifled the pages, studied the diagrams, artists' impressions, worked it out with what he knew of the area.

'It would go right through here,' he said, voice barely reaching a whisper. 'Take this whole estate away.'

They went through more pages. Donovan didn't understand most of them, being too technical or legal in their terms of reference. But he did spot something he knew well. A name.

Abdul-Haq.

Donovan and Amar shared a glance.

'His company,' said Donovan. 'They're behind this.'

'Is that how he fits in?' said Amar.

'Don't know. Must be.'

They looked around. There was nothing else demanding their attention. Through the blinds came headlights. Instinctively they both ducked down, Donovan turning off the torchlight. They both moved quickly to the door, looked out into the corridor. The car had gone past.

Giving one last look around, they left the building, got into the Scimitar and drove away slowly, not wanting to attract attention.

31

Donovan drove up the gravel drive to Lillian Knight's house. He and Amar had returned to the flat, sent Jamal off to bed and spent the night monitoring the phone lines. They had added Peta's to Whitman's. Amar and Donovan had taken it in turns, one grabbing some sleep on the sofa while the other sat at the desk. As soon as it was light they had both been wide awake and drinking coffee, their eyes red-rimmed and dark-shadowed. Donovan had waited until eight o'clock, then, throwing cold water over his face, he had driven to Peta's mother's house.

Amar had been left manning the phones and trying to reach Kev. Jamal had also been given a task.

Donovan pulled up in front of the house, switched off the engine and Richard Hawley asking whether his love could hear the rain. Donovan wished for rain. Plenty of it. The air was already hot, oppressive. Like a hand holding the city in place for a hammer to come down and strike it.

He looked at the house, tried to imagine a young Peta growing up here. Tried to imagine Peta anywhere, unharmed. Alive. Shook his head, wished he had managed some sleep. All his thoughts were of Peta. David had been put, reluctantly, on hold.

He pressed the doorbell. Waited.

Lillian Knight came to the door wearing a flowing, floaty dress and a worried expression.

Donovan introduced himself.

'Lillian Knight. Come in.'

She stood aside. Donovan walked through the hall, with the black and white checked floor, to the large living room. He took a seat on a battered brocaded sofa. She stood opposite him.

'Have you . . . have you heard?'

'Nothing yet,' said Donovan.

'Tea? Coffee?' She looked anxious, drawn.

'No, thanks.'

Lillian stood there awkwardly. 'I really shouldn't worry,' she said, arms moving uselessly at her side, like she didn't know what to do with her body. 'I mean, she's probably . . . They've gone off somewhere, talking . . . Getting to, to know . . . Yes, silly really to worry. Silly . . .' Her voice trailed away.

'D'you mean Peta and Trevor Whitman?'

Lillian nodded.

'Trevor received another phone call last night. We've heard nothing from either of them since.'

Lillian sat down in an armchair like a deflating balloon, as if air and hope were the only things holding her up. Donovan looked at her. Her face was drawn, her muscles taut. She seemed to have had a similar night to his.

'I think you'd better tell me what this news was she received last night.'

'I think . . . I think that's for, for Peta to tell you when she feels able.'

'We've gone beyond that, Lillian. Peta has disappeared. At the same time Trevor Whitman got a call from Alan Shepherd. It's time you told me what was going on.'

Lillian seemed about to shower Donovan with protestations but the look on his face silenced her. She dropped her gaze to the floor. Two wine glasses sat there, empty, the red wine dried on the sides, pooling in the bottom, the bottle next to them empty. She sighed.

'Her news was . . . is private, Mr Donovan. Really none of your business. As I said, if Peta wants—'

Donovan leaned forward, tried not to raise his voice, failed. 'Mrs Knight, Lillian, your daughter, my friend and colleague, has just gone missing. I've just told you your friend has received a call from a dead man and you haven't even blinked an eye. Let's stop playing, shall we?'

She looked again at the empty wine glasses, longingly, as if wishing them full. 'Trevor's disappeared as well. They were both together.'

'Together?'

'Yes. Peta had just found out that . . . her father wasn't the man she thought he was.'

Donovan nodded. 'Whitman.'

Lillian nodded. The weak morning light crept round the sides of the drawn curtain. It hit Lillian's face, turning her skin translucent. She looked ghost-like, as if nothing she said or did was real.

Lillian nodded. 'I'm having a cup of tea. I'd advise you to join me. I may be talking for some time.'

'Philip died four years ago,' said Lillian, settling back in the chair, mug of tea clutched before her like her strength and shield. 'It was hard for me, even though we knew it was going to happen for some time. People talk of death being some kind of blessed release. For both the sufferer and those around them. Not for me. I just wanted him back.'

Donovan sipped his tea, said nothing.

'It hit me hard, but it hit Peta hardest. You see, she had always been a daddy's girl, always wanted to be with him whatever he was doing, seek his approval in all things. Well, in most things.'

'She never favoured you?'

Lillian shook her head. 'I think we were too alike.'

'And you never had any more children?'

'Philip was . . . He couldn't. But he was a wonderful father to Peta. That was the most important thing.'

'Even though she wasn't his.'

'As I said. A wonderful man.'

'And he came along after Trevor Whitman?'

'Trevor Whitman and I were never actually an item, as you might say. You have to remember that the Seventies were a different time. It was the era of free love, of radicalism. *The Female Eunuch* and all that. We were liberated, there was no AIDS . . .' She sighed, lost in the past for a few seconds. 'Trevor and I were only ever occasional lovers. He was with Mary Evans for a long time, although such things as formal relationships were frowned on in our progressive, permissive little group.'

'Before she became a lesbian, I presume.'

Lillian almost smiled. 'We all experimented, one way or another.'

'And you found yourself pregnant.'

'Yes.' Another sigh, another sip of tea. 'And suddenly I wasn't so progressive or permissive. I was a university undergraduate flying high who suddenly found herself very earthbound.'

'So what did you do?'

'Well, first there was Mary Evans to consider. She'd already had two abortions through Trevor, both at Trevor's insistence, she always maintained. And when he found out I was pregnant I thought he would insist on me having one, but he said nothing of the sort. Have the baby, we'll bring it up. We'll manage.' She waved her arms about in a vague gesture. 'Whatever. Of course, Mary Evans was furious.'

'Because he seemed to think more of you? Jealousy? Had she wanted children with him?'

'I don't know about that, but she loved him. Passionately. Totally.' Lillian smiled. Her features softened, some of the worry folded away. 'He was a very easy man to love.'

'But you didn't take up his offer.'

'Philip was on the scene by then. And I didn't want my child aborted. I could, as they say now, talk the talk. But that was all. Also, the bombing had happened, the Hollow Men were in disarray and this utopian dream had suddenly turned very sour. Philip offered me security and safety, a future. Love and companionship. Naturally, I took it.'

'And he didn't mind bringing up another man's baby?'

'I think he may have been happier if the baby had been his, but, as I said, he couldn't have children and he knew that. A childhood illness, he always said. So in that respect he was happy. Families, he kept saying, are more than a question of biology. And he proved it.' Another wistful, sad smile. 'And he proved it.'

'And Peta had no idea.'

Lillian shook her head. 'To all intents and purposes Philip was her father. He brought her up, he loved her. She was his daughter. I never felt like I was lying to her, keeping anything from her. It's the same as if she had been a test-tube baby, or through a surrogate. It made no difference.'

Another smile. She seemed about to drift off. Donovan checked his watch. Bring her back. He had work to do.

'And then Trevor Whitman came back.'

She looked up, startled. 'Yes. Well, he'd been in the background all those years, at a distance, of course. That's how we wanted it. He sent money when he had it, presents on her birthday. She always had them but we never told her who they were from. We decided early on that Peta should never meet him while Philip was alive.' Another sigh, heavier this time.

'And with Philip dead he came back on to the scene.'

Anger flashed across Lillian's face. 'It wasn't like that. Never so cut and dried. Trevor was in a bit of a fix. He had discovered something, something awful, and needed help. When he told me what it was I invited him up here straight away.'

Donovan sat back. 'So what had he discovered?'

'He started to get calls. At first he didn't know who they were from, didn't recognize the voice. South African. But they used code words that only an ex-Hollow Man would know. And gradually this person revealed himself. Alan Shepherd. Well, Trevor was stunned. And scared.'

'Why?'

'Because he was a maniac. They were going to throw him out of the Hollow Men when he went off on his own and blew the pub up. They were blamed and he disappeared. Trevor was never prosecuted because he didn't do it. Maurice's father paid for the legal team. There was no evidence and they all had alibis. But the police tried their damnedest. My God, they tried.'

'And now he's back.'

'Yes. But you should know Shepherd doesn't care about the money, or the project. Shepherd just likes to get people to dance to his tune. He's a Fascist. And a psychopath. Put the two together and he's a big problem. All the unrest we've been having recently. Alan's behind it.'

'Why?'

Lillian sighed. 'Trevor says it's Alan's idea of fun.'

'Why didn't Whitman go to the police with this?'

Lillian gave a sad smile. 'Would you believe it? Coming from someone with his track record? Plus, he had no evidence. All he could say was he was getting phone calls. He had to find another way to force it into the open.'

'So that's when you brought in Peta. Gave her some cock-and-bull story and sent her off.' Donovan felt his anger rising. 'What did you expect her to find?'

'Trevor was going to hire a private detective. Snoop around, see what evidence they could uncover. If not that, then stir things up, bring them out in the open. And then we thought of Albion. It was perfect.'

'Except Albion weren't together. So you set your own daughter up. I suppose that was Whitman's idea of irony.'

Lillian slammed her mug down on the floor, spilling tea over the rug. 'We had to do something! People would lose their lives. People have lost their lives. We had to do something . . .' She trailed off, covering her face with her hand, hoping Donovan wouldn't see the tears.

It didn't work. The sobbing overtook Lillian. She curled inwards, shoulders heaving as grief took over. Donovan placed his mug by the side of the sofa, stood up. He wouldn't be getting anything more out of Lillian Knight for quite a while. He turned, made his way to the door.

'Mr Donovan . . .' Her voice was small, weak.

He turned.

'Please find them. Please find Peta. She's my daughter and I love her . . .'

Donovan saw himself out.

Jamal knocked on Peta's door without expecting an answer. He wasn't disappointed. Looking up and down the street, seeing no one, he got the key out, let himself in.

The house had been ripped apart. Furniture overturned, split open, books pulled from shelves, covers ripped off. CDs and DVDs scattered, ornaments shattered. A comprehensive, gleefully destructive job.

The devastation hurt Jamal. Once, in what seemed like another life, he would have been happy to do the wrecking. But not now. Seeing something like this reminded him of how far he had come in such a relatively short space of time.

He went through to the dining room, the kitchen. The same carnage in there.

They had been looking for something, he thought. He had no idea whether they had found it.

Then: a noise from upstairs.

He looked round, trying to think on his feet, decide what to do next. Options flew through his mind like darting sparrows. It might be Peta. Alone and hurt. It might be the people who did this, waiting for whoever came in next. It might be—

'Stay where you are!'

Jamal turned. Three uniformed police officers came running down the stairs carrying batons, wearing protective vests. Another two rushed in from the back of the house. Jamal looked quickly round. He had to do something.

'Stay exactly where you are!'

'Do not move!'

He looked at the front door, made a dash for it. They rushed forward, were on him straight away, pushing him to the floorboards, holding him down, twisting his right arm up his back.

'Thought I told you not to move, you little cunt,' he heard one of them say.

'Next time you'll fuckin' do what you're told, won't you?'

They stepped back. Left him lying there, handcuffed. Jamal screwed his eyes tight shut, waited for the blows to come down on him. It wouldn't be the first time.

'Leave him.'

A voice, female, familiar. He tried to turn his head, couldn't.

'Get him up.' She sounded weary.

He was pulled on to his feet, the handcuffs taken off. He turned round.

There stood Detective Inspector Diane Nattrass. Paul Turnbull's old partner. Joe Donovan's old sparring partner.

Jamal didn't know whether that was good news or not.

She smiled at him. 'Hello Jamal,' she said. 'Long time no see. Mind telling me what's going on?'

32

'Well,' said Donovan, looking round, 'quite the party.'

He stood in the living room of Peta's house. Detective Inspector Diane Nattrass was sitting on the sofa. She was one of the constants in Donovan's life, always the same. No-nonsense suit, hair pulled unfussily back from her face, little or no make-up. All business, unsexed for work. But she had a good heart, Donovan knew. And a razor-sharp brain.

There had been run-ins before. They weren't friends but neither were they enemies. Each had a strong mutual respect for the other. But neither would let that come before their work.

Jamal sat in an armchair opposite her, rubbing his wrists. Neither looked happy. Donovan looked round, took in the devastation. Felt something deep within him dislodge.

'Did you lot do this?' he said.

'What d'you think?' said Nattrass.

Donovan looked at Jamal. 'You OK?'

Jamal looked at Nattrass, thought of speaking, decided against it. Gave a noncommittal shrug, went back to sulking.

'Anyone put the kettle on?' said Donovan.

'Be my guest,' said Nattrass. 'If you can find it. Sit down, Joe. You'd better tell me everything about the case you were working on.'

'And a happy long time no see to you too, Diane,' said Donovan. He sat on the armchair by Jamal. Looked again at the devastation. Thought of the times he had sat in that room, drank coffee, watched DVDs . . .

'Joe?'

He looked up. Nattrass was looking at him, professional-ism softened by concern. 'Tell me what's going on.'

'How come you were here? In Peta's house?'

'A neighbour reported hearing noises, saw men running away from the house. Thought there must have been a break-in, phoned in.'

'Bit mob-handed and high-ranking for a break-in.'

'I saw whose name the house belonged to.'

'And your spider sense started tingling.'

'Just tell me what's going on, Joe.'

He told her about Alan Shepherd and the NUP. Their part in the recent civil unrest. She listened, nodding as he finished.

'Feel free to tell me that's all bullshit.'

'No. It would fit.' Nattrass looked around, seeing the other members of her team, Jamal, making her mind up. She looked back at Donovan. 'We've come across some . . . dis-crepancies in the investigation.'

'How d'you mean?'

Before she could say anything further, a young, sharply suited policeman stepped forward, looked at Nattrass with concern. 'Ma'am,' he said, throwing uncharitable glances towards Donovan, 'with all due respect I strongly advise you not to give details of police business to—' he looked again at Donovan, tried to find an appropriate phrase for him. '—this . . . member of the public.'

Nattrass looked up, surprised at the interruption. Donovan smiled.

'Paul's replacement?' he said.

Nattrass nodded. 'Detective Sergeant Fenton, Joe Donovan.'

Fenton nodded. If his facial expression were a tempera-ture it would have been sub-arctic. Donovan smiled, gave a little wave, looked at Nattrass.

'Very earnest.'

Fenton stepped forward, a look on his face showing Donovan what he would like to do with his opinions.

Nattrass spoke, her voice authoritative. 'He's my new DS. And a bloody good copper. Have some respect, please.'

'Sorry,' said Donovan.

'Good.' Nattrass looked at Fenton. 'Thank you for your input, Stevie. I'll be the judge of who I talk to and what about.'

Fenton, suitably chastised, shrank backwards. Nattrass said nothing until he was out of earshot.

'You were saying?' said Donovan.

'Yes, irregularities. Sooliman Patel, the student who was murdered. We thought it was just a racist attack. Hauled Rick Oaten in, went through everything he had. Not one single shred of evidence linking him or anyone in his party to the attack. Clean as.'

Donovan shrugged. 'So? Maybe he got someone else to do it.'

'Maybe. But with no means and no motive, we couldn't take it any further. And then it got even stranger. We found the car he must have been abducted in. A Rover. Stolen out of town. Torched on some wasteground outside Durham. Forensics went over it. Nothing. Clean.'

'CCTV?' said Donovan.

'Showed four hooded youths in the car. Or rather, four hooded individuals. Gloved, faces covered. No way to tell how old they were or even what race they were. The whole thing seemed like a professional hit. Why, we don't know.'

'Fits in to what I've told you, though. Everything done for a purpose. Get people angry. Stoked up. Destabilize the NUP.'

Nattrass nodded. 'That was the first. Then there was the suicide bomber. Or supposed suicide bomber.'

'What about him?'

Nattrass looked grim, her face taut. 'Safraz Rajput. More inconsistencies than you can mention. Not his car, not his area, nowhere near surfacing on any intelligence profile. It looked like someone had just taken him from where he was, plonked him in a car and blew him up.'

'Jesus.' Donovan tried to imagine it. 'So, instant hate figure, fear on the streets, that sort of thing. The other side destabilized now.'

Nattrass nodded.

Donovan almost laughed. 'I told Peta. She said I shouldn't take a Metro anywhere, leave the house. I told her not to be stupid, that it was all not real.' His voice tailed off. 'I told her . . .'

'Did you know she committed suicide?' Nattrass said eventually.

'Who?'

'The wife of the bomber. Rani, her name was. Rani Rajput. Killed herself. During the night. We've just heard.' Nattrass looked straight ahead while she spoke, her face matching the grey of her suit. Like the sun couldn't reach her.

Donovan sighed. 'This is so fucked up. Have you made any arrests yet?'

'Arrest who? All we've got are niggling inconsistencies. Nothing concrete. No suspect. We've hauled in Abdul-Haq even, but again it was like he'd been taking lessons from Rick Oaten.'

'Not such a daft idea.'

'No. And the attack on the vigil, they'd all been drilled, trained. It was more like a professional hit than a yob attack.'

'So what do we do?' said Donovan.

Nattrass looked up sharply. 'We? We don't do anything. We stop playing cowboys and leave it to the police to sort out.'

'Be my guest,' said Donovan.

Nattrass raised an eyebrow. 'Really? Is this the same Joe Donovan who never passes up an opportunity to get involved in police business and tries his damnedest to fuck up ongoing investigations?'

It was Donovan's turn to smile. 'Ah, that's the old me. Threat of court action, loss of earnings, sharpens the mind. I've learned my lesson. Plus, you're the best there is at what you do, Diane.'

'Why do I not believe you?'

'I don't know. But it's the truth.'

Nattrass reddened slightly. She didn't take compliments well.

'What you going to do next?' said Donovan.

'Bring in Rick Oaten. See what he's got to say for himself so soon before the elections.'

Donovan shook his head. 'He'll be all briefed up by now. You won't get anything out of him. Sharples is the one you want. If you can find him. He's probably disappeared.'

'Out of the region. On business. Apparently.'

'What about pulling in Abdul-Haq? Mary Evans?'

'On what charge? Your say-so? Think about it. Abdul-Haq's a prominent Muslim spokesman. How's that going to look? Mary Evans has lots of friends in the Civic Centre. And she's off on holiday for a few days – we checked. Anyway, I can't go bundling them all off the street, can I?'

'You could pay them a visit.'

Nattrass was getting angry. 'You telling me how to do my job?'

Donovan shook his head. 'No. I'm just . . . Find Peta, Diane. Please.'

Nattrass looked at him, her anger subsiding. 'I'll do my best.' She stood up. 'We'll need you to make a full statement. If you—'

'Not at the moment. I'm just . . . Not at the moment.'

'Come out to the car. One of the uniforms can do it.'

Donovan, seeing he wasn't going to get out of it, reluctantly nodded. He stood up. She ushered him out into the street.

'Oh, by the way,' said Nattrass, looking at the school opposite, the parked cars, anywhere but at Donovan. 'Thanks.'

Donovan frowned. 'For what?'

She looked up. 'Giving Paul a job. He needs something like that.'

Donovan shrugged, tried to pretend it was nothing. 'He's a good bloke. Despite his faults.'

'Which are many.'

'True. But it's a delicate job. I needed someone I could trust.'

Nattrass smiled. 'You're not such a bastard after all, are you, Joe Donovan?'

Donovan smiled. 'I am.'

They reached the car. 'Come on, let's make this as painless as possible.'

Donovan gave his statement. The police cleared out of Peta's house. Donovan saw them go. Jamal watched them, mistrust and dislike strongly etched on his face.

Donovan finished up, went back to the house. Jamal was waiting for him by the doorway. Nattrass caught up with them.

'Now remember,' she said, 'leave this to us. Don't go looking for her yourself. Am I clear?'

'As a beautiful mountain spring.'

'Good.'

She left. Donovan and Jamal watched them drive away. Once they were gone, Jamal turned to Donovan.

'Did you mean that?'

'What?'

'About not going looking for Peta?'

'Did I fuck. Come on, let's go.'

Donovan pulled Peta's front door closed. Gently, like she was inside sleeping and he didn't want to disturb her.

Jason Mason lay on the floor again. He didn't dare move. Not without being told to.

They had been in again. His body was bruised, broken and sore where they had worked on him. Now he lay there, not knowing if it was day or night, not caring, just hoping they wouldn't come back, start again.

But they always did.

The door opened. Jason lay still, eyes closed, tried not to move. Not to breathe, even.

'Get up. Stop fucking around.' That voice again. Major Tom.

Jason stood up. The blanket dropped to the floor. Jason tried not to shiver. Remembered what had happened to him the last time he had shivered without permission. Major Tom crossed the floor, stood before him.

'Bend over.'

Jason bent.

'Stand up straight.'

Jason stood up straight.

Major Tom smiled. Jason didn't move.

Major Tom reached behind his back, brought out two knives. Jason recognized them straight away. Had used them on carcasses enough times. Knew what they could do to skin and tissue.

'See this?' said Major Tom, dancing a blade before Jason's eyes. 'Know what it is? You should do. You're the Butcher Boy.'

Jason nodded.

'Can't hear you.'

'Yes,' he said.

'Better.' He moved in closer. 'I'm going to peel off your skin. Centimetre by centimetre. And you're going to stand there and let me do it. Aren't you?'

Jason was trembling, ready to fall. He knew he couldn't.

'Aren't you?'

'Yuh-yes.'

'Good.' Major Tom placed the blade on Jason's chest. He felt it pierce the skin, felt a trickle of blood run down his front. He wanted to scratch himself; it tickled. He didn't move.

Major Tom laughed. 'You'd let me too, wouldn't you?'

Jason said nothing. He didn't think it was a question that needed an answer. The blades disappeared. In their place was Major Tom's revolver. He spun the chamber, put it to Jason's forehead. Jason's heart was going into overdrive, pounding hard enough to wear itself out. He couldn't let it show. Didn't let it show. Knew what would happen if he did.

He felt the cold metal on his cold skin. Didn't even blink. He closed his eyes.

'Keep your fucking eyes open.'

He opened them. Tried to look past Major Tom's grinning face, tried not to lock eyes with him. Failed. Caught the gaze, flinched away.

Major Tom took the gun away from his face, swung it at the side of his head. Jason went down.

'Don't fall down until I tell you to fall down!'

Jason didn't see the blood spurt from the wound on his forehead, didn't feel the pain that went with it. Only heard the voice. Knew he had to obey the voice.

'Stand up.'

Jason shakily pulled himself to his feet.

'That's better.'

Another blow, this time to the other side of the head. Jason staggered, wanted to fall, stopped himself. Remained on his feet.

Major Tom smiled. 'Good. Nearly there.' He turned, walked towards the door, turned back to Jason. 'I'm going out now. Don't move.'

He went through the door, locking it behind him as he went.

Jason stayed where he was. Standing on legs that felt ready to give way at any second. He ignored the blood running down his face and neck, snaking down to his chest. Ignored the shaking in his legs that threatened to topple him over.

He didn't move, didn't shiver.

Stayed exactly where he was, did exactly as he had been told.

33

Peta opened her eyes. Light stung them closed again. She lay still, breathing shallowly. Pain suffused her body with each intake of air.

She opened her eyes again, slower this time. She squinted, acclimatizing against the light. Tried to move her arms. Tied behind her back. Her legs. Tied at the ankles. She breathed lightly, tried to keep calm. Remembered her police training. Assessed her situation.

She was lying on a floor. Concrete or stone flagging. Cold and hard. She moved her head slowly, tried to look round. Felt knives of pain twist at the base of her skull, blades skewer her back and brain simultaneously, nausea swirl round her head. Blinked, focused. Walls of rough brick and stone, small, filthy windows dancing with dusty light, wooden beams, rafters. Farming and garden implements round the walls, old and rusted. Smelling of decay and neglect.

Peta tried to pull herself into a sitting position, felt blood pounding round her head. Another wave of nausea hit her. She was wearing a gag; she couldn't be sick. She swallowed down hard, and again, willed her chest to stop palpitating. When she was sure the sickness had passed, she put her hand on the floor, balanced her weight on it, began to push herself up.

Sitting, she took another look round. The door at the far end looked big, old. But solid. Locked.

Peta weighed up her options. She wasn't dead. Yet. Either

they wanted her for something or hadn't decided what to do with her yet. She clung to that fact like a life raft.

She tried to trace the sequence of events after she had entered Mary Evans's office, looked for clues, combed her memory for a key, something she could work with, when she heard something. Bolts were being moved on the other side of the heavy door, locks turned. She stared, waited, barely breathing. The door opened. A figure entered. Peta recognized the figure.

Mary Evans. She crossed to Peta, undid her gag.

'Mary?' Peta's throat felt rusted over. 'What's, what's going on?'

Mary Evans looked quickly round as if being observed. 'This wasn't my idea. Any of it. I just want you to know that. OK?'

'What? What are you talking about?'

'You know what.'

'No, I don't . . . What's happening?'

Mary Evans strangled a laugh. 'Oh, come on, you know. Don't pretend to be stupid.'

'I'm not stupid. I don't know. One minute I'm investigating nuisance phone calls, the next . . .'

Mary Evans's expression changed. She didn't look like the same person Peta had met previously. 'You think anyone was fooled by that story?'

'Story? It was my job.'

'No.' Anger was rising in Mary Evans. 'It was a useless cover story. And he couldn't resist. Couldn't have sent a clearer message if he had used UPS. So fucking manipulative. Even with you.'

Peta said nothing, tried to think.

'What did I tell you? When you came to see me? About the past?'

'That it was dangerous. You warned me.'

'And you didn't bloody listen, did you?'

'You phoned me, wanted to meet me . . .'

'Because you wouldn't do what you were told. Wouldn't listen.' Her voice came in hissy stabs.

Peta frowned. More came back to her. Whitman. Her mother. She groaned. 'Oh, my God . . .'

'What?'

'Whitman. Trevor Whitman . . .'

Mary leaned closer, interested. 'What about him?'

'He's . . .' She didn't want to say it. She still hadn't come to terms with it in her own mind. 'Nothing.'

'Your father? That what you wanted to say?' Mary Evans's voice was dark-edged, an obsidian knife. Her eyes caught the dull light from the blades on the wall.

Peta nodded.

Mary Evans smiled, experiencing a twisted triumph. 'And everyone knew but you. Even your own mother.' She spat the word out. 'Even she wouldn't tell you.' Still kneeling, she reached out her hand, touched her face. Her fingers felt hard and cold. She locked eyes with Peta. There was no tenderness like there had been the previous time she had done this. No light in her eyes, only its absence. 'He didn't want children with me. Not good enough for him. Your mother was beautiful. I was just . . . available.'

Peta said nothing.

Mary Evans continued, her voice small, contained, the measured ticking of a timer on a bomb. 'You know he made me pregnant?'

'No.'

'Twice. Wouldn't let me have them. Forced me to get rid of them.' Still stroking. 'Stopped me from ever having any more. Took that away from me. A whole part of my life gone because of him. I blame him. And I hate him.' Her hand gripped Peta's chin, her grip surprisingly hard. 'So beautiful. Like your mother. Like your father. I'll have to hate you as well.'

'It's not my fault.'

'No. It's not.' She shrugged. 'But what can you do?'

'He's not my father,' said Peta, anger giving her strength. 'My father's dead. He died four years ago. Trevor Whitman's nothing. Just a fucking sperm donor.'

The light intensified in Mary Evans's eyes. She almost smiled. 'You don't like him.'

'No.'

The smile blossomed on Mary Evans's face. Hard, containing something beyond anger, something dark, twisted, unreadable. 'He's a bastard. A manipulator. A user. A hurter. And he deserves to fucking suffer for it. And he will. He deserves everything that's—' She reined herself in, stopped talking.

'What? What's going to happen to him?'

'Don't worry about that.' The anger gone, her face closed once more. 'Worry about yourself, not him.'

Peta shook her head. 'I was just working for him. Just a job . . .' Peta closed her eyes, too overwhelmed to continue. 'What's going on? Please. Just tell me what's going on.'

'You just pretending you don't know? Getting me to talk, like he would?'

'No. I really don't know. Why are you here? What d'you get out of this?'

Mary Evans looked at her, deciding whether she was telling the truth or not. Gave her the benefit of the doubt. 'I had objections at first. Of course I did. I was against, fighting it all the way.'

'Fighting what?'

'Don't pretend you don't know. The redevelopment.'

Peta frowned. 'In the West End? People are killing each other, bombing, kidnapping, because of that?'

Mary Evans nodded. 'More jobs. Better housing. They've given me assurances.'

'Assurances. You can't reconcile what's going on with what you're going to get out of it. The ends don't justify the means.'

'Just because I want a better tomorrow I'm not some soft-headed liberal. There's more than one kind of revolution. Remember what I said when you came to see me. By any means necessary. But this is different. This is personal.'

'How?'

'They wanted me in. Sway the local community, convince them it was a good plan. I couldn't. But then Trevor Whitman became involved. And they know what I think of him. So they offered me a deal. My cooperation in exchange for the chance to destroy him. And I will.'

'How?'

'Through you.'

Peta's heart flipped like a dying fish cleavered on a wooden slab. She looked into the eyes of Mary Evans and saw the dancing dark lights of madness.

Peta's voice was so small and weak it could barely make it out of her body. 'What's going to happen to me?'

Mary Evans looked at her as if about to speak again. From the look on her face, Peta wasn't sure she wanted to hear it. She re-gagged Peta, stood up, looked again at the door.

'You should have listened, Peta. I can't be held responsible for what happens to you if you don't listen.'

Mary Evans left, closing, bolting and locking the door behind her.

Peta sighed, sank back to the stone floor.

Tried hard not to scream.

Failed.

★

Donovan felt like Superman.

Staring down at the model before him, he was a child again, reading his comics. It reminded him of the miniature Kryptonian city Superman kept in his Fortress of Solitude. Contemporary yet futuristic, and on a staggering scale.

'Impressive, isn't it?'

Donovan turned to look at the owner of the voice. Colin Baty stood next to him, beaming down like a proud father at a just-born son.

'Very,' said Donovan. 'I'm sure people would kill to get in on this.'

Baty laughed like it was the funniest thing he had heard all day. All week, even. Donovan winced. 'I'm sure they would, Mr, er . . .'

'Donovan. Joe Donovan. And thank you for seeing me at such short notice. Especially today. I'm sure there's plenty of other things you should be doing.'

'Always have time to talk to one of the press.'

Donovan smiled, said nothing.

They were standing in a room in the Civic Centre. Donovan had turned up to see Baty using his journalist disguise once again. Told him he was interested in the unique new vision he had for the West End of Newcastle. Baty, his vanity immediately flattered, had ushered him deep into the building, down wood-panelled corridors lined with glass display cases and green leather banquettes. He had stopped to greet seemingly everyone they came across with a handshake or a kiss, a joke or a mock insult, all delivered at the booming pitch of a hard-of-hearing Brian Blessed. The man, thought Donovan, was a walking bonhomie machine. Or at least a politician the day before election day.

'This,' said Donovan, still looking at the model, 'is going to be huge. Has it got planning permission yet?'

'Not yet. But I think it will. It'll mean jobs for the city, for an area that's crying out for them. Employment, housing, leisure, it's going to be wonderful.'

'Looks huge.'

Baty smiled, accompanied it with a rumbling, smoky chortle. 'It is. Going to rewrite the map. They thought the Metro Centre was something. Wait till they get a load of this.'

'But aren't you worried,' said Donovan, crossing his arms, adopting his best journalist pose, 'that it's going to tear the heart out of the local community? That the jobs and housing will go to those outside the area? That it'll just be another extension of the urban gentrification taking place in the city centre? Another nail in the coffin of the indigenous working class? Isn't that why there are all the protests against it?'

Baty frowned. 'Who did you say you worked for?'

'I didn't.'

'You look familiar. But I haven't seen you on this beat before. Where do I know you from?'

'We bumped into each other the other day. Just briefly. Abdul-Haq's offices?'

Whatever was left of Baty's bonhomie drained completely away. His forehead gathered into a suspicious knot. 'Who are you?'

'I work for a company called Albion. My name's Joe Donovan.'

The frowning face turned openly hostile. 'This is nothing to do with, with this.' He swept an arm out over the model. 'I know what this is about.' Now he no longer had to keep up the friendly veneer, his voice dripped threat, carried the ugliness of violence. 'Had one of your lot come to see me the other day. Told her where to get off too.'

'And now she's disappeared.'

'Good. Best place for her. Like what's going to happen to you when I phone down to the front desk.'

'You don't understand. She disappeared after asking questions about Trevor Whitman.'

'And you think I took her?'

'No. But she was asking the people you've been getting involved with over this project.' He chanced his arm with a lie. 'Abdul-Haq?'

'What about him?'

'She disappeared after talking to him.'

A look of horror passed over Baty's face. He shook it off. Put himself back in control. 'And you think he did it? Rubbish.'

'You do know Abdul-Haq used to be in the Hollow Men with Trevor Whitman? Hasn't stopped you from making deals with him.'

'I know he was. He's come a long way since then. And he had nothing to do with my brother's death.'

'Neither did Trevor Whitman.'

'Bullshit.'

'The person you want is Alan Shepherd. He's back. He's working for the NUP now. Who are hotly contesting your seat in tomorrow's election. Funny how these things have a habit of joining together.'

'Bullshit. Now get out of here or I'll have you thrown out.'

Donovan didn't move. He felt a desperate anger rising, tried to channel it, control it. 'Her name is Peta Knight.'

'I know.'

'She's Trevor Whitman's daughter.'

Surprise registered on Baty's face. He quickly smothered it. 'So? You that worried, call the police.'

'I did. Detective Inspector Nattrass is handling the case. An old friend of mine. She was very interested in what I had to say about Abdul-Haq. And Alan Shepherd.'

'Get out.'

'I think you can expect a call from her some time soon.'

'Get out.'

Donovan still didn't move. 'Course, you can tell me all about it now. Get it off your chest. What you know.'

Baty's red face had turned almost purple. He turned towards Donovan. 'That's it. I don't need security, I'll throw you out meself, you little cunt.'

'Don't worry, I'm leaving. I'll see myself out.' Donovan made for the door, turned. 'And if I find you've got anything to do with my friend's disappearance, you're going to wish you'd never seen me. Oh, and good luck tomorrow.'

He was off before Baty could do anything else. Down the stairs and into the car park. Jamal was waiting in the Scimitar. He looked up as Donovan got in.

'Well?'

Donovan shrugged, sighed. 'I'd say he doesn't know anything. He's a bastard, but he doesn't know anything.'

'So where next?'

Donovan turned the engine over. Peta's face kept jumping in front of his eyes. He wished he could see her, talk to her. David swam into vision also. He felt guilty because he hadn't been giving his son all the attention. But he would. As soon as he found Peta. Made sure she was safe.

'We wait for a break,' he said.

'An' when will that be?'

'I wish I knew.'

34

Abdul-Haq stood on the cobblestones of the Mill Dam conservation area on the south side of the River Tyne in South Shields. The river was before him, lapping along past the ferry terminal and the ship repair and fit-out yard. Behind him was the old, stone-built 1860s Customs House from when South Shields was a thriving dock, now a Grade II listed building turned theatre and restaurant. Harton Staithes, the old coal depot turned retail, leisure, business and housing development, was at the side of him. Market Dock was further along, all offices and housing. Everywhere he looked he saw money. His money. God is indeed great.

But, substantial though it was, it was nothing compared with what he was going to make out of the West End of Newcastle. It was the most ambitious project he had ever undertaken, both in terms of scale and financial reward. He had been looking for something to stand as his legacy, a way to leave his mark for history. And this was it. A once-in-a-lifetime deal. So close to fruition. So close. He just had to keep his nerve, play his designated part. Nothing could be allowed to go wrong. Nothing.

He had dressed down so he couldn't be identified: jeans, trainers and a short-sleeved cotton shirt. Eyes squinting behind sunglasses. Arms folded, standing still. The car, an anonymous Fiesta, behind him. Further up the bank were Waqas and Omar, sitting behind the darkened glass of their 4×4. Tooled up, ready for trouble. They had checked he hadn't been followed, wasn't being observed. He wouldn't be. They were good at their jobs.

He wasn't alone long. Moving slowly over the cobble-stones, coming to a slow halt beside the Fiesta, a Vauxhall Vectra, as anonymous as the Fiesta. The back door opened slightly. Abdul-Haq took that as his cue. He crossed to the car, got in the back, closed the door behind him.

Mr Sharples sat beside him, Major Tom in the passenger seat, one of the rank and file driving, a woollen hat covering his bald head.

'You were not followed.' Mr Sharples spoke the words as a statement, not a question.

Abdul-Haq replied he had not been.

'Good.' Mr Sharples nodded. 'Congratulations on bringing in Whitman's daughter. A clean operation.'

'The fence is dead.' Abdul-Haq tried to keep his voice flat.

Sharples shrugged. 'I doubt the police will be overly troubled by that. But Whitman is still out there.'

'So is this Joe Donovan. My boys failed to drive him off the road.'

'Unfortunate. But we work with the situation as it stands.'

'Where is Whitman?'

'Where we can see him,' said Sharples, voice as cold, as smooth, as always. Unruffled. 'He's got Richie with him. Richie Vane.'

Abdul-Haq couldn't keep the surprise off his face.

'He must need all the allies he can get.'

'And he must be really desperate.'

'Perhaps not. Whitman has Richie out on the street. We think he's looking for something.'

'What?'

'We don't know yet. But the situation is being monitored. I have someone ready to step in if needs be.'

Abdul-Haq nodded, wiped his brow of sweat. 'And no doubt Joe Donovan has contacted the police about the daughter's disappearance.'

'No doubt. Oaten will soon be brought in for questioning.'

'But—'

Sharples turned to him, sun glinting off his round glasses, making them look like miniature spinning blades. 'Are you worrying, Gideon? Hmm? Wanting to back out? Getting too much for you?'

'No, no . . . It's just . . . things are coming to a head. I'm just . . . anxious.'

'Don't fuck up on me, Gideon. Not now.'

'I won't. You know I won't.'

Sharples scrutinized Abdul-Haq, who tried not to move or even blink while he did so. He must have found what he was looking for in his face. He gave a small nod.

'Good.' Sharples sat back. 'Oaten's brief is on standby, ready for the call. He'll be with Oaten the whole time, insist on an interview at the office so no media can be alerted. It's taken care of. Whitman and Richie are being monitored. Action will be taken when it is deemed appropriate.' Another look at him. 'Don't worry, Gideon. Everything is in hand. Just play your part.'

Abdul-Haq nodded, ready to ask more questions.

'Time to go,' said Sharples. 'I'm supposed to be out of the region on business while Oaten is questioned.' He smiled. 'I've enjoyed our little chat. We don't do it often enough.'

The driver came round to the side, opened the car door. Abdul-Haq got out. The driver got back in, drove away. Sharples had his briefcase on his lap, looking through papers. Didn't even acknowledge Abdul-Haq as he passed.

He waited until the car was on the road and gone before he got back in to the Fiesta. Sweating from more than the heat.

He turned over the engine, said a silent prayer for strength, drove off. Waqas and Omar behind him.

Amar was back in Camp David. The lunchtime crowd was different from the night-time one, more relaxed, mixed. Lunch-breakers of all genders and persuasions mingling with hardened cruisers. Some buttoned-up suits making tentative fantasy forays over a beer and a sandwich before going back to work, their office cubicles as cramped and confined as their closets.

Amar nursed his Becks, measured out his sips. Waited. He had spent the morning monitoring the phone lines, hunting without success for Whitman and Peta, listening for anything that could have been relevant, and above all trying to contact Kev.

He had left message after message but his mobile was turned off. Eventually, when Amar had been about to give up, a call. Kev. Amar told him he needed to see him. Tried not to be too heavy; he didn't want to spook him. He suggested Camp David. Kev was all for it.

Amar kept checking the door every few seconds, time crawling slower than a slug on gravel. Eventually Kev arrived.

He saw Amar straight away, gave a smile so wide and natural, like showing off a skill he had only recently acquired.

'Hi,' he said and kissed Amar on the mouth.

Amar was almost too surprised to respond. He looked at him. Kev seemed almost a different person from a few nights previously. Then introspective, tormented, striking a chord with Amar. Now bouncy and happy, a human Labrador. He was even dressed differently. Still jeans and boots, but a new, long-sleeved T-shirt in a darker, softer style.

'You look well,' said Amar.

'I feel great,' said Kev. 'For the first time in, oh, ages.

Ever.' The happy puppy smile again. He reached out, placed his hand over Amar's, clenched it. 'Great.'

Amar ordered another two Becks, handed one to Kev. 'So where've you been since I last saw you?'

'Here and there,' said Kev, necking the bottle. 'I came down here again, hung around, met lots of interesting people.' His eyes twinkled. 'Know what I mean?'

Amar knew.

'I've packed in my job, I'm . . .' He stopped, a darker thought passing through him. 'I'm looking for somewhere else to live. I feel good.' Another squeeze of the hand. 'All down to you.'

'Glad to hear it.'

'Right.' Kev looked round, smiling again, expectant, as if ready to embark on an adventure. 'So. What's happenin'?'

Amar looked him square in the eye. 'I need to talk to you.'

Kev shrugged. 'So talk.'

Amar looked around. 'Not here. Let's go back to mine.'

An even bigger smile this time. 'Thought you'd never ask.'

'Not for that. This is serious. Drink up.'

Amar drained his bottle, Kev, looking confused and slightly wary, did likewise. They left the bar.

Richie Vane sat on a bench at the bottom of Westgate Road, staring over at the Lit and Phil Building, eating a Mark Toney's sugar cone as people walked past him. The sun was shining, the girls wearing short skirts and pretty dresses. No one had asked him to move, no one had stared at him, called him names, made fun of him. Usually, he would consider that to be a good day.

But not today. Not with everything else that was going on.

He had made some calls, hooked Whitman up with a guy
he knew dealt in guns out of the back of a motorbike shop
on Westgate Road. Richie hadn't wanted to accompany
him, not wanting to even be near guns, never mind firing
them. Instead he had walked round for a bit, finally settling
on the bench, trying, with his ice cream, to enjoy the day.
And failing.

Two women walked past. Young, nicely dressed, with
clean hair and strong smiles. Richie watched them go past.
They either didn't see him or tried to ignore him. He licked
his cone, closed his eyes. There would have been a time, in
a past so distant and unreal it felt either dreamed or seen only
in a film, when girls like that wouldn't have ignored him.
They would have smiled, might even have talked to him.
Given him their phone number and even expected him to
call. Another life. When he was young and handsome. Not
old and invisible.

Richie wasn't thick. He knew what was going on. With
Mary and Gideon and Alan. Trevor had told him. And what
his old friends were doing was upsetting him in a way that
no amount of sunshine could compensate for. He could feel
his hard-won consciousness and serenity begin to fragment,
drift again. The bottle was pulling at him again, telling him
he shouldn't be sitting here with an ice cream in his hands.
He needed something proper to take the worries away, rein-
troduce him to those small, sustainable euphorias he had
tried not to miss so much. And the weed was calling too.
Ready to provide him with, if not answers, then the
becalmed need not to ask so many difficult questions. His
refuges, his comfortable caves. The last places he should go
to.

Trevor Whitman didn't need him. Not really. He was
only getting in the way. Why not just get up, walk away?
Trevor wouldn't notice him gone. And Peta, well, he'd made

a promise but he hadn't been able to keep it. Just another one. Join the queue. Walk away. And he could properly enjoy the day then.

Yeah, that sounded about right. Cool.

He got up, thinking of St Hilda's Trust, the people who had patched his life back together. Who could do it again. He threw his ice cream in a litter bin, thought how good it would be to hold a can right now, a real cold, real strong one, Carlsberg Special, Tennants Super, something like that. He closed his eyes, shook his head, not wanting to be seduced. Opened them again.

And there stood Mary Evans.

'Hello, Richie.' She gave a smile that matched the day.

Richie was too startled to speak. He just stared.

Mary Evans kept smiling. 'What's the matter? Not pleased to see me?'

Richie frowned. He should run back up the hill, get Trevor. Tell him who was here, bring them together so they could talk.

'Trevor . . . Trevor's just up there . . .' He pointed up Westgate Road.

'I know. But it's not him I want to see, it's you. How you doing, Richie? Haven't seen you in a while.'

'No . . . Good. Yeah, I've been good.'

'They been treating you right at St Hilda's?'

Richie nodded.

'Good.' Mary Evans looked around. 'Were you off some-where, Richie?'

'Yeah, I was, was goin' back there.'

'St Hilda's?'

'Yeah.'

Her smile was still dazzling. 'I'll give you a lift. Come on.' She stretched out her arm, touched his. He made to walk away with her but something stopped him.

'What?' she said.

There was something, a niggle in his brain . . . Something not right . . .

'What's the matter, Richie? It's me. Mary.'

She smiled again, even brighter if it was possible. He had always liked Mary. She had been a good friend to him. He had wanted her to be more than a friend at one point, but she had always told him that was impossible. So they had become friends. Just friends. And she was a good person. Despite what Trevor said.

He returned the smile.

'Come on, then.'

Richie allowed her to lead him away, her hand tenderly placed on his arm, like a mother guiding an errant son back to safety.

Later, Trevor Whitman stood on the same spot, looking round. A greasy old Tesco's carrier bag clenched in his fist. He had half expected Richie not to have waited, to have wandered off somewhere, but it was still irritating now that it had happened. But he didn't have time to think about that.

He took his mobile out, found the number he wanted. Started calling.

Wondering what he would say when Joe Donovan answered.

35

Kev sat on the sofa at Amar's flat, waited expectantly. His buoyant mood had subsided the further they had gone from the bar as he picked up the tension coming off Amar. Amar hadn't spoken on the walk. Kev perched on the edge of the cushion, like a death-row inmate waiting for a pardon, knowing that, in the battle of hope and experience, hope always lost.

It's AIDs, Kev thought. That's what he's going to tell me. Just started enjoying myself, finding out who I really am, then this.

Amar emerged from the kitchen, two mugs of coffee in his hands. He set them down, joined Kev on the sofa. Tried a smile. Didn't reach his eyes.

'Just tell me,' said Kev. 'Say what you've gotta say. I know what it is, anyway. What you're gonna say.'

Amar frowned. 'What?'

Kev took a few deep breaths. 'AIDs. It is, isn't it? It is. You can tell us.'

Amar almost laughed out loud. He shook his head. 'No, Kev. Nothing like that.'

'What, then?'

Amar looked at the coffee mug in front of him. 'I know who you're involved with. What you've done, what you're doing.'

The slight euphoria Kev had allowed himself to feel at Amar's AIDs denial dissipated completely. This was worse than AIDs. His heart felt like a stone in his chest, his legs unable to support him if he stood up. He said nothing, waited for Amar to speak again.

'The NUP. You're a member, aren't you?'

Kev tried to keep his breathing under control. 'You know that. You saw the tats the other night. We talked about it.'

'Yeah, I know, but it's more than that, isn't it? You're more than just a member. Just a voter.'

Kev swallowed. His throat was dry, ashes. 'Not any more. When I left my job I left the party. An' everythin' I was doin' for them. That's a part of me life that's over.'

Amar sighed, nodded. 'Shame. Because I need your help.'

'To do what?'

Amar put down the mug that had been on the way to his lips. 'I've got to trust you. I mean, really trust you.'

Kev was confused, wrong-footed, mentally running to keep up with the way the conversation was going. 'I'm not a thief nor nothin'. Not gonna run off with your PIN number, like.'

Amar managed a smile. 'Never thought you were.'

Kev relaxed at the sight of the smile. But only slightly.

'You know the other night, when I told you I worked in IT? Well, I didn't tell you the whole thing.'

Kev shrugged. 'Did you not think I'd see you again, then?'

'Not like this. I use computers but I also do surveillance, monitoring, all sorts of stuff. I work for an information brokerage. We're like—' he shrugged '—private detectives. But a bit better.'

Kev's eyes widened.

'We're working on a case at the moment. And it's become very . . . complicated. Not to mention dangerous.' Amar stopped talking, let that sink in.

'How?'

'We think the NUP have taken one of my colleagues. Kidnapped her, I suppose. We don't know whether she's . . . if she's OK, or anything. But they've got her. We want her back. And we need your help.'

'But I've left them.'

'They've taken my colleague. They might have taken someone else, we just don't know. They've tried to kill another colleague of mine. They've also murdered a fence on Westgate Road and kidnapped a boy.'

Kev felt butterflies in his stomach. 'Which boy?'

'His name's Jason. He's the one we think you and your gang were looking for.'

The name hit Kev like a hammer. 'They've got him? Aw, no . . .'

Amar frowned, confused by Kev's reactions. 'Why are you upset? You were looking for him.'

'Yeah, but . . . I was gonna, gonna let him get away again . . .'

Amar's eyes lit up. 'Did he stab you?'

Kev, his face downcast, nodded. 'I let him. It was, was the only way to let him escape.'

'They wanted you to do something, or make him do something and you couldn't, that right?'

Kev nodded again.

'They've got him now.'

Kev looked up. 'And your friend.'

Amar nodded. 'We know they've been behind all the racist attacks recently. They're planning something big to coincide with the election. Something that could tip the city over the edge, start a full-scale war on the streets. My partner Peta, we think she found out what it was and they've taken her. How am I doing so far? Am I right?'

Kev felt his whole world collapsing around him. His face was screwed up as if in pain, like he was dodging falling

shells, exploding walls and ceilings, dead and dying bodies.
Bodies aflame, screaming . . .

'Kev?'

He looked up. Amar was staring at him, concerned. Kev
felt tears well in his eyes. Fought them back. 'You're right,'
he said, his voice dry from dust and debris, 'that's what
they're plannin'. Major Tom's had everyone at the farm for
weeks, drillin' them like they were marines, gettin' them to
be like an army. An' I . . . I was part of it.'

'To what end?'

'Send them out on the streets on election night. Where
the, the immigrants an' that lived. With guns. Real guns
with real bullets. An' anyone who gets in the way, we were
gonna get rid of them.' He looked at his cooling coffee in
disbelief, as if he couldn't believe the words that were
coming out of his own mouth, as if he had been part of it.

'Jesus . . .' said Kev, as if suddenly seeing daylight after a
lifetime under ground. 'Killin' all those people . . .' Kev felt
a wave of emotion build within him. He tried to hold it
back, couldn't. 'Oh, God, I'm sorry, I'm sorry . . .'

'What are you sorry about? What did you do?' Amar's
voice was quiet, a priest in the confessional.

Kev saw the student again. Sooliman, his name was.
Lying on the floor. Breath leaving his body for the last time.
Major Tom smiling, putting down the bat, wiping his forehead. Hard work this, he had said. We'll have earned our
beer tonight. The others laughing. Kev joining in, wanting
to be one of them, but inside knowing that he had crossed a
line. A line he desperately wanted to get back behind.
Knowing that he had become something else, something he
didn't like, couldn't face. Knowing in that moment that he
wanted out.

'Kev?'

'I can't . . . You wouldn't . . .'

'You can tell me.'

'It's awful. That student, that boy . . . I know who killed him. I was, was with them.' Tears sprang to Kev's eyes. He made no effort to hold them back.

'Jesus . . . You . . .'

'Major Tom. The guy in charge. It was him. I was just, just there. But I may as well have killed him. I did nothing to stop it.'

Amar said nothing.

'I'm sick, I'm disgustin' . . . I'm . . . I'm . .' Kev cried. Let it all out in huge, racking sobs. 'So,' he said eventually, 'what you goin' to do with me? Turn me in? Hand me over to the cops?'

'Why would I do that?'

'Because I'm a, a murderer, a killer . . .' The tears started again.

Amar sat in silence until Kev was cried out. He wiped his eyes with his sleeve.

'You handin' me in, then?'

'No.'

Kev looked up.

'Wuh-why not? I need to be punished.'

'Seems like you're punishing yourself enough for that. Let it go, Kev. You did something horrible. Now's your chance to atone for that.'

Kev looked at him, light in his eyes.

'I need your help, Kev. You can turn yourself in later, but I need your help.'

Kev said nothing.

'The farm? Where's that?'

'In, in Northumberland.' Kev sniffed back the remaining tears. 'Major Tom's runnin' it.'

Amar nodded. 'D'you know where it is? That's probably where they'll be holding Peta.'

'And Jason.' Kev thought. 'Shit, Jason . . . I know what they were goin' to do with him . . .'

'What?'

'Aw, Jesus . . .'

'What?'

'Make him a suicide bomber. A martyr for the cause.'

'Shit . . .' Amar rubbed his eyes, like he couldn't believe what he was hearing. 'This is . . . this is so fucked up . . .'

'So what d'you want me to do?'

'Go back to the farm,' he said. 'Find Peta. Get her out of there.'

'And Jason.'

'Him too.'

'Then get back here. We'll inform the police.'

'Wuh-what about me?'

Amar smiled. 'You'll be a hero. Does that sound like atonement?'

Kev tried to smile. It didn't go far. Back to the farm. Back to his old life. His heart sank at the thought. He knew what they did to traitors and spies. Especially spies.

Kev thought of the student again, saw the flames. And through the flames, thought of that atonement. Peace. He could make up for what he did in the biggest and best way possible. He had no choice. He had to do it.

'Yeah,' he said, 'sounds simple.'

Amar smiled, put his hand on Kev's leg. 'Thanks, Kev. You're doing the right thing.'

Kev said nothing. Didn't trust himself to speak.

'Right,' said Amar, taking his hand away and making to stand up. 'Let's get—'

'Just a minute.'

Amar looked at Kev.

'Put your hand back where it was.'

'Kev, we don't have time for—'

'Please.'

Amar looked into Kev's eyes. Saw what was going on there. Understood.

'Please.'

Kev moved closer. Amar felt a hand on his body, a mouth on his mouth. Felt a need emanating from Kev that was more than just sexual.

Amar knew what Kev wanted, knew how to help. That torment that Amar had first recognized was still there. The same need he recognized in himself.

They came together, their mutual needs too strong to resist.

Mary Evans sat on the bank of the Tyne, looked at Richie. He was staring out ahead. She didn't know if he saw the green trees and fields of Ryton Willows on the other side of the river, or something else entirely, something not in the physical world.

She had brought him to the Tyne Riverside Country Park. A green and naturally beautiful part of the city, surprisingly just a few minutes away from the West End of Newcastle. Nature reserves, trails, a leisure centre and restaurant. Space. And peace.

And it would all go when the new development went through.

She summoned up a smile. Felt any remaining warmth, empathy slide off like a silk dressing gown falling to the ground. Concentrated on what she was here for. What she had to do. 'Remember when we used to come here, Richie? When we were students?'

Richie, still staring ahead, nodded.

'We used to lie here, just you, me and as many mushrooms as we could find. Remember?'

Richie gave a small laugh, nodded, rocking back and forward.

'We used to say that when we were in charge, we'd make all the drugs legal, put them on the National Health.'

Another nod, rocking. 'I tried . . . I wanted you to be, to be my girlfriend. This is, is where I asked you . . .'

She sighed. Tried to ignore the residual fluttering in her chest. No time for sentimentality. This was work. This was important. 'I know. I remember.'

'An' you . . . You said no.'

She felt impatience rise within, tamped it down. Kept her voice sweet. 'That was then, Richie. Things were, were difficult then.'

Richie said nothing, continued to rock.

'But they were good times, though. Wished they had never ended.'

Richie stopped rocking. Turned to face her. 'Why did you bring me here?'

The fluttering became a beating of fierce wings. She swallowed hard. 'Because . . . because this was always our special place. And because I've always, always liked you, Richie.'

She reached across, touching his greasy hair, stroking it, trying not to let her revulsion show.

Richie looked at her outstretched arm, felt the touch of her hand. His eyes widened, he began to shake. 'But not . . . not like that. You said. Then. You were never my girlfriend. Always Trevor's.'

Mary Evans sat forward, stroked her hand down his equally greasy face and on to his shoulder, kept a smile on her face, tried to calm him. 'It, it could be like that, Richie. It's not too late.'

He stopped rocking, looked at her.

'Really?'

Mary Evans nodded, concentrating, keeping the mask in place. This was the difficult bit. 'Yes, Richie. Just a, a couple of things to get out of the way first. Then we can be together. Properly.'

Richie frowned. 'But you're, you're a, a lesbian.'

Mary Evans smiled. She noticed her hand was shaking. She thought of what she had to lose, had to gain. The shaking stopped. 'People change,' she said.

Richie turned to look at her, a pathetic hope in his eyes, brightening up his ruined face. There would have been a time when that look would have touched her, made her waver. But not any more. The things she had done, would do . . . She was far beyond that now.

'There's just something you've got to do for me first.'

'What?'

'Trevor . . . he's got something in his head at the moment. Something he's doing, am I right?'

Richie nodded.

'He's . . .' Richie stopped himself, looked at Mary Evans like a guilty child caught doing something he shouldn't have. 'I promised not to tell.'

Another smile. Those wings beating, tearing to get out. 'It's OK, Richie. You can tell me.'

'He said you're . . .' Richie's features darkened. 'You're doin' somethin' bad.'

Mary Evans fought with the rising tide of emotion building in her chest. Kept smiling. 'Is that what Trevor said? Oh, come on, Richie, it's me. Mary. Do you think I'd do something bad? Honestly?'

Richie frowned, thinking hard. Jesus, he looked pathetic, she thought. He quickly looked up, shook his head.

'That's right. Now, you can tell me what Trevor's doing, can't you?'

Richie looked at her, unsure. She gave another smile.

'Come on, Richie. If you can't tell me, who can you tell?'

Richie made his mind up. 'He's . . . It's about some land or houses or something. An' his, his daughter . . . She's been taken.'

Mary stiffened at the word 'daughter'. The wings inside her flapped a different beat. She wanted a cigarette. 'Right. Anything else?'

Richie screwed up his face in concentration. Again he looked childlike, this time a child who desperately wants to please. 'An' he's, he's got a gun.'

Mary Evans tensed. 'What for?'

Richie looked straight at her. 'Dunno. Protection, he said.' His voice was tiny, cowed.

Mary Evans stared at him.

'I . . . I was just goin'. Leavin' them. Goin' back to St Hilda's. I didn't . . . didn't want to be with him any more. It upset me too much.'

'Don't worry about that.' The words came out absently. Mary Evans's mind was spinning, calculating her next move.

Richie frowned again. 'I . . . I was watchin' you, you know. Lookin' out for you.'

Those wings, back again. 'What d'you mean?'

'The way you looked out for me, y'know, looked after me. I was at your office. I saw that girl go in. Peta. She's Trevor's daughter, you know.'

'I know.'

'Aye. She went in. An', an' them two blokes come out. An' then Trevor. He was there. That's why I went with him. 'Cos he was there.' He gave a shy smile. 'So is that it? Are we boyfriend and girlfriend now?'

'Not quite.' She struggled, kept her voice even.

'How d'you mean?'

Mary Evans took Richie in her arms. Confused at first, he nestled into her arms, snuggling down. 'I looked after you for years, Richie. Made sure you got help, somewhere to live. You were like a . . . child. A son, I suppose, that I felt responsible for.' She kissed him on the forehead.

Richie rocked backwards and forwards, a soporific smile on his face.

Then abruptly she pulled away from him, stared straight into his eyes. She had stopped smiling. Her eyes were hard, cold. Like a look from them could freeze the Tyne. 'But you're not, are you, Richie? You're not my child. I'm not responsible for you.'

'What . . . what d'you mean?'

'You're an adult. An adult who fucked up his life. And has no one to blame but himself.'

She stood up, throwing him off her in the process. He looked up at her like a dog about to be beaten.

'What . . . what . . . I don't understand . . .'

'No, Richie, you don't. You never did.'

'What . . . what you goin' to do to me?'

'Me? Nothing.' She looked round. Two men detached themselves from behind nearby bushes. Waqas and Omar. They moved towards Richie.

'Goodbye,' said Mary Evans. 'I used to like you, but you're too pathetic for words.' She walked away.

Didn't see the look of incomprehension on Richie's face as it turned into fear, into pain. Didn't see or hear any of that.

She took out a cigarette, lit it, took the smoke down deep into her lungs, exhaled.

Watched the smoke leave her body, rise up into the sky.

Watched it dissipate into the hot air.

36

Trevor Whitman pulled his daughter's Saab up in the car park, killed the engine, tried to get his head straight.

Washington Services on the A1. Southbound.

He sat, drumming his fingers on the wheel, looking round, checking for watchers. No one. Or no one he recognized. He looked at the bag on the seat beside him. Thought of what it contained.

A rap at the window. He jumped, looked up, startled, grabbing instinctively for the bag on the seat. Relaxed. Lillian Knight's face was looking back at him. He sighed, opened the passenger door, placed the bag behind the seat. She ran round, got quickly in. She fell into his arms. He grabbed her, held on like she was the only thing keeping him from falling off a very steep precipice.

She pulled away, looked at him. 'Peta, have you . . .?'

He shook his head. 'They've still got her. But I'll . . . Did you bring what I asked you?'

She had placed a briefcase between her legs. She patted it.

'Good.' He stroked her face. Even now, her features creased, coarsened and reddened by worry, stress and tears, she looked beautiful. 'Try not to worry. It'll all work out. It will.'

She sighed, her eyes pleading for his words to be true. Knew she wanted what her heart was feeling to win out against what her head was telling her. Knew it wouldn't.

He put his arms round her again, pulled her hard to him. Held her.

'I don't . . . don't want you to go,' she said.

He said nothing.

'Let me come with you.'

'No, Lillian. It's safer if you go home.'

She pulled away from him again. 'Not for me. I have to sit there, on my own, waiting . . .'

'It won't be long now. I promise.'

They clutched each other like drowning mariners.

'I, I love you, Trevor.'

Whitman's eyes locked with hers. 'I've got to go,' he said.

She pulled away, the move hiding any sadness that he couldn't match her declaration. 'You're a brave man,' she said. 'And selfless.'

Whitman looked away. 'Not long now. Then we can get on with our lives again.'

Lillian nodded, her gaze averted. She sat up, wiped at the corners of her eyes, pulled her clothing straight. Opened the car door.

She walked to her own car, got in, drove off. He rubbed his face hard, dug the heels of his hands into his eyes, fought back fatigue and tiredness, myriad emotions crashing through him like a winter storm. Breathed deeply, screwed his eyes tight closed, opened them again. Shook his head to clear it, turned the engine over. Another check over his shoulder and off to his next meeting.

Unaware that a black 4×4 with tinted windows waited until he was almost on the road before, at a discreet distance, following him.

Joe Donovan sat in the bar of the Cluny, took another mouthful of beer, checked his watch. It had once been an old whisky warehouse and still held traces of its former life in the high ceilings and exposed stone and brickwork. Donovan could remember, twenty years ago, attending illegal warehouse raves in the same place. There had been live music, DJ sets, a trestle table bar selling only cans of Red Stripe and with parts of the floor roped off where the wood was rotten and unsafe.

Then the Ouseburn Valley in Newcastle had been run down and ex-industrial; now, as part of the regeneration of the area, the Cluny had been transformed into bar/art gallery/music venue. A community theatre was based next door, along with artists' studios, and the Seven Stories children's literature centre was further down, with more things promised. A neo-industrial-styled bar sold a huge variety of beers and whiskies, the kitchen did some of the best pub food in Newcastle and the floors were solid. It was one of his favourite haunts and the perfect place to arrange to meet Trevor Whitman.

Donovan sat on an old leather sofa in an elevated section of the bar. It was quiet, the early-evening drinkers not yet arrived. The only movement from roadies as they carried gear through the bar and into the other hall, setting up for the band playing that night.

Jamal was waiting in the car parked across the street, phone at the ready to warn of any unwanted attention. Donovan sat back, paperback book in front of him for camouflage, trying to look like a relaxed punter. Knew he probably looked anything but.

He didn't have to wait long. Whitman entered. His suit looked like it had not only been slept in but partied in and worked in for several days. His hair and beard matched. He was carrying a leather briefcase. He saw Donovan, walked hurriedly over, sat down. Stared at him, warily. Donovan returned it.

Silence.

'Well,' said Donovan, throwing his book on the table, trying to control his anger, 'what's to stop me leaning across this fucking table and planting my fucking fist right in your fucking smug fucking face?'

'Ah,' said Whitman. 'Like that. Right.'

'You have got some fucking explaining to do.'

Whitman said nothing.

'Peta's gone missing, you fucked us about with your cock-and-bull story, and all the time you knew what was going on.'

Whitman sighed. 'What do you know?'

'That Alan Shepherd's back from his sabbatical. That he's going to turn the streets into a war zone tomorrow night.'

Whitman almost smiled. 'That it?'

Donovan's features hardened. 'You've fucked me about enough. You got something, tell me.'

'You know why? You know who else is involved?'

'I've got some ideas.'

Whitman leaned forward. 'Let me tell you. I presume you know about the plan to redevelop the West End of Newcastle?'

'Which Abdul-Haq's company is behind.'

'Right. They, along with prominent people on the city council, think the area is in desperate need of redevelopment. Been left to die. A slum. Fit only for asylum seekers, immigrants housed by the council. No one would move there voluntarily. So there was a proposal made to redevelop the area.'

'Which is what all the fuss is about now.'

'Right. But despite having people like Colin Baty on his side, old Gideon didn't have enough backing to be taken seriously. So he needed something else. A way to focus attention on the shortcomings of the area, make those in power think his idea is a credible alternative to the status quo. In fact, the only alternative. So he and Shepherd came up with the idea of a race war.'

Donovan almost dropped his beer. 'What?'

'You heard. A race war. Shepherd would start his own party. Make them a credible, electable force. Gideon would increase his profile as community spokesman. Both would appear to hate the other. And the incidents would fan the flames of that hatred.'

'Incidents?'

'Flashpoints. Stage-managed events to stir things up. The beating and burning of that student in the street. The supposed suicide bomber. The riot at the candlelit procession the other night. Their incidents. Their catalysts. To get ordinary people to take sides. Become politicized. Get out and vote.'

'That's just . . . fucking ridiculous.'

'Think so? Know what Alan Shepherd was up to in South Africa all that time?'

Donovan waited.

'Remember Eugene Terre'Blanche? The Afrikaner Resistance Movement?'

'Yeah.'

'South African Nazis who didn't want apartheid to end so they started a terror campaign to spark a race war.'

'This was in the early Nineties, right?'

'Right.'

'And Shepherd was involved?'

'A fully paid-up member. An activist. Part of a gang who tried to bomb the Calvary church school in Nelspruit in 1992. A mixed-race school. Fortunately, the bomb didn't go off. Shepherd was caught. Got a twelve-month suspended sentence.'

Donovan said nothing.

'He was also linked to the murder of Chris Hani, the South African Communist Party leader, in 1993. Released without charge. And now he calls himself Sharples and is behind the NUP.'

Donovan shook his head. 'South African Fascists in Newcastle?'

'More around than you think. When things went tits up in South Africa, they came to Europe. The BNP have quite a few. Check. It's a matter of record.'

'But the NUP aren't organized enough for that. They're just street thugs.'

'Right again. But Alan Shepherd brought someone with him.'

'Who?'

'A mercenary called Tom Bascombe. Major Tom. Ex-British army, he used to work with him out there. He's the one behind the bombings, the beatings . . . everything. A very dangerous man.'

Donovan's head was swimming. 'But . . . why?'

'The area's heavily ethnic. They want to destabilize and frighten the populace. Get both sides angry and scared enough and they'll vote in the extremists. And that'll be a charter for them all to rip each other apart.'

'And the council see what's happening, get a guilty conscience for not acting sooner, come begging to Abdul-Haq to step in. So with their blessing he buys up as much land as possible as cheaply as possible, chases out the extremists, puts his plans into action and saves the area.'

'Exactly. All so a small amount of people can make a large amount of money. A very large amount, leaving lots of innocent people injured or even killed as a result.'

'How did you find out about this?'

'Shepherd wanted to cut me in. That's what the phone calls were about. Old times' sake.'

Donovan frowned. 'What d'you mean?'

'They were all in on it. Shepherd, Gideon, Mary Evans—'

'Mary Evans?'

'Apparently. Don't know what she's got to gain from it.

But her idea of social action is all pragmatism and blind eyes, so who knows?'

'What about—' Donovan thought for a second '—the other two? Richie Vane? Maurice Courtney?'

'Richie Vane has nothing to do with it. But I wouldn't be surprised if Maurice Courtney's not in there somewhere.'

Donovan thought about his meeting with him. He hadn't got the impression Courtney was lying. But his car had been forced off the road on the way back . . . 'You mentioned Colin Baty. Where does he come into this?'

'I think he's Gideon's plan B. If this fails, Colin Baty will be there to mop up. He's convinced him that it'll mean jobs, better quality of life for his constituents, that sort of thing. But Gideon might not need him. As you said, Shepherd's planning something big for election day.'

'D'you know what?'

'Haven't been able to find out. But it has to be stopped. So this is the situation. We've got to work our way out of it. In this briefcase is everything I've got on the project. It's taken me ages to put it all together, follow the paper trail. And there's a set of plans of the new development.'

He opened the briefcase, took out an old Tesco's bag, which he hurriedly put at the side of him, slid the case across the table. Donovan looked directly at Whitman.

'If you had all this, if you knew all this, why didn't you just go to the police?'

Whitman sighed, ran his hands through his hair. He looked like he was about to collapse, nervous energy being the only thing keeping him going. 'Because it's not complete. It's not the smoking gun. It's all supposition. They're very good; they're professionals at this. I'm an academic. That's why I needed . . . needed someone to help me.'

'Then why didn't you say all this in the first place?'

'Because . . . I didn't think you would believe me. I thought it best you found out for yourself. I knew it all and I didn't believe it.' Another sigh. 'I don't know why, though. If the world's greatest superpower can start a war in Iraq just for cheap oil and lucrative rebuilding contracts, then this shouldn't surprise me in the slightest.'

Donovan said nothing, just kept staring. Whitman looked nervous.

'Have you, have you heard anything from Peta?'

'We've got someone looking into that.'

Whitman sat forward. 'And?'

'I said. We've got someone looking into that. We think we know where she might be.'

'Well, get her. Tell the police—'

'Just keep out of it. You've done enough damage.'

Whitman sank back into his seat, an expression on his face of thorough chastisement. Donovan pulled the briefcase over to his side of the table.

'So what am I supposed to do with this?'

'Keep it. Take it to the police. We just need to stop it.' Another sigh, another riffle through his hair. 'It's election day tomorrow. It'll be too late after that. You've got to do it now. Please.'

Donovan stared at him. 'You're coming with me.'

'I can't. There's . . . things I have to do.'

'Yeah. Like sort out this mess you've created.'

'You're right. That's why there's things I have to do.' He leaned across the table, eyes red-rimmed, black-edged but imploring. His hands were clasped in front of him, shaking. 'I started this. I have to end it.' He stood up. 'I know you must . . . What you think of me. But do it because it's, it's the right thing to do. Please.'

Donovan kept his eyes on Whitman, took the briefcase. 'We'll have words. When this is over.'

Whitman nodded, sighed again. 'Right. Whatever.' He looked round the pub. 'I'll better be—'

Donovan's mobile rang. He pulled it from his pocket, flipped it open, read the display. Jamal.

'Yeah?'

'Listen, man, you got trouble headed your way. Big trouble. Two Indian guys, both got muscles like Arnie, one looks like he's been caught in a explosion. You better move it, man. They walkin' like they mean business.'

Donovan snapped the phone shut, grabbed the briefcase. 'We've got company. Where you parked?'

Whitman gestured to the front doors.

'Right. Let's go this way.'

Donovan walked briskly along the length of the bar, up the flight of steps at the far end. Whitman, the rolled-up carrier bag clutched in his fist, followed behind. At the top of the steps, Donovan turned. The double doors were pulled open. One burned, one scarred. Donovan recognized Waqas and Omar immediately.

'Come on,' he said to Whitman, turned and made his way round the corner. He heard the sound of running feet behind them, a shout from one of the bar staff. A roadie was coming towards them from out of the music hall, carrying what looked like a foldback speaker.

'Here,' said Donovan quickly, 'let me help you with that.' Before the roadie could argue or resist, Donovan had thrown the briefcase to Whitman, taken the speaker from him, turned to the top of the steps. Waqas and Omar were at the bottom, just ready to ascend.

'Catch,' he shouted, and threw the speaker as hard as he could.

Waqas saw it coming and put his hands up in a futile attempt to catch it. It hit him square in the chest, sending him backwards into Omar, who fell to the floor.

Donovan turned around. The roadie was beginning to get angry.

'Not music lovers, I'm afraid,' he said. 'Don't worry. They'll pay for any damage.'

Before the roadie could say anything else, Donovan had dodged round him and made it through the double doors. Whitman threw the briefcase at him.

He ran round the corner of the building to where he had parked the car. Jamal was waiting in the passenger seat. He had started the engine. Donovan jumped in, threw the briefcase on to Jamal's lap, floored the accelerator and they were away.

'I keep sayin', man,' said Jamal, when they were under way, 'you should let me drive.'

Donovan, concentrating, said nothing.

Whitman, moving quickly, watched Donovan round the corner, disappear. He looked around, unfamiliar with the area, tried to think of the best way back to his car. He had parked it up a hill, the Byker viaduct looming huge above it.

He checked both sides of the street, behind him. Ran across the road.

The car was just ahead, a black 4×4 in front of it. He heard sounds behind, knew without turning round that his two pursuers had made their way outside. He looked again at the car, made up his mind. It was too risky to run for it; he wouldn't be able to get behind the wheel and drive away before they reached him. He looked behind him again. They had spotted him. Holding hard to the carrier, he ran.

The area was quiet, even for early evening. Up the steep hill and underneath the viaduct was an urban country walk through the Ouseburn Valley leading up to Byker. A winding path leading through trees, bushes and overgrown weeds.

It was deserted. He ran towards it, knew they would be following.

Up the first part, rounding a huge bush. He ran off the trail, hid, waited. Panting hard for breath, sweat on his face and body. He knelt down, opened the bag, took out what was inside. An automatic. He checked it was loaded, clicked off the safety. Waited, trying to control his breathing.

He heard them easily. They sounded like a mini stampede. He waited until they had passed him, then stepped out. Gave a quick glance around, making sure of no spectators. There were none. He stood in the middle of the path, gun raised.

'Hey,' he called. 'You looking for me?'

They both stopped, turned. At first they didn't see the gun, charged straight at him.

Whitman fired. He missed. Again. And again.

Waqas flew backwards as if he had hit an invisible wall. His leg buckled under him and he crashed hard on to the pavement. Blood geysered from his thigh.

Omar looked at him, his face a mask of shock. Then back to Whitman.

Whitman's arm felt sore. He hadn't been expecting such a kickback from the gun. He also hadn't been expecting such a thrill. Adrenalin and testosterone surged through him. More power than he had felt in a long time, perhaps ever. He levelled the gun on Omar. Fired.

Omar saw what was happening, turned and started to run. He made one step, two, then the bullets hit his left ankle, bringing him down. With no time for his arms to come up and absorb the impact, he too hit the pavement hard, his face crunching and thudding on to the gravel.

They had both screamed when the bullets hit, and now were both lying there, writhing, gasping and moaning in agony. Whitman stared at them, at what he had done to them. At the power he had felt and continued to feel. He looked at the gun in his hand, felt its lethal grip. Thoughts sped through his brain. A reluctant trip to Las Vegas that he had ended up loving. Because he had understood how it worked. Casino chips. So seductive, so tactile. They had wanted to be touched, stroked, toyed with. Most of all, they demanded to be played with, used. The higher the amount, the more tactile. He had felt superhuman, playing dice with the cosmos. The gun was the same, but more so. It didn't just grant the power of chance; it conferred the power of life and death.

He wanted to stand there all day and all night, take on any and all comers, show them who was the strongest. He took aim at the bodies, felt his finger squeeze the trigger, felt a smile on his face.

Stopped. Looked around. He had been lucky so far. But someone could come along at any second. And what would he do? Shoot them? His luck wouldn't hold for ever.

He quickly put the gun in his jacket pocket, picked up the spare clip, turned and ran. Back to the car. Into the car and away. Thinking fast. Planning his next move.

Knowing, now that he had used the gun, that there was nothing he couldn't do.

Nothing.

37

Kev silently unlatched the door, swung it open as soundlessly as possible, stepped out into the dark, warm night. Closed it quietly behind him, waiting until the lock gave a barely audible click before moving away.

He had just left the bunker, the corrugated metal shed that the foot soldiers of the revolution, himself included, slept in. Or had been billeted in, as Major Tom said, giving them more of a sense of themselves as a disciplined military unit and not the disenfranchised bunch of losers and outsiders they really were.

Kev tried not to dwell on the fact that until recently he had been one of them. Told himself that his heart wasn't sinking to be back, that he was there for a reason, he had work to do. And more than work, atonement.

He had phoned up late in the afternoon, told them he was ready to come back if they wanted him. He was picked up, brought to the farm, brought before Major Tom. Questioned. About where he had been, who he had been with. Why had he not been there when they needed him. He told Major Tom that his wound had been playing up, that he needed to see a doctor and was worried about what the doctor would say, whether he would be fit for the task ahead, so hadn't wanted to tell anyone this. The doctor, he said, had cleaned the wound, given him some antibiotics; he was good to go. Not only that, but his brother had needed sorting out with his addiction.

Kev stood there, waiting to see if his words would be

believed. If they checked up on him, he was fucked. He hadn't been home for days; his brother could be dead for all he knew.

Major Tom had scrutinized him, long and hard, giving him some speech about how highly recommended he had been, the glowing report from Rick Oaten, how there was a place for him, but he had to prove himself. Kev had eagerly told him that his loyalties were with the party. That he was fit and ready for what was to come.

Major Tom had, not without reservations, believed him. Sent him off to the bunker with the other men.

Where he had hoped they would fall asleep so he could start investigating. But they were on too much of a high, overexcited about what was to happen the next day, so none of them were sleeping. The air was thick with heat and tension. Kev had got up, told them he was going for some fresh air. Was told to give the password if challenged, there were sentries patrolling.

He stood in the farmyard, looked around. Wondered where to start. The farm belonged to a party member and sympathizer who had gladly hired out his land to the NUP. He and his family lived in and worked out of the main house. Major Tom had a Winnebago on site and the foot soldiers the bunker. Deep in the secluded hills of Northumberland, miles from anywhere, the arrangement worked out well.

There were older stone buildings near the main house. Milking pens, a barn, storage areas, the slaughterhouse. From the old days, when animals were killed on the farm, not taken to abattoirs. Now used by Major Tom as the punishment block. Kev checked left and right, made sure there were no sentries patrolling, crossed the yard.

The door was locked, a thick padlock holding it in place. He pulled it, hard. No good. Checked above the doorframe for a key, at the side, on the ground. He didn't think he would really find one. He was right.

Along the side of the building, one-time windows had been bricked and breeze-blocked up. If Peta and Jason were being kept anywhere, it would be in here. Kev gave another look round, then walked slowly down the length of the building. Checking for gaps, other doors, anything that could get him a way in.

He rounded the corner. What had once been another outbuilding was linked to the punishment block. Its windows had been sealed too but not as thoroughly. Wood and board in place of brick and breeze block. It had been done quickly, hurriedly. He looked around, checking for sentries. No one. Tried the handle. Locked.

He looked again at the windows. Put his hands on the corners. They were nailed shut, new, thick nails holding the wood to the frame. But the frame might be rotten, thought Kev. Old and worn. Pushing his fingers round the edges, he pulled. No movement. He tried again. Felt the old wood give, splinter slightly under the new wood.

Kev smiled to himself, pulled harder. The nails squealed. He stopped, looked round again. Hoped the noise hadn't alerted anyone. Stood absolutely still, felt his heart hammering in his chest.

Tried again. Heard the nails squealing again. Stopped, waited.

Heard footsteps. Saw a flashlight.

Kev looked quickly round, scanned for a hiding place. Couldn't find one. If he ran he would be seen and possibly shot; if he stayed where he was he would be seen. And challenged.

He had no choice. Stay where he was, front it.

The flashlight-holding figure approached. Kev was standing against the side of the outbuilding, hands in pockets, looking up at the stars. Trying to be as casual as he could.

The figure drew level, stopped. He wore a handgun at his side. His hand was twitching to make use of it.

'Password?'

'Thor's Hammer.'

The flashlight was shone in Kev's face. He put his hand up to shield his eyes.

'Kev? What you doin' out here?'

Kev squinted, tried to see beyond the glare. 'Ligsy? That you?'

'Aye.'

Ligsy put the flashlight down. Kev's one-time lieutenant was frowning. It made his face look even more simian.

'What you doin' out here?'

Kev tried to sigh. 'Couldn't sleep. Thought I'd get a bit of fresh air.'

Ligsy said nothing, kept looking at him. Kev felt nervous under that animal gaze.

'Just thinkin', you know? Calm before the storm an' that.'

Ligsy's face split open in a smile. 'Hey, Kev, you were always the clever one. I said that. In wor gang, Kev's the clever one.'

Not hard, thought Kev. 'Yeah,' he said.

Ligsy looked round as if checking he wasn't being over-heard, then leaned in closer. 'Word to the wise, though. Do your thinkin' somewhere else than here.'

Kev's turn to frown. 'What d'you mean?'

'In there,' said Ligsy, pointing to the building Kev had been trying to break into, 'they've got somethin' in there.'

'What?'

'Top secret. Hush hush, an' that. It's for tomorrow. Some secret weapon. Cheggs reckons it's a bomb, like.'

'A bomb?'

'Aye. But I don't.'

'Why not?'

'I heard noises. Voices. Dunno what they've been doin' in there, but I wouldn't want it done to me.'

Jason. Kev knew what they wanted him to do. He could imagine how they would go about doing it. He tried not to let his anxiety show on his face or in his voice.

'Right,' he said. 'Keep away.'

Ligsy didn't move. Kev realized it was his cue to go back to the bunker. He stretched, faked a yawn. Said something about turning in for the night. Still Ligsy didn't move.

Kev had no choice. He had to leave Ligsy, walk back to the bunker. Get in bed, feign sleep.

And try to stop thinking about what was happening in that outbuilding.

But he couldn't.

It was going to be a long night.

Peta heard the padlock being tested, sat straight up. She waited. Nothing. No one came in.

A squeaking noise from nearby, then voices. Then nothing. She lay back down again. Tried to sleep. All she had done since Mary Evans's visit.

She knew how hostages must feel. How terrorism works. The incarceration was bad enough, but guessing at what her eventual fate was to be and waiting for it to happen was awful. She had tried to cry but was beyond tears. She was beyond hope, beyond everything.

She closed her eyes. Prayed that someone would come and rescue her.

Tried not to think how ridiculously hopeless that sounded. Even to herself.

Turnbull looked at the photo on the dressing table in the hotel in Bishop's Stortford. His wife. Two kids. Himself. All smiling. He had examined that photo for hours, days, months. Over and over. Ever since she threw him out. Ever since they left him.

But for the first time in a long while he didn't feel bad when he looked at it. Didn't feel that grinding, churning emptiness inside him, that abyss threatening to devour him. Because for the first time in ages he felt hopeful.

Hopeful that he would be the husband and father that he should have been. Hopeful that a new chapter of his life could begin.

This job for Donovan was the cause. It had pulled him out of his self-pitying rut, given him dignity and respect. He remembered that this was something he was good at. This was his passion. He didn't need the police force, he could go into the private sector, set himself up there. Build up his own client list. Be a success on his own terms. Demonstrate how he had changed. Earn the right to have his family back.

That's what he would do. As soon as this job for Donovan was out of the way.

Matt Milsom had been lying. Too many inconsistencies, vagaries in his story. Wouldn't the school have been informed if Jake was HIV-positive? Wouldn't he have had a Romanian accent? Those were the main points that stuck out. There were other things too. Milsom's body language had been all wrong. He had aimed at being relaxed, just two blokes chatting over a couple of whiskies. Been open and friendly in response to the questions. It was too much. Too studied. Overplayed. And that made Turnbull suspicious.

He knew what he had to do next. There was no need to creep around any more. He would make an appointment at the school, talk to the head teacher. Explain who he was and what he was doing, find out for definite about Jake. Depending on the outcome of that, he would confront

Milsom again. It was time to escalate, to move to the next phase. He looked at the photo again. Then, hopefully, it would be time to go home.

The room was comfortable but nothing more. He needed some exercise so, slipping his wallet and phone into his jeans, he left the hotel.

The streets were deserted. Bishop's Stortford was a small ex-market town, not famed for its nightlife. He had found a pub he liked and, although it was quite a walk from his hotel, felt like treating himself to a drink there. Maybe get talking to a few locals, see if anyone could give him background on the Milsoms. Or even just have a chat.

The night was creeping in. He walked through the park, the swings and slides empty, too late for children to be playing. Over the bridge and through the trees. Feeling good about himself, his work.

Too good to notice the figure slip from the bushes behind him. And when he did hear a noise and turned, it was too late. Something was constricting his throat, stopping him breathing, something sharp and hard. Pulled tight, tighter.

He put his hands to his throat, tried to get the constriction away. The wire just dug in, harder. Broke skin. Felt blood running down his neck.

A desperate thought flashed through Turnbull's mind: grab the assailant from behind, find something to twist, pull, injure. No good. He was too busy pulling the garrotte from his throat.

Black fireworks went off at the sides of his eyes, became bigger, more frequent. Their impact heavier. He scrabbled frantically at his neck, gasped and gurgled. He felt his legs give way, his body sink to the ground. He was mentally screaming: get up, get up . . . No good. His body wouldn't listen.

Turnbull gave in. He no longer had the strength to fight. He lay there, looked up. Saw his attacker. That black floppy hair, those glasses. That friendly, bland face, friendly no more.

Matt Milsom.

Turnbull just had time to put together what had been done to him before his body conceded defeat and the air left him for the final time.

Never to go home again.

PART FOUR

THE DEMOCRATIC CIRCUS

38

Election day.

The cars were out, the loud-hailers on. Councillors and candidates canvassing door to door, only local but treating it like a national, telling voters and potential voters to get out and do their duty. The same phrases trotted out like tired old mantras:

Get out and vote or THEY'LL get in again.

Stand up for what YOU believe in.

One person CAN make a difference.

Over and over, covering the whole spectrum, Colin Baty's Labour to Rick Oaten's NUP. Smiles, suits and rosettes. Leaflets and lifts to the polling station. Rictus grins and righteous speeches. The democratic circus had come to town.

The summons had arrived when Kev was getting ready. Queuing to wash his face, brush his teeth, from a standpipe by the barn. The foot soldiers lined up, laughing, horsing around. Hiding nerves, building up testosterone, storing adrenalin. Psyching each other up. Kev not joining in, his bandage showing, his side still aching, the knife still turning in the wound. One of the troops ran up to him. Looked only about twelve, thought Kev. Young kid with bad skin, bad teeth, bad attitude in his eyes. The message: Major Tom wants to see you.

The turning knife started spinning, gouging. Shit, thought Kev, this is it. I'm caught. Someone saw me nosing around last night. Reported me. They're going to want to know what I was looking for. Make me tell the truth. Any way they can.

He put down his tin cup, not giving his hand time to start shaking, and followed the foot soldier across the yard to the main house and into the kitchen. The room was small but busy, the scene one of sharp contrast: dishes drying by the sink while a military operation was planned on the kitchen table. Major Tom and his two lieutenants filled the room. The lieutenants buzzed around, checked coordinates on the map laid out across the table with pieces of paper at the side. Testosterone and adrenalin were building here too, but more concentrated, more focused than in the men outside. Major Tom sat at the table, head down, studying papers, unmoving, the eye of the storm. Dressed in full fatigues, ready for action. Kev stood before him, waited for him to look up.

Major Tom kept his eyes down. Kev felt sweat prickle his back, his legs. Didn't dare move. Knew what was coming, tried not to imagine it. The eventual reality would be bad enough. He backed away, until he was flat against the sink. Something prodded into him, something sharp. He moved a hand silently behind him, tried to move the obstruction out of the way. Felt the blade of a knife. A sharp one for skinning, paring, cutting.

Looking down at Major Tom, seeing his attention was still on the work before him, Kev surreptitiously slid the knife, blade first, up the sleeve of his jacket, stood again to attention. Eventually Major Tom pushed away the paper he had been reading, turned the same scrutiny on to Kev. A hard, unblinking stare.

The look said intimidation, and Kev felt he was expected to crumble. Fall to his knees and confess. Yes, he was a spy, no, he wanted no part in what they were doing. Take the consequences stoically. But another image lodged itself in his mind. Of himself in another time. The future. Away from the farm, the party, away from the flat and his father and brother and instead in a bar with Amar, laughing and joking and having a good time. And Kev felt anger well up inside, anger because he was so near to achieving it yet so close to having it snatched away. So he didn't crumble, he didn't flinch. He returned the gaze second for second.

Major Tom smiled, broke eye contact.

Kev said nothing. Waited.

'How's the wound?'

Kev looked down at his side, surprised by the question. 'Healin',' he said.

'Good.' Major Tom looked at the map, back to Kev. 'Don't want you to join the others yet. Could be too much of a liability. Got a job, though. You up to it?'

'Yes, sir.' The response automatic.

'Good. Come with me.'

Major Tom rose, crossed to the door. Kev, still wary, and checking the knife was in place, followed him. Out into the farmyard, over to the locked outbuilding. Kev's heart began trip-hammering. It was all a show. He was going in here too.

Major Tom produced a key, undid the padlock, opened the door.

They stepped inside. Kev recoiled from the smell. The building was unlit, the windows boarded up. The dust and must and overpowering stink of human waste attacked his throat; he started to cough.

'Get up.'

Major Tom stood before a blanket-covered bundle huddled against one wall, gave it a kick. The bundle groaned, moved. Jason got robotically to his feet, stood to attention.

Kev's eyes were adjusting to the gloom. He looked at the boy, tried to stifle the look of horror he knew had sprung up on his face. Jason was filthy and naked. Livid welts, sores and bruises his only clothing. His expression was completely blank, eyes staring straight ahead. A human robot waiting for commands. This wasn't what Kev had been expecting. It was worse.

Major Tom turned to Kev. 'More pliant than the last time you saw him, wouldn't you agree? Not about to stab you.'

Kev, not knowing whether he was supposed to answer or not, felt his fingers touch the blade of the hidden knife. Major Tom didn't wait for a reply, turned back to Jason, cupped his chin in his hand. 'Our secret weapon.'

Jason said nothing, allowed himself to be examined.

Kev stepped up alongside Major Tom, looked into Jason's eyes. No recognition. 'What have you done with him?' He tried to keep his voice neutral.

'What we planned. Taken an angry, disenfranchised kid, turned him into a human time bomb. Process we developed in Lebanon. Perfected, even. Worked every time.'

'And he's . . . he's ready?'

Major Tom turned, smiled. 'Oh, yes. Today's the day when he will strike a blow for freedom. And you're going to be his nursemaid.'

'What?'

Major Tom turned away from Jason, gave Kev his full scrutiny once again. 'His control. We can't let him out on his own.' He frowned. 'Problem?'

'No, no . . .' Kev looked between Jason and Major Tom, tried to keep his face as straight as Major Tom would expect it to be. 'What do I have to do?'

'Come back to the house. You'll be briefed.'

Major Tom turned, walked out. Kev gave one last look at Jason. Shivered. Jason blinked at him. In recognition, he was sure of it. He looked at Jason, waiting for something more.

'Come on.' Major Tom was standing at the door, key in hand.

Kev joined him. The door locked, they walked back to the house. Kev gave a glance towards the other building. No movement. Peta had to be there. If that was what they had done to Jason, what had they done to her? He had to get in there. Find a way.

He had somehow to contact Amar and his crew.

But he could do neither.

He fell into step beside Major Tom, walked back to the house.

The knife still hidden.

'You'll need to wear this.'

Amar handed Donovan an earpiece. 'Bluetooth?'

'Better than that. This is the king of Bluetooth. It'll keep us all in touch. Like our own personal network.'

'Great,' said Donovan. 'Very *Torchwood*.'

'Bags I John Barrowman,' Amar said, a faint smile on his lips. It disappeared as he resumed explanations. 'I'll be monitoring the phones. If Whitman gets another call or calls out again, we'll get him.' He pointed to a laptop on the table. It was hooked up to a piece of hardware. The screen was showing a gridded map of the city, a box at the side showing numbers moving rapidly along, up and down. 'And then I'll be straight on to you.'

Jamal smiled. 'I get one?'

Amar took another one from its plastic wrapper, handed it over. 'Here you go.'

Jamal, grinning, stuck it straight in his ear, posed as if he was holding a gun with both hands. 'Man, this is so cool. I be, like, Jack Bauer now.'

'Right.' Donovan put the earpiece in place. 'So where did you get this?'

'Had it a while. Been waiting for a chance to use it. Would have happened sooner if someone hadn't had a queeny fit and disbanded Albion.'

'Yeah, OK. Let's not go there.'

'Quite. Did a favour for a friend a while ago. Called it in. Top-of-the-range stuff, this. The real-deal industrial espionage, international spy kit.'

'Do I get to know what this favour is? Or do I not want to know?'

'Not what you're thinking,' said Amar, mock aggrieved. 'Client from the old days. Runs an advertising agency. Was having a bit of trouble keeping campaign plans secret. Asked me to look into it, money no object. As many toys to play with as I wanted. And I wanted a lot.'

'Right.' Donovan adjusted the piece in his ear. 'So this is going to be on all the time.'

'Yep. Whitman gets a call or Kev phones with some info on the farm, or Peta or her mother, and I'm on to it. It's relayed through here and I can track it down with my handy GPS system.' He gestured to the laptop. 'Then I call you, tell you where the call's coming from.'

'Then we go an' smoke those terrorist motherfuckers,' said Jamal, shooting his imaginary gun at the wall.

'Boys, eh?' said Donovan.

Donovan had delivered Whitman's briefcase to DI Nattrass the previous night. Once he had put sufficient distance between the Cluny and himself and Jamal, he had parked the car in a secluded spot behind the Central Station, opened the briefcase, read the files. Pages and pages of plans, figures, invoices. Photocopies of documents, some printed off. It meant nothing to him and he didn't have the time to go through it and find connections.

'Means nothing to me,' he had said. 'Let's see what Nattrass makes of it.'

Jamal pulled a face. 'I'll wait in the car.'

'It won't take long.'

'Police stations are like hospitals, man. I go in one, I ain't never comin' out.'

Donovan had phoned Nattrass, told her what he had for her. She wasn't happy that he had met Trevor Whitman and not informed her and had told him so as strongly as possible, but still arranged to meet. Donovan, thinking of Jamal's remark about police stations, insisted on a neutral spot. The café bar at Baltic, the contemporary arts centre.

She walked in, saw them straight away.

'Bring back memories?' said Donovan.

'Yes,' she said, 'none of them pleasant.'

She ordered a double espresso and joined them. Donovan didn't need to ask if she had had a tough day. One look at her tired eyes was enough. She knocked the coffee back, moved the cup and saucer out of the way. Donovan swung the briefcase on to the table.

'Here,' he said, and told her who he had got it from.

'Thanks.' Nattrass took it, put it at the side of her chair. She leaned forward, a question forming. 'When did you get this?'

'This afternoon.'

'Where?'

'I said on the phone. From Trevor Whitman.'

'I mean where as in location.'

'Oh.' Donovan was about to answer but sensed caution. 'Why?'

Nattrass aimed for casual. Missed. 'Just wondered.'

Something was up. But he trusted Di. And he had done nothing wrong. 'The Cluny.'

She sat back, unable to stop a triumphantly vindictive smile breaking out on her face. 'Really? And what else happened there?'

Donovan thought of the chase, tried to keep his face blank. 'Nothing.'

'Want to give me more detail about nothing happening?'

Donovan leaned forward. 'Want to tell me why?'

'Two of Abdul-Haq's men were taken to hospital from there. Both with gunshot wounds.'

The look of surprise on Donovan's face was genuine. 'And you think . . .'

'If not you, what about your . . . contact?'

'I don't . . .' Donovan thought. The carrier bag Whitman had been so protective of, the way he had clutched it as they ran . . . 'I don't know what you mean. I don't think so.'

Nattrass looked at him like she didn't believe him but didn't want to pursue it further. His look of genuine surprise had given him credibility credits. For a while.

'Got something for you, though.'

Nattrass sighed, like she knew it was going to be trouble. 'What?'

'The guy running the NUP. The power behind Rick Oaten's throne. Calls himself Sharples.' He told her about Alan Shepherd, where he had been, what he had been up to in the intervening years since he had blown up the pub in Newcastle.

'Jesus,' she said when he had finished. 'Quite a story. Can all this be proved?'

'Presume so. Ask Whitman.'

'I will. When I find him.'

'And there's something else. When Shepherd came back he brought a friend.' He told her of Major Tom's history and what he was currently doing. Nattrass listened, her eyes widening as he went along.

'So,' she said, when Donovan had finished, 'he's going to lead a gang—'

'Platoon, please. Let's get the terminology correct.'

'—gang of thugs on to the streets to do as much damage as possible.'

'Operation Thor's Hammer,' said Donovan. Jamal shivered. 'Kristallnacht all over again. In Newcastle.'

Nattrass groaned. 'Oh, God. The overtime . . .' She rubbed her eyes. 'Any chance this information might be false?'

'None at all. They're also planning something else.'

'What?'

'We don't know yet. When we do, we'll let you in on it.' Nattrass rubbed her eyes.

'You going to arrest Rick Oaten yet? That'll look good on election day.'

'On what charge? Your say-so? I would love to, but we'll have to wait. No doubt he's made himself untouchable for this. We just wade in with no evidence, nothing happens and we have to let him go. How does that make us look? One–nil to the Fascists, I think. Not a good result.'

'So what you going to do?'

'What I can. Strong riot police presence. Be prepared.'

'They're going to be armed.'

'Oh, God . . .' She looked up. 'Leave it to me.' She looked at her watch. 'I'd better be off.' She gathered her things together. 'Oh, have you heard from Paul?'

'Not a dicky bird. Tell you the truth, I've been too busy with this to chase him up. Which I feel guilty about. You?'

Nattrass shook her head. 'Same. When this is out the way I'll give him a ring.' She looked at the briefcase. 'But thanks for this. You've managed to make my job both easier and harder at the same time.'

Donovan smiled. 'Any time.'

Nattrass stood up, back to business. 'But you hear from Whitman, or in fact if you hear anything else, I want to know. The second it happens. Got that?'

'Loud and clear.'

And she was off.

After that, Donovan and Jamal went to get something to eat and went back to Amar's, bringing him up to date on what had happened. Donovan spent the night on Amar's sofa, Jamal in his usual place in the spare room. Donovan, tension pounding through his system like a noseful of class-A, thought he would have added another sleepless night to the previous one. But his mind had been so jumbled, his body so tired, he had eventually just given out. He had woken early, feeling decidedly unrested. And despite the shower and caffeine boost from two mugs of coffee, he wasn't refreshed.

'So what do we do in the meantime?' said Donovan, trying out the earpiece again.

Amar looked at the phone, willing it to ring. 'Nothing we can do. We wait.'

39

'You found us all right, then?' Sharples smiled at the rare, if unfunny, joke.

Abdul-Haq didn't smile. 'I found you.'

The two men were in the meeting room of the offices of the NUP. Beyond the closed door the office was alive with activity. Phones were being worked, voices cajoling, all was movement, hustle. Throwing out promises, threats if they helped. All with one aim: trying to squeeze the most possible votes out of as many people as possible. The staff, volunteers, all full on.

Sharples was out of the region, supposedly coordinating events from afar. Phone and internet. Too hot for him, too chancy. The police may choose today for that chat they so desperately want to have. So he had hidden in the last place anyone would look for him. The NUP headquarters.

To most people he was absent, but to those in the trusted inner circle he was in a meeting and had given strict orders not to be disturbed. By anyone. Things were critical and his business partner had requested a meeting. Face to face. He needed some fears allaying.

Abdul-Haq had been negotiated through a back entrance. No one but Sharples knew he was in the building. He sat, again, in chinos, casual short-sleeved shirt, loafers. Sunglasses tucked into his top pocket.

'And you're in disguise as well,' Sharples added.

'We all become the masks we wear,' said Abdul-Haq.

'Quite,' said Sharples. 'Let's talk.'

'Waqas and Omar are hospitalized,' said Abdul-Haq, lean-ing forward on the chesterfield. 'The police have been round to my offices. I can't talk to them, I . . .'

'You're safe here. This is the last place they'd look for you.'

'Thank you. I know, but . . . We've underestimated Whitman.'

Sharples's expression was grave, his face lined and creased, carved out of granite. 'Perhaps.'

'So what do we do about him?'

'Don't worry about him. After today he'll be powerless to stop anything.'

Abdul-Haq threw up his hands. 'Tomorrow is too late, Alan. I've got the police asking questions, and Whitman could still undermine everything. Do you know where he is? Are you still watching him?'

Sharples said nothing, the crevasses in his features increas-ing.

'You've lost him, haven't you?'

'Not I. We. And you know it. Waqas and Omar were watching him, Mary was detailed to Richie. Yes, it's bad, but there's nothing he can do.'

'He could go to the police.'

'He could have done that a long time ago. But he didn't. I have something in mind if needs be.'

'Tell me.'

'Mary planned it. A little icing on the cake. Involving his daughter.'

Abdul-Haq shifted uncomfortably in his chair. His sweat-slicked clothes were sticking to the leather. 'She disturbs me, Alan. There's something lacking in her.'

'We need her.'

'She isn't a professional. She's a civilian. A believer. She's not one of us. Not any more.'

'I have her on a tight leash. And if that fails, which it won't, there's always his lover.'

Abdul-Haq stared hard at Sharples. 'Keep a sense of perspective, Alan. Don't let this get out of hand.'

Sharples grinned and Abdul-Haq saw the old Alan Shepherd. 'Out of hand? There's too much at stake now to let it get out of hand. By any means necessary, Gideon – isn't that what we agreed?'

Abdul-Haq said nothing. Sharples continued.

'Things go forward as planned.'

Abdul-Haq opened his mouth to argue; Sharples talked over him. 'Just keep your nerve. Once the elections are over, things move into a crucial phase. Just—'

The door opened loudly, swinging back on its hinges, hitting the wall. The two men looked up, startled.

'Secretary tellin' me you're in a private meetin' and not to be disturbed.' An angry Rick Oaten stood framed in the doorway. 'Told her, I said, this is my fucking party. There's no such thing as a private meeting without me being there. I—'

He stopped talking, saw who Sharples was talking to. Or rather, what Sharples was talking to. An Asian. A Paki.

'What the fuck's goin' on? Who's this? What's he doin' in here?'

Sharples stared at him, swallowed down his anger, tried to ride it out constructively. 'Why aren't you out trying to win an election, Rick? Haven't you got babies to kiss and hands to shake?'

'But . . .' Oaten pointed at Abdul-Haq. Incomprehension was coagulating round his anger.

Sharples stood up, crossed to him. 'What, Rick? Have you something to say? Something on your mind?'

Oaten didn't notice the menace, the danger behind Sharples's words. He kept staring at the Asian man. 'I know

you,' he said, trying to regain his voice. 'You're, you're
Abdul-Haq.' Oaten frowned, looked from one man to the
other. 'Abdul-Haq . . . what, what the fuck . . .'

Abdul-Haq shifted uncomfortably. He looked across at
Sharples, who had a gleam in his eye and a curl to his lip.
Abdul-Haq had seen both things before. Usually as a prelude
to someone being hurt in some way. And to Alan Shepherd
enjoying it.

Oaten's voice returned. He slammed the door behind
him so there could be no enquiring faces, turned back to the
two men in the room, pointed an accusing finger at Abdul-
Haq. 'What the fuck are you doing here? Here?' Oaten
laughed. A harsh, ugly sound. He looked round to the door,
summoning unseen support. 'You must have a fuckin' death
wish, mate, comin' here like this.'

'He's here as my guest, Rick,' said Sharples.

Oaten looked at Sharples, back to Abdul-Haq, back to
Sharples, his words sinking in. 'What? Your, your fuckin'
what?' He was blinking quickly, twitching.

'Guest, Rick. And I gave orders not to be disturbed.'
Sharples's voice had dropped in register. Flat, menacing.

Oaten either didn't notice or ignored it. He gave another
sharp laugh. 'Well. I see now that, that . . .' He tailed off, lost
for words. He shook his head, regained his thread. 'Get out.
Go on, get out. You've got no place here. And take the
fuckin' Paki with you.'

Sharples stood, immobile, looking at Oaten, smiling.
Abdul-Haq sat rigid, braced for a storm to hit.

'Oh, Rick,' said Sharples, a weary sadness to his words, 'I
had hoped it wouldn't come to this.'

Oaten stared. 'This is my party, this is my room. Get
out.'

'Rick . . . you're pathetic.' The smile faded from
Sharples's face.

'What?' The tics started to jump again in Rick Oaten's cheek. 'What did you call me?'

'Pathetic. Your party, your room.' Sharples moved slowly towards him, talking all the time. 'This was never your party, Rick. This is not even your room. You're only here because it suited my purposes to have you here.'

'What—'

'Listen. It's about time you heard a few home truths.' Sharples was face to face with Oaten. 'I chose you to do a job. A very specific job. I found you, trained you, educated you. Made you what you are. And what are you? A tool to do my work. A puppet to do my bidding.' Sharples smiled. 'A fool.'

Oaten's face went red. 'What are you fuckin' . . .' He wanted to be angry but there was too much doubt, too much confusion racing through him.

'Your room, your party? Only because I let you believe it. Only because it suited my purposes.'

'What . . . what purposes?'

'Business, Rick. Purely business. Same as my colleague here.' He gestured to Abdul-Haq.

Oaten looked round, agony in his expression, confusion in his gestures. He raised his fist to Sharples. Abdul-Haq was off his seat, behind Sharples, backing him up.

Sharples laughed. 'You going to hit me, Rick? I wouldn't recommend it.'

The fist dropped.

'That's better.'

'But you, you . . . believed . . .'

'No I didn't. I don't believe in what you believe. I don't care what you believe in. You suited my purposes.'

'You . . . you used me . . .' Oaten sounded like he was crumbling away.

'That's right, Rick.'

'Why? Why me?'

Sharples shrugged. 'Why not? I needed someone and you ticked all the boxes. If it hadn't been you it would have been someone else. Some other fanatic. True believer. They're the easiest to manipulate.'

'Like the Danish cartoons,' said Abdul-Haq.

Rick Oaten looked between the two of them, confused. 'What? What?'

'Good point, very educational. The Danish cartoons of Mohammed,' said Sharples. 'Got all the Muslims up in arms. Thing is, the ones they were complaining about weren't even there originally. They were only put in later to exploit the potential for hatred. It's very simple.' He looked at Oaten's uncomprehending face. 'Probably too simple for you to understand.'

Oaten again looked between the two. His body crumpled. He looked around, pulled at his tie. Tried to move, couldn't. Didn't have anywhere to move to. 'I don't, don't know what to do . . .'

'I'll tell you, shall I?' said Sharples, putting his arm round Oaten's shoulder and smiling. 'You go back out there, you say nothing of what's gone on in here and you win your election. That's what you do.' Sharples adjusted Oaten's tie, fastened his top button. 'Chin up, smile.'

Oaten just stared at him.

A dark light twinkled behind Sharples's eyes. 'What alternative have you got, Rick?'

Oaten looked round the room, at the two men, at the door he had entered through. 'None,' he said.

'That's the spirit,' said Sharples, giving his shoulders a squeeze. 'Look like a winner, feel like a winner, you are a winner. And if you're not a winner, or you want to tell someone about this, it's not too late to replace you. Permanently.'

Oaten looked into Sharples's eyes. He understood.

'Now go.'

Oaten turned round, made his way to the door, slinked silently through it. Sharples and Abdul-Haq waited until he had gone before speaking.

Sharples gave another rare smile.

'Like I said, nothing to worry about.'

Abdul-Haq nodded.

Sharples checked his watch, looked at the darkening skies outside. 'Polls should be closing soon,' he said. 'And since you and I aren't going anywhere for the foreseeable future we may as well watch the election results here.'

Abdul-Haq looked towards the door. 'Won't—'

'We won't be disturbed.'

Sharples settled himself on the chesterfield. 'Whisky?'

Abdul-Haq gave a small smile, tried to commit himself to looking relieved. Failed. 'Don't mind if I do.'

40

The polls had closed. The count was starting.

Politicians and would-be politicians could relax their facial muscles, let their rictus smiles go. Get on with the business of waiting. All around the country bins were emptied, armies of volunteers got to work, voting slips were counted by hand.

On TV David Dimbleby settled into his studio, readying himself for an all-night shift before an audience of students of politics and insomniacs.

At the farm in Northumberland they were getting ready to move out.

The foot soldiers were lined in the barn, listening to Major Tom give their final instructions before getting into the backs of the four white vans. There was no pushing or jostling. No joking, name-calling, rough-housing. Just concentrated, focused men standing to attention, listening. All dressed in uniform of combats, boots and black nylon bomber jackets.

Major Tom had a map of the West End of Newcastle in front of him, a pointer in his hand.

'A team,' he said, gesturing to the first four men, 'will be stationed here. B team here, C team here and D team here.' He looked round the group. 'Don't worry about the names of your groups. It doesn't mean anything. Just something to identify you all by.'

The men said nothing. A well-drilled, well-trained platoon.

'I want you all to wait for my signal. It'll come over the radio. I'll be in the central command vehicle. When you hear that, you go into action as planned.' Another look round the group. 'Any questions?'

There were none.

'Good luck, everyone. Pick up your weapons from the armourer and off you go.'

The men filed out. No talking, no shambling. Straight lines all the way to the milking shed, where they were each given a firearm. Some were rifles, some shotguns, some handguns. They had been familiarized with them, trained, and they weren't tempted to play about with them. Then on to the waiting vans.

Kev, standing with his back against the door of a black 4×4, watched it all, mobile hidden in the palm of his hand. Surreptitiously, he captured the scene, disguising the camera's click with a small cough.

He had kept the camera with him all afternoon, trying to find a way to phone Amar and failing. Major Tom had banned the use of mobiles; no one was to know where they were, what they were up to. He had introduced the strictest penalties for anyone caught breaking that rule. So Kev had had to think on his feet. He had kept it hidden, taken pictures of the farm, the layout of the camp and, from a discreet distance, Major Tom and his lieutenants. He had been lucky so far. But he knew that luck could run out at any moment. And he didn't want to endure what would happen to him then.

He felt the stolen knife, wrapped in cloth to protect his skin, nestling at the small of his back. That gave him some consolation. It was something he was familiar with, something he knew how to use to the best advantage. He drew comfort from having it there, strength.

Another click, another cough. Then Major Tom came striding towards him.

He hurriedly flipped the camera shut, slipped it into his pocket, swallowing hard, hoping Major Tom hadn't seen him do it. Major Tom drew level.

'Right,' he said, checking his watch. 'Shouldn't be long now. You may as well get in the car.'

'Right, sir.' Kev got into the car, tried not to let his reluctance show. Because Jason was in there waiting. Sitting, staring straight ahead, the blink of his eyes, the slow rise and fall of his chest the only indications that he was actually alive. Kev had tried to talk to him. Jason had said nothing. Shared memories, told him jokes. Nothing. Eventually he had given up, sat there next to him, staring alongside him. It had become too much. That was when he had climbed out of the 4×4, started taking photos again.

That was bad enough. But worse was the plastic explosive strapped to Jason's stomach. Kev didn't know how much was there, but knew it was a lot. Enough to do a great deal of damage. Jason's jacket was zipped up to his chin, no wires showing.

Kev sat back next to him, sighed. Wondered how his life had come to this.

'All right, mate?' he said to Jason.

No reply.

Kev felt like the relative of some comatose car-crash victim, sitting at his bedside, talking to him in the hope that something he might say, some trigger, might bring him back to life. He looked at Jason, who hadn't even acknowledged his presence. Kev went back to looking out of the window.

And saw something.

A separate white van had backed up to the door of the outhouse where he suspected Peta was being held. He saw that scary, strange, wizened old hippie woman who had been wandering around for the last few days go to the door, open the padlock with a key. He took the camera out again, glanced round for sight of Major Tom. He was off talking to one of his lieutenants. Good.

Kev opened the door a little, placed his camera hand on the crack. The back doors of the van were opened, obscuring Kev's view. He tried to crane his neck, see around them. He caught glimpses: what looked like a bound figure being helped, if that was the word, then thrown into the back of the van.

Click. Cough.

And again.

Then the doors of the van were slammed shut. Kev looked to the front of the van, angled the camera at it, hoped he had got a shot of the numberplate. He closed the door, sat back, began to go through the phone, see what he could do about sending the photos.

'They're not allowed.'

Kev jumped, almost dropped the phone. He looked round. Jason had pulled his gaze away from whatever it was he had been looking at and turned to face him.

'What?' Kev was almost too stunned to talk.

'If they find you with that,' he said, voice small and distant, like it was coming down a transatlantic phone line, 'they'll be really angry with you. You'd better get rid of it.'

Kev swallowed. 'You're not going to tell them, are you?'

Jason looked like he was making up his mind. 'No,' he said eventually, although he didn't sound convinced.

'Look, Jason, I can get you out of here. I can. But you've just got to trust me. Can you do that?'

Jason said nothing.

'Can you?'

Jason frowned, like he was receiving thoughts he didn't know how to process.

'Can you?'

The front door of the 4×4 opened and Major Tom got in.

Kev quickly shoved his phone into his pocket. Major Tom looked round, his eyes flashing down to Kev's hand. Kev didn't know whether he had seen him or not.

'Not long now,' said the major.

Kev waited for him to get up again but he stayed where he was, in the passenger seat. Jason had resumed staring into space.

Kev, not knowing what was going to happen next, joined him.

Peta landed on the floor of the van with a thump. Her shoulder, already sore, ached further. Her hands were still tied behind her back, her ankles similarly bound. A gaffer tape gag over her mouth. She couldn't move, had given up all hope of escape.

She had lost all track of time, and had alternated between impotent anger and real hopelessness. After Mary Evans's visit she had been left alone, just food and drink brought in and left by the door, one hand freed to eat with, then the plate taken away, her hand retied.

She had spent all the time in her head. Thinking of child-hood holidays with Lillian and Philip. Her real father. Imagining those days were with her again, ignoring the tears on her face when she came out of her fantasies, realized where she was.

She made deals with a God she had long since ceased to believe in: I'll never drink again. I'll be the daughter my mother wants me to be. I'll find a man, settle down. I'll never go looking for trouble again. I'll go to church every Sunday.

Bargains she hoped she would one day be in a position to make good on but doubted that would ever happen.

She was going to die. She knew it. Everyone was going to die, but Peta knew that her death would come sooner than most. She had tried not to torture herself with thoughts about who and what she would be leaving behind. Instead tried to be brave, even philosophical about it.

No good. She couldn't do that. She imagined she knew what her friend Jill must have gone through several months ago when she had been kidnapped, tortured and finally killed by a serial killer. She would never read a Thomas Harris novel again.

Add that to the list of impossible bargains.

And then they had picked her up, thrown her in the van. When they had opened the door, her heart had momentarily risen. But now, as she lay on the filthy floor of the van, she wasn't so sure. She looked around. At each side of her, piled high, was something that, although not an expert, she recognized.

Explosive. And lots of it.

Her heart sank again, lower than it had ever been.

The door was still open. A figure stood in the doorway. Peta recognized her immediately.

Mary Evans.

'And how are we today?' she said. 'It doesn't matter. Because you're soon not going to care about things like that. Remember I said we had something planned for your dear old dad? Well, this is it. We're going to make sure you give him something to remember you by. Smile. You're going to be famous.'

She slammed the door shut.

Peta felt like she had been locked in a tomb while she was still alive. She looked at the explosives.

But not for long.

Amar sat staring at the screen. Jamal and Donovan were on the sofa, the TV on, David Dimbleby marking time until he had something to talk about.

Nothing would start until the polls had closed. They all knew that. But they had monitored, nonetheless. Now they just had to wait. There was a limit to how much tea, coffee and Coke could be drunk, how much pizza could be eaten in one night and they were all discovering it. Not that they had appetites or thirsts. It was just something to fill in the time with.

They knew the best thing to do was wait, but it didn't come naturally to them. Donovan wanted to go tearing round the streets, knocking on doors, talking to people. But he knew it would yield nothing. So he had joined the others, eating pizza, waiting. Hating it.

They had discussed courses of action, made their plans. Nattrass would be informed as soon as they heard anything pertinent to her. Anything concerning Peta they would deal with themselves.

But there had been nothing. David Dimbleby was interviewing politicians and political editors who knew as much as he did. The phone hadn't rung.

They waited.

41

Trevor Whitman stood by the entrance to Stowell Street, Newcastle's mini Chinatown, looked along it.

The street consisted of two strips of Chinese buildings, mainly restaurants, interspersed with supermarkets, stores and Chinese community associations. He took out his phone, dialled a number he had learned by heart. Lillian answered.

'Hello.' Her voice was fraught, sharp. On edge, waiting for news.

'It's me.'

'Joe, Jamal,' said Amar turning round and slipping the head-phones on, 'we've got something.'

Donovan and Jamal rushed over to the table, joined him at staring at the laptop. The figures made no sense to Donovan.

'Here,' said Amar, turning up the volume, 'listen.'

'There's no news,' Whitman said. He had heard that catch in Lillian's breath, knew what she had been about to ask. Her silence was his response. 'But I'm working on it. I'll have answers soon. Very soon. Then it'll all be wrapped up.'

'Soon? What? Where are you?'

Whitman laughed. 'Stowell Street.'

'Least we don't need to trace him,' said Amar.

*

'Remember,' Whitman was saying, 'one of our first proper dates was here? Chinese restaurant. Saved up for months. Poor students.'

Lillian's voice became warm. 'You said you would only eat food from a left-wing country that cared for and respected their workers.'

Whitman gave a small laugh. 'Shows what I know.'

She joined him in laughing, longer and harder than the joke warranted. She sounded like she had been drinking. Whitman couldn't blame her. The laugh died away.

'Why?' he said, a plaintive edge to his voice.

'Why what?'

'Why target one ethnic minority for hatred and not another?'

'What d'you mean? What are you talking about?'

'The Chinese,' he said, slightly slurring his words. 'They've been here as long as I can remember. But, you know, apart from that casual, ignorant everyday British racism, no one bothers them.'

Lillian's voice filled with concern. 'Trevor, have you been drinking?'

'I mean, who decides?' he said, ignoring her question. 'Who says, yeah, Indians and East Europeans, but not Chinese. Who draws up these lists? The right-wing political parties? The right-wing media?'

'I, I don't know, Trevor.'

'Should write a book about it,' he mumbled, then sighed. 'Something else I wouldn't get round to doing.'

'Trevor, come home. I'm worried about you.'

'No, Lillian, this has gone on long enough. It's time for this to end. Tonight.'

'But, Trevor . . .'

'Don't worry. It'll all be over soon.'

Lillian sighed.

'I'm going back to where this all started. Get it sorted out.'

'Where it all started?' said Donovan.

The other two looked at him, frowning.

'Then find Peta. Make sure she's safe,' said Lillian, that catch returning to her voice.

'I will,' he said. He sighed, building himself up for something. 'Look, Lillian, I've got to go. But I just . . . I just wanted to say . . .'

Lillian waited, her breath fast.

'I love you.'

Silence from Lillian, then a gentle sob, sniffed away. 'Thank you,' she said, her voice small and soft. 'The first time you've ever said it.'

'But not the first time I've ever felt it. I didn't want to say it until I was sure. And I was sure that you'd accept it.'

'I do. And I love you too, Trevor.'

Another sigh from Whitman. 'I've got to go. Just wanted you to know.'

'I think I knew already.'

There was only a little bit more. She wished him luck, he accepted it. With great reluctance, he broke the connection.

Pocketed the phone, walked away from Stowell Street, checking the gun in his pocket, his stride becoming more purposeful the longer he walked.

Amar turned to the other two. 'Don't know about you, but I felt a bit pervy listening in to that last bit,' he said. 'And not in a good way.'

'Know what you mean,' said Donovan. 'But what did he mean? Where it all started. What does that mean?'

'The Chinese restaurant?' said Jamal.

'No,' said Donovan, 'he was already there. He'd have mentioned it. I think that was just some romantic memory between the pair of them. No. Where it all started . . .'

'Dunno,' said Jamal. 'Man sounded out of it.'

'Sounds like he's been trying to build up the courage to do something. Getting angry on purpose. Think.'

'What about the pub?' said Amar. 'Where the bomb was?'

'That's it,' said Donovan, his heart beating faster, his breathing getting heavier. 'The pub.' He looked around for some case reference material. Nothing there. He'd left it all at his own place and Peta's. 'Right. Which pub was it again?'

'Major Tom, can you come over here a moment, please?'

'Won't be a moment.' Major Tom looked at Kev and Jason, got out of the 4×4. That look had been held a bit too long for Kev's liking. He felt Major Tom suspected him of something.

Kev looked through the window. Major Tom was talking to one of the van drivers. It looked like they were checking and coordinating routes. He had a minute, two at the most. He took the mobile out, clicked through the menu. He had to find Amar's number, get the photos off to him. Call him or text him, let him know that Peta was definitely there and was being transferred. Let him do something about it. Call in the cavalry.

He clicked through, trying to find it.

'Please don't.'

He jumped. Jason was watching him. 'All right, mate? Don't worry. Just get this done, then I'll get us out of here.'

'Please, just do what they want. If you don't they'll . . . they'll really hurt you. I know what they do. Please . . .'

Kev found the number, began sending the photos. 'Don't worry, mate, it's all right.' Kev looked to see where Major Tom was. Still talking. Good. As his attention came back to the phone, his eyes strayed to the front of the 4×4. The keys were still in the ignition.

An idea hit Kev, sent a thrill through his body. Drive the 4×4, get away with Jason. Give Amar the news in person. A smile spread over his features. Brilliant. How was that for atonement?

He flipped the phone shut, ready to get out, slip into the driving seat, drive off.

The door slammed. Major Tom was back in. Kev hadn't heard him. He looked at the mobile in his hands.

'What the fuck's that? What are you doing?'

Kev looked up. His heart started thumping. Terror flooded every cell. He had been caught. Beside him, Jason silently closed his eyes. Tried not to whimper.

'I'm . . .'

'I said no mobiles. You think you're exempt?'

'No, no,' said Kev quickly. 'It's just . . . me dad and, an' brother. I just wanted to check they were OK. They, they rely on me. Me brother's got this, y'know, problem. Drugs. Got to make sure he's, he's sorted, y'know?'

Major Tom's features softened slightly. Kev pressed on.

'I'll, I'll . . . You're right.' He turned the phone off. 'They can do without me for one night.' He pocketed the phone. 'There. Gone.'

Major Tom stared at Kev, his features hard, unreadable. Kev felt his hands shake. He began to sweat. Eventually Major Tom turned away from him. But the look remained on his face. Kev sensed this wasn't over with yet.

'Right,' said Major Tom. He looked out of the window. 'Here's our driver. We're ready to go. Onward to victory.' He gave a bitter laugh.

The car started up. Jason still had his eyes closed. Kev didn't dare move. His knife wound was hurting again. But that was the least of the pain he was feeling.

The convoy of vans, led by the 4×4 pulled out of the farm and headed for Newcastle.

42

Trevor Whitman stood on the opposite side of the street, looking at the offices of the NUP and imagining what used to be there. He should have expected it to come down to this. There was no other option. It had to.

Light seeped out from behind the boarded front windows. He imagined the party faithful in the office, watching the TV, waiting for results. He looked beyond the present, into the past. Saw the building burst into flames, windows blow out, the explosion causing a lethal hailstorm of glass, wood and brick. The screams, shouts, cries, sirens. Movement all around. People rushing, outside, burning. Staggering into the street, bloodied, dazed. Some missing limbs, parts of faces. All uncomprehending.

He shook his head, tried to dislodge the memory. It was reluctant to budge. The noise still intense, the images still vivid. And he had stood, where he was now, and watched it all. Entranced by the horror. Knew it would haunt him for the rest of his life but still unable to look away, walk away.

And Alan Shepherd knew that. Was counting on it. He had to be. Shepherd was inside the building, waiting. Just for him. A spider deep within the web of the building, sitting there, smiling, beckoning him in. In this place, at this time. Just waiting for the correct moment to pounce, to kill. Expecting him to just walk in through the front door.

Well, thought Whitman, sorry to disappoint you. He felt

the gun in his pocket, crossed the road, moved down a side
street.

Looking for a back entrance.

'Found it.'

Amar looked up from his computer. The three of them
had been poring over screens, checking the internet, utiliz-
ing every search engine, trying to find the name and location
of the blown-up pub.

The other two came over to join him. He had gone
through Wikipedia, found an article linked to the Hollow
Men. 'Up in Fenham.' He checked the road. 'Near the
police station there. That must be it.'

'Page down a bit,' Donovan said, pointing to the screen.
Amar did so. 'There. Read that.'

They did.

'Jesus,' said Amar. 'Now headquarters to the NUP. The
leylines are connecting.'

Jamal frowned. 'Wha'?'

'Never mind,' said Donovan. 'I'll bet that's where
Whitman's on his way to. And where Shepherd is. Or
Sharples. Or Shithead or whatever he calls himself now.' He
stood up. A thought struck him. 'Can you check for own-
ership on there?'

'What d'you mean?' said Amar.

'Can you find out who owns the building?'

'Course I can. Pay enough for these subscription services
I'm not supposed to have.' Amar opened another tabbed
screen, hit some keys, waited. 'Here we are.' A list appeared
on screen. He scrolled down. 'It should be . . . here. What
d'you think?'

Donovan looked at it. Laughed. 'Fuck me.'

'It's a kind offer,' said Amar, 'but you're not my type.
What does it mean?'

'The company that owns it. It's Abdul-Haq's.' He looked at the other two. 'Now why am I not surprised?'

Whitman pulled hard, fingers scrabbling and sore, managed to lift his body up on top of the brick wall. He balanced his body, fingers holding on, chest aching and trying to pant quietly, not wanting to be heard, gathering strength for the jump down. He could smell the stale alcohol on his breath, knew it wasn't a crutch, like fuel for his engine.

He slung one leg over, the other, lowered himself indelicately down, scraping his suit against the rough brickwork as he did so. He landed on the ground, stood up, checked for noise. Nothing. Good.

He had walked all round the NUP headquarters, looking for a way in, found nothing except the back alley, a seven-foot brick wall with a locked, wooden gate set into it.

He was in a concrete back yard, nothing in it but bins, old cardboard and bottles. At the back of the building, a door, half-glassed, with a window beside it. He tried the door. Locked. Checked the window. Locked from the inside but loose in its frame. Heart rising, blood pumping faster, he wedged his fingers under the hinged window frame, pulled hard. It rattled but didn't budge. Pulled harder. Heard the splintering of rotten wood. Pulled harder. The window opened.

He wiped his brow. He was sweating, shaking. He wiped his hands down the front of his jacket, checked the gun was still where it should be, pulled himself up on to the windowsill.

He managed to climb inside the window, get his feet on to the floor on the other side. He stood up. Still shaking, still sweating. He hadn't felt so unfit for years, but he doubted that was the main reason.

Ahead of him was a hallway with a staircase leading upstairs. He drew his gun, set off quietly down the hallway. A small kitchen was to his left, a toilet to his right. He walked on. Another staircase, a doorway ahead. Noise coming from beyond the door; people drinking, watching the TV. Slowly he made his way up the stairs.

On the landing were more doors, light seeping from under one of them. That was Shepherd. He knew it. Could feel it. He tried the handle. Locked.

Bastard. He thought hard, tried to work out what to do next. He had come this far, he couldn't just stop now. The action was taken out of his hands. Movement in the room. Someone coming to the door. Whitman's heart began pumping even harder. He looked round, desperate for a hiding place. Couldn't find one. Flattened himself by the side of the door, waited, gun in hand, for it to open.

It did. The key was turned. Whitman's breath caught. Alan Shepherd stepped out. He would have recognized him anywhere. The hair was gone and the face was lined, but the eyes were the same. If anything, they were worse.

Shepherd stepped through the door. Whitman put the barrel of his gun against Shepherd's temple.

'Don't move, cunt.' His voice was shaking and breathy. Whitman struggled to control it.

Shepherd stopped moving, smiled. 'Trevor. How nice. Would you like me to put my hands up too?'

'Why not?' Whitman's voice was getting stronger. 'Back inside.'

'I was on my way to the toilet.'

'Then you'll just have to cross your legs. Back inside.'

Shepherd did as he was told.

Whitman followed him in, the gun trained on his back.

Shepherd was trying to act casually, but his shoulders were tensed and hunched as if he knew where the gun was aimed.

'Look, Gideon,' said Shepherd, 'look who it is. The hollowest of Hollow Men.'

'Alan? What . . .'

Whitman looked down. It took him a few seconds, but he recognized the figure on the chesterfield.

'Jesus,' he said. 'Gideon.'

'Trevor.' Abdul-Haq's face drained of colour. 'What are you doing here?'

'Come to watch the election results, like the rest of us,' said Sharples. 'Why don't you put the gun away, pull up a chair. Have a drink with us.'

Whitman sneered. 'What, all old friends together?'

'That sort of thing.'

'Sit down, Alan. Or I'll shoot you.'

Shepherd stayed standing. He turned round, faced Whitman. 'Really.'

Whitman tried to keep his grip tight, his hand steady. He remembered his earlier shooting, tried to draw strength from that, from the gun itself. 'Yes, really. I've already shot two people today. Want to make it a third?'

Doubt flickered briefly across Shepherd's face, then was gone. He moved over to the other chesterfield, sat down. 'There. Happy?'

'Ecstatic.' He held the gun tight. His hand wasn't shaking now. 'Now—'

He didn't get to finish his sentence. His mobile rang.

Amar motioned Donovan across the room to the laptop. 'Whitman's phone. He's got a call coming in.' He turned the sound up so the other two could hear.

'Recognize the number?'

'I think . . . give me a minute.' He went looking through his lists.

Whitman answered his phone.

'Hello, Trevor.'

'What? Who is . . .' He thought for a moment. The voice was familiar.

'Oh, come on,' said the voice on the phone. 'Don't say you've forgotten me.' There was anger in the tone and also bitterness.

Whitman placed it. 'Mary. Mary Evans.'

On the sofa, Alan Shepherd smiled.

'Yes. Hello, lover. After all these years. Surprised to hear from me? You should be.'

Whitman looked at the two on the sofas, back to the phone. 'Right, Mary. It's great to hear from you, and I would love to spend some time catching up, but I'm a bit busy at the moment. Why don't we—'

'Always busy.' The anger was there again, accompanied by a manic edge. 'Busy, busy, busy. Always got something better to do than talk to Mary. Spend time with Mary. Give some respect to Mary.' The last few words were almost spat out.

Whitman gave an exasperated sigh. 'What d'you want?'

She laughed. It wasn't pleasant. 'Just some of your time, lover man. Got a little job for you to do. Take you on a trip down memory lane.'

'Look, Mary, like I said, I'm a bit busy at the moment.'

'Don't fucking patronize me! You'll listen to me when I'm talking to you! Listen! Right?'

'Mary—'

'If you want to see your daughter alive again, you'll fucking listen.'

Whitman's mouth fell open. The words that had been about to come out died in his throat. 'What?'

Again, that laugh. 'You heard.'

He looked at Shepherd and Abdul-Haq. He had been sure they had Peta. 'But, what . . .'

'It's very simple. Even an ageing pretty boy like you can understand. I've got your daughter. Now she's alive at the moment and she'll stay that way. But you have to do something for me.'

'What?' Whitman was shaking again, sweating. He tried to stand still, hold the gun upright. But his hands were slick, his legs shaking.

'Run an errand. Down memory lane. Relive the story of our love. Then you can see your daughter again. Alive.' She laughed again.

'What?'

'Remember how we were always going to the cinema? We saw everything together. Remember *Dirty Harry*? Clint Eastwood?'

'What about it?'

She laughed again. 'You'll see.'

He looked again at the two on the sofa. 'What? What d'you want me to do?'

'Go to the Quayside. By the Guildhall. Underneath the arch of the Swing Bridge. There's something there waiting for you. Go and get it.'

'But—'

'The clock's ticking. The longer you wait, the more chance you have of not seeing your pretty daughter alive. There's a public phone box there. Be waiting for a call. You've got ten minutes.'

The line went dead. He put the phone down, looked back at Shepherd, who was openly grinning.

'Leaving us, Trevor? And so soon.'

Whitman stared at him, the gun still trained on him. 'You knew. You were expecting . . . expecting that call.'

'Of course. I've left nothing to chance.' He held up his mobile. 'Had a text waiting, just ready for you to turn up. That was the signal.'

Whitman stared at Shepherd. The gun was starting to get heavy.

'Hadn't you better be running along?'

'Yes . . . yes . . .'

Whitman's phone rang again. This time, Shepherd was as surprised as Whitman. He answered it, clumsily putting it to his ear, still holding the gun outstretched.

'Yes?'

'Trevor, it's Joe Donovan.'

Whitman groaned. 'Look, this isn't—'

'I just heard the call. From Mary Evans.'

Whitman wasn't sure he had heard correctly. 'What? What d'you mean? I've just . . .'

'We've been listening in. I said we were good. Where are you now? Have you reached the NUP place?'

'But how did you . . .'

'Like I said, we're good. Are you there yet?'

'Yes, yes, I am.'

'And who else is there?'

'Alan Shepherd. And Gideon.' His composure began to return. 'They're not going anywhere. I've got a gun on them.'

'Brilliant.' Donovan sounded exasperated. 'Don't do anything stupid, Trevor. Just don't let them get away. They'll be arrested before the end of the night.'

'What?'

'Don't panic. Just listen to me. We have a plan. I'll go down to the Quayside, keep the appointment for you.'

'But—'

'Don't argue, Trevor, and just listen. We think we know what she's doing but we're running out of time. I'll go down to the Quayside, wait for the call. We'll have to keep in contact. Can you get another phone?'

Whitman looked around. Shepherd's mobile was still on the table between the two seated men. He waved his gun at Shepherd. 'Give me your phone.'

'What?'

'Fucking do it!' He moved closer, stuck his gun in Shepherd's face. Shepherd handed over the phone.

'What's the number?' said Donovan.

Whitman asked Shepherd for the number, repeated it to Donovan.

'Right,' said Donovan. 'I'm going to call it.' It rang. 'Answer it. Put it on speakerphone, keep it near you. That's how we keep in touch. Right, I'm going now. I'm counting on you. Peta's life depends on you. Don't fuck up.'

Donovan rang off. Whitman put his phone down, kept the gun on the other two. 'Well,' he said, 'looks like I'm going nowhere for the time being.'

Shepherd and Abdul-Haq exchanged glances. This wasn't the plan.

This wasn't the plan at all.

43

Amar sat at the desk, watching numbers tumble down the screen, counting, analysing them as they went. Cross-reference them with the mapped-out grid on the screen next to him, try to pick up Mary Evans's location and, by extension, the location of Peta.

Donovan and Jamal had set off moments earlier on foot, running down to the Quayside. They hadn't had time to test out the Bluetooth earpieces. Amar just hoped they worked as they were supposed to.

They had all agreed not to phone Di Nattrass until they had something more concrete to tell her. Whitman with Shepherd at the NUP headquarters was one thing, working with Whitman to free Peta quite another. If Mary Evans was as unstable as they suspected her to be, the presence of police might just be thing to tip her over the edge. And they had no idea what she might do to Peta.

His mobile, sitting on the coffee table in front of the TV, began playing Rufus Wainwright's 'Release the Stars'. Amar's ringtone for an incoming text. He started to get up from his chair, cross the room, answer it. Then stopped. The screen had come up with a partial match for Mary's number.

He sat back down again, pressed some keys, watched, waited. The box sprang up: nothing.

He sighed, sat back. Kept staring. Kept hunting.

The mobile on the table forgotten for now.

★

The 4×4, with the vans in tow, drove into Newcastle, sticking one mile over any given speed limit so as not to arouse suspicion. Once in the city centre the convoy split up. The vans headed off down the West Road towards Arthur's Hill. The 4×4 continued down to the Central Station, negotiated the traffic system around it, skirting the Arena and, thankful there was no concert on that night, down Forth Street behind the station. It came to rest outside a lock-up in one of the old railway arches. The driver got out, unlocked the old wooden doors, drove the 4×4 inside, locked up behind him.

Major Tom got out, flicked a switch. Striplights flickered into life overhead, casting a bare, depressing glow throughout. 'Here we are,' he said. 'High command.'

Kev, his stomach lurching, got out. The place was dusty and dirty. Empty. It carried the ghosts of bad things on its musty air. Jason stayed where he was. Major Tom turned to him, beckoned with the slightest crook of his right index finger. Jason immediately scrambled from the car.

'Good. Let me check the equipment.'

Jason unzipped his bomber. Like an oversized version of Batman's utility belt, the bomb was strapped round Jason's waist, high explosive distributed evenly in packs, interspersed with containers of nails and shrapnel. In place of a buckle was a timer on the front of a detonator. Wires connected the detonator with the rest of the bomb. It had been designed to look home-made and lethal. Exactly the sort of thing a deranged loner would come up with.

'Good,' said Major Tom as Jason stood silently to be examined. He stood back. 'Zip up.'

Jason did as he was told. Major Tom checked his watch, asked his driver the time. Quarter to midnight. The platoon's watches had all been synchronized. Major Tom reached across the seat of the 4×4, brought out the corded mic of a field radio. He depressed the button, spoke into it.

'A team, B team, C team, D team, can you hear me, over?'

Static and crackle, then each leader reporting in, answering in the affirmative.

'Good,' said Major Tom. 'This is an order. Repeat, this is an order. Operation Thor's Hammer is ready to go on my signal.' He checked his watch again, waited for the seconds to tick by, hit zero. 'Go. All units go.'

The A team were stationed on Nun's Moor. Their leader, Kev's old lieutenant, Ligsy, switched his mobile off, turned to the troops. Eight of them, standing to attention, weapons visible. Like attack dogs straining on too short leashes. Almost gave him a hard-on just to see them.

'That was the order,' he said. 'Let's go.'

They didn't need to be told twice.

Major Tom dropped the mic on the front seat, turned to the driver and smiled. 'Tomorrow belongs to us, and all that.'

The driver, not understanding the reference, nodded.

'Right,' said Major Tom, 'now for tonight's other major contribution to democracy.' He turned to Kev. 'D'you know what you're doing with this?'

Kev nodded, not believing what he was about to say. 'Taking Jason up to the Civic Centre, wait for the signal, arm the bomb.' He swallowed, felt something stick in his throat. 'Send him in.'

'To be a martyr to the cause.'

Kev swallowed again. The obstruction wouldn't shift. 'To be a martyr to the cause.' His voice was unsteady. 'Sir.' Said too loud, too forcefully.

Major Tom frowned. 'You feeling all right?'

Kev cleared his throat. 'Fine. Sir.'

'Big ask, this. Big opportunity.'

'I know, sir.' Kev moved his feet uncomfortably. Felt the knife, tucked into the back of his waistband, dig in slightly.

'You up to it?'

Kev nodded. Major Tom kept staring at him, quizzical. 'How long will it take you to walk up to the Civic Centre? Fifteen minutes? Half an hour? An hour?'

Kev shrugged. 'Fifteen minutes, I reckon. Sir.'

Major Tom nodded. 'Right. Well, just in case.' He stepped towards Jason. 'Unzip.'

Jason unzipped his bomber jacket. Major Tom armed the bomb.

'What you doin'?' said Kev. 'It'll go off now.'

'No, it won't,' said Major Tom. 'I've set it to detonate in thirty minutes. It can only be disarmed by inputting a code. That code is known only to me.'

'Why?'

Major Tom smiled. 'Just in case you got any ideas. Just in case you decided to run off.' His gaze hardened. 'My gut feeling with you, Kev, is that you're not one hundred per cent a team player.'

'What? Sir?' Kev's anxiety was increasing. He wished for the knife in his hand. He had to get out.

'Too unreliable, too flaky. If I could have used someone else for this I would have done. But it's too late for that. You'll have to do. Oh, and don't try and tamper with it. Cut the wires, pull them out, undo it, anything like that. It'll blow up in your face.'

Kev was speechless.

'Oh,' said Major Tom, continuing. 'I'll have your mobile too.'

'No.' Kev couldn't believe he had said that. Not to Major Tom.

From the look on his face, Major Tom couldn't believe it either. 'What? What did you just say to me?'

'I said no. You . . . you can't have it. No.'

Major Tom advanced on Kev. Jason closed his eyes. 'Oh, yes I will.'

Kev drew the knife from the back of his jeans. It slipped into his hand like it was an extension of his body. It felt good, right. He drew comfort from it, strength. And he knew how to use it.

'I don't think so,' he said, and ran forward, plunging the blade through Major Tom's ribcage. Deeply in, twisting it, snapping the metal, leaving only the handle in his hand.

Major Tom staggered back in shock, his hand going to his chest as blood began to pump out.

'I got you in the heart,' Kev said, watching him fall to the ground. 'I might know nothin' else, I might be flaky, I might not be a team player, but I know me cuts of meat.'

Major Tom slid to the floor, his mouth wide, his eyes staring, unable to believe what was happening to him. Then his features changed. Fear entered his eyes, bringing with it the realization that he was about to die. He began grasping, flailing about, trying desperately to grab on to something, anything, that would anchor him in the world. His grasp was too feeble, his fingers wouldn't hold. The world slipped away from his blood-slicked fingers.

The driver, standing at the front door on lookout, saw what was happening, moved towards Kev.

'You want some an' all, eh?'

The driver stopped walking, looked round uncertainly. Then, watching Major Tom writhing and gasping on the floor, blood flowing from his body like dark, red water, he opened the door and ran.

Kev looked down at the twitching body, the knife handle in his hand, at Jason standing dumbfounded to the side of him. Panic welled within him. He didn't know what to do.

He grabbed Jason's hand and pulled him to the door. Started running.

It was only when he had gone halfway up Forth Street without stopping for breath that he realised he had just killed the only person who knew how to defuse the bomb Jason was wearing.

He grabbed Jason, kept running.

44

Donovan and Jamal ran along Neville Street, round the bottom of Westgate Road, along past the cathedral, down the Side on to the Quayside. They reached the Guildhall out of breath, grateful for their run being mostly downhill.

Donovan's chest was burning. He put his hands on his thighs, bent over, thinking he was about to be sick. Jamal, next to him, was doing likewise. His vision was spiked with dayglo swirls, his legs shaking. Donovan turned to Jamal.

'You OK?'

Jamal, too winded to speak, nodded.

'Good.' Donovan straightened up, looked round. The Guildhall was in front of them, the massive arc of the Tyne Bridge just to their left. 'Come on.' Donovan trotted over to the water's edge. Drinkers walked along the front, making the most of the extended opening hours, bar-hopping the night away. Dance music was carried on the air, giving the night a heartbeat of its own.

Donovan checked the railing. No Mary Evans, no Peta.

'Whitman,' he managed to get out between gasps, 'she's not here. Peta, Mary. Neither of them.'

Whitman's voice came down the line. 'What? Has she left something?'

'Like what?'

'I don't know. A . . . key, or something? A map, some directions?'

Donovan directed Jamal to check the area. 'Why here, Trevor? Why did she want you to come here?'

'She . . . wait. Wait a minute.'

Donovan heard the other phone ringing. Whitman answered it. Donovan pressed a small button on the earpiece, changed channels.

Whitman put the phone to his ear. In front of him, Shepherd and Abdul-Haq sat uneasily. As he moved the phone, Shepherd moved forward. Whitman raised the gun. Shepherd sank back.

'Are you there yet, Trevor?' Mary Evans's voice was in his ear. Already he hated the sound of it.

'Yes.'

'You don't sound very out of breath.'

'Stop fucking about, Mary. Tell me what you want.'

Silence while she digested the rebuke, then that voice again. 'Have you found it yet?'

'What am I looking for?'

'You know fucking well what you're looking for. We had just started seeing each other. We had our photo taken down there. Asked some passer-by to do it. We had two copies made. Said you would keep it for ever, treasure it. Did you?'

Whitman tried to think. Photo? He couldn't remember . . .

'Right,' he said. 'The photo.'

'It's there. Have you found it? It's got a message on.'

'Photo,' Donovan hissed to Jamal.

They both began looking. They checked along the front, by the bollards, on the windows of the Guildhall itself. Couldn't find anything. Donovan switched the channel on his earpiece.

'We can't find it. Ask for another clue.'

★

'I can't see it anywhere, Mary,' he said, turning his head so no sound would bleed through from the other phone. 'Give me a clue.'

'It's where it was taken.'

Whitman shook his head. He had no idea.

Mary Evans laughed. 'Time's running out, lover boy.'

'I can't . . .'

'You bastard. Did I mean so little to you? The underpass beneath the Swing Bridge. You fucking idiot. You're losing minutes for that.'

Donovan ran to the location, searched around. Tucked into a crack between the brickwork was a photo.

'Found it.'

'Found it,' Whitman said.

'Good. Now read the message to me.'

Donovan looked at the photo. It showed a young Trevor Whitman with his arm round an equally young Mary Evans. They were both smiling. There were no hints at how things would turn out, no seeds to be interpreted from it. He flipped it over, read out the inscription on the back.

'"Where you first fucked me, with a view of the Tyne." Got that?'

Whitman repeated it to Mary Evans.

'Right,' she said. 'Go there. You've got, ooh, six minutes.'

The phone went dead.

He picked up the other one. 'Donovan, you've got to go, you've got to go.'

'Where?'

'The . . . the pub . . .' He couldn't remember the name of it.

'Which one?'

'By the . . . the bridge. The High Level. The Bridge Hotel. That's the one.'

'You fucked her there? Classy.'

Whitman's face reddened. 'Don't fuck about. Just get there.'

Donovan pocketed the photo, turned to Jamal.

'You OK to do this?'

Jamal looked like he was ready to collapse. 'For Peta, innit?'

Donovan gave a grim smile. 'Yeah.'

'We're bein' Dirty Harry, like you said.' Jamal frowned. 'Who is Dirty Harry?'

'Film with Clint Eastwood,' said Donovan quickly, not wanting to take up any time. 'Early Seventies. Bad guy has a girl hidden somewhere and he sends the good guy running round the city looking for clues.'

'Right.'

'Shit.' A shiver went through Donovan.

'What?'

'Just remembered. The girl was dead when he found her.'

Jamal looked horrified. 'What we fuckin' waitin' for then?'

Jamal ran off. Donovan joined him.

On the chesterfield, Shepherd started laughing.

'Think you can keep this up? Hmm, Trevor?' Shepherd's eyes were glittering darkly. 'How long before she finds out? How long before she gets bored? We're not dealing with the most stable of people here, are we?'

Whitman looked at him, anger and confusion etched into his features. He kept the gun pointed. His arm was really aching now. 'What's she doing this for? Eh? What does she get out of all this?'

Shepherd's features darkened. Any trace of a smile disappeared. 'Revenge, Trevor. This is all about money and power, yes, but also revenge. For what you did to her. For what you did to me.'

At his desk, Amar leaned forward.

'To you?' said Whitman. 'What d'you mean? I didn't do—'

'Oh, spare me.' Shepherd spat the words out. His face was contorted with anger. It had none of the cynical sheen he had used up until that point. He looked wounded, enraged. 'Fucking spare me the holier-than-thou act. It may wash with your readers or your students, but not with me. Not with the person you fucked over all those years ago. Whose life you ruined.'

Whitman closed his mouth. Whatever he had been about to say he had decided was unnecessary.

'Yeah, Trevor. I took the blame, all right. For blowing up the pub, killing the policeman. But we know who made the bomb, who planted it, don't we?'

Whitman said nothing.

'I said, don't we?'

Whitman nodded his head. 'Yes,' he said, voice small and defeated. 'I did it.'

45

Amar, listening in, recovered from the shock quickly. He stuck another wire into the side of the laptop, attached a digital recorder.

Pressed RECORD.

The foot soldiers were on the march.

Down Wingrove Road into Nun's Moor Road. Ligsy leading, head specially shaved and oiled so it gleamed in the streetlights, more like steel than skin, automatic pushed down the waistband of his jeans, motorbike chain wrapped round the knuckles of his right hand, swinging the loose chain like some medieval flail. Muscles like taut, metal rope. Shoulders straight, chest out, cock nearly hard and leading with it.

The others followed him, all on their lookout for targets. And that could be anyone, as long as their skin was a different colour or they didn't understand the Queen's English.

Ligsy loved it. This was what it was all about. No other feeling in the world like it. Better than sex. Better than anything.

The A team rounded the corner. And there they were. Pakis. Tooled up. Waiting for them. Word must have gone round. They were expected.

Ligsy stopped the march. They could have taken them out easily, just pulled out the guns, let them have it. But there was a better way. More fun, more honest. More brutal.

The Pakis started chanting: 'Nazi scum, leave our streets. Nazi scum, leave our streets . . .' Over and over.

'Come on, lads,' said Ligsy. 'We're not gonna let a load of fuckin' Pakis shout louder than us, are we?'

They weren't. They shouted back: 'Wogs out, *Sieg Heil.*' Doing the actions to accompany the words, moving forward all the while.

Both sides' eyes burning with hate.

Anticipation like a big hard python coiled in Ligsy's guts, waiting to get released and spread terror. A big hard-on waiting to come.

The chanting rose. And rose. Both sides getting louder, nearer, both sides psyching each other up for what they had to do.

Then it came. No more verbals, no more posing. Adrenalin pumped right up, bell ringing, red light on. The charge.

The python was out, the hard-on spurted.

Both sides together, two walls of sound clashing. A big, sonic tidal wave ready to engulf them all in violence, carry each one under with fists and boots and sticks.

Engage. And in.

Fists and boots and sticks. Ligsy and his boys took. Gave back double. Twisting and thrashing, swimming in anger. Up for air, then diving back in again, lungs full. Screaming the screams, chanting the chants.

Then Ligsy wasn't swimming. Liquid solidified round him. And he was part of a huge machine. A muscle and bone and blood machine. A shouting, chanting cog in a huge hurting machine. Arms windmilling. Boots kicking. Fuelled on violence. Driven by rage. Lost to it. No more individuals. Just the machine. They had never felt more alive.

He saw their eyes. The fear and hate and blood in their eyes. Fed on it. Hate matched hate. Hate gave as good as hate got.

Gave better. The machine was too good for them. The

other side were going down. Red blood on brown skin. The machine was winning. Cogs and clangs and fists and hammers. The machine would always win.

Then it stopped.

The police were there. No one had noticed them approach. They had let the fighters tire, moved in to pick them off one by one. Batons raised, shields up. Batons down. And again. And again.

The machine fell apart; components became selves again. The police were the machine now, moving forward inexorably, dragging off bodies to waiting vans, throwing them in the backs.

Ligsy grabbed the butt of his gun, ready to pull it out, start shooting. He stopped. A little red dot danced on the handle. He tried to grab it; it went with him. Understanding, he looked up. On rooftops were silhouettes, crouching, lying, streetlight glinting on telescopic sights, rifle barrels.

Armed police. No chance. His hand dropped. He turned, tried to run. Went straight into the baton of a waiting riot police. He went down.

He stayed down.

Similar scenes were happening all over the West End. The resistance had been crushed. The foot soldiers of the revolution were beaten.

Kev was running. Away from what, towards what, he didn't know. He remembered being told once of a man, an associate of his dad's, a one-time hard man, who started to have a heart attack while he was driving. He knew it was going to be fatal so pulled the car off the road and ran into a field, screaming all the while, ripping at his chest, trying to outrun it. He didn't make it.

Kev felt exactly the same.

He ran, pulling Jason by the hand, along Forth Street, up

on to Mosley Street to the bottom of Grey Street. He stood there, forcing air into his blazing lungs, looked up at the huge Georgian buildings, all beauty and elegance, and knew he would never have anything like that in his life.

Rage and self-pity built up inside him, mingled with fear. He wanted to scream, to run, to rip himself apart and start again. He knew that would never happen now. Even without Jason he was looking at life in prison for murder.

He grabbed Jason's hand again. 'Come on.'

'No . . .' The voice almost inaudible.

Kev turned, looked at Jason. 'What?'

'No, I'm . . . I can't run . . . any more . . .'

Kev grabbed him by the shoulders. 'You're talkin'. You're back. Look, d'you know what your name is? D'you know who you are?'

'Yeah,' said Jason, panting. He almost smiled. 'I'm the Butcher Boy . . .'

Kev hugged him, felt tears forming in his eyes. Then remembered the clock.

'Come on,' he said. 'We've got to get you somewhere, get that bomb defused.'

Jason shook his head. Started to cry.

'Come on,' said Kev, although he felt no better himself. 'Let's . . . let's see if we can find somewhere, someone to help.'

Jason nodded. 'Oh–OK . . .'

'Good,' said Kev. He held out his hand again. 'Come on, then.'

And they were off again, Kev all the while trying to think where they could go, who they could find to help them in the time they had.

Feeling more and more like that dying man running across the field, ripping away at his own chest.

*

Whitman held the gun on Shepherd. It felt heavier than ever. In the background the TV was still playing, results starting to come in. David Dimbleby was talking about wanting to go over to Newcastle West but there being some kind of delay. No one in the room was listening to him.

Shepherd's phone sat open and ignored by Whitman's side.

'So,' Whitman said, 'this was all for revenge.'

Shepherd made a harsh, grating sound that could have been a laugh. 'Don't flatter yourself. If it had been left to Mary, yes. But not when there's so much money at stake here. She wants payback. I want a payday. And after all I've suffered over the years because of you, I think I'm fucking entitled to it.'

'So why the phone calls?'

'To fuck with you.' Shepherd enjoyed saying the words. 'Some of us—' he shot a pointed look at Abdul-Haq, who looked away '—actually wanted you in on it. For old times' sake, all that shit. I just wanted you to know what we were doing. Fuck with your mind. Destroy you.' His voice wavered. 'Like you tried to do to me.'

Whitman shook his head. 'No, Alan, it wasn't—'

'What? Wasn't what? Your fault? It never was. Face it. You planted the bomb. You wanted to see how far you could take things. Then someone died, you got scared. And I was missing, already planning on baling out. Because I'd got your number. I knew what kind of fake you were.'

Whitman said nothing, just held the gun as straight as he could.

'Wasn't much of a leap, was it? Shift the blame on to me. Get Mary to lie about where you were that night. She ended up with a fucking mental breakdown from covering up for you. She's been on medication for years, can't function without it.'

'I . . . I'm sorry.'

'Bit fucking late for that, isn't it?'

On the TV David Dimbleby was reading out a news report about trouble on the streets of Newcastle. Gang fights that the police had broken up. Nothing serious. Shouldn't delay the result from Newcastle West for too much longer.

No one in the room heard him.

'I had to move out of the country. All because of you.'

'You went to work for Eugene Terre'Blanche. A Nazi.'

'Work is the right word. He paid me. By that time I didn't care who I worked for. Your betrayal killed any ideal-ism I might have once had. I'm just in for the money, Trevor.' Another laugh. 'I sold out.'

'Why are you trying to stop this?' said Abdul-Haq. 'Why couldn't you just leave us alone?'

'Because of him,' said Whitman, gesturing at Shepherd with the gun. 'Yes, I set the bomb. He's right about that. But I've paid for that. I've had years of nightmares, of burning figures talking to me, of guilt . . .' He shook his head, tried to clear it. 'But what you're doing is wrong. I didn't want another mistake made. More lives lost. I had to do some-thing about it. Something to stop it.'

'Bullshit,' said Shepherd. 'You heard I was back in the country. You knew I'd be pissed off. That I might say some-thing to someone about who really bombed this place. And you didn't want that to happen, did you? Could still go to prison for it. So you make out you're all liberal and con-cerned about the redevelopment deal. And something must be done. You were fucking clever, I'll give you that. But not clever enough. You see, there's a race war starting tonight. A whole platoon of NUP foot soldiers are taking to the streets. They're armed. They're out to cause trouble. And there'll be retaliation. So you see, it doesn't really matter who wins this election. We just step in and mop up.'

'That's bullshit,' said Whitman. 'It won't work.'

Shepherd checked his watch. 'Should be happening now. Just after the polls closed. Like I said, not clever enough.'

'Really?' said Whitman. It was his turn to laugh. 'Then how come it's me holding the gun?'

Shepherd smiled. 'Your legman hasn't reached the Bridge Hotel yet, has he?'

The gun felt even heavier in Whitman's hand.

Amar couldn't believe what he was hearing. He wished he had someone to share it with. He could call Joe, tell him – his mobile. There had been a text and he had ignored it. He took the headphones off, crossed the room, picked up the phone, checked the message. Kev. Looked at the photos.

His eyes widened. His heart began to beat faster.

He picked up the landline, speed-dialled. Di Nattrass's number.

Hoped they weren't too late.

46

Donovan ran, Jamal just behind him. They had passed the point of collapse some time ago. Their legs were shaking, chests burning, limbs aching. Every time one of them had felt like stopping, listened to their body telling them they couldn't go any more, they had thought of Peta, pushed on, eked out a little more stamina. Neither wanted to think that Peta hadn't been saved because they put themselves first.

The run had been all uphill, Donovan leading Jamal along the Quayside and up the Castle Stairs, the old Georgian route that linked the quay to the old castle keep. Taking them two at a time, dodging the pools of vomit, trying not to startle any post-pub fumblers in darkened doorways.

He reached the top of the steps, went through the old stone arch into what was left of the castle. Most of it had gone, only low stone walls and an oubliette built into what would have been the flagged stone floor but what was now, with wooden benches, a spot to sit at and enjoy the view along the Tyne.

But not tonight. The Bridge Hotel was just above, backing on to the castle remains. Leaving Jamal by the wooden bench getting his breath back, Donovan ran to the front doors of the pub. They were locked, the windows dark, the last punter long since drunk up and left. He looked around, tried to find a clue, something that jumped out at him, that he could tell Whitman about.

Nothing.

'I'm, I'm here,' he said into the earpiece. 'The Bridge Hotel.'

Whitman's voice came over the line. 'Have you found anything? What's there?'

'Nothing. What happened here, Whitman? You had sex with her, that right?'

'Yes,' he said. 'It was a thrill, for both of us. Out in the open, at night, looking down on the Tyne. We were the only ones there.'

'You're a classy date, Trev. And then what happened?'

'I . . . I don't know. I can't remember.'

'Think. There must be—'

Whitman's phone rang. 'That'll be her,' he said.

Whitman answered his phone. Shepherd sat before him, listening to every word. His grin back in place.

'Are you there?'

'Yes,' said Whitman.

Shepherd looked like he was about to speak. Whitman pushed the gun at him as a reminder. Shepherd said nothing.

'This is the next chapter in the story. Our story. What do you see?'

'Erm . . . nothing.'

'Then you're looking in the wrong place.'

'Where, where should I be looking?'

'Where you fucked me!' Her voice raged down the line. Whitman took the phone away from his face, could still hear her. 'Where you fucked me and made me pregnant!'

'Right,' he said. 'There. The ruins. By the oubliette.'

'That's right. I've left you a present . . .'

Donovan turned from the front of the pub, made his way down the stone steps. Jamal was staring at the oubliette, a look of disgust on his face.

'Oh, man,' he said, 'that . . . that is well fucked up.'

Donovan drew level, saw what he was looking at. And agreed. He told Whitman what it was.

'What?' said Whitman.

'A foetus. In a jar. Tiny one. Human.'

'Oh, my God . . .'

Abdul-Haq shot a concerned glance towards Shepherd, who ignored it. He looked at Whitman, enjoying the man's discomfort. Mary Evans was back on the line.

'D'you recognize it? Do you?'

'It's . . . it's a foetus, Mary. Where did you get this from?'

Her voice was on the verge of breaking up. 'It's our baby. The one we would have had together if you hadn't forced me to have it aborted. The first one you had me kill.' Anger pulled it back.

Whitman looked frantically about the room, breathing heavily, sweating. Abdul-Haq and Shepherd sat on their respective sofas. Shepherd was smiling. He knew exactly what she was saying to him.

'What d'you think of that, Trevor?' asked Mary.

'I think . . . think you're sick.'

'One of us is. One of us ruined the other one's life. And not just mine. Alan's. The policeman you killed. And God knows how many more. Does it revolt you? Does it?'

'Yes.'

'Good. Because you disgust me.' There was mad satisfaction in her voice. The deranged vindication of a long-held grudge given well-plotted revenge. 'I hope you're suffering. Just like your daughter's going to suffer if you don't get to her in time.'

'Where . . . where's next?'

'Where d'you think?'

'I don't . . . I don't know.'

'Our story's about to come to an end. Boy meets girl, boy gets girl pregnant, boy kills girl's babies, boy runs off with other girl.'

Whitman thought. 'A march, a demonstration. The Haymarket.'

A sad sigh from Mary Evans, like she had been wounded. 'You can remember where you met her. But not me. The war memorial, Barras Bridge. Six minutes.'

She rang off.

Whitman felt like he was falling apart. 'Did you get that?' he said into the other phone.

Donovan placed the glass jar carefully back on the oubliette, stepped away. Jamal was already standing well back.

'Loud and clear,' he said. He turned to Jamal. 'Come on, let's go.'

Jamal looked pale.

'You OK? You going to be sick?'

Jamal shook his head but seemed unsure.

'It's fine if you want to stay here,' Donovan said. 'I'll go on alone.'

Jamal shook his head. 'Nah, man, she some twisted bitch, you get me? I wanna see this one through. Get Peta back safe. Dirty Harry or no Dirty Harry.'

Donovan smiled. 'Come on, then.'

They set off running again.

Kev couldn't run any more. He stumbled forward, collapsing into a shop doorway on the way up Westgate Road. Jason went with him. They sat there, staring out, trying to get their breath back. Kev checked his watch. Less than fifteen minutes to go.

He watched the cars go by. People with boring, ordinary lives. Maybe been round to someone's for dinner. Maybe coming home from work. How he wished that could have been him. Now it would never be him.

Self-pity and sadness hung round his neck like a granite necklace. He couldn't go any further, couldn't go anywhere. He sighed. No one was going to help them, nothing was going to happen.

He stole a glance at Jason next to him. Almost catatonic, staring ahead, grunting and wheezing as he breathed, the beginnings of lung trouble in later life. Except he wouldn't be having a later life.

Impotent anger thrashed within Kev. It was so unfair. It shouldn't have come to this. Life should have been better than this. Another look at Jason. An idea came into Kev's mind. He could get up, walk away. No, run away. There was nothing stopping him. Jason might have to die, but that didn't mean Kev did. He'd feel guilty, sure. But that would go. Eventually. What was guilt compared with being alive? Guilt he could live with. Anything he could live with.

He checked Jason again, moved his body forward, ready to get up. A hand shot out, clutching his arm.

'Don't go. Please. Stay with us.' Jason's arm gripped tighter, like holding on to Kev was the only thing stopping him from going into freefall.

Kev jumped, startled. 'I'm, I'm not . . .'

'Please, Kev, don't go. You're all I've, all I've got . . .'

Kev settled back down again.

'Kev,' Jason continued, 'you're like me dad an' me brother . . . like I always wanted them to be.'

Kev put his head down. The words hurt more than punches. Each one guilt-edged. 'Thank you.'

Jason was crying now. 'I just, just wanted to say, say thank you.' Tears took over him. Kev put his arm round him. Jason fell into him. 'I don't wanna die, Kev, I don't wanna die . . .'

'I know, Jason, I know.'

Jason was sobbing uncontrollably. 'I duh-don't . . .'

Kev held him.

'I'm goin' to, aren't I?' said Jason. 'We're nuh-not goin' to get help. Not now.' Tears and snot were flowing down his face.

Kev sighed. 'It looks that way, mate.'

Another round of crying. 'Please, Kev, don't leave me. Please, Kev . . . I duh-don't wanna die on me own . . .'

Kev felt his own tears welling up inside. 'I won't leave you, Jason. Don't worry.'

Jason burrowed into his side, kept sobbing. Kev stared ahead. This is what it's come down to, he thought. This is it. This is life. And death. And none of it matters. He shook his head. And was hit by an idea. An idea born of anger and injustice. A way to balance things up.

'Jason,' he said. 'There is somethin' we can do.'

The boy looked up, hope in his eyes. 'What?'

'We can't do anythin' about the bomb, but we can make sure it takes the people who are responsible for this with it. What d'you reckon?'

'Yeah,' said Jason. 'Whatever. Just as long as you stay with me, Kev, please.' He clutched harder. 'Please . . .'

'Don't worry Jason. I'm going to stay with you.' Kev took out his phone. 'Just got something to do first.'

He dialled. It was answered.

'Hello, Amar.'

'Kev' said Amar, checking the screen for the call signal. 'Where are you?'

'Listen,' said Kev. 'Just listen. I've got somethin' to say. An' I haven't got long. Don't interrupt.'

Amar listened.

Kev looked at Jason before continuing.

'You're not goin' to see me again, Amar. After tonight.

But you're gonna hear about me. I just want you to know
that it's not my fault. Not my choice. I wished . . . wished—'
he felt his voice crack, held it together '—things could have
worked out. I could have . . . could have loved you, Amar. You
said I could be a hero. This is, is the only way I can think to do
it. Goodbye. I—'

He cut the connection, couldn't say any more.

Amar stared at the phone.
  'Kev? Kev?'

Kev switched the phone off. The last call he would ever make.
He stood up, pulled Jason to his feet. Set off for Fenham.
  And the NUP head office.

It wasn't going as Whitman had planned. He was starting to
feel dizzy. The buzz from the earlier alcohol had disappeared, leaving only a sluggish disbelief in what he was
doing. The noise of the TV was droning on in his head, like
a fly trapped inside and trying to batter its way out. He
blinked, his gun hand slipping, his focus going.
  And that was when Abdul-Haq pounced.
  Whitman didn't realize until Abdul-Haq was on his feet
and coming towards him. Hands outstretched, ready to grab
his gun, wrestle him to the ground.
  Whitman's response was instinctive. He fired.
  The bullet tore a chunk out of Abdul-Haq's side. He
spun, his body flying backwards with the force, flinging him
round until he landed in an awkward heap on the floor.
  Shepherd was straight out of his seat and on the floor
with him. Abdul-Haq was still breathing, his eyes circular
with shock. Shepherd looked up at Whitman.
  'You fucking idiot.'
  Whitman was staggering, the recoil from the gun having

sent painful shock waves up his arm again. He swung the
gun at Shepherd.

'Leave him, get back, sit down . . .'

Shepherd didn't move. Whitman squeezed the trigger.

'All right,' said Shepherd, getting slowly to his feet. Abdul-
Haq lay there, blood haemorrhaging from his side.

'Call an ambulance,' he managed to wheeze out.
'Please . . .'

'Do it, Alan.' Whitman kept the gun on him.

'No.'

Whitman stared at him. Abdul-Haq couldn't believe what
he was hearing. 'Please, Alan. Call an ambulance . . .'

'No. The police would be called. They'd find him here.
They'd ask too many questions.' Shepherd looked at him, his
eyes hard, flinty. 'Sorry, Gideon, can't be done. You'll just
have to grin and bear it.'

'Then I'll do it,' said Whitman.

'No, you won't,' said Shepherd coolly, as if he were the
one holding the gun. 'Because police will mean questions.
About you. About who shot him, for one thing. About
how those bullets will match the ones taken out of Gideon's
associates this afternoon.' He leaned forward. 'And how will
that help you find your daughter?'

'Shut up,' Whitman shouted aloud. 'Just shut up. All of
you . . .'

He needed to think. He needed space and time.

He looked down at the floor, at the twitching, spasming
body of Abdul-Haq, the pleading eyes of his one-time
friend. Knew he had to do something, act quickly. But he
didn't know what.

On TV David Dimbleby talked of the imminent move
over to see the results for Newcastle West. Whitman didn't
hear. He just held on to the gun as if that was the only
thing that could save him.

47

'What was that?'

Donovan on Percy Street with Jamal, stopped running, shouted into the earpiece. No one answered. 'Whitman? What happened?'

Whitman's voice came on the line eventually. 'Nothing. Nuh-nothing. Everything's . . . everything's fine. Now. It's fine. Just keep, you know, going.'

Donovan checked his watch. They were ahead of schedule. He nodded to Jamal and they set off again.

They made it to the war memorial in front of St Mary's Church in less than a minute from where they had stopped. He checked his watch again. Still ahead of schedule. He flicked the switch on the earpiece.

'Amar? How you doing locating Mary Evans's phone?'

'Yeah,' said Amar, staring at the screen, 'I'm on it. Nearly . . . nearly there . . .' He punched in some more numbers, looked at the screen. The map of Newcastle had a grid over it. He was trying to get three green lines to find a spot to converge on. 'I'm in the area. You just need to keep her talking so I can triangulate the right location.'

'OK,' said Donovan. He flicked the switch. 'You hear that, Whitman? Keep her talking. We've nearly got a fix on her.'

'Oh, OK. Right.'

Whitman didn't sound right to Donovan, but he didn't have time to worry about him now. The war memorial was directly in front of the church. On the opposite side of the road was the Newcastle Playhouse, home to Northern Stage, and behind the church was the Civic Centre. The lights were on there, the place humming with activity. Donovan looked at the circular tower, saw the sea horses lit up. The night would have been beautiful under other circumstances.

'Check round,' he said to Jamal. 'See if you can find anything.'

They looked all round the memorial. Donovan spoke to Whitman again.

'What should we be looking for?'

'This was where I met Lillian. On a peace march here. For Vietnam,' he said.

'Was Mary here too?'

'Maybe. Probably.'

Donovan could see why Mary Evans had taken such a dislike to the man.

'But we used to go there all the time. All of us, when we were students, sit around on the green by the memorial.'

'Doing what? Anything in particular?'

'Just sitting. We . . . Wait. I . . . Let me think. Mary always said it was a special place for us. That's why she was so annoyed that I met Lillian there.'

'What made it so special? Think.'

'It was where we made our plans. Talked about the future. Destroying the old order, getting the corrupt bastards out. This was in the days of Dan Smith, remember? Mary loved it, she was on fire for it.'

'And how were you going to do that?'

'By . . . Oh, my God. By blowing up the Civic Centre. Fuck.'

Whitman's phone rang.

'Keep her talking,' said Donovan.

Whitman answered his phone. 'Yes.'

'Are you there yet?'

He sighed. 'Yes. The war memorial.'

'Know why I picked that place?'

'Because we once sat there and talked about getting rid of the old order. Blowing up the Civic Centre. And because that's where I met Lillian.'

There was silence on the line. He didn't think he had been expected to get the right answer. 'Very good,' she said eventually.

'So what have you got there for me to find? A bomb?'

Mary Evans laughed. 'A map. Find that and you find your daughter.'

Whitman looked over at the chesterfield. Abdul-Haq had pulled himself on to the sofa, taken his shirt off and was holding it against his wound. It was sodden with blood. He was sweating. He didn't look good. Shepherd was next to him, staring at Whitman, hatred in his eyes.

Whitman just wanted it all to be over.

'OK,' he said.

Donovan and Jamal were looking round the memorial, checking under stones, looking up at the top.

Donovan saw a folded piece of paper sticking out of the soil. He bent down, picked it up. Opened it.

'Found it,' he said.

'Found it,' Whitman repeated.

'Good,' said Mary Evans, a sick excitement in her voice. 'It's a white van. That's all I'm saying.'

She rang off.

★

'A white van,' said Donovan, reading the paper.

It was a map leading from the war memorial, down by the side of the Civic Centre to the car park at the back. He and Jamal exchanged a glance. Another voice came over their earpieces.

'Found her,' said Amar. 'She's at the back of the car park by the entrance. Unless the phone's being bounced off somewhere else. And that white van, that's the one Peta was in. I've got the registration number here.'

'How did you know that?' said Donovan.

'Kev came through for me. Got a pen?'

Donovan wrote down the number. He and Jamal moved round to the back of the Civic Centre.

Whitman put his phone down. Shepherd was still staring at him.

'Haven't you worked it out yet?' he spat. 'You really are a thick bastard.'

Whitman rubbed his eyes, tried to clear the buzzing in his head. Failed. 'Tell me.'

'She wants to see you. She wants to see you opening the doors of the van. She wanted you to run round Newcastle, revisit your old haunts. She wanted to break you. Then she wanted you to look at your daughter, see her lying there helpless. Realize what your life's come to, then blow you both sky high.'

'What? How?'

'A bomb, you fucking idiot. Radio controlled. It's all sorted. We've got a white Nazi suicide bomber going in through the front doors. We've got a bomb in a white van that has the planted DNA of a Muslim extremist all over it.' He gave a bitter laugh. 'You have no idea. You're pathetic.'

On the TV the action had switched to the Newcastle West results. The camera was surveying the podium. Rick Oaten was standing there. The results were imminent.

'Ka-boom,' said Shepherd.

48

Kev stood outside the NUP headquarters, looked at it.

'Come on,' he said.

Jason didn't move, just stared resignedly at the front door. Kev looked at him. 'What?'

Jason was choking back tears again. 'I just don't want to die, Kev. I don't want to die . . .' The tears flowed. 'I just . . . I always wanted, wuh-wanted somewhere to, to belong. A home, a fam-family. Someone. That's all I wanted. Belong . . .' His words dried up, choked them off.

Kev put his arm around him. 'Me too, mate. Me too.' He thought of Amar. His words. About being a hero. About atoning. He took a deep breath. Another. Checked his watch. Almost time. 'Come on, mate. Let's do it.'

He led him across the road and through the front door.

There was silence from the storefront as they entered, then Kev's raised voice, muffled by the boarding. Then silence.

Then screaming, as the few remaining party faithful, those still in the office watching the results, made their way to the front door and out into the night, as fast as they could go.

Mary Evans sat at the top of the slope that led down to the car park behind the Civic Centre. Watching. Barely able to contain her excitement.

The culmination of years of planning, of waiting, of imagining. And it felt good. Making Trevor Whitman suffer.

Arranging his death. And knowing there would be no consequences for her. Living out the perfect revenge fantasy.

She looked at the two phones beside her. One for making calls, the other purely for pressing a button that would blow the van and its occupant and its opener sky high.

She couldn't wait. Had even brought her binoculars to get a close-up of his face as he opened the doors.

Wouldn't be long now.

She looked at the phone on the seat.

Just one more call to him . . .

Whitman picked up on the first ring.

'Are you there yet?'

'Nearly,' he said, head pounding. 'Just coming round the corner.' He closed his eyes. 'I can see it.'

She picked up the binoculars, focused on the back doors of the van. She smiled.

Waiting. Not long . . .

She touched the other phone, ran her fingers over the button.

Closer, closer . . .

The returning officer was standing on the platform, candidates behind him. Rick Oaten was at one side, Colin Baty the other. David Dimbleby had cut the voiceover, allowing the pictures to speak for themselves. The returning officer was about to speak.

'Here we are,' said Shepherd. 'This is what it's all about.' He laughed. 'The timing couldn't have been more perfect.'

Abdul-Haq's eyes had rolled into the back of his head. He was going into shock. Whitman didn't know what to focus on first: the phone, the bleeding body, even the TV. He looked from one to the other, frantically. He had to tell

Donovan about the bomb. Had to . . . He didn't notice Shepherd rise off the chesterfield, cross the room, come towards him. Until it was too late to do anything about it.

Shepherd was on him, kneeing him in the stomach, bending him double. Whitman fell to the floor, clutching his groin. The gun was snatched from his grasp. He hit the floor, curling up in a foetal ball. Shepherd kicked him hard. Once. Twice.

'Here. That kicking I've always promised you.' He laughed.

From outside the room came screams, the sound of running. Shepherd looked at the door. The screaming continued out on to the street. He looked back at the TV. Whatever was happening to the few stragglers in the front office, watching the results, chugging back lager, he didn't care. Nothing was going to stop him savouring his moment of triumph.

Footsteps came running up the stairs towards the room.

Shepherd ignored them.

Mary Evans kept her eyes on the van, holding her breath, waiting for him to appear. A shadow moved round the corner of the building. She sat up straight, squinted through the binoculars. Stroked the button.

'Yes.' Her words hissed out through clenched teeth. 'Yes . . .'

The figure drew nearer. Her finger hovered over the button.

'What?'

She looked at the figure, refocused the binoculars. Looked again. It wasn't Whitman. Nothing like him. It was a teenager, a light-skinned black youth. He checked a piece of paper in his hand. She recognized it. The map she had left for Whitman. He checked again, walked towards the van.

She looked at the button beneath her finger, looked again at the black youth. He was opening the back doors of the van . . .

'No . . .'

The returning officer opened his mouth to speak. Behind him, Rick Oaten adjusted his tie. Shepherd thought he looked ashen, drained. Like the fight had been knocked out of him. Or he was no longer fighting for what he believed in.

Shepherd smiled. Purely academic. In a few minutes it wouldn't matter at all.

At his feet Whitman stirred, sat up.

'Should watch this, Trevor. This is where I win. The final countdown, you might say.'

Whitman groaned, tried to pull himself up. Shepherd watched the TV.

The returning officer opened his mouth to speak, started speaking, but a commotion in the crowd distracted him. He looked down to the floor of the packed hall where someone was making their way towards him. A woman, dressed in a business suit, followed by a similarly dressed younger man made their way on to the stage. Shepherd didn't know who they were, but from the cut of their clothes he knew what they were. Cops.

The female detective introduced herself over the mic. 'I'm Detective Inspector Diane Nattrass,' she said, holding up her warrant card, 'and I am arresting Rick Oaten on charges of abduction, conspiracy, attempting to pervert the course of justice and murder.'

The crowd gasped.

'What the fuck?' Shepherd's face turned scarlet.

On the floor, Whitman laughed.

'Shut up! Fucking shut up!' Shepherd began kicking him,

hard. Whitman took the blows, felt at least one rib break with each kick he took.

On the screen, they were cuffing Rick Oaten and leading him away.

'Bastard!' Shepherd kept kicking.

The door was flung open. Shepherd looked up. He just had time to recognize who was standing there and what it meant before Kev shouted something about love and hate and the whole world turned a blinding white, then to nothing.

The building went up.

Not with a whimper, but with a bang.

Mary Evans put down the binoculars, confused. Angry. She didn't know what to do. This wasn't the plan, this wasn't how it was supposed to work out.

The black youth was opening the van doors.

'No . . .'

She grabbed for the phone, made to press the button. The car door was pulled open and the phone was snatched out of her hand. She looked up.

'This what you want?'

An out-of-breath man was standing there, wearing a superhero T-shirt and an angry but triumphant expression. She reached out, made to grab it off him.

'I wouldn't do that if I were you.'

She jumped out of the car, screaming like a wounded animal, hurt and rage in her eyes, trying to claw at his face, grab the phone back from him. He punched her square in the face. She fell backwards, blood springing from her nostrils.

He punched her again.

She saw stars, then blackness.

★

Joe Donovan looked down at the prone body of Mary Evans, then at the phone. Then at his sore hand. He flexed his knuckles. It would hurt in the morning.

Punching her had been completely instinctive. He had no qualms about hitting a woman. Not this one, anyway. He turned the phone off so it could do no damage, hauled her body into the boot of her car and locked it.

Then walked across the car park to where Jamal was helping Peta out of the back of the van. A voice came on in his ear.

'Joe? Joe? What's happening? Are you OK?'

'Yeah, Amar, we're fine, Peta's OK,' he said. 'I'm just going to get her.' He smiled. Felt tears prick the corners of his eyes. Saw his two best friends in front of him, heard the other one on the end of a phone line. 'We're all fine.'

EPILOGUE

HOME LAND SECURITY

The weather had broken. The heatwave was over. The rain was falling.

Donovan stood in David's room and looked out of the window.

Three weeks. Since he and Jamal had pulled Peta out of the back of the van.

Three weeks. Since all the deaths.

Nattrass had phoned Donovan after election night. He thought she was going to thank him for his help but it was another reason entirely.

'Paul Turnbull's dead,' she had said, voice beyond weary.

Donovan was too shocked to speak.

There was more. Much more.

Turnbull's body had been discovered in Bishop's Stortford and a murder investigation launched. Both Nattrass and Donovan cooperated. Donovan had brought in the lawyer, Sharkey, when it seemed the prime suspect was Matt Milsom.

But Matt Milsom had disappeared. Both he and his wife Celia and the boy they had called Jake were gone. The house they had lived in had been stripped, scrupulously cleaned, then torched. Forensic teams had launched a search for DNA, but their chances of recovering much that was usable was slim.

This had brought the focus of the investigation on to the Milsoms themselves. Which was where the surprises really

began. The couple who had bought that house were not
Matt and Celia Milsom. The real Matt and Celia Milsom
had emigrated to the United Arab Emirates. Matt Milsom
had been a TV producer but had left several months before.
He had never worked, as much as anyone knew, in Eastern
Europe.

Donovan had been stunned at this news. He didn't know
what to think, how to feel. He had phoned Sharkey straight
away.

'Why wasn't any of this picked up on the initial investigation? Why just now?'

'Because they were very clever,' said Sharkey. 'They stole
the Milsoms' identity subtly and without raising suspicion.'

'But surely—'

'Joe, the watchword of this investigation was discretion.
The Milsoms didn't come to our attention until they turned
up in Hertfordshire with the boy in tow. A full background
check was undertaken. As far as was allowed. No one could
storm into their workplace and demand to know whether
Matt Milsom was who he said he was.'

'So who were the couple who claimed to be the
Milsoms?'

'No idea.'

'And what did they want? What did they hope to gain?'

'Again, we don't know.'

Donovan had taken a deep breath, asked his most important question. 'Was the boy David? Was that my son?'

The school the boy known as Jake had attended had been
contacted. They confirmed that he kept himself to himself,
that he seemed distant. Did he have an accent? They didn't
know. But not Romanian, nothing like that. Somewhere in
this country. HIV-positive? It was the first that they had
heard. Did they have to test the rest of the school now?
Because if word of that got out . . .

Sharkey had sighed. 'We ... I don't know, Joe. I just don't know.'

Sharkey had given him assurances that his team would keep looking, that no stone would be unturned, that they wouldn't give up, but Donovan had just put the phone down.

Gone into David's room. And talked to him until the tears stopped falling.

Turnbull's funeral had taken place in his local church at Westerhope soon after that. Donovan had attended with Nattrass. Turnbull's estranged widow kept her distance from them both. That suited Donovan just fine.

'Lots of his old mates from the force,' Donovan said afterwards. 'He'd have been pleased with that.'

Nattrass had nodded. She looked shell-shocked.

'I think you should take a few days off,' he said. 'Have a rest.'

She turned to him, about to let loose with some cutting remark, tell him to mind his own business, something like that. But she saw the look on his face, realized his concern was genuine. She sighed. 'Maybe I should. Maybe I will.'

'I feel like shit over this,' said Donovan. 'I asked him if he wanted to go. Gave him the job.'

'It's not your fault,' she said. 'You didn't know what would happen. None of us did.'

'No.' Donovan left it like that. But he couldn't shift the feeling of guilt so easily.

There had been a call for Donovan on his mobile. From a girl called Claire.

She had described herself as a friend of Turnbull's and been given his number if Turnbull wasn't around and she got into trouble and needed help. She hadn't heard from

Turnbull in ages so Donovan would have to do. Could he meet her?

He had gone to meet her at the specified time and date, but she didn't show up. He waited for two hours. Eventually he went home.

She never called again.

Another election had been announced, the results of that one declared null and void. Rick Oaten had been arrested and was being held in police custody as he was considered a serious flight risk. The redevelopment plan had been shelved. Indefinitely. Money instead to be put into new community schemes to tackle integration. Mary Evans had been arrested. The last Donovan had heard, she was going to declare herself insane.

And Albion was going back into business. The office was being refurbished, all previous investigations would be dropped. While officially the city couldn't condone the actions they had taken, they had to admit they had helped stop a vicious terrorist act.

'But I'm still keeping my eye on you, cowboy,' Nattrass had told Donovan.

'Sure you are, sheriff,' he had replied.

Whitman's funeral had been next.

Lillian had requested the release of his body, wanted to see it buried properly after its untimely cremation. There was so little of him left and what there was had been fused with other artefacts in the explosion that it was more of a memorial service than a funeral. However, Lillian had insisted on a full-size coffin, wanting to honour the memory of the man as she remembered him, rather than his final state.

The crowd in the small parish church in Ryton, where Lillian lived, was also full-sized, swelled by journalists and ghoulish rubberneckers; the church had never seen such activity.

A human storm of bodies, cameras, mics, cables, lights and vans was outside in the rain. Inside, at the eye of the storm, Peta had sat next to her mother, Donovan, Jamal and Amar, all black-suited, a discreet number of rows behind. The vicar talked of him in glowing but impersonal terms, obviously having never met the man. He told what a debt of gratitude the region owed to this man, who had selflessly sacrificed himself in order to save more lives.

Donovan and Amar tried hard not to exchange glances.

There were words from his work colleagues, and Lillian gave a Bible reading. He had not, it transpired, ever got seriously involved with another woman after her. She had held herself in check admirably during the service but afterwards, as the mourners filed out with Jimmy Cliff's 'Many Rivers to Cross', Whitman's funeral song of choice, playing over the speakers, she broke down. Peta supported her all the way to the graveside. Lillian had wanted him buried beside where she lived. Wanted him near her.

Standing away from the party around the grave, watching the vicar say his final few words, Amar whispered to Donovan. 'I've still got that recording.'

Donovan nodded.

'What should I do with it?'

Donovan looked at Lillian, barely holding herself together at the graveside, Peta with her arm firmly around her, hiding whatever conflicting emotions she was experiencing, being strong for the sake of her mother. Amar's eyes followed Donovan's.

'Lose it,' said Donovan.

Amar nodded.

After the service, Peta came up to them. 'Thanks for coming, guys.'

Donovan smiled. 'What are friends for?'

Peta nodded, gaze averted. She wiped the corners of her eyes, looked back at him. 'You coming back to the house?'

'D'you want us there?'

'Of course.'

'I have a feeling,' said Donovan, looking over to Lillian, who looked lost without her daughter to lean on but nevertheless giving him an unpleasant look. 'I have a feeling that your mother won't make us all that welcome.'

'She's just a bit . . . She wants someone to blame. For what happened.'

'And it can't be Whitman.'

'He's not here,' said Peta, her voice fracturing slightly.

'I think we'll be off,' said Donovan.

Peta nodded. 'Oh, Joe, guys. I think . . . I think I'm going to take a little time off. Go away somewhere with Lillian. Spend some time together. Things we need to talk about.'

'Good idea,' said Amar.

'But I'm still one of the team,' she said, trying to summon up a smile.

'You're damned right,' said Donovan.

He pulled her to him, embracing her in a tight hug. She let her tears go. He held her until she had ridden them out. Then it was Amar's turn, then Jamal's. She pulled back, looked at the three of them.

'Best friends I've ever had,' she said, and went back to rejoin her mother.

Kev Bright's funeral was different again. A run-down, soot-blackened old church in Scotswood, only three present including the vicar. Amar had paid. He felt it was the least he could do.

He watched the coffin go into the earth alone but for the vicar. There had been an older man there during what service there was, but he had left straight after, saying something about looking after Joey.

'Would you like to say a few words?' the vicar asked Amar.

'No, thanks,' he said. 'I've said plenty to him while I've been standing here. If he heard them, he heard them. I don't need to say them out loud.'

The vicar nodded, understanding.

Jamal had been sitting on the sofa one night, a thoughtful, disturbed look on his face. He turned the TV off. He wanted to talk.

'What's up, kidder?' said Donovan.

'Was thinkin' 'bout Jason,' he said.

'What about him?'

'It's sad, y'know? He had no one. All that shit, that Nazi shit, it wasn't who he was, what he wanted. It's just what came to him. His way out. He just wanted to try an' fit in, y'get me? Be, y'know . . .'

'Loved,' Donovan said.

Jamal blushed. 'Yeah. Loved.' He sighed. 'But, like, not everyone get that, yeah? Not everyone can be lucky.'

'That's right, Jamal. It's a cruel truth. Not everyone can be lucky.'

Jamal said nothing, sat thoughtfully. Eventually he put the TV back on.

Donovan stood in David's room, stared at the rain. Three weeks.

He had promised Abigail, his daughter, that he would have some news for her. He couldn't phone now. Not just yet. He couldn't tell her what had happened. He wasn't sure himself what had happened. He just had to keep going. See what the next job for Albion would involve, see—

He stopped dead. There was movement in the house.

He looked round. The door to David's room was closed. Jamal was in town with Amar, staying overnight, so it couldn't be him. He checked the window again. No car outside. He hadn't seen or heard anyone drive up.

Another sound. Someone moving through the front room, making their way to the stairs.

He looked round, tried to find anything that he could use as a weapon. Nothing there. He checked his pocket for his mobile, make a call for help. Not there. He had left it charging downstairs.

The footsteps came to a halt on the landing. There was someone outside the door.

He took a deep breath, another. Then pulled the door open.

Donovan froze.

Standing there with his black, floppy fringe and his black-framed glasses was Matt Milsom. Or the person who claimed to be Matt Milsom. He smiled.

'What the—'

Donovan got no further. Milsom's fist crashed out, connecting with Donovan's face. He fell backwards, hitting the bare floorboards with a hard thump. He looked up. Milsom was standing over him. He took something from behind his back, something black and heavy-looking.

Donovan didn't have time to move out of the way. Milsom's face twisted with rage as he brought the cosh down on Donovan's head.

Stars exploded.

Then there was nothing.

Just darkness.